**From her high refuge she heard the chains
that raised the gates,
opening the fortress of her protection,
the stronghold that guarded her heart.**

Spurs, scraping metal on stone as he took the stairs to reach her, rang out with his fierce intention. She knew he would not, could not, waste a minute more to hold her, bury his need in her until they both cried out in their joining. The scents of leather, sweat, and musky male melted her bones and she leaned into him to keep from falling. Sapphire flames searched her face. Long fingers traced the line of her jaw and traveled to her neck, where her pulse beat in counterpoint to her panting breaths. "It has been too long, *Muirnín.*" His whisper settled like a butterfly's wing on her ear. "I want you now, Katie..."

"Katie...wake up, sleepin' beauty. It's supper time."

Brandon sat on the bed and brushed her hair out of her face. "I'm sorry. I meant to wake you sooner."

"Oh...oh, dear...I was having this dream." *My God, what a dream.* "I thought I was in that castle." She pointed out the window at the medieval fortress that was now a silhouette in the evening sky. "And you were there." *How much am I going to tell him?* "Well, it was...amazing."

"It's called Carraigdún." His fingers combed through her mass of curls. "Do you know, you have such beautiful hair? It reminds me of a lioness—like you—wild and unruly."

She smacked his hand away, dropping the quilt and exposing the rise of her breasts. "Brandon, I'm not dressed."

He traced the line of her collarbone with one finger. "You might have forgotten, but I've seen you in less than this."

Hot Flash

by

Clare Austin

Hot Flash

COPYRIGHT © 2009 by Máire Clare Austin

Cover Art by *Rae Monet*

The Wild Rose Press
PO Box 708
Adams Basin, NY 14410-0708
Visit us at www.thewildrosepress.com

Publishing History
Last Rose of Summer Edition, 2010
Print ISBN 1-60154-725-0

Published in the United States of America

Dedication

To the people of Santo Stefano di Sessanio,
L'Aquila, Abruzzo, Italy,
who suffered the loss of their beautiful hilltop town
in the earthquake of 2009.

And, to my husband. *Tá mo chroí istigh ionat.*

Chapter One

"WS HS." Was his! The little blue Beemer with vanity plates had become a symbol, the only thing Kate Aiello wanted from her erstwhile husband that he'd resented giving her. She didn't particularly like the fancy roadster, but its new license plates sent a message to the world.

Driving along the back roads from her suburban Baltimore neighborhood to the rural countryside, she perceived a twittering in her belly—excitement, anticipation, fear? Or was it a warning bell her unpredictable thermostat was about to work it's evil on her again? Kate took a deep breath and tried to concentrate on driving.

Tears choked in her throat and stung her eyes. Wasn't it insult enough she was turning fifty and being left at the side of life's road by her philandering husband? Now she had to contend with her body's betrayal...hot flashes!

Today the dissolution of her marriage would be final. Kate's life would begin to be her own. She was no longer Catherine Waldon, or Mrs. Jeffrey Waldon. She was once again, after twenty-five years, Kate Aiello. And, just as Jeffrey had promised, she would never want for anything money could provide. Her attorney called it 'a very profitable divorce'. Unfortunately, where her heart had once resided, there remained only a big black hole.

That was the moment it hit her—the tingling in her face, a million fine needles pressing into her flesh, heat spilling from her pores, pulse intensifying.

1

Distracted by her rebellious body, she didn't see the squirrel until the last moment, but she was sure they had made eye contact. As he scooted to the right then to the left, she swerved to avoid rendering him road kill. The next several seconds slowed to a ballet of disaster. Brakes squealed, tires bumped over the bewildered varmint in their path, and she was thrown forward and then snapped back. A sickening sound of metal on metal pierced the atmosphere and her cranium smacked hard into the headrest.

Aghast, Kate took assessment. She was stunned but not hurt. Her hands gripped the steering wheel with pale knuckles, and her seat belt pressed into her chest with such force she could barely breathe.

That is when she heard him.

Muttering in a mix of English and a language unfamiliar to her ears, a voice rose and fell in anger and frustration. "Jaysus. *Céard atá ar bun agat?* Do ye see what ye did to me pick-up?" He pointed at the grill of his truck. Then, as if it were an afterthought, he asked, "Are ye hurt?"

Kate unfastened her seat belt and, on shaky limbs, as elegantly as possible stepped out of her car. The back quarter panel of the Beemer was smashed and one tail light bobbled, looking like a dislodged eyeball hanging from its optic nerve.

"Your truck? It isn't even scratched. Look at my car. I was trying to miss the..." She looked at the pavement and screamed at the horror that lay there. "Ahh! I've killed him! Oh my God." She had completely flattened the squirrel, his bloodied corpse a bleak reminder of her own vulnerability.

In counterpoint to her rising panic, he appeared to calm himself. "If you could see it in yourself to settle down—I think we should exchange insurance information," he said, raking his hand through his thick, black hair.

Kate silently counted to ten, cleared her throat and modulated her voice to hide her alarm. "Yes...yes we should do that." She reached into the glove box, retrieved her card and handed it to him. "I hope my car will run. I have an appointment."

"Sure, an' that makes two of us." He wrote her information on the back of an envelope, showed her his driver's license and handed her his business card, which she was too shaken to read.

He stepped cautiously around her, and surveyed the damage to her car. "I think you can drive safely with this, but get in and start her up. I'll wait until you're sure you can get down the road."

Tears again began to well up in Kate's throat. *No, no, no way...I will not cry in front of this man. No man will ever see Kate Aiello's tears again.* She swallowed back the convulsive, wracking sobs threatening to consume her. This person had no right to be angry with her. He'd run right into the back of her car. He should have been paying attention. Didn't he see she was trying not to murder an innocent forest creature?

She had to get out of here. Now that she'd calmed down, the man, with his riveting sapphire eyes, chiseled jaw and lean body, was having a strange effect on her. It was not an altogether unfamiliar feeling, though it had been quite a while since she had experienced it.

It must be hormonal.

She had to get a grip. Kate was determined to move on. She was headed to her first horseback riding lesson with the desperate hope some magic would transform her back into a whole woman.

As she drove away from the scene she had whirligigs in her stomach. Her cheeks were pinked and glowing, and she feared it wasn't from a low ebb of estrogen.

****

3

The entry to the barn office blew open and Brandon Sullivan burst through like a squall off the Irish Sea. He slammed the door behind him so hard two framed photographs bounced against the wall and crashed to the floor.

"Who am I riding?" he shouted, grabbing a pair of breeches and his tall black boots from the chair where he had left them last night.

"Ah and it's himself come to grace my day." The red-haired woman who sat at the desk peered with intense green eyes over her bifocals.

"Sorry, Annie girl, it's been one hell of a mornin'." He stepped into the small bathroom and closed the door, kicked off his shoes and stripped the grey wool trousers off his long legs. "Let me start over," he called, trying to regain his manners. He knew he would get nowhere with his sister if he was brusque. "What horse, my dear, am I riding next, if you please."

"That's better." She spoke up so she could be heard through the door. "I believe that would be Penny Lane. Barbara has her ready and warmed up for you. All you need to do is get your skinny arse in the saddle. And, just to increase your pleasure, Penny's owner is here to watch you perform your charms on her mare."

"Grand, just grand," he muttered with disdain. "The woman is a royal pain in what you call my skinny arse." He stepped out into the office, tucking his shirt into the breeches, and threw his slacks in a heap on the desk. "Give me those boot pulls." He pointed to the shelf behind Annie.

"Get 'em yourself. I keep your books. I'm not your feckin' servant."

Brandon did get the boot pulls himself and sat down to slide his feet into the worn leather boots, wanting to curse but holding his tongue. He stood, grabbed his helmet off its hook on the wall and

4

turned to leave.

"Bran," she said, stopping him. "Did you remember you have a new student at eleven?"

"Dammit, I don't want another student. Give me a horse to train, not a human. Jaysus, tell him to go to some other barn."

"Well, even an audience with the Pope isn't getting you out of this one. I'm an accountant, brother mine, but I'm not a miracle worker. You need this student just as much as you need to ride Mrs. Dalwhinny's mare. So stop your belly achin' and get to work."

"Ok, ok. I'm going. When the student gets here, send him out to the arena." He started to leave and turned back to plant a kiss on Annie's cheek. "Thank you. I don't know what I'd do without you here to kick my bum."

"I'll do that. And, Bran, it's a woman. Your new student is a Ms. Aiello."

"Great, more hormones to deal with. Don't American men ride? What's the matter with this country?" He exited the office and strode in determination toward the jump arena.

Brandon knew he had to leave the events of the morning behind. When he put his foot in a stirrup, all the troubles had to stay in the dirt at his feet. Usually, this was not hard. Riding was in his blood, his bones. It was respite from the world and the one thing he could turn to when everything came crashing down on him. But today had been a day from hell.

It couldn't have started with more of a bang, literally, right into the back end of a fancy sports car. More likely than not, Brandon's insurance would be cancelled when they received this claim. The BMW's driver was obviously a nut case. The screaming, weeping woman with wild brown eyes and hair like a lion's mane had taken his breath away, making it hard for him to collect his thoughts. She'd been hysterical, for God's sake, and blamed the whole incident on him.

Squirrel, my arse. Damn thing had probably been rabid. And the woman—bloody lunatic, she was. She'd fretted about the damn squirrel like it was her long lost cousin. If she hadn't been going on so, he might have thought she was pretty.

Well, she was. He noticed such things, even under stress.

He'd dutifully given her one of his cards and looked at the insurance card she'd presented, at his request. He'd made a mental note of her name, Catherine A. Waldon.

Brilliant...just fuckin' brilliant. She'd given him one more thing to deal with, and him on his way to the bank and late for his appointment with the loan officer.

And, Mr. Sullivan, what do you do for a living?
I ride horses.

There it was, that is what he did, he rode horses, trained them. To the average banker it sounded like a hobby, not a living. But it was what he did, and he was good at it.

"Is she ready, Barbara darlin'?" He smiled at the young woman dismounting from the big grey mare.

"Walked, trotted and cantered. She feels soft today." She patted the horse's sleek neck. "Be a good girl for the boss." She handed Brandon the reins.

Penny stood obediently as Bran adjusted the stirrup leathers for his long legs and then checked the girth. He often teased his clients that he should be able to ride balanced enough to leave the girth completely loose, but he had nothing to prove on this day. He didn't worry about impressing the owners. They knew little about what he was teaching their horse and even less about the sport of Three Day Eventing. His main concern was for the animal on

6

which he sat, and as horses went, he liked what he saw and felt in Penny Lane. She was a talented dressage horse and a fabulous jumper. She was also incredibly brave, a necessity for a cross country mount. Whether it be a steep drop to a water obstacle or a massive rock wall in the trees, this mare never hesitated. Brandon had been riding since before he had memory, and with Penny he knew he had a winner.

He picked up the reins and gave a squeeze with both legs. "Barb, raise the oxer and give it more spread, would you dear. Did you take her over those X's?"

"Yeah."

He sat deep in the saddle and moved Penny into a canter, lengthening and shortening her strides, testing her mood and sensitivity. She felt magnificent—muscles bunching and stretching under him, her mouth soft and her ears perked forward in anticipation. He played a bit and asked for her one tempi changes, feeling the smooth bounce from lead to lead as she danced across the arena. It made Bran smile, and he'd had precious little to smile about this last year-and-a-half.

As often was the case when the boss was up, other riders had gathered, on and off their horses, to watch. Brandon Sullivan was captivating in the saddle, and it was always a show.

Turning the big grey toward the first fence, Brandon rode her to the perfect spot where she lifted off the ground, stretching like an archer's bow over the rails. Their landing was exact. They made a lead change and turned to the vertical. It was a huge wall of blocks that would easily fall if she even tipped them with a front foot, but in her usual, careful way, Penny leapt over the barrier meticulously.

Obstacle and barrier they jumped and turned— the mare pushing off the sandy footing with her powerful back legs and Brandon moving with her in complete harmony. Focusing on the task at hand, he didn't notice the Montego blue metallic BMW convertible pull in and park. He didn't notice the dark-haired woman in the buff-colored breeches until he glanced over to the groupies at the rail.

He damn near fell off the horse! It was *that* woman. What was she doing here? *Jaysus in a bathtub.* It was the Waldon woman, the nut case, the *loolah*!

His chest squeezed and his pulse raced. He picked up his reins and nudged the mare into a gallop, rapidly eating up the ground to the oxer and taking it with air to spare. They pounded down the rail and turned for the combination. Penny had plenty of speed and Brandon didn't think to rate her or set her up. She took a tight spot to the first fence, one huge stride between, where she should have put in two and catapulted over the second, a monstrous triple bar, catching the top rail with a back leg and sending the brightly colored PVC poles crashing like Pick-up Sticks to the ground. All the saints in Ireland must have held him in their hands, because even Brandon Sullivan had a moment of thinking he would be jumped right out of the saddle and launched like a javelin.

He slowed to a gentle trot to let them both catch a breath, sending a look to Barb meaning "Get that fence back up. We're coming through again." He turned and approached the combination once more. He used his body to balance the horse and she left the ground exactly where he asked, put in two tidy strides and spanned the triple in a fluid arc. Feeling redeemed, and not a little chagrined that he'd let anger fog his judgment, he patted Penny on the neck and told her what a good girl she was. He dismounted and handed the reins to Barb. She looked as though she might be biting her tongue to squelch the urge to ask him what the hell that was all about.

****

Kate sat on a park bench under the big elm and watched the rider who had the attention of every human and equine within sight. Two young women were chatting while the pair circled to the next fence.

"Damn, why can't I ride like that?" a cute, dark-haired woman sighed.

"Forget riding. I'd like to be ridden like that," replied her companion.

"Well, go for it. He's single, straight and he doesn't seem to be dating anyone. At least no one we know about."

"Oh, yeah, I can imagine how it would work. A little quickie in the tack room between rides. God, can you imagine!"

"Hey, it might be worth it."

"Sure, then I'd have to find another trainer when we have our first lovers' quarrel. Good trainers are hard to come by. No thanks. The last student who went there got her butt kicked right out of Willow Creek."

Kate watched with rapt attention this man and horse moving as one being, turning, leaping, like gymnasts doing a floor exercise. All they needed was music, she thought. The horse was beautiful and the man, well, she might be divorced but she wasn't blind. She decided she liked the idea of riding breeches...on this man. He had long, slender but muscular legs and the tightest backside she had seen in a long time. She couldn't see his face, obscured in the shadow of his helmet and dark glasses, but his upper body was obviously strong and supple. She noticed he wore no riding gloves and his hands held the reins like he was caressing little birds between those long fingers. He had finesse

9

about him.

The rider dismounted, removed his hard hat and started to walk toward where she sat. He ran his hand through his black hair and a chill of déjà vu tickled the back of Kate's consciousness. She stood, ready to shake his hand and introduce herself. The woman in the office had said this was the man who taught the lessons. Well, for better or worse, this was why she was here. She was eager to get started.

But, as he came closer, a cold hand gripped Kate, and her heart began to throb in her head. A python had a stranglehold on her throat; she gasped for air that failed to reach her lungs.

It couldn't be. But it was, and she was trapped like a rabbit in a snare.

Brandon walked straight to Kate, blue eyes searing through her. "Ms. Waldon," he said with studied control, a fist clamped around the crop in his hand. "Please join me in the office."

"Certainly, lead the way." She squared her shoulders, tossed her hair back and followed, needing to almost jog to keep pace with his long strides.

"After you." He held the door for her and closed it behind them. "I can't believe you would track me down and come to my place of business. I gave you my information. Do you think I wouldn't follow through?"

Kate knew the signs of male temper. She had grown up in a house full of brothers. The way this man's jaw clenched was a clear warning of escalating anger and he didn't appear to be slamming on the brakes of his approaching tirade.

No way was this bombastic Irishman going to shout her down. She stared straight into his eyes and waited.

"Why would you come here? To be sure your precious sports car is fixed? It will be, I assure you.

But, truth be told, you were the cause of your own damage. I was simply trying to drive like a responsible person." He took a breath to continue, when Annie stepped through the door.

"Oh, Bran, I see you've—"

"Excuse me, Annie. I've something to attend to here," he all but shouted. He turned to Kate. "As I was saying, Ms. Waldon—"

"Bran, this is Kate Aiello." Annie tried to stop him, but he was on a roll.

"Ms.Waldon—" he repeated, his voice a tremor of frustration, modulating to a higher decibel.

"Aiello, Kate Aiello...your new student, Brandon Padraig."

Kate sensed a tone of warning in the woman's voice.

"This is Ms. Aiello."

"What? What are you talking about?" His brows furrowed.

Kate took a deep breath and extended her hand. "Kate Aiello. I've signed up for riding lessons."

"But, you...who's Catherine Waldon?" he stammered.

"I've been recently..." She couldn't say *divorced.* The word caught in her throat. "I recently changed back to my maiden name."

"Oh. I thought you... Sorry...uh..."

Annie, with an ease that must have come from years of saving her brother from himself, stepped in. "Well, Kate, I'll have some paperwork for you to fill out. You can start with the release of liability and there is also an emergency contact form. Here, you just have a seat and I'll get you all fixed up. Bran, why don't you decide which horse will be best suited to our Kate?" Her eyes pierced him like green, gilt-edged daggers.

"Excuse me, Annie...Ms. Aiello, Kate..." Brandon made his retreat as graciously as a male ego would allow.

Kate was mortified and completely justified in being furious. But she had made a decision and everyone, from her mother to her therapist, expected her to bail or fail. She wouldn't do either. She would get this done or go out in a blaze of glory trying. Brandon Sullivan was the best. She needed the best, could afford the best, and wouldn't compromise. She wasn't going to marry the obnoxious oaf, just let him put her up on a horse and give her some tips.

How hard could riding a horse be, anyway? All kinds of people rode. Bo Derek had ridden naked on a beach and scored a *10*. Kate had watched for hours while her own daughter, Laura, trotted 'round and 'round in a little arena on her rented pony.

"This is our liability release. Please read it carefully." Annie handed Kate a three page legal document. It read in part: "Under the Law of the State of Maryland, an equine professional is not liable for an injury or death of a participant in equine activities resulting from the inherent risks of equine activities."

Death? Not responsible for death? All right, Kate, don't panic. Who dies riding a horse?

She signed page after page, agreeing to wear an approved hard hat and a chest protector on cross country. Of course, the stipulations were moot. She would never ride on cross country. People who did were completely insane. Men and women, galloped wildly, jumped felled trees of enormous proportions, braved precipitous drops into deep ponds, and spanned ditches rivaling the Grand Canyon.

They Kate filled out the emergency contact card and wrote a check for a month of lessons, in advance. It occurred to her, with these fees, if Mr. Sullivan had more than a few students, he must be doing all right for himself. Handing the papers to Annie, she announced, "Well, I guess I'm ready to start."

****

Brandon strode out past the paddocks and into the hay barn where he let out a stream of foul language, English as well as Irish, unsurpassed by the devil himself.

When he had expended every last word in his lexicon of profanity, Brandon flopped down on a hay bale to think. Considering his behavior, he thoroughly expected, even with Annie's sweet cajoling, Kate Aiello was history.

If she had any sense she would take her fancy backside, put it in her pricey sports car and go down the road to Twin Oaks for her lessons. Good riddance to her. He had no patience for a woman like her. She was not a serious rider. She was dabbling. He didn't do dabblers. He taught the skills one needed for Eventing, the most challenging equestrian sport known to man or horse. He had no time for Kate Aiello.

Of course Annie would kill him if he didn't take the woman on. They were going broke, for God's sake. Every opportunity to increase business must be accepted. If he didn't pull Willow Creek out of its current doldrums he would be looking for work on someone else's farm before the year was through. His dear sister had come here to Maryland to help him get back on his feet, to help him cope, to help him grieve. He owed it to her to give this last great try. And he owed it to Fiona, God rest her soul. His lovely Fiona—hot-headed, beautiful Fi, who would be kickin' his arse from here to County Clare if she knew how close he was to quitting.

Bran stood, took a deep breath, brushed the hay from his breeches and walked back to the office to face the consequences of his stupidity.

As Annie led Kate out the door of the office, Brandon walked up from the paddocks. With a satisfied *okay you jackanapes I've saved you once more* look, Annie pulled herself up to her five-foot-two and smiled. "Kate is all signed up and ready. Who's she riding?"

"That would be Murphy. Come with me and I'll introduce you." He turned to Kate, peering down at her feet. "Did you bring riding boots?"

"Yes, they're in my car. Should I get them?"

"You'll be fine for now. Let me explain how this works around here. I will be your primary instructor, but I have a working student, Barb Matthews, who will help you with grooming and saddling...and cooling your horse down when you're done."

Grooming? Saddling? Kate had pictured this somewhat differently. For the amount of money she had agreed to pay, she'd expected someone else to prepare her mount. She'd figured she'd get on and ride, then hand the reins over to a trusty lackey when she was done. "Oh. That sounds...delightful," she said with as much sincerity as she could muster.

In the main barn, smells of hay, wood shavings, leather and horseflesh struck her with the reality of what she was doing. Brandon stopped in front of a stall with a Dutch door, the top half open to the barn. A reddish brown horse with a shiny black mane and tail stood with his back to them, turning his head to peer over a pile of hay. He greeted his visitors with a snort.

Brandon reached in his pocket and pulled out a piece of mint candy. When Murphy heard the cellophane crinkle, he nickered and approached the door.

"If you ever need to get this boy out of the pasture, he'll come a runnin' if you have a mint in your pocket. Spoiled he is." Brandon patted the sleek neck as the horse picked the morsel carefully out of his hand. "Murph, say hello to Katie."

Katie? No one had called her "Katie" in thirty

years. When Sullivan said it the name had a different sound, an extra syllable, it seemed. It occurred to her she should correct him. She didn't. "Murphy? Well, hello."

Brandon handed her a mint. "Give him this and he'll be your friend for life." He smiled.

Kate's tummy did a back flip. Brandon Sullivan, when he wasn't having a raving melt down, was a handsome man. She reminded herself she was a terrible judge of men.

"Murphy will take good care of you. He belonged to my wife."

Belonged? Wife? A cold stab of anger cut right through Kate and she stiffened. Here was another man who'd left his wife behind. And this arrogant bastard had gotten a horse in the settlement.

"Bran...Annie said you needed me."

Kate recognized the young woman who had been setting up the jumps in the arena.

"Ah, this must be the new student. I'm Barb Matthews. Great to have you join our little bunch. You'll like it here."

"Barbara, Ms. Aiello—Kate—will be riding Murphy for her lessons. Would you show her around and go over the basic ground work?"

"Sure, no problem. Do you want us to saddle him up?" Barb had a concerned look on her pretty face.

"Well, Katie, what do you think?" He lifted a brow in query. "I don't know if you have the time, but you are certainly welcome to take a short ride today and we will start in earnest tomorrow."

"Yes, please, that would be...nice." She felt a wave of fear pass through her and stroll off down the aisle. "I haven't ridden before but I'm here to learn."

Brandon rhythmically tapped his leg with a crop he had been carrying. "Barb, I'm on Caduceus next. Meet me out in the dressage arena." He nodded at Kate and strode off.

"Well then, Murphy, let's get you all dressed up." Barb grabbed a halter and handed it to Kate. "We'll start at the beginning." As Barb opened the door to the stall, Kate couldn't help but feel she was stepping though a time warp. She was stripping down and rebuilding herself into an independent woman who would learn to be a partner with this animal and, if she were lucky, an ally to herself.

Barb took her time and explained all the techniques Kate would need to prepare her horse for a day of riding. It surprised Kate when she was handed a sharp metal hook and told to clean Murphy's feet, but the horse was compliant and she found she was tentative but not frightened. There was so much equipment; saddle, pad, girth, bridle, and these Velcro-on boots Barb applied to protect the horse's front legs. Kate had to write notes to even hope of getting it right by herself. Barb reassured her she would have assistance until she felt completely comfortable with tacking up before she would be left on her own.

They hand-walked Murphy to the dressage arena just as Brandon finished working Caduceus. "Just in time," he called across the expanse. "Barbara darlin', if you'll take Caddy and cool him out, I'll help Katie get mounted." He vaulted off the horse with the grace of a gymnast and handed the reins to Barb.

Kate stood holding Murphy's reins, her feet rooted to the ground, watching the tall slender man striding in her direction. He moved like a feline, she thought—a stalking cat, muscle and sinew, lean and lithe. He removed his sunglasses and gave her a hint of a smile she thought might have a sense of humor behind it.

"Are you ready?" He stood closer than Kate's comfortable social distance.

"Ready? Oh, yes...yes I am. Uh, what do I do

first?" She felt dumbfounded and his proximity had her a bit rattled.

"Come over here to this step...we call it a mounting block...and put your left foot in the stirrup." She complied. "Now just give a little push with your right leg and hop up into the saddle."

Left foot, right foot, hop...she realized too late the hop wasn't big enough to get her right leg over the saddle. She felt his hands...around her waist, giving an extra boost to her efforts. "There you go now." One hand strayed to her calf and he adjusted her foot in the stirrup.

A bolt of electricity ran through Kate with such fury she was sure all her wiring had been fried. Hard enough to be sitting on a horse for the first time, but Mr. Sullivan was making her dizzy and not a little disconcerted.

He showed her all the necessary details and then snapped a long line on Murphy's bridle. With himself as hub, he sent the horse out on a circle. "I want you to get the feel of walking on the lunge line before you ride by yourself," he explained, and urged Murphy into an ambling walk.

They spent nearly an hour, and by the time they stopped Kate had managed to walk and trot this circle around Bran without disgracing herself. Though she still thought of him as an arrogant Philistine, Mr. Sullivan *was* a good teacher.

He offered to help her down from the saddle. Again his hands encircled her waist as she swung her right leg over the back of the saddle. His arms were strong as he set her on the sandy footing and she thought he kept his hands on her middle a bit longer than necessary, but decided she would let it slide for now.

"Oh, my legs feel like jelly." She laughed. "I think I might be sore tomorrow." It wasn't just her legs she was sure would ache. Kate was amazed at how much muscle effort it took just to stay balanced on a moving horse. Brandon had run her through a series of mounted exercises—windmilling her arms, standing in the stirrups with her hands stretched out to the sides and up over her head. She was required to do all these contortions at a standstill, at the walk and finally the trot.

"You have a lovely seat, you know."

"Thank you." Kate knew he was referring to the way she sat a horse, not complementing her bum, but it made her blush all the same.

"As a sort of apology...for my unforgivable behavior this morning...how about I put Murph up for you? So you can get along home...to your family."

"Thanks. That would be nice. I should be getting back." *I don't have anyone to go home to.* She didn't even have a cat or dog. The house would be deathly quiet. "I'll be here tomorrow. I signed on for three lessons a week."

Brandon smiled. "See you at eleven then...and a pleasant evening to you, Katie. Safe home, now."

When Kate pulled the Beemer into her garage she was covered with horse kisses—smears of green slobber adorned her white blouse. Her hair was tangled from the wind after being matted to her head under the helmet she had worn, and her breeches and formerly shiny new boots were covered with the fine dust of the sandy arena. Her legs ached, her backside felt blistered and she could not get the smile off her face.

She filled the jetted tub and lowered herself into the hot, bubbly water. She lay back, letting the pulses massage away her soreness—the well-deserved aches of accomplishment. She hoped to sleep tonight without nightmares, without lying awake kicking herself for twenty-five years wasted on the wrong man. She had the distinct feeling she'd found a chink in the wall of loss she had been trying to scale to reach herself on the other side.

****

By the time Brandon finished the last of his lessons it was after eight P.M. He was exhausted but had managed to get through the rest of the day without pissing anybody off. He hated to admit it but he was glad Kate Aiello had decided to forgive his contemptible behavior enough to want to continue at Willow Creek. He found her refreshing, different from the typical horse owners and riders he was used to dealing with. Hoping the bizarre behavior she had displayed on the road that morning was not a common occurrence for her, he tried to look at her as an effective rider. She had a good rider's body—legs long in proportion to her torso, the potential for strength without bulkiness—and a willingness to try what he asked of her.

Brandon thought of himself as an honest man, and he had to admit he found Kate rather attractive. She had the kind of womanly body he liked, with enough flesh on her bones to soften the curves. The horse world was full of women who worked harder at staying thin than they did at staying in the saddle. When he cuddled up to his woman, he wanted a welcoming female who fit to him and melted the hardness of his body into hers.

Fiona had been such a woman—fair-haired, petite and curvy—until chemotherapy stole her hair and the demons of illness wracked her body. Brandon fought the images of those last months when Fi had been so thin and weak. He wanted to remember her as the strong and gentle woman who could charm a man or a horse into doing her will. The mother of their two children had been a force to contend with when she was determined to have her way, but the one thing she could not defeat was the disease that took her life.

The look of concern on Barb's face when

Brandon told her Kate would be riding Murphy had chilled him. Since Fiona's death, no one but Bran had ridden the gelding. The horse had been Fiona's. Horse and woman had been bound at the heart.

At twenty years of age, Murph was as fine a specimen of horse flesh as ever there was. A Connemara-Thoroughbred cross, fifteen-and-a-half hands, the sleek bay still moved as elegantly as the day they purchased him at the horse auction in Claremorris, and he was safe enough for a beginner. The time had come to put sentiment aside and let Murphy earn his keep. Brandon had no room for equine barn ornaments.

The early autumn sun had set and Brandon walked the short distance to his house. He loved living right here near the horses. It was going to be very hard to leave this place. He hated to be all gloom and doom about his prospects, but the meeting at the bank had not been encouraging. The loan officer had looked at Brandon's debt-to-income ratio and sighed loudly.

"I see on your credit report you have a large outstanding balance at the University Hospital." He looked at Bran over his glasses.

"Yes, I'm trying to get that paid. It was all unavoidable, my wife was very ill." *Dammit man, have a heart. No one counts the cost when a loved one is dying.*

"You have some college loans. Are these for your children?"

What a stupid question. Who else would he be putting through college, for God's sake? "Yes," he replied. "I have a son, Kevin. He's a senior at Georgetown. My daughter, Brighid, is in her first year at the University of Maryland."

"Hmm, this is going to be very challenging, Mr. Sullivan. I don't believe I can offer you what you are requesting here. I might be able to get a very small loan approved, but it is hard to see how that will help you at this point." His voice was dour as he continued to peruse the paperwork on his desk.

Brandon's stomach was in knots as he gathered his papers together and started to rise from his uncomfortable perch. "I'm sorry to have bothered you." He extended his hand. "Thank you for your time."

"Well, now, Mr. Sullivan, let me just see. A short-term loan with your farm as collateral...this might work. I do have to warn you, though. This can be risky for you. You could lose your home and your farm."

"I don't see that I have much of a choice."

Now he could only hope his luck would change. He had a few good horses in training, and one, Penny Lane, backed by a lucrative sponsorship. Being a success in the business meant making a name for one's self. You did that by winning the big ones—Rolex, Fáilte, the World Equestrian Games— and becoming an Eventing icon like Davidson, O'Connor or Dutton. The Sullivans had been close to the dream before Fiona's illness, but losing her had stopped him in his tracks. Now he needed to recapture the vision.

He'd promised her. He'd also pledged Kevin and Brighid would finish college. The difficulty had come when Fi had taken his hand in her cool, frail one and made Bran give his word that he would seek a future without her.

"You are too full of love, my sweet man, to stop giving it away." Her breath had come in sorrowfully weak gasps. "You have to assure me you will allow...another into your heart. I...I have the easy part here, *Leannán*."

Leannán. Lover.

For more than half his life he had been that to her and she to him.

21

Laying his head gently against her chest, hearing her heart struggle to continue its life-sustaining burden, Brandon Sullivan had made the pledge and wept.

Chapter Two

The turquoise of the sea called, singing a siren's song past the rocks, shoals and the craggy cliffs. Cool salty breezes caressed her skin like gentle fingers, coaxing a moan of contentment from her throat. She stepped into the translucent water, letting it pool and weave around her slender ankles. Smooth pebbles glittered like precious gems tossed from the heavens. One of the jewel-like stones called to her and with trepidation she picked it out of its sandy bed. The pebble became a ring, a golden circle that turned hot to the touch and burned her palm with its stinging bite. The heat spread from her hand and settled in the center of her, near her heart. Like flames licking in concentric circles it broadened to breasts, arms, thighs, and out the tips of each limb.

This sea became a roiling tumult, matching the ache, reached into her chest and pulled her heart from its fragile moorings. A pyroclastic flow covered her like a blanket, as she struggled to free herself from the sweat-soaked sheets.

She was paralyzed. Kate couldn't move her legs. It was a nightmare. She would never walk again, never ride a horse. *Ahh...okay, Catarina, you can do this. Just roll over and start slowly.* Her back ached like she had been in labor for three days, her butt muscles were pummeled to mush and her legs cramped from thigh to ankle.

Gingerly, she rose and sat on the side of her bed. The pain in her spine elicited a wave of nausea threatening to render her helpless. She longed to remain supine for the rest of the day, ensconced in

23

her bed, eating chocolates and washing down Ibuprofen with diet soda. But she had a riding lesson at eleven and she would die rather than wimp out.

A shower helped soothe her agony. In a moment of clear thinking she decided going to the gym for a gentle workout and lots of stretching would be wise. She dressed in black spandex leggings, a T-shirt and running shoes, pulled her unruly mane into a ponytail and hobbled out the door. She threw her riding clothes in the trunk of the car so she could go straight to Willow Creek from the gym.

"Hey, Kate, how's it goin'?" Ginny, a bouncy blonde, with a bosom requiring major support, jogged in place between machines.

Though Kate had never been much for nurturing female companionship, she liked this group of women who met every other morning to pump, sweat and grimace as well as laugh and gossip. Their ages ranged from adolescence to one foot in the grave and the other on a banana peel, and they came in all shapes and sizes. The motto on the wall read, "No men, no mirrors, no make-up required," and if you were having a *fat* day, this was just the place to put it in perspective.

"Well, Gin, I had my first riding lesson yesterday and I'm feeling my age…all thirty-nine years of it," Kate joked as she raised her arms over her head and started to stretch. "I'm going to take it easy today."

Cher rocked from the speakers as Kate maneuvered the first of the machines, slowly at first and then pushing to her limit.

"Change stations now," the overhead recording prompted.

Kate moved to the mat between machines and jogged in place. Yeah, Cher girl, no shit, he shot me down for sure, the arrogant bastard.

"Change stations now."

As her heart rate increased, so did her anger. She'd given Jeffrey her best years, when she was young, vibrant, still attractive to other men. Now she felt used up. Kate pushed the hydraulics of the exerciser to her max, thinking of it as assailing the smugly pudgy face of her former husband.

Cher sang on about crying over *her* man.

Kate would not cry. Her jog in place became a challenging cardiac run. *Screw him!*

"Change stations now," came the disembodied voice.

If resentment was good for anything, it was a motivator. Ginny had once told Kate looking good was the best revenge. *Well, eat your cholesterol-clogged black heart out, Dr.Waldon, because I'm on a roll here.*

"Stop and check your heart rate, ten seconds, starting...now."

She didn't stop to count her pulse. Mocking sensibility, she pushed on until she had completed the three circuits of her routine. It was invigorating and the energy expenditure and spilling of rage made her forget her aching muscles.

After her workout, Kate sponged the perspiration from her face and armpits, and changed into her breeches and a long-sleeved knit shirt. Catching her reflection in the glass of the door, she decided she liked the way she looked. It was liberating to be this casual about her appearance. Her hair, free of its constraining scrunchy, sprang wild about her face, and her complexion glowed. She felt more alive than she had yesterday morning.

At Willow Creek, Kate sat on the bench near her parked car. She pulled and stomped until her feet were solidly encased in her tall boots. How did anyone walk very far in this torturous footwear? Standing, she stumbled on stiff ankles toward the barn.

The barn aisle was dark and cool, making Kate feel almost reverent, like she was entering a church. Only the sounds of contented equines disturbed the quiet inside. Hearing muted voices behind the wall, she headed in that direction to find Barb, but the scene that met her gaze at the door stopped her dead.

His back was to the open door and he towered over the small form of a woman. With tanned hands braced against the wall on either side of her, he was grinding his hips seductively.

Stunned into immobility, Kate watched as he lowered his head for a kiss and groped under the woman's shirt.

It was Barb Matthews!

The scum bag, the low life, the reeking sonofabitch! Jesus, the girl is young enough to be his daughter.

Kate spun on her heels, planning a hasty retreat. She would demand her money back. She would not associate with this villain, this...this child molester. But as she stepped forward she came reeling headlong into a hard body. *Brandon Sullivan.*

"In a hurry?" he questioned, catching her in his arms to keep her from falling over him.

"Ahh! Oh my God." Confused, she shot a glance back toward the farrier's stall. "Who?"

Brandon followed her gaze and a hint of a smile lifted his lips. "Kevin Flanagan Sullivan!"

"Yeah, Dad?" came the response.

Kate heard a giggle and some scrambling about, and Barb rushed out the side door. A young man, red-faced with either embarrassment or passion denied, stepped toward Kate and Brandon.

She blinked her eyes shut and when she opened them he was still there. He was the image of his father, black hair, blue eyes, the same slender build, tight ass and swagger to his walk.

"Kevin, I thought you came to ride some horses for your old da, not to be messin' with the barn help." Bran raised a brow in question.

"Sorry, Dad...couldn't stop myself."

"Kate." Brandon nodded toward his son. "This is my firstborn, God help me. Kevin...Kate Aiello, our new student."

"Nice to meet you, Kate." The young man shook Kate's hand and smiled, showing perfect teeth and a twinkle in his blue eyes. "Hope my dad's been behaving himself. It would be nice to keep you around for a while...dress up the place."

Kate returned his smile, relieved to discover she'd jumped to a wrong conclusion. He was terribly charming, apparently a family characteristic.

"Enough, Kev," Brandon interrupted. "Get to work. And fetch Barbara for me. She's to help Katie get ready." When Kevin walked away, Brandon laughed. "College isn't teaching him any manners and apparently I'm not a good example."

"Does he live here, with you?"

"No, only here for a few days. He's at Georgetown University, a senior, but comes home whenever he can. I can always use extra hands around here."

"And, his mother, does she live nearby?" Kate knew it was none of her business, but she was curious about the former Mrs. Sullivan. After all, she was riding the woman's horse.

The blue of Brandon's eyes darkened and his smile faded. His hardened, clenched jaw transformed his face into one she could only describe as fearsome.

"No."

Was it anger? Disdain? Kate had no idea what had set him off, but Brandon grabbed a lunge line and continued to the arena without further comment.

It took a full half hour to get Murphy ready. The saddle slipped. Kate's hands failed to grip the leather girth billets. The horse raised his head and avoided her lame attempt at placing the bit in his mouth. He refused to pick up his feet to be cleaned.

Kate felt incompetent, but Barb assured her Murph was only testing and when he was certain who was boss, he would comply without question.

Brandon was waiting when the women approached, Kate leading a reluctant Murphy.

"Well now, let's get started." Moving out of the way of the horse, Bran stopped Barb as she started to help Kate mount. "Uh, no, she's got to do it by herself this time."

Kate turned her back on Bran and stepped up to Murphy. "Huh! You don't think I can, do you?" She put up a brave front, but whispered to the horse, "Okay, good boy, stand nice and still now and don't let me look like an idiot." Gathering the reins in her left hand, she took a deep breath and slipped her foot in the stirrup.

Bran stood so close she could feel his breath on her neck. Kate tried to distract herself with the idea that he was simply poised to intervene if she miscalculated and failed to get herself into the saddle. Her legs felt like cooked noodles but she managed to swing herself up in one graceful try.

"Perfect," he praised. "Now we're going to do what we did yesterday...start you on the line. After we're done, you can ride on your own a bit." He turned to Barb. "Saddle Clancy for me, if you would, please."

The first several minutes felt good to Kate. She let her back and pelvis swing along to the rhythm of the walk. Trotting was more daunting. The jarring, jolting pace bounced her feet out of the stirrups and threatened to launch her into the stratosphere. Bran taught her the trick of it, how to rise to the beat of the trot, and life became bearable again. The warm autumn sun caressed the exposed skin on her arms and a slight breeze cooled her at the same time.

She wasn't quite sure when the pleasant sensation started to change. The coolness became a sickening chill that settled in her gut and turned rapidly to a searing hot orb. Her thighs and seat were damp with sweat where they touched the saddle, and beads of perspiration formed on her scalp and trickled from under her helmet and down her neck.

She gave an involuntary gasp. "I have to stop. Please, Brandon, I need a break."

"Sure now and are you all right?"

"Yes, I'm just a little...uh...out of breath. I left my water in my car...Oh..." She actually felt faint, and the damnable hot flash wasn't passing as quickly as usual. *Take a deep breath...don't you dare fall off this horse in front of this man. Get a grip, Aiello.*

Brandon gathered up the lunge line and stepped to Murphy's side. "Do you need to get down?"

"No!" she all but shouted. The thought of hopping off and having him see sweat stains on her breeches horrified her. *He'll think I peed my pants.*

Bran called to Barb. "Hey, darlin', leave Clancy with me and get our Katie a bottle of water, would you, please."

She handed the big, black-bay thoroughbred over. "Sure, I'll be right back." Kate heard her whisper, "Is she okay? She looks like she's gonna keel...or hurl."

"My thoughts exactly. Hurry on, will you?" And he turned back to Kate.

Kate wiped her brow with her shirt sleeve and tried to smile. "I'm okay, now." She didn't want to be a sissy and quit. These episodes were, after all, going to be part of her life for a while. If she got off the horse every time her rebellious body threw her a fast ball, she'd never learn to ride.

"Here you go." Bran handed her the water bottle Barb had retrieved.

"Thank you. Do all your students get this kind of service?" Kate finally managed a genuine smile.

"No, only when they look like they need an ambulance," he teased. "If you really are feeling better, I'm gonna hop on my Clancy here, and we can take a walk."

"I'd love that. I'm fine now. Maybe I was just a little dehydrated. I worked out pretty hard at the gym before I came here."

She was lying. It wasn't that simple, but this man would never understand. After all, he hadn't stuck with his wife long enough to suffer through the change with her. She was most likely in the same boat as Kate—lonely, miserable and overheated.

"Just shorten those reins a bit. Murphy will stick to Clancy like glue," Brandon said as he swung up into the saddle.

They rode out of the arena and into the field surrounding the property. The hay had been cut for the last time this growing season and lay waiting to be baled. They ambled along between the parallel cuttings and out to a track that bordered the area.

Neither spoke. Kate listened to the meadowlarks call, the distant sound of a tractor working a field and the hum of life around her. An overwhelming contentment washed over her as quickly as the surge of unwelcome heat had gripped her minutes earlier. The freshness of mown hay, clarity of air and scent of warm horse calmed her body and soothed the pain in her still freshly-bruised psyche. She thought of this as therapy—mental, physical and spiritual—and if she allowed herself to have a little fun along the journey, all the better.

Bran finally spoke. "So, Katie, tell me...why riding lessons?"

Shaken from her reverie she took a moment to answer. "Well, I guess it has to do with taking care of myself, doing something just for me." How much did she want to share with this stranger? "My daughter is grown, she lives in D.C. I'm on my own and, well, I just thought it was time to do something new."

"Hmm. Hard to imagine why a woman like you would be alone, if you don't mind my sayin' so, Katie."

"It's Kate." She corrected him.

"What?" He looked genuinely confused.

"Kate...my name...it's Kate, not Katie." She wasn't sure why it bothered her that he liked to call her that. Maybe it felt a little too personal. Jeffrey had never called her anything but Catherine.

"Ah and why not? Katie suits you well, a good name for a beautiful woman."

Nervous laughter welled up in her. "You have that 'charming Irishman' thing down to a fine science, don't you? Go ahead, call me anything you want." Obviously, the man had his own opinions. It was most likely fruitless to try and correct him. She should have resented it, but his arrogance fit him like those breeches he wore. From another man, his attitude would have felt patronizing, but coming from him it was...well...titillating.

He said nothing, just looked directly into her eyes and smiled a slow, lazy grin that made Kate shiver deep in her bones.

Chapter Three

The house was quiet except for the ringing of the phone. Kate dropped her bag of barn clothes on the kitchen floor and grabbed the receiver, answering just as the machine picked up. "Hold on, don't hang up," she said over the automated message.

"Catarina, are you there, Cara? Catarina?"

"I'm here. *Ciao*, Mamma. I just walked in the door. How are you?"

A wave of guilt passed over Kate. She hadn't called her mother in a week. It was painful to keep rehashing the situation with Jeffrey, and Kate found it easier to just not call. But it wouldn't work for long. Her mother counted the hours and the days between communiqués.

"Oh, well, you know, Cara, how I worry about you if you don't call. It's been a week, you know."

"I know and I'm sorry, Mamma. The time just gets away sometimes. How's everyone? Is Joey there tonight?" Joey was Kate's youngest sibling. He was thirty-five, still single and happy to let his mom fuss over him. His two older brothers teased him and called him *mammone*, an Italian mamma's boy, but Kate was glad he spent the time with their mom. Joey was a good kid.

"No, he had a date. I got it in my head to make gnocchi. I'll have to freeze most of it and you know, Catarina, it's not good after it's been frozen."

"Yes, Mamma, I know. I'm cooking for one now myself." *Oh shit.* She hadn't meant to let that slip. But it was too late.

"*O Dio.* My poor bambina...that man...how

could he treat you so? You should come home. I have room for you here. Catarina...you should not be alone."

"Mamma, I'm fine. I like living by myself...really. And, I have plenty of friends. Actually, Mamma, I have to go now because I'm supposed to meet some friends and have dinner. They're taking me out for my birthday." She looked at the kitchen clock. She had an hour.

"Your birthday, yes, I remembered. I put something in the mail for you. Oh, I can't believe my bella Catarina is fifty years old. *Buon compleanno*, Cara."

"Thank you, Mamma. I've got to go now. I'll call you soon, I promise. I love you."

After ten more minutes of promises and I love you's, Kate hung up the phone and went upstairs to shower. She did love her mother, but she was so sick of trying to make her feel better about the divorce. There was no way Silvana Aiello would ever understand. She was, after all, not just an Italian, she was seventy-two years old. Life had been hard, harder than anyone of Kate's generation could imagine. Marriage, family and the Church were the only constants in Mamma's life and in her mode of thinking it should be the same for everyone. No, Silvana Gondolfo Aiello could never comprehend divorce.

Kate showered, dressed and headed to Dimitri's to meet her friends. She felt a bit like she was driving to her own funeral. For God's sake, who would willingly celebrate a fiftieth birthday? But, Ginny had insisted and Kate never wanted to disappoint anyone. She even got dressed up for the occasion—soft, wine-colored wool trousers and a creamy silk blouse that complemented her complexion, pearls that had belonged to her grandmother and ear studs to match.

In one last attempt at festivity she had painted her lips dark red, dusted her eyelids with shadow and highlighted her cheeks with deep mauve blush. Kate took a good long look at her reflection in the rear-view mirror and tried not to be negative. Not too bad, she decided. The make-up that would have made a paler woman look like a street walker, actually made her look quite elegant, and she was pleased with the overall impression.

The parking lot was full when she arrived and the restaurant was packed. Kate found Ginny, Angie and Marietta at a corner table where they had already emptied a full bottle of wine while waiting.

"There's the birthday girl now," Ginny yelled, so there was no hiding the fact that Kate was indeed the honored guest. "Sit, we've ordered your favorite wine. You look fabulous."

There were several gift bags on the table. Kate feared the candles would light the tissue paper and the whole table would go up like the Space Shuttle. "Thank you, Ginny." *Please lower your voice. I'm dying here.* "Thanks Marietta, Angie...this is...great."

"Have a glass of this...you'll love it. It's just what the doctor ordered." Marietta laughed at herself. She *was* the doctor, after all, a pathologist who had worked in the same hospital as Jeffrey. Kate knew Marietta's opinion of Jeffrey was little higher than pond scum.

"Well, Dr. Johnson, how much of this booze do you recommend?" Kate wasn't much of a drinker, and she needed to be sober enough to drive home, but she could allow herself a glass or two of the Assyrtiko. "Have you ordered yet?"

"No, we're waiting for you," Angie said and waved at the young man serving tables. "Damn, he's a cutie. Too bad he's the same age as my son."

"Haven't you heard? Geez, it's all over

Hollywood, all those aging actresses hooking up with the twenty-something guys. Oh my God, can you imagine?" Ginny laughed. "I wouldn't mind young and hard one more time, before it's too late."

"When is it too late? Not 'til I'm in my grave, sister." Marietta added.

Kate sipped her wine and couldn't help but smile. Maybe it wasn't too late, but where does a woman over fifty find romance? Didn't a statistician a few years back say it was more likely to be kidnapped by terrorists than for a woman over forty to find a man? Kate figured that meant she would have a better chance of being abducted by space aliens.

Somehow they managed to eat dinner between all the laughing, gossiping and telling crazy tales from their misspent youth. Kate did have her two glasses of wine and was feeling relaxed and possibly even happy for the first time in months.

"All right, Kate, we've waited long enough. You don't get dessert until you open your presents," Ginny announced.

"Yeah, I'm actually a little frightened," Kate admitted, reaching for one of the bags on the table. "Is this something I can safely open in public?"

"Oh, sweetie, that one's from me. It's just a boring 'real' present." Angie reached over the table and hugged Kate. "Happy birthday, girlfriend."

"Oh, Angie. Oh, I'm going to cry." It was a framed photo of Kate and her daughter, Laura, when they had all gone to the sea for a day trip. The sun was behind the two women and they looked like sisters, one dark, one blond but with the same classic features. "This is perfect. I didn't know you had a picture of us. Thank you."

"Okay, okay enough of the poignant stuff. Here's one from me." Marietta handed Kate an envelope and a small box. "Go ahead now, it won't bite. Well, not right away, anyhow. Open the envelope first."

"You're scaring me." She peeked inside the envelope and pulled out a card. Okay, not too frightening. A slip of paper slid out of the card. "What's this?" She read and started to laugh.

"You have to read it out loud," Marietta insisted.

"It's a prescription for a colonoscopy, from Dr. M. Johnson. Why, I can hardly wait. Do I get a matching mammogram with this?"

"You greedy girl." They all laughed like fools. "You didn't open the box. It's something to wear to the colonoscopy."

In the little box, a pair of ruby ear studs glittered. "These are beautiful, Marietta. Thank you. You're a good friend."

"Dear, you are the bravest woman I've ever met. And, if anyone asks me how I know, I'll tell them because I know your ex-husband. And, by the way, you look like a million bucks tonight. Here's a toast to Catarina Aiello, a fine-looking babe." They all raised their glasses and drank.

"There's one more." Ginny smiled a mischievous grin and handed her a brightly colored bag.

"Are you going to give me a hint?" Kate asked.

"Sure, you don't have to feed it, it provides hours of fun and it doesn't require the presence of a man. How's that for hints?"

Kate closed her eyes and took a deep breath. She reached into the bag and looked at Ginny with total bewilderment. "Am I looking at what I think I'm looking at? Ginny?" She extracted a bright yellow rubber ducky from the bag. "Tub toy?"

"Squeeze him," Ginny suggested.

When Kate pressed her fingers into the yellow plastic she expected it to quack. Instead, like a duck having a seizure, it shook in her hand. "Ginny, it's a...vibrator...oh, my God. Where did you find such a thing?"

"Never mind where I found *him*. All he takes is batteries, you don't have to cook for him and he'll never leave you unsatisfied."

Kate wasn't sure if she would die of embarrassment or lack of oxygen from laughing. She squeezed the ducky into action and set him in the middle of the table to watch him dance about in a head-bobbing frenzy among the wine glasses and gift wrappings. "*Now* I want dessert."

The women were well into baklava, crème caramel and cheesecake when a party of four was seated at the table next to them. Kate's back was turned and she didn't see the group, but then she heard his voice. There was no mistaking that musical lilt; it was Brandon Sullivan, and he noticed her before she even had a chance to lick the baklava crumbs from her lips.

"Hey, look who we have here. It's our Katie." He turned to Kevin, Barb, and Annie. "Ah and you find the best folks out'n about some evenings."

"Brandon, what...what a surprise...uh...let me introduce my friends," she fumbled. The wine made her feel loose and disjointed. His sudden presence threatened to unhinge the last of her decorum. He was dressed, not in his usual breeches or tattered jeans, but in dark trousers and a crisp white dress shirt open at the collar. He had his jacket draped casually over his shoulders. His eyes drifted lazily over Kate. How she managed to get all the names straight was a miracle she did not want to have to repeat.

"It's Kate's birthday," Ginny blurted out, looking at the man like she had just been offered additional dessert.

"Is it now? Well then, happy birthday, Katie." Before she could even think of a response, he bent over her and kissed her on the cheek. His lips were warm and soft and he smelled of expensive whiskey and clean maleness. "You look beautiful tonight," he whispered, his breath tickling her ear and eliciting a shiver that spread through her body and settled in places she had forgotten existed. He said good evening to the other women and joined his family at their table.

Kate was not normally so lacking in vocabulary, but *stunned* was too weak a word to describe her state of being. She tried to smile serenely at her friends, who were just staring googly-eyed at the man now sitting and chatting companionably with his family, looking intently at a menu.

"Kate, have you been holding out on us?" Ginny whispered, then giggled.

"He's just my riding instructor," she tried to convince them with the truth. "Really."

"Well, if you don't want him, send him my way. Or the young one who looks just like him." Marietta spoke under her breath.

It was clear to Kate that she was not going to get them to stop their teasing and she imagined Brandon knew what they were all laughing about. She was also pretty certain he had done what he did for its effect on her. *Why was he flirting?* "Okay, enough, I've really got to get home. Thank you all for the great party."

They all stood, hugged and kissed before Kate headed to her car. The cool night air began to clear the fuzziness out of her befuddled brain. Why had she reacted like an inexperienced adolescent? It brought back memories of being twelve years old again, when she had a crush on a young parish priest. The guilt was devastating and she couldn't even share her troubles in the confessional because she was terrified he would know she was speaking of him. And now she was right back there, a giddy school girl. Did she give herself away? Did Brandon Sullivan see how she responded to his touch? *Jesus, he most likely comes on to anything with a pulse. The man is hopeless.*

****

To Brandon it had been just a happy birthday peck on the cheek—no different from a kiss he might give his son, daughter or Annie on a special day. He came from a demonstrative family and a vibrant culture where emotions were worn like a vulnerable breastplate. The Irish had joy and love, sorrow and despair woven so tightly into their history in story and song it seemed a waste not to share it with the world.

If he had been entirely honest, he would have admitted to the others at the table, as he had already admitted to himself, he wished he had kissed her lips, red, moist and sweet with the honey of the baklava.

Annie echoed his thoughts. "Well, didn't Katie look lovely tonight? Gallant of you to control yerself and not just kiss her on that tempting mouth of hers."

Kevin agreed and Bran squirmed under his gaze. He wasn't sure how his son would react if he were to become seriously involved with a woman. Earlier that fall Brandon had, in what he now knew was a despondent moment, taken one of the women at Willow Creek out to dinner. He had been desperately lonely and had, in a blaze of stupidity, kissed her. She all but chased him around the barn for weeks after that and he finally had to tell her it was time to move her horse to another stable and leave him be. She was incensed, while he was embarrassed and swore he would never let loneliness influence his judgment again.

His children had not been privy to the oath Fiona had elicited from her husband in those last days. God knows he would have promised her anything to give her peace. But, surely if Kevin knew, he would understand. Brighid might be a different story. She had taken her mother's death as such a devastating blow that Brandon had feared for the girl's physical as well as mental health. Oddly, worrying over his daughter had been one of the catalysts in transforming his own grief into an almost bearable pain. But the sound of Brighid's voice, the curve of her cheek, the way she gestured with her delicate hands when she spoke were so much like her mother that Brandon, more than once, had to reach for her and touch her to be sure she was not Fiona's ghost. No, Brighid would not take it well, her da with a woman who was not her mam.

Brandon knew he should mind his p's and q's with Kate. After all, she was his client, his student and, although it was not uncommon for romance to bloom in the close knit community of a riding stable, he was the boss and jealousy abounded wherever few men and many women congregated. But he wasn't a man who courted denial and he knew he liked the look of Kate Aiello.

He wasn't sure if he preferred Kate with the wild chestnut mane flying about her face, sable eyes flashing a warning, passion simmering so close to the surface he could feel the heat from across the room or the shy, bewildered and softly feminine Katie, who shivered at his touch and veiled her ardor like a forbidden jewel.

"Dad," Kevin's voice broke into Bran's thoughts, "you got any big plans you're not telling us about?"

"Plans, what plans?" *Why would I have plans?* "Oh, for the coming season, yes...Well, Kevin, what do you think of Penny Lane?" *Jaysus, I thought he was reading my mind.*

"She's a nice one. Of course, you haven't let me take her over a fence, so I'll hold my opinions until that day." Kevin was a talented rider and a damn good cross country jockey. He needed more miles in the saddle and the kind of patience only years could teach, but he had the love. Bran could see it.

"I'm thinking she's as good a mount as I've got for the coming season. She'll jump the moon for me if I ask and has good speed. I'd appreciate your help with her conditioning." Bran knew he had to be careful. Mrs. Dalwhinny had made it clear that she wanted no one but Brandon Sullivan on her horse, save for Barb to warm the mare up. However, one person couldn't do it all and conditioning took precious time out of a trainer's day. Kevin was more than capable and he was willing.

"Sure, Dad, but it'll be mostly on weekends until semester break."

"That'll do. Thanks." He couldn't tell his son just how much it meant. Hiring another person to exercise horses would surely speed him down the slippery slope of financial disaster faster than he was already tumbling. He had to last until next spring. He needed to get into the winner's circle or he'd be just another poor, landless Irishmen downing his pints and bragging about the good ol' days.

Chapter Four

Autumn had never been one of Kate's favorite times of the year. She had always started to feel the pressure of the holidays looming like a wolf in the woods ready to catch her unprepared. Nightmares of forgetting someone or something, disappointing her family or one of the numerous volunteer organizations she supported would haunt her sleep. While it seemed that all around her were enjoying the festivities, Kate fretted and obsessed over every detail.

As she watched the leaves color and the days shorten this year, it all took on a different perspective. A chilly day was more about fitting long underwear beneath her breeches than picking out just the right outfit for the hospital auxiliary party. Storm clouds meant deciding whether to ride in the indoor arena or risk getting soaked by a sudden cloud burst, not how she was going to fight the traffic at the mall during peak shopping hours. Her little car became a rolling collection of clothes, boots and laundered saddle pads and the family room coffee table no longer had space for the large Metropolitan Museum of Art folio; horse tack catalogues usurped the area.

Her riding skills progressed and she was now able to ride a twenty-meter circle with acceptable accuracy at the walk and trot. She had wept the first time she cantered Murphy alone, without the lunge line to guide her. The floating feeling of freedom, his body moving under her at her bidding, was like flying without the need for wings.

Brandon had been gentle with her when she was hesitant, but firm when she needed a push. The first time she took a tumble—when she had badly miscalculated the bouncy nature of Murphy's trot, lost her stirrups and flopped ungracefully into the dust—he rushed to her side in concern. Once satisfied that she was shaken but not injured he said, "Back on the horse, Aiello. This is not a sport for wimps. Oh, and by the way, you owe me for that one."

She, momentarily, hated him and thought of him as a boorish oaf, but she knew he was right and thanked him for not allowing her to fail. Now she understood why she would occasionally see a gaily-wrapped bottle of Chardonnay or a beribboned decanter of Jameson on Bran's office desk. If you fall, you owe him. It was the tradition.

It was a chilly Friday in mid-November. Autumn leaves picked up by the wind scudded along the ground like fleeing varmints. With no lesson scheduled, she had decided this would be a day when she and Murphy would share some quality time. She loved the cold days when she would tie him in the barn aisle and brush him, breathing in the earthy scents and hearing him rumble and nicker to her as she fussed over him.

****

Brandon pulled in and parked next to the BMW. His heart accelerated a notch when he saw she was there. It was not her lesson day, which meant she had come simply because she liked being here. The thought of it made him warm inside. He had suspected from the first that she could be a real horsewoman disguised as a housewife. Now he was sure. Any woman who preferred to be in a cold, damp barn full of equines blowing horse snot on her clothes to being at a spa getting a massage or her nails polished was a true daughter of Epona.

He was congratulating himself on his astute people skills when he noticed the left rear quarter panel of Kate's car had been repaired. There was no sign of the damage his truck had done that fateful day she had swerved to miss the squirrel, causing their lives to intersect with a bang and a crunch of metal. Hmm...odd, he thought. He hadn't heard anything from the insurance company. He would have to ask Annie about that. He headed for the office.

"Good morning, Annie. How's my favorite sister this fine day?" He gave her a kiss on the cheek as she sat at the desk.

"If you mean to say 'only sister dumb enough to keep your books,' I'm frustrated...if ye must know." Her smile belied her genuine concern for their financial state. "How much longer do you think I can put off paying this hay bill?"

"I've got a little something here for you that should ease your mind." He handed her a bank deposit receipt. "This should cover it." He took a seat at his desk and started to shuffle though the papers that littered the small space.

"What are you looking for?"

"Well, I must have gotten a notice from the insurance for the fixin' of Katie's car. Now I can't find it. Have you seen anything like that? I'm sure they plan to cancel my policy." He was tossing paper and unopened mail around to no avail.

"I never saw anything from the insurance. Are you sure it was reported and all?"

"Yes, of course, how else would she get the car fixed? I had better ask Kate. I'll be right back." As he reached for the door, it opened and Kate stood smiling on the other side. "Well, just the lady I've been lookin' for. Come in."

"Why were you looking for me? Hi, Annie. Brandon, I owe you this."

She handed him a bottle of Bushmills Single Malt. "For my unplanned dismount."

"Umm, I like a woman who knows her Irish whiskey. Thank you, but don't land on yer bum too often or you'll render me a drunkard." He loved his sister, but right now he wished she would disappear and leave him to enjoy Kate's company unobserved. He'd almost forgotten why he had wanted to talk to her. "Katie, I never heard from the insurance about fixing your car. I'm afraid I must have misplaced the correspondence."

The softness of her lips hardened and the smile in her eyes turned to concern. "I...uh...well you won't be getting any notice. I didn't report the damage. I decided to get it fixed on my own."

Brandon's jaw clenched and his throat tightened. "I told you I'd take care of it. You shouldn't have, Kate. I...well, I'm a man of my word. Did you think I wouldn't take responsibility for the situation?" His voice raised a notch.

"It wasn't that, Bran, I just thought—"

"You just thought I would not or could not follow through?" *Why am I doing this?* Stupid pride spurred him into a gallop toward calamity. He rushed headlong to put one foot and then the other squarely into his big mouth. "I was fully prepared to take the responsibility for the damage, even though I wasn't at fault..."

"You what? Just a minute here, *Mister* Sullivan. Are you saying *I* was not driving safely?" Kate's eyes sparked with anger and her hands waved in the air emphasizing every spoken word. "Just you listen to me. I got the damn car fixed because I wanted to do it myself. It had nothing to do with your silly male pride."

"My 'silly male pride' is it now?" He took a step that put him within either kissing or strangling range and stood with his hands balled at his sides.

Annie rose from her desk. "Brandon. Kate. Excuse me, but as an innocent observer here, I'd like to point out that you are both being completely unreasonable." She slipped her arms into her coat. "I'm going to step outside for a breath of fresh air, while you two try to see eye to eye." She left, closing the door behind her.

Brandon wanted to move back, away from Kate, where he couldn't smell the scent of her hair and feel the heat off her body, but he was unable. She must be some kind of enchantress, a *selkie* come to steal his soul away and carry him out to sea. "Katie?"

"What?" The sharpness had left her voice.

"Katie," he said again, liking the way her name tumbled from his tongue. "Why are we doin' this?" His feet moved a half step toward her.

"I don't know. Do you?"

He was so close he could see into her eyes, dark as semi-sweet chocolate, with tiny golden sparks around the irises that shifted with the shadow of her long dark lashes. Her mouth was parted as if she were about to speak, luscious full lips that appeared to turn up at the corners even when she tried to be serious. "I think I might—"

"Dad, I'm finished..." Kevin stopped halfway in the door. "Oh...uh...sorry...excuse me..."

Brandon turned away from Kate and ran his hand through his hair in an attempt to regain his brain. "No problem, Kev...you're done you say. Good...good. I'll come out with you, I wanted to check Penny and see if we need to wrap her legs tonight. She worked hard today. Kate, I'll catch up with you later." And he rushed out the door like a man with the devil himself at his coattails.

****

Kate could not move her feet. She was rooted to the spot, welded right to the floorboards from the heat of that man. Her fault? He thought the damage

46

to her car was her fault? Well, that was one of the reasons she paid for the repairs herself, but she wasn't about to admit it to him, not when he was being such a pig about the whole thing. She had started to feel guilty as hell about her role in the collision and, if truth be known, she had been *driving while impaired* one might accuse. The wounds of her loss had been fresh that morning and her body's thermostat had gone mad. Everything happened so quickly, and yet in slow motion.

"Ah Kate, ye'er still here." It was Annie, returning to retrieve the bloody remains of her brother. "And where's Bran?"

"He went with Kevin to check on Penny."

Annie smiled her sweetest smile. "Well now, I hope you didn't injure him too severely, he has to make a livin', ye know. Have a seat and join me, it's too chilly out there to go fussing with old Murphy now, anyway."

Looking at Annie, Kate tried to see a family resemblance to the Sullivan men. It was hard at first. Annie had flaming red hair sprinkled with silver and fair skin with just the slightest hint of freckles over the rise of her cheekbones. Her eyes were sea green. Kate had wondered at first if they were enhanced with colored contact lenses, but the honeyed sprinkles radiating from her pupils were definitely the real thing.

Apart from the diversity of her coloring, she did have a look that she shared with her brother. It was a presence that made one want to stand at attention and salute, a demeanor of confidence buffered with a loving heart and a sense of humor.

"He was all in one piece when he left. I think he owes Kevin his life." *And possibly mine.* Kate's eyes scanned the office as they talked. She had been in this small room dozens of times and it never stopped amazing her, the number of awards, plaques and certificates on the walls. Behind Bran's desk she had seen a photograph that she was sure must be of Kevin, sitting on a dark horse that looked like a younger version of Clancy. Kate squinted at the date in the left hand corner of the image—*April 1978 World Three Day Event Championships*. Bran, youthful and handsome, with that same look of defiance she had seen in his face this morning.

"Annie, this is *Bran*."

"Oh that, yes, his first international event. An historic moment actually. That competition became the Rolex Three Day, still goes on every April."

"Did he win?" It sounded like a big deal, the way Annie described it.

The other woman laughed. "Ah, no, for sure. He didn't get eliminated, but he was way down in the standings...no...the gold medal went to Bruce Davidson and Tango. Bran should have been happy to complete the course, but he wanted a better finish. He's a perfectionist, you know."

"That couldn't be Clancy."

"No, that's Clancy's sire, Carrick. Ah and he was a brave one Carry was, would have given his heart and his last breath for Bran. Clancy's a fine jumper, but just never had the speed. Big disappointment, but that's the world of horses."

Another photo caught Kate's attention—a gleaming bay in flight over a monstrous rock wall. Kate's imagination would never even have dreamed that a horse could leap over such an obstacle. "Annie, who's this?"

"That?" She removed her bifocals and looked at the photo with an expression Kate could only describe as reverent. "That's our Fiona and her Murphy. What a pair they were."

He still had a picture of his ex-wife? Well, maybe they had an amicable divorce. It did happen, Kate had heard. "So, that would be Brandon's *ex*?"

"Ex? Why no. What would make you think that?" Annie looked perplexed. "Fiona, God rest her soul...she's gone from us. It'll be two years ago this coming spring."

A chill ran through Kate that started with a knife thrust to her chest and ended with goose bumps on her arms. *Gone...as in...dead?* How could she have been so wrong about Brandon? Then, the thought struck her like a ball peen hammer knocking from inside her cranium; what stupid things had she said? When had she implicated him as a callous lout who had left his wife and taken her horse and probably her heart? What stereotype had she pasted on Bran? He wasn't Jeffrey and she should have seen that, but she'd assumed. *Assume,* as one of her college professors liked to say, *ass-u-me, don't ever go there if you can help it.* Now she tried to reel back and remember if she had actually said anything derisive to Brandon's face or had she just thought awful things about the poor man.

"I...had no idea. I'm so sorry." She truly was. "Do you mind if I ask...what...happened?"

"Ah, no, I don't mind at all. Fi died of ovarian cancer. Fought it like the dickens, she did, but it took her from us all the same. Bran and Fi, what a pair they were, married almost twenty-five years, those two. That's why I came here, to be with my brother and his children, and with Fiona."

"Annie, what did you do before you came to help Bran?" Kate had wondered if the woman had been married, had children of her own. She never mentioned any.

"Ha! You mean it isn't written all over me?" She laughed. "Sisters of Clare. I spent a good many years in Belfast, during the worst of the Troubles. Planned to change the world, I did. I taught school. Tried to teach tolerance to children who had grown up only knowing violence and hatred. Oh, and maybe I had a bit of a hand in the peace that came, but when Bran needed me...well, he's family."

Kate was astonished. "You left the Church? They let you do that?"

"I made a choice. I'm the oldest, you see. I had served the Church my whole adult life, but if I hadn't come? It was a hard choice, Kate, breaking my vows. There's no going back."

Tears welled in Kate's dark eyes. She knew what family loyalty meant. Her family was so close-knit she often thought she'd smother in its warmth and she had to wonder how far her family would go to help her through a crisis.

"Annie, I'm glad you're here. It is nice to have another woman to talk to. I've been alone now for a while." She did not want to say more. Her troubles seemed minor compared to the despair and sacrifice the Sullivans had endured. Kate had an irrational thought that she wanted to hold Bran in her arms and comfort him, and she sorely regretted her earlier erroneous judgment. "I'd better get going. Would you let Brandon know that I need to be out of town next Wednesday and I'll miss my lesson?"

"Sure and he's planning to take Thanksgiving off, but yer welcome to come out and ride if ye like."

"I might, if I get back in time. We have a big family get-together at my mother's in New Jersey." A guilt trip, Kate called it. "Well, happy Thanksgiving to you all." She reached for Annie and hugged her.

"Same to you, Katie. Enjoy your trip."

Chapter Five

Joey and Mark met Kate as she stepped off the jetway. Both wore full Hackensack Police Department uniforms and broad Aiello smiles. One and then the other hugged their big sister, lifting her off her feet and swinging her around until she begged to be put down.

They looked like the Italian version of the Bobbsey twins in dress-up, she thought. Tall and big-shouldered, with nearly black, short, curly hair and golden brown eyes. "This is quite the welcoming committee. Police escort, no less."

"Joey wanted to cuff you and scare everyone, but I thought that was going a little too far with our authority," Mark said in his booming baritone.

"Thanks for saving me. So, how's Mamma? Cooking her brains out, I suppose." Silvana was determined to do everything herself if it meant dropping over dead from exhaustion at the end of the holiday. There was no way to dissuade her and all had stopped trying years ago.

"Well, of course. Maria is trying to help, but you know how that always ends up. And with two teenagers whining to go to the mall for last minute shopping, Maria has her hands full anyway," Mark offered as they made their way to the car.

"How are the girls?" Kate asked. Mark had twin daughters, sixteen going on twenty-one, driving him crazy with their bare midriff fashions and iPods stuck in their ears from morning to night.

"I don't know how you got through those years with Laura without goin' nuts, Kate. Maria says they're just normal teenagers, but I think I'm raising Madonna and Janet Jackson's evil twins." He laughed, opening the door of the white Crown Vic with the blue badge on the side.

"Oh, come on you guys, the cruiser? You couldn't come and get your sister in a real car?" Kate wasn't really embarrassed, but she did think her cop brothers were incorrigible.

Joey spoke up. "I'm actually on duty until midnight. So, sorry...if I get a call, you're my back up. Hey, if I remember my younger days, you have quite the left hook, big sister. Any bad guys who try to hurt me, I'm gonna hand 'em over to you."

They drove the few miles to the Hackensack neighborhood where they had grown up. Nothing had changed. The street, the noise and the house full of laughter, food and music were all reminiscent of every Aiello family gathering Kate could remember. They greeted one another with a traditional Italian kiss on each cheek and huge hugs.

"*O Dio*," Mamma shouted as she emerged from her kitchen. "My Catarina, my daughter, come here and let me get a good look at you. Cara, you are so thin, are you well?"

"Yes, Mamma, of course I'm fine. You know I've always been on the skinny side." Kate never heard the end of her mother's concern over her slim build, like it was a sign of poverty or pestilence. She tried not to let it get to her. Being grumpy never got her anywhere.

Mamma was fussing and cooing over Kate when the front door opened and Kate's gaze fell on her next younger sibling, the one she had been, and still was, closest to.

Frankie was a contrast to his brothers in body and soul, and Kate had to admit she loved him more than anyone else who bore the Aiello name. He was tall and elegantly handsome with black hair and eyes the color of good Italian coffee in a face of classic Roman features. Kate had often watched Frank's hands when he spoke; his sweeping gestures emphasized his smooth eloquence. She had always thought he would marry a beautiful woman and have the best looking babies in creation. The day he came to his sister and confessed his plan to go into the priesthood, she had cried. She was so afraid it meant she would lose him: his warm presence in her life, the fun they had, the adventures. But Frank hadn't changed and they had stayed close, always able to confide in one another on any subject.

"Ah, *mia sorella*...here at last." He gathered her into his arms and held her. "We need to talk," he whispered in her ear and gave her hand a squeeze.

She looked at Frank with concern. *We need to talk?* It worried her. Was he upset about her divorce? Frank knew she had not wanted out of her marriage and it wouldn't be like him to blame her, but the thought uppermost in her mind was that maybe her family believed she had not tried hard enough to keep her husband from straying. "Sure, Frankie, maybe we can get out of here for a few...later, when everything calms down a bit."

The evening with her family had been great. She went to bed exhausted from emotion and her face hurting from speaking Italian. Kate slept in her old room, which hadn't changed much in the last thirty years. Her diplomas still hung on the walls and her collection of Nancy Drew books remained on the shelves. She did not know whether to laugh or cry. Here she was, fifty years old and back in the bed she had slept in the night before her wedding, with the pink ruffled comforter and her favorite doll sitting in the dolly highchair in the corner.

Laura had always loved sleeping in this room when they had visited over the years. It pained Kate that in the twenty-five years of her marriage, Jeffrey had only come to this house a half dozen times and rarely had he stayed over night. He always had a reason: office hours, surgeries, meetings, something that called him back to Baltimore and prevented him from spending time with her family.

Maybe it was being home or the need to hide her stress in front of her family, but at one A.M. Kate awoke with the dreaded *should haves* and *could haves* running circles in her head, tap dancing on her fragile shred of self-esteem.

It should have been obvious to her that her marriage was doomed when she had to bribe Jeffrey for sex with promises of his favorite breakfast. When his performance in bed had flagged, Kate took it as a personal assault to her womanhood. She tried harder to remain attractive for him, to be more openly loving, to give him reasons to be more affectionate toward her. Nothing she did seemed to be enough. Jeffrey was not interested in her amorous advances. She was an abysmal failure.

When she found the Viagra in his travel kit, it should have been a wake-up call; but she thought she understood. He was having a problem, a health issue. That explained it all. To her dismay, he still shunned her attempts at romance.

She could have insisted that they see a marriage counselor before things deteriorated to an appalling level. Finally he agreed, after some serious hysterics on Kate's part, to schedule a visit with a psychotherapist. Jeffrey Waldon, M.D., was certain it would change nothing. He, after all, did not have a problem. But Kate was unrelenting and over time she thought they would start to have more spark in their marriage, find again the love they had pledged to one another all those years before.

Kate thought she might die of embarrassment when she recalled the fateful day in the office of Dr. Glenda Steinberg. She and Jeffrey had sat and calmly discussed all the ways they could make their marriage more satisfying. They were always polite, always positive in their approach to these discussions.

"Well, now, Kate...Jeffrey...our time is just about up for today. Is there anything else either of you wants to contribute?" Glenda looked at the couple sitting on her office sofa.

Surprisingly, Jeffrey Waldon, who rarely had anything to say during these hour-long sessions, cleared his throat. "Yes, Dr. Steinberg...I do have something I want to add."

"Jeffrey, turn and speak directly to Kate," Glenda insisted.

"Certainly. Catherine, I want a divorce. I'm in a relationship. I dare say, I am in love and there is nothing you or these sessions can do to change the way I feel."

A bolt of hot pain hit Kate right in the middle of her chest and exploded in the center of her head. She looked at the therapist, who appeared as astounded as Kate was confused. "What? What, are you talking about? Divorce? I don't want a divorce, Jeffrey...Glenda?"

Coldly, as if he were talking to someone he had only met that morning, he continued. "You will be well taken care of. You can have the house and I will certainly compensate you financially. You will never want for anything."

"Jeffrey, I don't want money, things...I want our marriage..."

"It's too late. I am moving out this afternoon. I have a place in Baltimore, near the marina. I've bought a yacht." He was unmoved by the tears that trailed from Kate's brown eyes and down her cheeks.

Kate continued to see Glenda at regular intervals, trying to get a grip on her new persona, one that did not include the overpowering presence of Dr. Waldon, Chief of Staff of the cardiovascular surgery department of Baltimore's most prestigious hospital. Who was left when the appellation of 'wife' no longer defined her?

She got her hair trimmed and her grey covered. She joined a health club. All these little fixes were fine, but she still had to face the nagging truth—she had not done anything in the last twenty-five years entirely for herself. Every move she had made was for the happiness and fulfillment of her husband or her daughter. It was even possible, she had to admit, that her whole life had been a voyage through a sea of satisfying others, from as far back as she had memory.

Kate rolled onto her side and looked out the window at the night sky. "Oh, mamma, you didn't warn me about this." This what? This depth of sorrow, this loneliness, these damn night sweats? She struggled to choke back a flood that would wash her overboard and she couldn't remember how to swim.

****

Kate was awakened by the sound of traffic on the narrow street, shouts of people greeting one another on the sidewalk below her window and the sounds of the open market a block over, the vendors calling in a cacophony of diverse languages. It was always a bit of a shock, the hum and clatter of the city. She liked the way this neighborhood purred and pulsed with humanity and it was a welcome change from the stillness of her suburban home.

"Catarina," she heard her mother call. "I have a cappuccino and cornetto for you."

"I'll be right there Mamma." She sat on the side of her bed for a moment and prepared for the onslaught of the day. *Hang in there, Kate, you can do this.*

Silvana was already in a frenzy of unrelenting

cooking when Kate sat down at the kitchen table.

"Mamma, would you come and have coffee with me? The turkey can wait a few more minutes." She pulled the vinyl-covered chair out from the table. "Sit, please. I want to thank you for having Thanksgiving a day early, so Laura can be here and still spend time with her dad."

Silvana finally settled in a chair and Kate got the clear impression that her mother had something she wanted to say, but was hesitant. "Mamma, are you troubled over something?" she asked, hoping it wasn't illness she was fretting over.

"Catarina, you are a beautiful woman. You should not have to spend the rest of your life alone."

"I'm not unhappy...really, I wish you would try not to worry. This was all a shock, but I'm doing some things to help get back on my feet, emotionally." Nothing she could say would ever satisfy her mother.

"Did I tell you Zia Livia called from L'Aquila? We had a long talk. I was glad she was paying for the call. You do remember Livia?"

"Sure I do. We stayed with her family when I was...what eighteen, between high school and college when we went to Italy for the summer holiday." Zia lived in the mountains of Abruzzo. Kate remembered it as a wild and mysterious region and had thoroughly enjoyed her time there.

"Do you remember Sergio, her son? He is a distant cousin to you. Well, he is coming to America for a holiday."

Kate had a strong suspicion that her mother was not coming out with the whole story and tried to be patient. "That's nice, Mamma. Yes, I do remember Sergio. He was about my age, and he was into motorcycles, if I remember him correctly."

"*Si, si, si*, that was Sergio, lovely boy, never married, you know."

Okay, mother, spit it out, what is going on here?
"Will he visit you?" Kate tried to remain calm
although she dreaded the idea of wining and dining
a distant cousin from Italy, lovely though he might
be.

"Cara, I hope you will not be angry with me. Zia
asked me how you were and I just could not tell her
that your husband...well...that he..."

"Say it, Mamma, divorce. It's not a dirty word
you know." She was going to lose all charity in about
ten seconds if her mother didn't get to the point.

Silvana, who would be struck dumb if she had
her hands tied behind her back, gestured wildly as
she spoke. "I just couldn't disgrace you by telling her
your husband...divorced," Kate thought mamma
would choke on the word. "That he left you for
another woman. I told her he...died...in a gardening
accident."

"Jesus Christ, Mamma! You can't tell her that.
It's a lie." This was unbelievable to Kate. Her mother
must have said a thousand Hail Mary's for this tall
tale. "You have to call her back. You have to tell her
the truth." Anger mixed with disbelief stirred her
stomach into a fiery jelly. Kate was sure she would
explode and bits of her would stick to the walls like
overcooked spaghetti.

"Now, Catarina, I can't do that. It will be all
right. You will see. Sergio might make a good
husband for you..."

"Oh my God, Mamma, tell me that's not why
he's coming to visit. Mamma, I'm not...this is
insane." She was trapped, tears threatened and she
couldn't breathe. About the moment she thought she
would actually faint from lack of oxygen the kitchen
door swung open.

"Hey, Nonna, don't you answer your doorbell
anymore?" It was Laura.

"Oh, Mom, it's so good to see you. I've missed

you so much." She hugged her mom and then her grandmother.

Kate stroked Laura's shoulder-length blond tresses and looked in her daughter's bright blue eyes. "I've missed you, too, sweety. It's been weeks. How's school?"

"Oh, not bad...busy...but I'm happy." She looked quizzically at her mom. "I'll put my stuff in the bedroom and be back to tell you all about it."

Kate stood and tried to get her bearings. She felt like she'd been shot with ice pellets since her mother's disclosure. "I'll help you get settled. We can catch up. Mamma, I'll be back to help you with the turkey."

By afternoon, the house was full of people, eating, laughing, telling stories of childhood misadventures. Mark and Joey entertained them all with some of the goofy stuff that went on down at the precinct. After an indulgent mix of American traditional and Italian *festa* fare, the men dozed and watched football while the women cleaned up the kitchen. Laura and her twin cousins talked of fashion and boyfriends. Kate and Silvana avoided the subject of Sergio.

"Kate, take a walk with me." It was Frank. He took her hand in his and led her out of the stuffy house and into the cool autumn evening. "I thought I'd never get you alone," he confessed.

"I've wanted so much to talk to you, Frankie." Tears choked in the back of her throat. He stopped and put his arm around her shoulder. "It's been just awful." Her voice cracked and the tears spilled down her cheeks.

"So, talk now or cry, that's why I wanted to get you away from Mamma for a while. I know how hard it is between the two of you right now. Don't even hope she will understand. She won't. But, I do...on several levels."

"Well then, are you here as my brother or my priest?" She tried to smile.

"Unless you feel that you need a priest, I'm just Frankie, the kid brother. Kate, what Jeffrey did was his mistake, his weakness, his poor judgment. I know you, maybe better than anyone. You turn yourself inside out to make sure everyone around you is content. Sometimes I've wanted to stop you and force you to consider yourself, but your unfaithful husband had nothing but the best from you."

"I keep thinking I could have done more, even though I know that's ridiculous. Now, I'm trying to put myself first, but it's not my habit and it's hard."

"Yes, I hear you've taken up horseback riding. Mamma is sure you're going to fall and be crippled for life."

"Well, Frankie, I have fallen, bruised my butt pretty bad, but no crippling injuries. I'm having fun for the first time in a very long time and I'm pretty good at it. According to my instructor...get this...he says I have a nice seat." She laughed thinking of Brandon's appraisal of her.

"He does, does he? And what's he like, this riding instructor?"

"Frank, I know what you're thinking and I am not 'involved' with Brandon Sullivan."

"Oh, Sullivan is it? Irish Catholic?

Kate punched her brother hard in his upper arm. "You're hopeless," she said. "Let's walk off some of Mamma's cooking."

They continued to meander around the streets where they had played so many years before, where Kate had joined the boys throwing the football and playing sand lot baseball. She was sassy about the fact that she could outrun her three brothers and not break a sweat. Once, when Frankie had said she was *just a girl* and girls couldn't throw a ball straight, she wrestled him to the ground and made him cry like a baby. He'd had nothing but respect for her abilities since that day. Now, she was thankful for him, here at her side, allowing her to grieve in her own way and not blaming her.

Late that night, Frank drove Kate to the airport for her flight home. "Please call me, Kate. I'm never too busy to talk to you. And don't worry about Cousin Sergio. He probably won't have the nerve to show up on your doorstep."

"Jesus...I hope not. What will I do with him?"

He kissed her on each cheek, held her close for a moment and bid her farewell. "Tell him you've decided to join a religious order."

Chapter Six

Headlights glanced off the bay window of the Sullivan dining room and startled Brandon from a well-fed stupor. He looked at the clock on the mantel. It was quarter past eight. Who would be coming in at this hour, on a holiday?

"I'm goin' out to check the horses," he called to Annie. "When I get back, we should have pie."

"Sure, Kevin and Barb should be back from their walk by then," Annie replied from the kitchen.

Brandon loved the late night checks, when the horses were munching softly on their hay, some of them flat out asleep, Clancy usually snoring. Bran started down the aisle, peeking into each stall, but stopped and held his breath when he heard her voice. It was Kate.

"Murphy," she whispered. "You won't believe what I had to endure yesterday. My mother is crazy. *Pazzo.* Do you remember your mother? You're a good horse, old Murph. Your mother probably wasn't nuts."

He knew he should make his presence known, but Brandon was transfixed. He waited and listened.

Kate spoke in a soft voice as if confiding in her closest friend. "I'm so glad I came to see you. I should have come earlier, but I had this urge to clean my house. Laura spent the day with her father and his new wife. Too bad Jeffrey didn't choke on the wishbone and fall face first into the mashed potatoes."

Murphy sneezed.

"Oh my God, now look at me. Oh hell...I really

don't care. You can get horse snot on me anytime. Just don't step on my feet, big guy." Her voice started to sound choked. "Damn, I was not going to cry anymore."

Bran realized he was holding his breath. *Okay, I've heard enough.* Humming a few bars of "When I Was a Lad on the Emerald Isle" to let her know he was coming, Bran walked toward Murphy's stall, He tried to act surprised.

"Who's there?" Kate called.

"Is that Katie? Well, what a treat. Come to give Murphy a holiday kiss?" He opened the stall door and went to her side. "And a happy Thanksgiving to you." He put an arm around her in a friendly half-hug. She shivered. "You must be freezing out here. Come over to the house, warm up and have a bit of pie with us. Kevin and Barb are here. Come, they have some news to share."

He didn't give her time to refuse. Bran took her by the hand and walked her straight to his house. She did not protest.

"Annie darlin', look who I found out in the horse barn. It's our Katie." He offered her a seat on the sofa and went to the sideboard to pour her a drink. "This is some fine Scotch whisky. Of course, you know they learned the art from the Irish." He handed her the glass of amber liquid.

"Thanks, Bran, but I don't really drink. I need to be able to drive home."

"Now don't you give it a worry, Katie, just a sip or two." He didn't want to have her drunk and on the road, but she seemed cold to her bones and emotionally tied in knots. He was genuinely concerned. What had happened over the last days to make her so fragile? Or had she always been this breakable, like a young filly who had been mistreated by rough handling?

"Ah, Katie, so good to see you." Annie greeted

her with her usual unadulterated warmth, just as Kevin and Barb rushed through the front door.

"Kate, we didn't know you were coming, great to have you." Kevin had his arm around Barb. "Did Dad tell you the big news?"

"It's your news to tell. I haven't said a word." Brandon joined Kate on the sofa and sipped his drink, looking at his son with a knowing grin.

"Barbara has agreed to be my wife." He kissed the tip of Barb's nose. "What do you think of that?"

"Wow, that's...wow." Words tumbled from her lips. "Congratulations."

Bran saw the color in her cheeks darken and little beads of sweat pop out on her forehead. He hoped that giving her the drink had not been a mistake. He had wanted to warm her up, not roast her alive. "Katie, are you okay darlin'?"

She held her glass out to him, "Could I bother you for another, Brandon *darlin'*?" He thought she'd had enough but she didn't look like she would take well to *no* as an answer. He filled her glass and watched her.

Barb and Kevin sat together on a pillowed bench by the fireplace. Annie brought a tray with plates of pie, whipped cream and coffee. As Brandon surveyed the room his heart squeezed and he felt tears sting his eyes. Almost perfect, he thought. Brighid had left right after dinner to get back to her studies and, he suspected, her boyfriend. Then a bolt of fatherly instinct shot through him. *If that bloke breaks my baby's heart I'll kill him.* He turned to Kate. "You just missed my daughter, Brighid."

"Yes, well...I'm sure she's as beautiful as the rest of you. My daughter was with her father today. I'm certain she had a good time. Jeffrey's new wife is only a few years older than Laura...they probably talked about...their prom dates." She laughed, but tears wet her cheeks.

"Kate, you should eat a piece of pie. Here you go." Bran tried to wrench the whisky from her hand and replace it with a fork and pie dish.

"Maybe I should, I haven't eaten today. Yesterday...my God...you can't imagine what an Italian feast day is like...my mother cooked...we ate. *'Mangia, mangia, la mia famiglia'*. One does not refuse Silvana Maria Gondolfo Aiello and live to tell about it. I don't think I'll ever need to eat again." Her voice was trembling. Bran thought she looked like she was going to blow a fuse right there on his sofa.

"Kate, dear, are you telling us you've had nothing to eat today. That's not good." Annie looked to Bran with alarm in her eyes. Two glasses of the Glenlivet on an empty stomach. No wonder the poor girl was inebriated beyond reason.

"Sweet Annie, you're so kind. Why are you so good to me?" Kate sniffled. "I have a funny story. Bran, you'll get a bang out of this."

He wasn't sure what was coming. "Kate, maybe I should take you home. It sounds like you've had a big couple of days." She was self-destructing before his eyes.

"No, no...you've gotta hear this." She slapped her hand down on Brandon's thigh for emphasis. He flinched but it wasn't from pain. Even in her current state, more than tipsy, laughing hysterically, tears streaming down her face, she was stunning. "My husband of twenty-five years, *Doctor* Jeffrey Waldon...well I can think of better things to call the jackal...but anyway...he tossed me over for a fucking...excuse the French...twenty-eight-year-old foozly...uh...floozy."

"Katie?" Bran did not know what to say. He wanted to stop her, he knew she would be mortified tomorrow when she, *if* she remembered tonight. But this was a safe place for her to vent and maybe that was what she needed to do. "Go on with your story, Kate."

"She's pregnant, you know...the foozly...yes... well, needless to say, my dear mamma doesn't believe in divorce. God no. Like she thinks I'd have chosen to be dumped on the ash heap of life...Jesus...she can't even say 'divorce' without crossing herself. So she goes and tells the cousins in Italy that I'm a widow. Well, I should have killed the bastard when I found the Viagra, but, Mamma. *'Oh Dio'* she likes to say. She tells them he died *in a gardening accident.*"

Kate took her whisky glass out of Bran's hand, gulped the remainder of the liquid and laughed, sounding panic-stricken. "Died in a gardening accident? Who the hell dies gardening? Like what, he was attacked and strangled by the clematis vine, or a bee flew up his nose and settled in his brain? You'd think *my* mother could come up with something more creative than that."

He hadn't meant to put Kate in a situation where she might embarrass herself. Now, she was sobbing uncontrollably with no regard for or awareness of the people in the room.

"Dad, Barb and I have to get going. Do you want us to drop Kate off at her house?" They both looked concerned for this woman they had grown to like and respect.

"Oh no you don't," Kate spoke up through her haze. "I can't leave my car here. I'll be fine, just point the way." She started to get up from the sofa, but her face went deathly pale and she sat back down. "Just give me a minute."

"It's okay. Kev, you take Barb on home. I can drive Kate in her car and I'll call you when I need you to come get me."

"But I'm not done with my story," Kate protested.

"That's okay darlin', you can tell me on the way home." Bran bent over her and she put her arms around his neck, her head lolling on his shoulder. He lifted her to her feet. "Come on now. Let's get you home to bed."

Fortunately, Kate was coherent enough to give Brandon directions to her house before she dozed off in the passenger seat of the Beemer. He drove the distance, wondering what he should do and deciding he would tuck her in her bed and—for fear that he even consider staying—he would call Kevin right away to come and get him.

The house sat back from the road. It was dark, but as the car passed through the driveway gate, motion-sensing lights illuminated the expanse of lawn, a well-kept garden and an enormous brick edifice. *Katie lives here?* Brandon was surprised, but he guessed that *Doctor Ex* had left her the house. It just did not look like the kind of place Kate would have preferred, too austere, empty and cold.

He parked the car in front of the door and reached over to awaken Kate, stopping just short of touching her upper arm. He watched her breathe. Her eyes were closed and her face was quiet, an unusual state for this animated woman. Her hair was a mess and she had a bit of whipped cream on her upper lip. He squelched the urge to lick it off. "Katie," he whispered. "You're home."

Brandon walked to the passenger door and helped her to her feet. "Where's your house key?" he asked.

She bobbled and he caught her. "We don't need a key. It's a key pad, on the door, there. Its one...zero...three...one." She started to tremble and he could feel the sobs start to well up from where his hands encircled her middle. "My birthday, I...was...born on Hallo...Halloween."

"Samhain eve?"

"What's *sawan?*" Kate asked, imitating Bran's pronunciation of the Irish word.

"Yer birthday, my good witch. Let's get you inside." He helped her into the marble entryway, his hand skimming over the wall until he found a light switch. The house was like a museum, he thought, huge, imposing and impersonal. "Where can I sit you down and get you a glass of water?"

She pointed in the direction of a dark hallway that led to the kitchen. There was an adjoining seating area with a comfortable-looking leather divan and matching chair. The mantel over the brick fireplace displayed family photos and held a few artistically placed objects with a nautical theme. This room, Brandon thought, looked more homey and inviting than what he had glimpsed of the rest of the house. He smiled when he helped her to the sofa and noticed a messy pile of horse books and catalogues strewn on the coffee table and falling onto the floor.

Brandon found the glasses and filled one with water. He joined her on the sofa. "Here, sip this. This is a big house. You could get lost in here."

"Yeah, I hate it. It's Jeffrey's house. I never wanted it. I thought we would be fine in a townhome, closer to Baltimore." She leaned into him. "Brandon...hmm, it's so nice of you to take me home."

"I think I better get you to your bed." His pulse was accelerating from her body brushing his. He ran a hand over her upper arm and settled it on her collar bone. Looking in her eyes was a mistake—seductive, deep, dark, pleading and wonderfully beautiful eyes.

"Brandon, do you want to kiss me?" Kate whispered. "You can't imagine how long it's been since I've been properly kissed by a man."

He did, of course, want to kiss her. Any man

who did not want to kiss her tempting mouth would have to be blind or light in his loafers. Brandon ached to do much more than that. He burned to bury himself in her softness, let the warm contours of her body soothe away the rough edges of his lingering loss. But he would not use her like that; he cared too much for her own hurt.

He took her chin in his hand and tipped her to face him squarely. "Katie, I would like nothing more than to kiss you, but, when I do, I want you to remember it and you, my beautiful fairy queen, are too far gone with the whisky to know what you really want right now." *Damn, Sullivan, you are a man of unmatched self-control.* "You deserve to be loved whilst sober."

"Why do you keep calling me beautiful?"

"Because I'm an honest man."

"Jeffrey never told me I was beautiful. He would say, 'you're a handsome woman, Catherine' and then he'd tell me to change my dress because he didn't like the color on me, or the fit, or whatever didn't please him at the moment." She shook and tears streamed down her face. He ran a thumb over her cheekbones, feeling the wet slipperiness on her smooth skin.

"Jeffrey was a fool. You're lucky to be rid of him." He knew he needed to get her tucked into her bed soon before his desire for her won the battle over his conscience. "Point the way to your bed, darlin'."

"Umm...I haven't had a man say that to me in years. Maybe never."

"You need a good night's sleep. Things might look a whole lot different in the morning."

"My bedroom is all the way at the top of the stairs. I can't go that far. I'll just sleep right here." She started to keel over on the sofa.

"Oh no, you won't." He scooped her into his arms and stood.

"Oh my god, you'll get a hernia and sue me. Put me down."

Her head was nestled into his shoulder and he could barely breathe with her lips moist against his neck. "You're not going to make this easy for me are you?" he asked, mostly to himself.

Her bedroom was, as she had said, right at the top of the stairway. It was a large room with a big sleigh bed. Brandon threw the covers back, sat her on the edge of the mattress to remove her shoes and then laid her gently back on the pillows. "Good night, Katie. I'll call you tomorrow to see if you're all right." And he kissed her on her forehead.

Her eyes were closed. He started to pull back and leave her to sleep when she grabbed his shirt with both hands. Like a woman drowning, she held on to him with such tenacity he couldn't move. "Please...Brandon, don't leave me." She sounded terrified. "I can't be alone again, please." Her voice cracked and she started to sob uncontrollably.

His hands stroked her, quieted her like he would a spooked horse. "It's okay, easy now, Katie girl, I'm not going to let anyone hurt you. Just rest now, I'll be right here." She started to loosen her hold on him. Her eyes closed and her breathing slowed. "That's fine. You just go to sleep now." He pulled the covers over her. "Everything will look better in the morning light." He lay down on top of the quilts and put his arms around her trembling form. He planned to stay until she fell asleep, until the demons that tore at her and wracked her soul receded into the oblivion of unconsciousness.

****

Kate rolled out of bed and staggered toward her bathroom. Instinctively, she knew she shouldn't turn on the light. She was afraid she might look as rotten as she felt and scare herself to death. Her mouth was fuzzy and dry, her bladder was about to burst and she had hammers behind her eyeballs tapping out a *Tarantella.* She vaguely remembered Bran driving her home and the strange dream of a man holding her in his arms. It wasn't a bad dream at all; it made her feel safe and wanted.

She peed, splashed water on her face, brushed her teeth and pulled off jeans and sweater, panties and bra. She crept back into her bed and pulled the covers up. Kate slipped into slumber hoping to have another episode of that dream she had left moments earlier.

When morning light played over her eyes, Kate resisted opening them. She had a headache the likes of which she had not known was possible. Her brain had liquefied and was sloshing in her cranium calling for her stomach to follow the dance. Moving would surely set off a chain reaction that would have dire consequences. But, if she lay very still, and just listened to the comforting sounds of the cat purring, she knew she would be fine. *Soft, breathy, rhythmic purring...so nice...but...a cat? I don't have a cat.*

Her arm reached out and hit something hard and alive. Forgetting her throbbing head Kate lurched from the bed.

"Aaahh!" she screamed and grabbed a pillow to cover herself. "Aaahh!" she screamed again, as if the piercing noise coming from her throat would make him disappear like a phantom in a nightmare. But he didn't vanish. He stood, shook sleep from his head and stared at her.

"Brandon...what are you doing in my bed?" Reality struck. She was bare-ass naked. "You...we...what...what happened here?"

"Calm down...nothing happened here. I put you to bed, that's all. You asked me to stay."

"You...you..." She dropped the pillow and pulled the bedspread off the bed, wrapping it around her like a suit of armor. "How did I...get undressed?

Oh...my...God. You didn't...?"

"No, I did not. You asked me to stay, you were all upset and you begged. I meant to wait until you were asleep and then leave, but I...well...dammit." He sagged into a bedside chair.

Kate stood, unable or unwilling to move in any direction. What had she said to him? What had she done? Was she supposed to believe that he could lie next to her all night and not touch her? She had a niggling memory of asking him to kiss her. But he didn't. What was wrong with her that he didn't even want to kiss her?

"I'm going to take a shower now." She started to back toward the bathroom.

Brandon watched her. "I'll go down and figure out your kitchen. I'll make coffee. We should talk, Katie."

Time stopped while the shower pulsed its soothing warmth on Kate's hurting body. Her head was pounding like a poor imitation of a conga drum and her fear that she had completely humiliated herself made her stomach twist and threaten to reverse. She made the mistake of looking at herself in the bathroom mirror. Her eyes were puffy and red, her olive skin had a ghastly yellow undertone and every muscle in her torso ached and throbbed. It was as though she had fought the devil and wasn't sure who was victorious. "*O Dio*, what am I gonna do with this?" Kate wanted to slap herself for sounding like her own mother.

Then, the final smack of mortification struck. He had seen her completely naked. Sure it had only taken a matter of seconds for her to cover herself but for that brief dreadful moment, there she was, in her birthday suit, the fifty-year-old edition, right in front of his eyes. Her heart sank into her feet and a wave of body hatred swarmed around her like killer bees at a church picnic. Well, that should clinch it. No red-blooded man with good eyesight would want her old carcass. She had been crazy to think he might find her attractive. So why did she remember him calling her beautiful? *That was with your clothes on, Aiello.*

She wrapped herself in a terry bathrobe and went downstairs to see if he was really making coffee or if he had escaped this mad house. As she descended the stairs the doorbell rang. *Crap, who would show up at this time of the morning?* Cold fingers of guilt clawed down her spine and paralyzed her legs as Brandon opened the door.

"I am a looking for a Catarina Aiello. Do I haves da correcta house?" The heavily accented voice spoke in barely understandable English.

She heard Brandon answer. "Yes, Kate does live here. Uh, and who, if you don't mind my asking, are you?"

"I ama Sergio Di Benedetto, *cugino di* Catarina from Italia."

Kate pulled the bathrobe tightly around herself, girding her loins for battle, and rushed headlong into the fray. "Sergio, *buon giorno,* welcome to America. Brandon, this is my cousin from L'Aquila." She thought she saw a resemblance to the nineteen-year-old she had once flirted with in the wilds of Abruzzo. He was not as tall as Brandon and broader of shoulder, but he was a classic, suave Italian gentleman down to the cut of his suit and the perfect trim on his wavy silver hair. He looked from Kate to Brandon with bewilderment in his golden eyes.

She knew this situation looked suspect. She was damp from the shower and barely clad, Brandon was rumpled, hair uncombed, and in his stocking feet. This information would be back to her mother by the speed of light as soon as Sergio got to a phone. She had better have a damn good explanation. She did not. Kate had never been successful at lying and when she had no time to prepare for duplicity, she was doomed to dismal failure. She would need to give it a try or Mamma would blow a blood vessel.

She invited Sergio to sit, have a cappuccino and biscotti. Kate spoke to him in Italian, to make him feel at home, and so that Brandon would not understand the outrageous deceit she was about to commit.

"Sergio, Brandon is my fiancé. It was all very sudden. We are both widowed, you see." She'd be in the confessional for a month explaining this one. She smiled angelically at Brandon, who simply smiled back in complete confusion. "Well, Sergio, I'd just love to have you stay and I can show you around."

She turned to Brandon and said with a sticky sweet voice, "Sweetheart, would you come upstairs with me for a moment. I have a light bulb that needs to be changed and I just can't reach that high." She grabbed his arm. "Sergio, we'll be right back."

Bran followed obediently, grin on his face.

When they got to her bedroom, Kate closed the door and turned to Bran. "Jesus, Mary and Joseph...what am I going to do?" She started pacing, running her hands through her tangled, wet curls. "He actually came here...my mother...she told Aunt Livia that Jeffrey was dead."

"You told that story last night. You didn't mention a cousin Sergio."

"You didn't let me finish...and then I guess I fell asleep. I don't remember. Sergio is single."

"So, we'll show him the glories of the U.S.A. and he'll go home a happy single man."

"You don't understand. My crazy mother...she fixed me up...with Sergio. I guess she actually thought I would consider marrying him."

"Why would you do that?" Brandon asked.

"I wouldn't of course. Don't be ridiculous. So, I lied just now." She had better tell Brandon of the ruse. He was going to be annoyed, but better to hear it from her, she decided.

"Katie, anytime you want to start making sense here, I'm ready to listen."

She took a deep breath and stepped back from him, just in case he burst into flames when she told him what she had done. "I told him we are...engaged. Well, look at us. He can come to his own conclusions. I'm half naked and you..." *Oh my God, you look like hell...or heaven...* "look like you just woke up...which you did..."

Brandon started to laugh. Kate stared at him like he had lost his mind. "What's so damn funny? My family will freak when the news hits Hackensack."

"Katie, why would they care? It's the twenty-first century. You're a grown woman."

"Okay, call me 'the adult child of an Italian mamma.' I'll never hear the end of it. Trust me...this won't play in New Jersey."

"I see your point. Look, I'll go along with it. What's the big deal? Cousin Sergio will stay for a while, we'll be the happy couple and when he goes off to wherever it is you said he came from, we'll 'break up.' We'll have a good laugh about the whole thing. Don't worry about your mother. If it makes her feel better about it, you can break up with me."

"Brandon...you'd do that for me?" It could work. *When it's over, Mamma won't have a thing to fuss about and I can live my life the way I want.*

"Katie, if it will make you happy, I'd be honored, but I think we need to seal the deal." He pulled her to him, encircled her slender waist with one arm and slipped his other hand into her hair at the back of her neck, coaxing her to look up at him. "You asked me to do this last night...I told you I wanted you sober. Are you sober, Katie?"

"As a judge." But she couldn't breathe, her heart

failed to pump enough blood to her brain and a sensation of heat that started at the place where his hand touched her back spread to her neck, trickled down her spine, across her belly and landed, softly, low in the cradle of her pelvis. She was certain that the source of *this* heat had nothing to do with waning hormones.

"Do something for me, Katie." His breath came in soft gasps against her ear. "Believe, even if it's only for now, when I tell you that you are the most beautiful woman who walks the earth." He brushed her lips with his. "Believe me," he whispered and kissed her again, his mouth soft, warm, moist and wanting.

And for that moment Kate did believe, while he tasted her, teased her with his tongue and lips. Kate Aiello, for the first time in half a century, made the conscious decision to believe that she was, for this unequivocal moment, the most beautiful woman on the planet.

Chapter Seven

Kate made sure Sergio was settled into the guest room, hoping he would want to sleep off the jet lag and giving her some time to regroup. She had to plan her next move, be certain she didn't step deeper into the mire she had caused herself. And she had to try not to think about her response to Brandon. The first kiss had terrified her...the second left her stunned. Kate was not sure she had ever been kissed like that, even when her relationship with Jeffrey was new. Brandon had awakened a part of her that had lain dormant, possibly since puberty, and he did it all with a graceful touch of his mouth on hers.

"Brandon, I'm going to drive you home while Sergio is resting, but I don't think I should be on a horse today," she said. He sat at her kitchen table, drinking tea and reading today's Baltimore Sun, the morning light spilling across his finely-sculpted features. He was muscle and bone covered with smooth bronze skin. She tried to picture him naked. Was he brown all over? Likely not. He was probably pale as a ghost where the sun's rays failed to color his hide. She tried not to think about whether or not she would ever know such details, and then chided herself on her speculations.

"Too hung over to ride? Probably a wise choice. I need to work Penny today. I wouldn't mind an audience, if you have the time and you aren't too tired from last night."

"I have a headache, but I'm not as trashed as I should be...considering." She sat at the table and poured tea from a china pot. "Thanks for the tea, and for seeing me safely home last night. I should be terribly embarrassed. I hope I didn't offend Annie and the kids." She had an indistinct recollection of spouting a litany regarding her recent marital demise and maybe something about her mother being crazy. Beyond that, the evening was a hodgepodge of tears and ranting juxtaposed against soft words of comfort and strong arms of support.

"Annie has seen me in much worse condition; and as far as Kevin and Barb go, I think they like you and aren't disposed to judging." He reached for her hand. "If you don't mind, I should be getting back."

They took the BMW. Brandon drove. They did not talk much. Kate watched the scenery. The hardwood trees were losing the last of their leaves and the bare branches stood in stark contrast to the dark green of the pine woods that bordered the road. She looked at Bran and tried to read him. It wasn't difficult as he was not a man bent on hiding his thoughts. Brandon wore his feelings right out in the open, like a badge of honor. Anger, pride, frustration, kindness, tolerance and gallantry were so deeply a part of him that it seemed never to occur to him to measure out doses of each. Jeffrey, in contrast, had developed temporomandibular joint stress from keeping his thoughts and desires locked away from Kate. He was a man overly concerned with decorum; yet he could betray her, seemingly without the slightest twinge of regret.

"Here we are." Brandon's voice stirred her from her daydreams. "Time to face the music."

"I'm going straight to the office and apologize to your sister." *God, the woman was a nun. She must be mortified.* Kate liked Annie and wanted to nurture a friendship, not offend her.

"Hey Dad." It was Kevin. "I waited for your call last night...finally gave up. Did you have a pleasant evening?" He gave his father a lopsided and slightly lascivious grin.

"Sorry, son. I wasn't sure how late it would be. I'm glad you didn't wait all night." Brandon shot Kevin a *this is none of your business* look. "If you want to give me a hand, I need to run Penny through the Grand Prix Special, make sure she has all the moves."

"I'll get her tacked up for you. Barb is on Caddy and she's got Doofus next." He jogged back toward the barn.

"Doofus?" Kate laughed, but it made her head throb. "What kind of name is that for a horse?"

"Well, that's not actually his name, and I wouldn't call him that in his owner's hearing. It's appropriate though. He isn't the sharpest knife in the drawer, you might say." He took her by the arm and they went to face *Sister* Annie.

"Mornin' to you, little brother," she peered at Bran over her bifocals. "Good of you to show up at work today. Ah, an' there's that Katie. Are you feelin' better, dear? I was worried about you. Were you able to get some rest?"

"Yes, Annie, thanks. I...please let me apologize for my unseemly behavior...I don't drink much...obviously I shouldn't." Kate's cheeks darkened in embarrassment.

"Oh now, don't you think a thing of it, darlin'. A woman needs to ventilate her feelings and who better to do that with than lovin' friends." She gave Kate a big hug. "Bran, you better get busy, and I need to see you when yer done."

"Yes ma'am. I don't get nearly enough respect around this place. Bran do this...Bran ride that...see me...don't see me..." He laughed and blew the women a kiss.

"Your brother is quite the comic. Must be a family characteristic, I've noticed it in Kevin, too."

Kate wondered what it was that Annie needed to talk to Bran about. "I'm not riding today...go figure...but I thought I'd watch Brandon work Penny. Thanks, Annie, for your kindness."

Kate sat down on the picnic bench at the edge of the dressage arena to watch. Soon Barb sat down beside her. Barb was cute in a pixyish sort of way Kate thought—short blond hair, fair skin, big blue eyes. She had a petite build that belied her true strength. Kate had seen her lift bales of hay and move jump standards with ease. Barb also had a quiet nature and off-beat sense of humor that made her a good match for Kevin Sullivan. She hoped they would be happy—and with a stab of cynicism she wondered how many well-wishers had thought the same of the young Waldon couple, oh so many moons ago.

They surveyed the scene in silence as Brandon and Penny traversed the arena. Kate did not see that Bran was doing anything, the man-horse team moved as one—intricate patterns, changes of gait, direction and bend. She watched his body, tall, long-legged, supple. When he rode the mare into her extended trot, Kate couldn't take her eyes off the way the man's hips moved in the saddle. She was glad no one could read her thoughts and hoped that her accelerating pulse and breathing weren't obvious to the young woman sitting beside her.

"Damn sexy if you ask me," Barb chuckled.

Kate was sure someone had just displayed her every thought on a jumbotron and the world knew her secrets. "They are quite a pair," she said, not wanting to say the alternative; *wonder what it would be like to have him move like that on me?* "How long have you known Kevin?" She not only needed to steer away from dangerous waters, she was curious about the Sullivan family.

"Oh, wow, I've known Kevin since I was in

fourth grade. He's a couple of years older than me, but I was friends with Brighid...we're the same age. I came here to ride horses with her and was hooked."

"The Sullivans have lived here for a while then?" Kate tried to imagine Kevin as a sixth grader...not much of a stretch.

"Well, yeah...maybe ten years or so. They were, you might say F.O.B., fresh off the boat, or 747 in their case, from Ireland. Kev's lost his accent, but every once in a while, he'll say something that just screams 'mick.' I just love to tease him about that."

Kate knew she was treading shaky ground but curiosity had her by the throat, so she asked, "You knew Kevin and Brighid's mother?"

"Sure, Fiona gave me my first riding lessons. Great lady, I miss her...she was like a second mom to me. I wish she knew about me and Kevin. I think she'd be happy."

"I'm sure she would be." Kate tried to stop the tickle of tears that settled in the back of her eyes.

"From the time I first came here, I had this mad crush on Kevin. He teased the hell out of me, laughed at the way I rode, would hide my grooming stuff, drive me crazy until I would cry. So, one time I greased the inside of his helmet with Vaseline so when he put it on it totally yucked up his hair. He was so mad...it was magnificent."

"When did you know, if you don't mind my asking, that you belonged together?"

"I thought I knew from day one. Kevin took his sweet time. When his mom was so sick...he just didn't know how to handle it. We spent lots of time just talking...and then it got serious, I guess you'd say, when Fiona died."

"Barb, I hope you don't think I'm prying." Of course she *was* prying.

"If you don't mind my asking you a personal question as well." Barb looked right into Kate's eyes.

"Do you think Brandon is totally 'hot'?"

Kate looked across the arena where Brandon was coaxing Penny into a canter pirouette. "Yeah, I do." And the two women laughed at their mutual observation, Kate pondering that age made no difference. Hot was hot, by any standard of measurement.

****

"You wanted to see me about something?" Brandon pulled off his sunglasses and dropped them on his desk. He hoped he was not about to get a lecture on their abysmal financial status.

"Have a seat Brandon." Annie swiveled her chair around to face him. "Now, you're a grown man, and I'm not inclined to tell you how to live your life—"

"But, you're going to anyway...," he cut her off.

"Now, just shut yer face and give me a proper audience here. I like Kate. She's a fine woman and I don't want to see her hurt, so I was alarmed when you did not come home last night."

"Annie, please, I was a perfect gentleman. She was drunker than a priest into the communion wine. You think I'd..." He tried to come up with of a plausible explanation. "I'm gonna be honest with you here, because you'd know in a heartbeat if I lied to you. I slept with her."

Annie's hand flew to her mouth to stifle a gasp.

"Yes, I tucked her into her bed, fully clothed, and I was about to leave. She...begged me...she didn't want to be alone. So, I stayed...but I promise you it was as chaste a night as ever a man had to suffer." He could just see the way Annie must have been with an errant school boy. "I care about Katie as much as you do—"

There was a knock on the door.

"Come in," Annie called and then turned to Brandon and chuckled, "you're dismissed, young Mister Sullivan."

"Am I interrupting anything?" It was Kate.

"No, my big sister was just humiliating me again." Bran's arm automatically reached around Kate's shoulder and pulled her close. "I've a wonderful idea. Kate, we should take Sergio out to dinner...show him around."

"Sergio?" Annie queried. "Who's Sergio?"

"My cousin from Italy. He just arrived this morning. I'm not sure how long he'll be staying. Sure, let's take him to a local joint. You pick one."

"Let me think on it. I'll call you as soon as I'm done with the horses on my list." He looked in Kate's eyes. "Are you okay? No headache?"

"I am remarkably recovered. I'll expect your call. See you later, Bran, Annie." And she left.

"Cousin Sergio is it? Does this have anything to do with Kate's husband dying in a gardening accident?" Annie's eyes flashed like Fourth of July sparklers.

"It does. And you're going to need a dispensation from the Pope himself if you decide to help us with this." He hoped his sister still had the Sullivan taste for adventure and a superb sense of humor.

Chapter Eight

Brandon called and suggested Trapeze. Kate was thrilled. She had been to the restaurant in Maple Lawn before. They had a nice variety of dishes which should please Sergio. Kevin and Barb already had plans, so it would be just the four of them—Annie and Brandon, Sergio and Kate.

She decided it would be fun to dress up a little but stood paralyzed in front of her closet, unable to get enthusiastic about anything that hung there. Finally out of sheer desperation and indecision she reached for a simple, black silk dress. It had been an impulse buy a couple of years ago. The garment had caught her eye, hanging on a mannequin in the boutique window. She rarely purchased anything without a specific event in mind, but when she slipped the shimmery, slippery fabric over her body, she instantly felt uncommonly sexy. She brought it home, hung it in her closet and had not taken it out again until today. *Well, little black dress, it's time you got out of the house.* This was as good an occasion as any to let her purchase see some action.

Kate hated high heels, but she had one pair of black satin pumps with heels she could manage. She could never understand why any woman would jam her feet into painful shoes and then pretend she was having a good time.

Standing back and assessing the overall effect in her full length mirror, Kate was not unhappy. The dress still fit like it was made for her, the hem was just above her knees and the thin straps left her shoulders bare. She wore an antique garnet pendant and matching dangly earrings. She added a touch of wine lip gloss and a dab of Shalimar, which she liked to think of as her signature scent. Her other scent, chocolate chip cookies, just didn't go with the dress.

She joined Sergio in the foyer. He looked incredible in his grey Armani suit, Versace tie and Bulgari sunglasses. Kate would not mind being seen on the arm of this man, in any place in the world. She could not help but be confused as to why he had stayed single all these years. She knew he wasn't gay, and she remembered he was a nice kisser. She wondered what he thought of the flirting they had indulged in when they were young. Well, it was too late now. Kate was not interested in shackling herself to another man, even if he had been the best kisser this side of heaven.

They pulled into the parking at Trapeze right next to Brandon's truck. Kate noticed with a wry grin that he had washed the old pickup for the occasion. Usually, it had bales of hay in the bed and the passenger compartment was a jumble of bridles, papers, coffee cups and riding apparel. Kate thought it odd that he did not own a car, but figured it must be some horsey guy thing.

The hostess showed Kate and Sergio to the bar where Annie and Brandon were waiting. When they entered the room and Brandon stood to greet them, Kate thought her knees would buckle. He looked good enough to eat and she suspected he knew it. She offered her hand and he pulled her to him in an embrace.

"We're supposed to be sweethearts. You should pretend that you like me," he whispered playfully, and kissed her cheek.

"Brandon, please...uh...introduce Annie to Sergio." She smiled at him and whispered, "Behave yourself or I'll break up with you."

"Sergio Di Benedetto, this is Anne Sullivan, my

sister." Bran put a brotherly hand on Annie's shoulder.

Sergio took her hand, bent over and kissed it, looking in her eyes the whole time. "*Bella* Anna, *buona sera.*" Kate thought Annie was going to faint. Her cheeks pinkened and her green eyes glazed over.

"*Si, buona sera, signore Di Benedetto, mi piacere,*" Annie answered in perfect Italian. The woman was full of surprises, Kate had to admit. Aside from her foreign language skills, Annie Sullivan looked stunning. Her red locks fell in a polished wavy curtain brushing her shoulders. She wore a teal green knit shift that flattered her abundant curves and made her eyes appear dark turquoise. She had skipped the ubiquitous bifocals and added a touch of peach blush to her cheeks and gloss to her lips.

"Your table is ready," the hostess said, and led them to the dining room.

Kate and Bran watched with amusement as Sergio seated Annie with the care he would have given royalty while never taking his eyes off hers.

Bran leaned over and spoke so only Kate could hear. "Your cousin is quite the Romeo. He'd better behave himself with my sister."

"I'm not sure Annie is the one in danger here," Kate replied and her own heart jumped at the feel of Bran's breath on her ear. Did he know he had that effect on her?

"Katie, you look incredible tonight. What are you trying to do to me?"

"I'm playing the part of a woman in love, until Sergio goes home and I dump you." She gave him a sweet smile.

"You are merciless. Are you ready to order?"

If he kept looking at her like that she was going to have to think twice before she *dumped* him. "Yes, I'll have the seafood pasta, the house salad and bottled water with a twist of lime."

"Umm, good choice, I like you sober."

They ate, laughed and talked about Sergio's trip. He wanted to see all the sights. Kate figured he sounded like he planned to stay for a while. "Sergio, how long will you be able to stay?" Kate lifted her water glass to drink.

"I have a decided, to a stay for you *matrimonio*."

Kate choked on her water and nearly dropped the stemmed glass. "Oh, Brandon...uh...well..."

Brandon looked like he was about to burst into hysterical laughter, but he recovered long enough to help her out. "We haven't actually nailed down a date for the big event yet, have we, Katie darlin'?"

"No! I mean, no, not yet. There's so much planning to do." *Jesus Christ he wants to stay for the wedding?* Kate tried to get a grip. Surely there were all kinds of reasons they could put the *wedding* off, until Sergio gave up and went back to Italy. She could handle this—it was only another pothole in the road of her wacky life.

Kate's hand was shaking. She felt too warm and a bit dizzy. The Beast hit her square on. With the force of a freight train bound for Hades, needles dipped in molten quicksilver pierced her face, her heart rate blasted into the red zone and she tried to mop the perspiration from her neck, hoping in vain no one would notice.

"I...uh...excuse me." She tried to stand on quivering legs. "Please, I...I'll be right back."

"Katie, what's wrong? Here, let me help you. Do you need some fresh air?" Brandon stood and tried to take her arm, but she pushed him away.

"I just need a moment." Her voice was nearly inaudible. He was trying to help her. Kate was so embarrassed she thought she might burst out weeping if she did not get away from him, and fast. She nearly ran from the table toward the ladies' room, leaving Brandon staring in her direction.

Kate mopped at her face with paper towels soaked in cold water, hoping to squelch the fire before she was consumed. Her hair was damp with sweat and she had a prickly, hot irritation that made her want to rip off her panty hose. She didn't hear the door to the restroom open and it startled her to see Annie's reflection next to her own, in the mirror.

"Oh, Katie dear, was it a bad one? Here now, let me help you." She took a towel and patted Kate's neck. "When I went through the change...oh heavens...I wanted to be taken out and shot. Add to that living with six other old nuns, all sufferin' with the flushes...well, I can tell you we spent a great deal of time in prayer, we did."

"It just happens, Annie. I have no control over it at all. I can't think...I say and do stupid things. Oh God, did I...was I awful to Bran?" She thought she remembered pushing him out of her way, and he was only trying to help.

"Oh now, don't you worry about my little brother, he'll live. It's you I'm concerned about. Are you feelin' better?"

"Yes, thank you, I am." Kate looked in the mirror. "But, look at me. I'm a mess. I can't let him see me like this. I look awful."

"Can't let who see you like this? Brandon? Brandon thinks you're lovely. He's not going to change his mind due to a bit of a flush. Come now, let's get back before the men start to worry that we've taken up with some younger fellows and gone dancing."

****

Brandon sat trying to make conversation with Sergio. Knowing only a few words of Italian, and those being epithets, he was at a loss. He was also alarmed at Kate's sudden distress. He tried in vain to keep images of Fiona out of his consciousness, but when he saw Kate, burning with inner heat and perspiration pouring down her neck, his gut twisted. When Fi had been waging war on her illness she was given drugs that bollixed up her internal thermostat. One moment she would be in fine fettle and the next she would be gripped by such a burning terror she wanted to die right there and then. He would bring her cold compresses and cool drinks, anything to quell her misery, but nothing helped.

Certainly Kate wasn't sick. She would have told him. Wouldn't she? With a sense of rising panic he realized she would not. She would not want him to know or to care. Kate was the kind of woman who cared for others. She did not take easily to letting others nurture her. Not while she was sober at any rate.

He was immensely relieved when he saw her returning to the table. "Katie?" He wanted to touch her but was not sure she would let him. He wished he could get her away, in private, for a few minutes. "There's a lovely veranda. Would you step outside with me? We can look at the stars." It was cloudy; there would be no stars and he was aware she knew that. He slipped her coat over her shoulders and offered his arm. "We'll be back shortly," he said to the other couple.

"Brandon...I'm sorry, for being so abrupt."

He had to ask, it was in his mind...a deal breaker. If Kate were ill, he was not sure he could allow himself to care about her, to start to love her, to let his heart be ripped out of his chest a second time. "Katie, are you...ill?" His hand brushed damp tendrils that clung to her face. He felt her shiver.

"Me? God no, I'm as healthy as an ox. A menopausal ox. But I've been told that as long as it doesn't cause me to commit a crime punishable by death, I should live to see the end of it."

Brandon laughed and pulled her to him. "You

scared me." He wanted to just hold onto her, feel her heart beat strong and sure against his, and know she was alive, vibrant and whole.

"Do you think we should get back inside?" She didn't try to move away from his embrace, but peered up into his face. "Annie looks so pretty tonight. I think Sergio is smitten."

"My sister, as far as I know, has never even had a boyfriend. This could get mighty interesting." Brandon ran a hand up Kate's back, enjoying the elegant curve of her spine under his fingertips. Did Kate know how pretty *she* looked tonight? When she walked into the bar, every man in the place turned an appreciative eye in her direction. It was the first time he had seen Kate in a dress and she was elegant.

"Do you need to have a birds and bees talk with her?" Kate laughed quietly.

"Jaysus, I hope not." A visual of his fifty-two-year-old virgin sibling and the charming, sophisticated Sergio flashed through his brain. He tried in vain to delete the image and started to laugh deep in his chest. He kissed Kate's still moist forehead and led her back into the restaurant.

It was midnight when Kate said good night to Brandon. She was tired and, surprisingly, happy. The evening had, except for her momentary temperature aberration, been perfect. She was glad she had come clean with Bran about her unruly body, because there was no hiding the unpredictability of it.

Her message machine was blinking. Kate thought at first she would just listen in the morning. She wanted to get in her bed and dream about a man's hands tracing a path down her backbone and eliciting tummy squeezing tickles in her girl parts. But her ingrained habit and overwhelming need to take care of loose ends did not allow her to leave flashing messages unattended.

"Catarina, this is your mamma. Sergio says you're engaged...to *un Irlandese...O Dio*. You must call me, Cara."

"Kate, this is Frank. Mamma thinks you're getting married. Tell me she's hallucinating. Call me when you get in, no matter how late it is."

"Mom, this is Laura. Nonna called me and...have you lost your mind? I'm coming home tomorrow to talk to you, please be there."

"Kate this is Ginny. You're not going to believe the rumor that's been going around at the gym. My sister's daughter's boyfriend is the roommate of your daughter's best friend's brother and...well...call me and tell me it's the hot guy from the Greek restaurant."

"This is a message for Kate. This is Dr. Glenda Steinberg. Sorry to bother you, but your daughter called and was very upset. Call me at your earliest convenience."

Kate flopped onto a kitchen chair and put her head in her hands. Her stomach churned and her jaws ached from the energy this duplicity required. *So, they think I'm getting married. I can tell a little white lie, I won't disappoint anyone, and when I break up with my intended they can all breathe a sigh of relief.* The only person she couldn't fib to was Frankie. He would know. She didn't want to lie to Frank.

She picked up the phone and hit her speed dial for the rectory of the church of St. Stephen the Martyr. "Frankie, it's me."

"Kate, Mamma has called me no less than a dozen times in the last five hours. What, if you don't mind telling me, is going on?"

"Well, Frank, first of all, I'm not getting married. But, I don't want you telling mamma yet. Let me see if I can explain it to you." *Think clearly,*

Kate. "Sergio just showed up on my doorstep. It was early. Brandon answered the door and..."

"Kate...hold it. Brandon? The riding instructor?"

"Well, yes. He went to the door...I was in the shower." *The shower? Why did I say that?*

"Uh, okay...go on."

"Frank, let me explain. I was drunk..." *That sounds terrible.*

"At that hour of the morning?"

"No, I mean, the previous night. Brandon had given me some Scotch...you know I'm a cheap date." *Ooh, I shouldn't say cheap.* "Well, it was so cold out and I went to see Murphy."

"Kate...hold it. Who's Murphy? Brandon Murphy? I thought it was Sullivan. Is there more than one man involved here?"

She knew she wasn't making any sense, her mind was whirling hopelessly like a leaf in a dust devil. Kate could not grab on to a coherent thought. "No...one man, one horse...Sullivan is the man. He took me home and I was...well, too impaired to remember much, but when I woke up in the morning he was still here."

"Oh my Lord, Kate, the man rendered you helpless...and then took advantage of you? Don't ever let Mark and Joey hear about this. They'll beat the crap out of your Irishman."

"Frank...it wasn't like that. I'm just not making myself clear. He...we..." *I'm a grown woman, why am I defending myself like I just lost my virginity?* "He stayed because I was upset and sad. And, if you must know, we haven't been intimate. Jeez, Frank, we're not in your confessional here."

"I'm sorry, Kate, I know how vulnerable you are right now. I don't want you to be hurt again. Anyway, how did you suddenly become engaged to the man? "

"That's what I'm trying to tell you. Sergio

showed up. Bran asked him in. I was in my bathrobe. It looked compromising and it seemed the best option at the moment to tell Sergio that Brandon was my fiancé." This sounded ludicrous, even to Kate. "Now, everybody knows, or thinks they know, what's going on in my life and it's out of control. Sergio thinks he's staying for my wedding. Laura thinks I've had a nervous breakdown and Mamma...oh my God. Mamma has probably reserved the church hall and started cooking already."

"Okay, just try to calm down. You can explain this to Laura. She has your sense of humor. She'll be fine. Mamma...well, leave her to me. Kate, one more question...if I may...are you in love with your Brandon Sullivan?"

Kate's first instinct was to laugh. The question was wildly ridiculous. But a twitter started in the vicinity of her diaphragm, flipping her stomach like a flapjack and settling somewhere below her belly button. "I...well...no, certainly not. He's a friend. His family has been nice to me...Frank...don't be silly." She hoped she sounded convincing to her brother, because she wasn't sure her answer rang true to her own ears.

"Friends are a gift; if that's what you have I'm happy for you. Kate, just remember, you have your whole life ahead of you and it's perfectly acceptable for you to live it on your terms. Mamma, Laura, Sergio...Brandon, you can't make any of them happy if you're miserable."

"Thank you, Frankie. Good night. I love you." She closed her phone and stared at it for a long time. Frank was right, of course, but it was so out of character for Kate to think of herself first. *Was that the mistake I had made with Jeffrey? Or was he simply a hopeless baboon and I would have realized it sooner if I had been able to look beyond his needs and consider my own.*

Kate dreaded it, but she had to make one more call. She opened her phone and hit the speed dial for her daughter.

"This is Laura's machine. I'm not in right now. Please leave a message."

Thank God, I can leave a message. Kate really did not feel like explaining herself to her child. "Laura, this is Mom. I got your message. Please don't worry, it all sounds worse than it is. You don't need to come home. Not that I wouldn't love to see you. Call me tomorrow. I have a riding lesson in the morning, but then I'll be home. I love you sweety."

That is the last time I speak into this demonic device tonight. Kate put her phone in her purse and left it downstairs where she wouldn't be tempted to use it again. Her impulse was to call and explain herself to everyone, set everybody's mind at ease, make sure all were satisfied with her answers. She had always tried to go out of her way to make sure her life was traveling along a road that pleased each person in his or her own way. That had been the life that had made Kate happiest, until now.

Kate stripped off her dress, panty hose and underwear and lay atop her bedspread, arms stretched out across the barren expanse. She had stopped wearing pajamas when she started sleeping alone—one less item to throw into the wash with her sweat-soaked sheets.

Lying here in the dark of her room, naked and solitary, it was impossible to grasp the fact that she was old, washed up, or that her life was over in any sense. She felt alive, young and physically unchanged by the years. It comes so gradually, she decided. It's not like you wake up one day and your face is full of wrinkles and your butt has sagged to the backs of your knees. The metamorphosis from young woman to wizened crone snuck up on you while you were busy living life.

Kate's hands glided over her breasts and down her rib cage to her belly. In the dark, to her touch, the landscape had not drastically changed. She tried to feel her stretch marks—she had secretly called them her badge of honor—those silvery streaks in the golden skin of her lower abdomen. Kate's pregnancy had been forty weeks of pure joy. She had not experienced the usual discomforts that her girlfriends had warned her would be inevitable. No nausea, tiredness or hemorrhoids for Kate. She was born to make babies. She had wanted a houseful, but it was not to be. Now, her reproductive years were ending, not with a whimper but with a bang.

For one gloomy moment it seemed to Kate that women were meant to be like flowers: beautiful, growing, blooming, reproducing other lovely flora and then fading, and blowing away, as ephemeral as a dandelion on the wind. She wasn't ready for that. She wanted to continue flourishing, even if she had to do it alone.

Chapter Nine

The road to the stable wound through the trees. Her little car seemed to have wings as it glided around each curve, wheels humming, the breeze blowing her hair into her face. But the coolness was replaced by a hot wind that blasted her with suffocating heaviness. She struggled to control her vehicle, steering into the skid, or was it steering away from the direction of the spin? She could never remember, so she closed her eyes to block out the distractions and when she opened them there he was...the squirrel, pale blue eyes staring, blond thinning hair falling into his pink face...Jeffrey? His eyes met hers and in one fleeting moment of decision, Kate swerved to miss him, hurtling herself over a cliff and into the black of night.

"Oh God." Kate rolled over and tried to focus on the clock that sat on her bedside table. "It's five A.M. I'll never get back to sleep."

She decided to get up and take a shower, wondering what time Brandon usually awakened. She didn't have to imagine what he looked like when he woke up; that she had been witness to. She had to admit he was kind of cute in that rumpled condition, needing a shave, his hair sticking out on one side and flattened to his head on the other. If she hadn't been in such a state of shock she might have relished the moment.

She had a riding lesson at nine. It was going to be hard to cool her heels until eight when she needed to leave for the stable. She planned to make a simple breakfast of coffee and cornetti for Sergio and give him the option of going with her. From what Kate saw last night, she would not be at all surprised if her cousin jumped at the chance to see Annie Sullivan again.

It seemed like more than two hours, but the clock struck seven and Kate made a decision that if Brandon was not already awake, he should be. She dialed the number to his house.

"Uhhh...hello...," a tired and gravelly voice muttered.

"Bran? Did I wake you? I'm...I couldn't imagine you a late sleeper." She was immediately sorry she'd called.

"Katie? Umm, Katie, I had a hell of a time getting' to sleep last night."

Kate could not think of why she called, but she had been watching the clock until an hour when it would be appropriate to give him a jingle. Now she felt foolish. "I actually didn't sleep well either. I'll be out for my lesson this morning. Are you going to be conscious?"

"Oh, yes, for my lovely fiancée, I'll even take a shower."

"That's gallant of you. I had phone messages from everyone and his brother, actually it was *my* brother, last night. News travels fast among the Aiellos. Brandon, anytime this gets too...if you get annoyed with the whole charade, I'll take care of it."

"What and miss all the fun? I hadn't had a good laugh in a couple of years, and then I met you. I am actually looking forward to meeting the rest of your family."

"Uh, we'll have to talk about that. You may have a chance to meet my daughter...very soon." *I hope she likes him.* "She left me a message saying she was coming to see me. She's sure I've had a mental collapse."

"Ah, well, once she meets the Sullivans she'll be

certain of it." His voice was as soft as if she had her head on the pillow next to his. Kate could picture how the little wrinkles at the corners of his eyes looked when he laughed and how he had a habit of licking his lips when he was deep in thought.

"I need to go check on my house guest. I'll see you soon."

"Yes, you will. And, Katie, be prepared, I have plans to work you hard this morning." The call ended.

Oh, I'll just bet you do Mr. Sullivan. And I'm ready for you.

****

Brandon did make her work and loved every minute of it. She was a fast study and he liked her attitude in the saddle as well as on the ground. He couldn't help but wonder if she would have the same sense of adventure and energy in bed. He told himself he had no business even fantasizing about her. He had nothing to offer a woman like Katie, except himself. Right now he wasn't sure he would even have a roof over his head in six months. Though she didn't seem to be a materialistic woman, the former doctor's wife was certainly used to a level of lifestyle that he could not provide.

"Katie, don't let him grow roots at the halt, he's taking advantage of your kind heart. Kick the lazy bum, or I'll have you carryin' a whip," he called from his seat in the corner of the indoor arena. "That's a good girl. Now, let me see how the trot is coming."

Kate nudged Murphy into a trot and turned a circle in the center of the ring.

"Katie...do you know what a twenty meter circle is? Did you take geometry? You've got to be more accurate than that...this is dressage, not a trail ride." He would not let up until she got it right. "You tell him, every step, where you want his legs, his body...don't you be lettin' him take *you* for a ride now."

"I can't believe I pay you for this abuse," Kate said through clenched teeth.

"Ahh, you love it. There...that's a circle. Good, not perfect, but respectable. Turn down the center line and give us a nice, square halt." He got off his chair and stood where he could evaluate the straightness of horse and rider. "That, darlin' is an *eight* and it's hard to get a better score unless you're sleepin' with the judge."

"That bit of information might come in handy someday." Kate patted Murphy on his sweaty neck. "Good boy, Murph. I have mints for you."

Brandon stepped to Murphy's side and whispered to Kate, "I don't know if you noticed, but you have an audience, and the young lady has an uncanny resemblance to a woman to whom I am, in a manner of speakin', betrothed."

Kate looked across the arena where a tall, elegant woman stood. She was illuminated by the morning sun, golden hair a halo of untamed curls framing her lovely and bewildered countenance. It was, of course, Laura.

It was time to face the music. Kate hoped it would be a slam dunk. Laura was not prone to hysterics. She would listen to what her mother had to say.

"Let me put Murphy away for you, Kate. You need to talk to your daughter." Brandon held the reins while Kate vaulted from the saddle.

"Thanks, do I owe you extra for this?" Kate said with a shaky smile.

"Oh no. Anything to promote family togetherness. I hope she has your sense of adventure."

Crossing the short distance to the arena door was like walking to the guillotine. Laura would either laugh or want to lop her mother's head off.

Kate wasn't sure what to prepare for, or which would be easier.

She hugged Laura, kissing her on both cheeks. "Sweetheart, it's great to see you, but didn't you get my message? Everything is fine. Nonna completely misunderstood what was happening."

"Mom, is there somewhere we can talk...privately?"

"Sure, sweetheart. It's a pretty day. Let's take a walk." Kate led her out into the hayfield and they walked silently for several minutes.

Kate thought she could hear wheels turning in Laura's head as she planned her interrogation.

"Momma, you've got to tell me what the hell is going on here. I get this crazy phone call from Nonna telling me you're engaged...then you call and leave this cryptic message about how I don't need to worry. How can I not worry?"

Kate had been holding her breath and had to remind herself to exhale as she pondered what to say to her grown child. "Laura, you know, I'm not done living. For half of my life I have awakened every morning, and my first thoughts were 'how can I take care...how can I please the most important people in my life.' Your father, and then you, were my complete focus. Nonna and your uncles, I never wanted to disappoint them either. I think I did a pretty good job. Would you agree?"

"Momma, you know I think you're the best. Why would you ever question that?"

"Have you ever thought about how it feels to be loved and how you would cope if that love were taken from you, forever?" Kate sat down on a log and invited Laura to join her.

"Look, Mom, I know you and Daddy splitting up was a blow to you. But, I love you. Nonna and the uncles love you. You will always have enough love in your life. You don't have to go looking for it...from strangers."

"Well, first...Brandon is not a stranger. Second, I'm not in love with him." The bewilderment in Laura's face reflected her own. "But, Laura, if I were...you would have to accept that."

"So what Daddy told me was true?"

Laura had an angry edge to her words that made Kate suddenly suspicious.

"That depends on what it is you're referring to."

"I shouldn't say anything, I guess it's none of my business, but he told me about you...seeing other men...while he traveled. I didn't want to believe him...but well...he said he forgave you."

Kate thought her brain was going to explode and splatter all over the field. She had been so careful, from the start of her marital problems to never malign Jeffrey to his daughter, but, apparently *daddy dearest* had no such scruples. Kate measured her words with as much precision as she could afford.

"Let me just set the record straight here, Laura. I never, in twenty-five years of marriage to your father, never even looked at another man in lust. If Jeffrey told you that *I* was unfaithful, he was mistaken. You can choose to believe me or not, but let me tell you something about myself. I'm not dead inside. I want to be loved, just like I did when I was your age. I still awaken in the night and want to reach out and have a man there who thinks I'm beautiful and tells me so, who wakes in the morning and is glad I'm part of his life."

"Mom, I don't want to hear this."

"Darling, you don't have a choice. You are going to hear it. You might not understand it now, and when you do, I hope it isn't because you've been hurt. Am I going to marry Brandon Sullivan? I wouldn't put money on it. But I might have dinner with him, go to a play or a concert...and Laura, I might take him into my bed. And, God forbid you should ever be as lonely as I have been for the last many years, but if you are and you meet someone as kind and loving as Bran, I hope you take advantage of what he has to offer."

Tears ran down Laura's fair cheeks. "Momma, I'm sorry."

Kate held her daughter in her arms while Laura sobbed for many minutes before Kate looked back toward the barn and saw Brandon watching them. She had to ask herself if she would, indeed, take this man to her bed, if the occasion presented itself.

While they walked back from the field, Kate explained the *engagement* scenario. Laura laughed and said she would get right into the act. She loved her Nonna, but knew how overbearing a woman she could be. And Laura admitted that if her mom was going to fake a love affair, she had certainly picked a hotty to do it with.

Chapter Ten

Kate had started to feel like she had everything under reasonable control. She had juggled like a one-armed paper hanger to keep her deception from spilling out of bounds and mucking up her life any further. But the inevitable glitch in the less-than-smooth workings of her plan presented itself before the month of November saw its last day.

"Catarina, I shoulda go to *'ack-in-a-sack* to see your Mamma. I will take *il treno*," Sergio stumbled in English.

Kate knew her mother would never forgive her if she put Sergio on a train and he got hopelessly lost in New Jersey. "No, Sergio, I'll drive you. It'll be fun." *Like a stick in my eye is fun.* She truly did not want to drive the two hundred plus miles, nor spend several days convincing her mother that she was not insane. Kate had to be honest, she would miss riding *and* Brandon.

She dialed Mamma. "*Ciao*, Mamma. How would it be if I came and brought Sergio to visit? We'll spend a few days."

"Oh...Catarina, *molto bene*. Bring your Mr. Sullivan. It is time he met your family. Your brothers are wanting to know that this is a good man for their sister."

A noose tightened around Kate's vocal chords and her voice came out in a strangled, squeaky, "Oh, I don't know, Brandon probably can't get away from his work...uh...this is a busy time for him."

"*Si, si, si*...well Cara, what does Signore Brandon do for a living?"

Okay, this should send her into a fit. "He trains horses, Mamma. I thought I told you that." *Or I avoided telling you that.*

"Trains horses? What kind of a living is that, Catarina? Can he take care of you? I must talk to him. You bring him with you."

"I'll have to ask Brandon if he can come." And then in a moment of brilliance Kate remembered. "But I don't see how it will be possible. My car only holds two people." *Dodged a bullet on that one.* "Sergio and I will come on Wednesday. See you soon Mamma. I love you."

"*Perfetto.* I will cook. I love you Catarina."

As Kate closed her cell phone, her home phone started ringing. She seriously considered letting it go to the machine, but her unyielding sense of responsibility won out over jaw fatigue. *I am so sick of explaining myself.* She sighed and picked up the call. "Hello," she grumbled, hoping it was a solicitor so she could justify hanging up.

"I must have the wrong number. I'm calling Katie and she never sounds that grumpy."

"Brandon? I'm sorry. I was just talking to my mother."

"Ahh, that explains it. What can I do to help? Set a date?"

"I think I'll join the next expedition to Antarctica. I hear that once they get you down there, you can't come home for months." Kate groaned.

"That bad, is it?"

"Yes, but I think I can handle it. My mother wants to meet the man who swept me off my feet. I called her to let her know that I'm coming to Hackensack with Sergio and she decided it would be just great to have you come along."

"And, you told her...what?"

"That my car isn't equipped to transport three people." Kate imagined him grinning that irresistible grin of his while he teased her with his questions.

"I wouldn't mind getting away for a few days. I could take the train and meet you there."

He's insane. Why is he offering to meet my family? "Brandon, you don't want to do that."

"Actually, I do. I'm intrigued. Your family sounds...fascinating."

Kate was not at all sure this was a good idea. Frankie was the only one who knew the truth, her mother would be a force to contend with, and her two youngest brothers...God, she didn't want to think of the impression those clowns would try to make.

"I'll pay your plane fare if you want to fly." I can't believe I'm letting this happen. Lord help me.

****

Brandon tried to convince Kate that they should all fly. The weather had been turning colder and he thought it would be the sensible thing to do. She disagreed and he backed down. Sergio, she explained, preferred not to fly and she did not want to displease him. But Brandon had made it his mission to worry for her safety and he was relieved when he saw the blue Beemer pull into the passenger pick-up at the Newark airport.

"Hey, handsome, can I give you a lift?" she called to him.

"I don't know, where are you plannin' on takin' me?"

"Hackensack and the best Italian food in all New Jersey. Get in. My mother hasn't left the kitchen in days. Hope you're hungry."

"A smart man never refuses a free meal." He almost reached over to kiss her but remembered he had no basis for such an action. Save it for the show he would be putting on for the Aiellos; the performance of a lifetime, if he played it right.

"Oh, *trust me* when I say 'there is no such thing as a free lunch'." Her smile made him melt from the center of his chest out to the tips of his extremities.

Kate chattered the whole way to Hackensack. Bran thought she seemed awfully nervous. After all, he was only going to meet her family, people like Kate—energetic, good humored, maybe a little crazy—he wasn't concerned. But passing through the front door was like being sucked into a storm surge. Spinning wildly in its center was a tornado of a small, grey-haired woman in an apron, dark eyed, with an ebullient smile. She rushed to Brandon and with both her flour-covered hands, pulled his face to hers and kissed each of his cheeks. She stood back and, hands on her hips, she exclaimed, "*O Dio!*"

"Brandon, this is my mamma, Silvana Gondolfo Aiello." Kate brushed the white hand prints off his face with a dish towel.

There was a short knock on the door and Bran turned around to see a priest who crossed to Kate and pulled her into his arms, lifting her off her feet in a bone-cracking bear hug. He grasped Brandon by the shoulders and kissed him, in the same fashion that Mamma Aiello had, on each side of his face. A priest? The woman has invited the parish priest? *Jaysus, this is lookin' mighty serious.*

Kate started to introduce the cleric when there was a pounding on the door and calls of "Hackensack police, open up!"

Brandon thought he saw Kate start to smile, but then she looked at the priest and back to Brandon, and muttered, "I can't believe it. Mamma, stop them."

The door was flung open and two uniformed police officers stood there—a matched set of big, burly, fierce-looking cops, hands on their holstered side arms.

"Is there a Mr. Sullivan on the premises?" one of

them demanded.

Kate opened her mouth, but all that she managed was "Ooh, noo..."

Brandon couldn't figure out why the police would want him. He didn't remember breaking any laws...in New Jersey. "I'm Sullivan." He stepped forward.

"Cuff him," the bigger of the cops growled and the other one grabbed Brandon and, pulling his hands behind his back, snapped the handcuffs onto his wrists.

Kate started to protest, "Frankie, stop them! Mamma, please don't let them do this. Brandon, I can explain."

"Katie, don't worry, whatever this is about, I can take care of it," he hoped. "Listen, fellas, I'm just here to meet the family. Let's be reasonable now. What do you think I've done?"

"Come with us, Mr. Sullivan. We're taking you in." The two police, flanking a very confused Brandon, marched him out the door. The priest followed, crossing himself and muttering a prayer in Latin.

As they put him in the back seat of their cruiser, Brandon could hear Kate yelling out the open window of the house, "You stupid buffoons, you can't do this. Come back here. I'll get you for this. You'll be sorry..."

****

Sergio sat studying his Italian-English phrase book while Mamma and Kate fussed in the kitchen over the dinner preparations. It was nearly eight; the Three Stooges and Brandon had been gone almost four hours when Kate heard the discordant strains of *That's Amore* being sung loudly in what sounded like a mix of Italian and Gaelic.

"Catarina, the water is boiling and I will start the pasta now that the boys are home. You can set the table."

"Sure, Mamma, I'll do that, right after I strangle my brothers." Kate hoped they hadn't gotten Brandon so intoxicated that he spilled the beans about the spurious engagement. She wondered why she cared. The whole story was so idiotic she wasn't sure her mother would believe either version, so what did it matter?

The door was thrown open so hard it bounced on its hinges with a loud crash, shaking the china cabinet so soundly Kate thought her mother's fine china would shatter. Sergio stood, apparently ready to protect the family from intruders.

"Where the hell have you reprobates been?" Kate shouted.

"Catarina, there will be no cursing in my house," Mamma yelled.

"Sorry, Mamma," Kate called and then her jaw dropped an inch when she saw Brandon. "What did they do to you?" He was completely disheveled, his shirt had slipped the confines of his trousers, he was missing his shoes. The way he was grinning, Kate was sure he had left part of his brain in some bar on a Hackensack street corner, courtesy of the Sons of Italy.

Mark and Joey were laughing stupidly and Frank—Father Frank, her serious, studious Frankie—was trying so hard to hold back the mirth that his eyes were streaming tears. "Kate, we can explain."

"Oh, can you now?" Kate shot back.

"Ah, Katie darlin', we just had a little male bondin' here, the brothers and meself. As we say in the west of Ireland, '*da craic* was mighty.'" Brandon stumbled toward her, pulled her into a clinch and looked into her furious eyes. "Uh-oh, boys, I fear the lovely Kate is not happy with us." She squirmed in his arms but he would not let her go.

Mark hooted and slapped Joey on the back so hard the younger sibling fell forward, barely catching himself before falling headlong into Kate and Bran. "Kiss her, you fool. That'll cool her off. Or maybe you don't want her cooled, ahh, whatta you think, Joey?"

"Kiss her, kiss her...," Joey chanted, hooting and whistling encouragement.

"If you kiss me I'll bite you, you drunken Irishman. Let me go," Kate hissed. "And, where are your shoes?"

"Catarina, is the table set? The pasta is al dente. *Tutti...andiamo,* come."

Silvana carried a huge platter of pasta to the table. Sergio, seeking a diversion, started to open the wine.

Kate was momentarily distracted. Brandon took the advantage and stole a kiss from her angry lips. She pushed on his chest and pulled back to look him square in his dizzy face. "Umm, you taste like Zuccherini." But even with the tang of the sugar cubes soaked in strong spirits, his tongue probing her mouth elicited pleasant twinges low in her belly. "You need to get some pasta in you, before you disgrace yourself any further."

They took their seats at the table and Frank asked the Lord's blessing and forgiveness, hoping to curry Kate's forgiveness as well.

All through the meal Kate endured the boisterous guffaws of her brothers and slightly bleary-eyed taunting from Brandon. "You know, sweet Katie, I learned things about you that only a proper fiancé should be privy to."

"Well, let me tell you, there's nothing *proper* about you tonight, so I shouldn't have to worry about what you might have learned." Kate tried to avoid looking at him and stabbed at her fettuccini.

"They told me about the time...which one of you

was it? Oh yes, Frankie took you to hear...uh..."

"Dan Fogelberg." Frank piped up, looked at Kate and mouthed, "Sorry."

"And the two of you got stoned and...oh..."

Kate was horrified, "Frank...you traitor."

Joey chimed in, "We had to tell him, Kate. He can't marry a woman who keeps secrets. It's not healthy."

"And, Giuseppe Aiello, if you actually knew anything about marriage, you might not be single at your age." Kate leveled her gaze, in warning, on her youngest brother.

But, Brandon was not done. "I heard all about Dan...oh...Danny Spumante..."

"Spelletti...Danny Spelletti...," Frank corrected him.

"How he broke your heart...in the third grade and you refused to come out of your room for dinner." Brandon leaned and whispered into her ear, "He was a fool, Danny Spumante was."

Joey, who never knew when he had pushed his big sister too far, had one more tidbit to share. "I forgot to tell you about the time Kate went skinny dipping..."

"Okay, that's enough, you jackass. Brandon, don't believe anything these yahoos tell you." She kicked someone under the table thinking it was Joey, but realized too late it had been Sergio when he yelped in pain. "Oh, damn, I'm sorry...I didn't mean..." She reached for her wine glass and raised it in a toast. She knew this was a lame attempt to steer the conversation away from her adolescent exploits, but she figured it might stand a chance. "To Cousin Sergio, who came all these many miles to visit us." They all clinked glasses, saying *"cin, cin"* and *"salute."*

To Kate's complete horror, Brandon started to stand, looking suspiciously like he was going to make an announcement. She grabbed his arm and her eyes met his in a pleading glance, but he just smiled and patted her hand. He raised his glass, "to the lovely Katie, my intended." He smiled down at her and winked, "and to the Aiello family. May your home always be too small to hold all your friends. *Sláinte!*"

Kate leaned into him when he sat, and whispered, "That was very sweet, but stop being so charming, or they'll be really angry with me when I break up with you."

"I can't help it. I *am* charming."

And he was, dammit. Kate's mother loved him, and her two youngest brothers thought Brandon was the best sport outside the donut shop. Even Frank, who knew the truth, was no help. Kate was afraid Father Frank would stand up at any moment and offer to bless the happy couple. She was going to have to put an end to the game, and soon. But how could she accomplish that and not disappoint half her family?

They ate, drank, laughed and talked for hours. Finally they ran out of words, food, wine and energy. "Mamma, let me take care of the dishes. You've done enough. Go, sit with Sergio and visit." Kate actually wanted to get away from the constant talk and noise for a while. She stacked the dishes and set to work putting away the few leftovers that remained. One sure thing with the Aiello men was their appetites. Rarely was a scrap of food wasted.

Kate slipped her hands into the soapy water and started washing the glassware, letting her mind float into a calming space, blocking out the craziness of the evening. She didn't hear Brandon and was startled when his arms reached around her waist.

"Ahh, you scared me." She tried to shove him away with an elbow. "You can stop playacting now. No one is watching." Kate's hands were trembling. A wine glass slipped from her grasp and back under the water. "You're going to make me break one of Mamma's glasses. Stop distracting me."

"Let me help you clean up. I'm actually fairly good at domestic chores. I'll dry."

"No...no, you don't need to. You should go visit with my mother. She likes you. Just back off on the 'engaged' scenario, if you don't mind. It's going to be hard enough when we split up." He still had his arms encircling her and his breath was hot on her ear. "Brandon, do you mind...uh...removing your hands?"

"Why?"

She did not have a ready answer. What was she supposed to say? You're making my knees turn to jelly? My heart can't take the palpitations at my advanced age? I'm not accustomed to the tingling feeling that is settling in my crotch? So she simply said, "You're spending the night at Mark's house and he needs to be getting home."

"I'm not sleeping with you?"

She gasped and turned to face him. "Are you crazy? My mother would kill me." It took a second to realize he was teasing. "You know what I mean. You need to go now."

"Okay, I'm sure you're right. Good night Katie." He kissed her just above her ear. "I'll see you in the morning."

Kate shivered from the warmth of his lips on her temple. She tried to tell herself she would react like that to any man who had the balls to be that intimate, it was completely understandable. Besides, she had been deprived of any physical affection for so long, it was like being starved, her body and mind were not very discriminating at this point. She would get over it, the physical reactions would fade, she would adjust.

Chapter Eleven

Morning drifted through the filmy curtains of Kate's childhood room, spilling golden light across her face and waking her from her fitful slumber. She had to wonder if the difficulty getting a restful night had anything to do with her hormonal changes or if it was just her unsettled life.

She crept softly to the bathroom, hoping to not awaken Mamma or Sergio. Kate wanted a cappuccino, solitude, and time to organize her thoughts. The house had one bath, no shower and walls that amplified every sound. She had never had a moment's privacy growing up, the only daughter in a house full of mamma's boys. She loved her brothers but had to admit they could be an overwhelming force in the family.

Kate dressed in jeans and a sweater, took her cell phone and went to the kitchen to make coffee. While the espresso steamed and the milk heated she checked for messages. There was only one and it was from Annie Sullivan.

"Katie dear, would you have Brandon call home as soon as you get this message. I have been trying to call his phone and he doesn't answer. Thank you. Oh, and give my regards to Sergio."

Why wouldn't he answer his phone? She looked at the clock. It was only quarter after seven, but she'd better call Mark's place.

"You have reached Mark and Maria, please leave a message." Damn, they were probably sound asleep. As much alcohol as the guys had put away and the mountains of food they had consumed, they'd sleep for a week. Annie sounded worried. Maybe one of the horses was hurt or sick, or, God forbid, something had happened to Kevin or Brighid.

Mark's house was two blocks away. Kate decided to go wake the lazy bums up and get the message to Brandon. She left a note for her mother, turned off the stove and grabbed a coat. Kate walked the short distance and used the key that she knew was hidden in a flower pot on the front stoop to let herself in.

Maria and the twins were visiting her mother in Queens, so Mark was bachelor king of his castle for a week. The house was a disaster area. Maria would kill him when she and the girls got home. Kate found Mark asleep on the couch. "Mark, wake up." She shook him. "Wake up. I need to talk to Brandon."

He rolled over and fell off the narrow sofa. "Jesus, Kate, what the hell are you doin' wakin' a guy up like that? Good thing I didn't have my weapon. I mighta mistaken you for a cat burglar."

"I need to see Brandon," she insisted.

"Uh, okay...you can't stay away from him for a few hours? Jeez, you're actin' like a school girl."

"Shut up, you dope. I have an urgent message for him." She looked down at her big little brother. "And why are you sleeping on the couch?"

"Ah...well...I don't like to sleep in the bed when Maria is away...it's lonely." He looked at his sister with a sheepish grin. "Brandon's in the girls' room."

"Go get him for me," Kate insisted.

"Hell no. He's your fiancé...go get him yourself."

Kate sighed, and made her way down the short hallway to the bedroom belonging to her nieces. Brandon lay on one of the twin beds, long legs hanging over the edge, quilt flung to the floor. He was wearing boxers and an undershirt, his dark hair a sharp contrast to the white linen of the pillowcase. Kate watched him for a moment, noting how his breathing was soft and even. Her eyes focused on the gold chain that encircled his neck. A ring, a simple gold band, had been slipped onto the chain and now lay just below the hollow of his throat. Kate's stomach clenched. He carried Fiona with him, usually hidden from view, but always next to his heart.

She felt like an intruder, standing there, watching another woman's husband as he dreamed. A wife who, though gone from this corporeal existence, still owned him with a love he would hold until his own life faded away.

"Brandon," Kate whispered. "Wake up."

His eyes opened and he smiled. "I've been awake, wondering when you were going to say something."

"Liar...you were snoring," she fibbed.

"I don't snore." He gave her a lopsided grin. "And what brings you to my bed so early in the mornin'? Can't live without me?"

"Don't flatter yourself. You have a call. Annie left a message on my phone. Apparently yours is turned off." She handed him her cell. "You'd better call her back. She sounded worried." She started to leave. "I'll make you some coffee, if I can find a clean cup in Mark's kitchen."

Kate washed the espresso pot and two coffee cups. She made the coffee, added steamed milk and walked to the bedroom to hand the cup to Brandon. Stopping just short of putting her hand on the door knob, she froze in place. It was not like her to eavesdrop, but as she listened she nearly dropped the mug from her hand.

"Listen, sweetheart, you know I love you. Kate is just a client...yes...yes...I know it sounds like that. But you are going to have to believe me when I tell you it's nothing."

I'm just a client? Well, I guess that's technically

true.

"I know...she's not my girlfriend, as you put it....Well, darlin', you have nothing to worry about. Look, baby...I can explain."

Baby, darling, sweetheart? Cozy.

"I'll be home tonight. I want to see you. No...no you don't have to drive to Willow Creek. I'll come to your apartment and we can talk. Okay? Love you...I'll call you from the airport."

He's going to see her...tonight? Okay, Kate...you fool. What were you thinking? That he might actually care? This is just a game for him. He's helping a client. Kate's hands started to shake so badly she thought the cappuccino might splash out of its cup and onto the carpet. She headed back to the kitchen.

"Brandon," she called as casually as possible, "coffee's ready." She nearly jumped out of her skin when she turned around and he stood in the door frame, looking no less delicious than the cantuccini on the plate in her hand.

He pulled out a chair for her. "Will you join me?"

"Uh...yes...well, I should be getting back to Mamma's, but..."

"Katie, what's the matter?" He took the plate. "You're shakin'. Is something wrong?"

"Why would you think that? Everything is fine...just wonderful." She nearly choked on a biscuit.

Brandon reached for her hand, but Kate picked up her cup as a diversionary tactic. "Something's come up, Kate. I need to get back home. I'm sorry."

"Don't be. I understand." She stood and started to leave. "I'll say goodbye to Mamma and Sergio for you. Mark can take you to the airport."

"Kate, sit down," he all but shouted. "I'll go see your mam. I want to thank her for her hospitality and I'd like to say 'so long' to Sergio."

"Whatever," Kate sighed in resignation. "I need to get back to the house...see you later." She stood and rushed out the door before he could see the tears that were brimming in her eyes. *You fool, Kate. You stupid fool.* She had let him get to her, make her feel pretty, desirable, sexy for the first time in years. She should have known that a good looking, single man, even one who still cared about his dead wife, would have a woman tucked away somewhere ready to satisfy his needs. Whoever she was, he was headed to see her tonight and quell any confusion about "Kate the client."

Kate hoped in vain that her mother wouldn't see her come in the door. She had no ability to stop the tears spurred by the humiliation of her folly. But getting past Silvana was like trying to sneak past a platoon of rabid guard dogs.

"*O Dio*, Catarina, what happened Cara? Who made you cry?"

"It's nothing, Mamma. Please, I just need to be alone." She knew this wouldn't work. Mamma thought no one should grieve in private. Kate would have to come up with an explanation. "Uh...it's just that..." Think Kate. "Brandon and I...well..."

"Oh, bambina, did you have a lover's quarrel? That's okay. What's a marriage without some good healthy fighting? When you make up...ah...it will be so good."

"Mamma, it's not like that. He's going home. Today." The street level door buzzed and she heard footsteps coming up the stairs. Kate ran to her room and slammed the door, locking it, but she could still hear the conversation in the front parlor.

"Oh, Brandon, I'm a so sorry you and Catarina had a little fight. My Cara, she has such a temper. She'll get over it. She always does."

"Mrs. Aiello, I just came to let you know I need to leave. What do you mean 'fight'? Kate told you we

117

had an argument?"

"*O Dio*...she ran to her room, crying like a baby. She said you had a disagreement. Maybe you should talk to her before you leave."

"Yes, maybe I'd better."

Kate heard his footsteps coming toward her room. Oh, crap, how am I going to get out of this without looking childish? What am I worried about? I was going to send him packing sooner or later...guess it's gonna be sooner.

"Katie?" He cajoled through the door. "Let me in, sweetheart. I'm not sure what I did, but I'll make it up to you. I'll sing you your favorite Barry Manilow tune."

"They told you *that*, too?" She was going to flog her brothers for that divulgence. "Go away. I'm done with males of my species. You're all horrible."

"Come on, Kate, I'm not playing here. Tell me what's wrong."

"Yeah, well, I'm not play-acting either. Go away." She blew her runny nose and tried to gain control of the quivering in her voice.

"Open the door, Kate. I have something for you."

"Anything you have you can just keep," she snapped. She wanted to send him a volley of stinging words, but she choked on her own silence.

"But kisses are no good for keeping, you have to share them." His voice was gentle, until he heard no answer from her side of the barrier. "Kate, I'm serious. Open up."

"Why should I?"

"Because I don't know why you're angry and I didn't mean to hurt you. Come now. I want to talk to you, but not through the damn door."

"Brandon, go home. I'll be back in two days. I'll see you at Willow Creek for my scheduled lesson." She gagged back a sob and pulled the bedspread over her head. *At least Jeffrey left me enough money that I can buy myself compliments and the occasional kiss. Kate Aiello, you are so pitiful.*

****

Brandon did ask Mark to take him to the airport. Though he did not want to leave while Kate was unhappy with him, he was not going to sit outside her door and plead with her. She did have a temper; he had seen it in action more than once. But he knew she had come to her senses in the past and he was certain he could figure out what had set her off this time.

By the time he arrived at the gate in Baltimore, his head hurt from his attempts to understand Kate, and his feelings for her. How could he explain the whole thing to Brighid, if he didn't know his own mind? He had only the bag he had carried on the plane, so headed straight out to the passenger pick-up.

"Daddy!" The voice of his daughter caught Brandon and pulled him back to real time. Brighid had pulled her Volkswagen beetle into a space and was waving wildly, hoping he would see her.

See her he did and, as always, he thought his little girl was beyond beautiful. She had her mother's fair skin, blond hair and eyes the color of the sea off the coast of County Clare. Those eyes could change like the weather from tranquil to rampant without warning.

They drove to a pub in College Park where Brighid often hung out with her friends from the University. She was quiet, and Brandon wondered if she felt she had gone too far this time, gotten too much into her father's personal business.

"Have you had dinner, baby?" he asked.

"No, but I'm not particularly hungry. I'll just have herbal tea."

He ordered a beer and cheese chowder for himself and the tea for her, sat back and looked at

119

her lovely face. "Are you ready for my attempt at an explanation?" he asked.

"Now I feel really bad. I didn't mean for you to cut your trip short on account of me. It's just when Kevin said you were engaged...fuck...oh, sorry...I mean, I don't know what's going on."

"And you wouldn't believe me if I said nothing is goin' on? So, let me ask you this. Do you think I should mourn your mother forever?"

"Well, you love her, don't you? I mean...you don't stop loving someone because they're gone. I'll always love mammy. I can barely get through my day without crying, I miss her so much."

Tears threatened to stop him, but Brandon had to make her understand. "I miss her, too. Sweety, your mam, she loved you more than life. I believe she had enough love in her heart to transcend death. She knew we would miss her and she made me promise her something."

"What promise? What are you talking about?"

"She wanted us to go on without her. She wanted to know we would be happy, that we would keep our hearts open to the possibilities that life would offer each of us." In one sense he dreaded telling his daughter these things; in another he knew she needed to know. "I don't want to hurt you or your brother, but I hope you can understand. I may have met someone...I...want to spend some time with." He wanted to mentally lash himself for not just admitting he was fascinated by Kate and wanted to spend *more than* time with her.

"But, Daddy, how can you?"

"Because I'm just a man, flesh and bone, human, and I have needs. I have you and Kevin, Annie, Willow Creek, but I'm lonely...for the kind of companionship an adult man needs." *Fiona, if you're listening, help me out here.* "I haven't been with a woman, other than to have dinner...since your mam."

"I sort of knew that. Daddy, wow...I hate to pry into your personal life like this, but if it's about sex..."

Damn, she was a straight-forward girl. Learned that from her mother, she did. "Um hum...I should tell you that is none of your business. No, it isn't entirely about...that, but it is part of being loved. I won't deny it."

"This 'Kate'. Would you...did you...?"

Brandon laughed. "That, young lady, *is* none of your business. I will tell you though, I enjoy her company and I think you would like her, as well."

"Yeah, Kevin said she's 'a babe'. Of course, I don't trust Kevin to make good judgments on these things. It did take him a while to realize what a prize he had in Barb." She reached across the table for his hand. "Da, I'm afraid...afraid that if I lose focus on mam, I'll forget her face." Tears made tracks down her cheeks.

Brandon stood and stepped around to Brighid's chair. He pulled her into his arms and held her while she sobbed. "Baby, if you ever think you have lost your mam, just look in the mirror, you'll see her in you." He held her close and the tears that wet her cheek were not hers alone.

Chapter Twelve

Kate hadn't quite recovered from her self-hatred when she decided she needed to get home. Sergio chose to stay with Silvana for the rest of the week. *Great*, Kate thought. It would give her time to catch her breath and get reorganized.

Her bouts of tearfulness, unexplained by the events of the last few days, were escalating beyond all rational explanation. After all, she had planned to give Brandon the boot. Now it was done. Of course, her mother and brothers just beamed when they talked of Kate's betrothed. It made her want to hurl things at them, like knives or shards of crockery.

She said goodbye, trying not to prolong the kissing and hugging. Kate wanted to get on the road. The weather report had been predicting snow and she had no desire to get caught in bad weather.

She took the New Jersey turnpike, giving her miles to berate herself and argue out loud. It was smooth sailing all the way to the outskirts of Baltimore. When her eyes started to glaze over, she stopped at a mini-mart for coffee. That's when she discovered she had forgotten her purse. She had enough tollway change left over to pay for her coffee, but she hoped her gasoline would hold out because she did not even have a credit card. Annoyed with herself she drove on, hoping to get home before midnight.

Had she learned nothing in the last half of her life? Why had she allowed Brandon to weasel his way into her heart and set up camp? Why had she acted like a foolish adolescent, crying, locked in her room when he tried to talk to her? Ripped through a time warp, she was fifteen again, out of sync with her body, her mind and the rest of the world. Her thoughts echoed, boomeranged through the decades and back to her present, where she had no excuse for her inanity.

Tears blurred her vision and hurt muddied her thoughts. The roads that lead to the Baltimore suburb where she lived were becoming ice-slicked. Kate hated her little useless excuse for a car and she detested the thought of going to the mausoleum she laughingly called home. She slammed her hands down on the dash and screamed, "I hate my life. Why do I have this meaningless existence?"

Her answer came swiftly, with a nauseating rip of skidding, sliding tires on the glassy pavement and a lighter than air whirling into space. The sickening sound of metal tearing and vague visions of sparks sheering past her window seemed to Kate a slow motion ballet in which she had no time to ponder her exit. Her neck was whipped back and the last memory before blackness tore consciousness from her grasp was of being hit, hard, by a gray mass and slipping down a declivity into an inky abyss.

Lights spun beyond sight like when she was a child and pressed on her closed eyelids. Voices came from a poorly tuned radio, so far away, barely understandable.

"Can you hear me? You're going to be fine. We just need to get you out of here."

I can hear you. But my mouth won't work. You're hurting me.

"I'm going to move you. Don't be afraid. No, don't move. Wait for me to help you."

I'm screaming, why can't you hear me?

"Okay. Hey Jack, check around for a purse or something. We need ID."

I'm Catarina Aiello, from Hackensack.

"I don't see anything. Look in the glove box."

"Yeah, here's the owner's manual. Hey, shine that light over here. It looks like a Jeffrey Waldon owns the car. This must be the wife. Yeah, there's a phone number."

No, I'm not his wife, you fool. Listen to me.

"Let's worry about that when we get to the E.R. They can track down the husband. Damn, she's a lucky gal. Look at the car."

****

When Brandon's phone rang at four A.M. his unconscious was tempted to ignore it. No one would be calling me at this hour, unless...and he was fully awake in one heart-pounding moment. "Sullivan here."

"Brandon, this is Frank Aiello. I thought you would want to be awakened..."

"Jaysus, Frank...what's happened?" His chest constricted and his mind wanted to blank out the fearful message he was sure was about to be delivered.

"Yes, there has been an accident. Kate...is in Frederick Memorial Hospital." Frank sounded professional, calm.

"God man, is she...is she badly hurt?" Brandon was grabbing his clothes as he talked. "I'm on my way."

"I'm flying in as soon as I can get a flight. I believe Laura is already with her mom. She's the one who called me."

"Good...hey, I gotta go."

"Brandon, she's going to be okay. My sister is tough."

"Thanks for calling me, Frank. See you later this morning."

By the time he hung up the phone Brandon was dressed, except for his shoes. He considered just leaving Annie a note, but knew she'd be furious with him if he let her know like that, so he awakened her. "Annie, there's been an accident and Kate is in the hospital. I'm going. I'll call you from there. Frank says she's gonna be okay."

"Oh my God in heaven, Brandon, I should go with you." She sat on the side of the bed.

"I'll call you as soon as I know anything. Please, I need to leave right now." He kissed his sister and rushed out of the house.

It was still black as midnight and the roads were treacherous. The thought of Katie hurt, in pain, afraid, ripped at him like claws. The only way he could function was to pull a trick out of his memory that he had used to get through each crisis with Fiona. He focused intently on the task at hand, like leaving his anxieties on the ground when he swung into the saddle. He planned each next step in a calculated manner. He would need to talk to the doctor, find Laura, comprehend the details of Kate's injuries. He should let Kevin and Brighid know so they could help pick up any slack at Willow Creek if he needed to be—wanted to be—at Kate's bedside. Annie could rearrange lessons. Everyone at the barn loved Kate; they would understand.

Brandon parked and ran the distance to the hospital entrance, pushed his way through the doors and straight to the admission desk. "I need to know where you have Kate Aiello." His words were unintentionally loud. "I'm sorry. I need to find her right away. She was in an accident and brought here." He tried to modulate his voice.

"And who are you, sir?"

"What difference does that make? I need to see her." He was trying to remain calm, but time was wasting.

"Well, it makes a great deal of difference. We don't give information regarding patients to nonrelatives; it's against our policy and it's the law."

"Okay, sure, I understand. I'm Brandon Sullivan. I'm Kate's...husband." He was about to say fiancé, but wasn't sure that had enough clout.

The receptionist eyed him suspiciously. "Sign in here." She handed him a clipboard. "She is in room 205. Up that elevator to the second floor, check in at the nurses' station."

When the elevator doors opened, he saw Laura Waldon speaking to a man with a professional demeanor and a stethoscope in the pocket of his jacket.

"Laura," he called and rushed to the girl. "Frank called me." He hugged her. "Where's Kate? Is she all right?"

"Brandon? Uh...well...she hasn't broken any bones and has no serious injuries, as far as we know. Brandon...," she turned to the man at her side, "this is..."

"Sure," he blurted out. "You must be Katie's doctor. Excuse me, I should introduce myself." He shook the man's hand. "Brandon Sullivan...I'm Katie's...," he hoped Laura would not mind the lie he was about to tell..., "husband."

Laura gasped. "Brandon, this isn't Mom's doctor. This is my father, Jeffrey Waldon."

So, this is the maggot who broke Kate's heart? Brandon had an almost overwhelming urge to punch the bastard in his smug face. "Laura, I'd like to see Kate. Is it okay if I go in?"

"Sure, that would be good for her." She laid a hand on his arm. "Brandon, she's had a pretty bad hit on the head. Just so you know she isn't quite with it yet."

He just gave the girl a nod, ignoring Jeffrey and strode briskly to room 205.

Intensive care units were a painfully familiar environment for Brandon, and he had a welling of nausea when he walked through the door and saw Kate. She was a frail sight with IV lines taped to her wrists, monitor leads coming off her chest and oxygen tubing in her nose. Her face was swollen and bruised and her lips crusted with dried blood. He pulled a chair to the side of the bed and gently took her hand.

"Katie, I'm here." He dampened a washcloth from the bedside table with water from the omnipresent hospital-issue carafe and blotted her dry lips. "Darlin', you won't be givin' any kisses with those tender lips for a while."

"Excuse me, are you a family member of Ms. Aiello?" An attractive, young black woman stepped to the foot of the bed.

"Yes." He stood, offering his hand. "I'm Brandon Sullivan." He really hated to continue the deception, but was cornered. He wanted to be privy to the details of Kate's situation. If she had him drawn and quartered for invading her privacy later, he would gladly take his punishment. Now he needed information. "I'm Kate's husband."

She eyed him appreciatively and welcomed him. "I'm Dr. Cason. Your wife is a very lucky woman. She has no internal injuries and no broken bones. The bruises and swelling to her face are superficial...from the airbag. She has a concussion, probably hit her head when the car flipped. But her MRI did not indicate any bleeding in her brain. I'm not her neurologist, but I think her semi-conscious state is simply from the concussion. I don't believe there will be any long-lasting memory loss."

"Memory loss?" he said with alarm.

"She might not remember the accident and events just prior. But it will all come back, eventually." She glanced at her watch. "I need to get going. I'm in the house all day. If you have any questions or concerns, have the nurses page me."

She shook Brandon's hand. "Stay as long as you like, talk to her. Patients who hear the sound of a loved one's voice often come around quicker."

****

Kate knew she was in hell. The heat was so intense she had no doubts that her lies and deceits had caught up with her. There was a torturous noise of water dripping, and a sound like rats scratching on walls. Clear tendrils snaked down, held her arms, and tickled her nose. She tried to speak but her lips were fused together and pain throbbed in her head. Trying to open her eyes and seeing only a vague shadow of what remained of the world, she was convinced of her condemnation. Jeffrey, pale, balding, pudgy-faced Jeffrey Waldon, stood over her, repeating her name. "Catherine." She tried to scream, *no*, but demons had taken her vocal chords. This is what hell is like, she thought, and Jeffrey is here, which means I'm shackled to him for eternity.

Just as she knew her devastation was complete and everlasting, she felt a gentle hand touch her cheek. Fingers trailed through her hair. Something damp and cool was pressed to her lips and soothing words, like a song, caressed her. *This must be a dream to tempt me, to give me a taste of glory before being plunged back into the void.*

"Wake up, my fairy queen; it's time to come back to me now. Katie, everything is all right." The voice was familiar, deep and comforting. Through the blur of her insensible state she realized this could not be eternal damnation after all. The contrary must be true. She must be in heaven, because no one in hell would be calling her *Katie*.

Chapter Thirteen

She dreamed that Brandon was there, and then his face was replaced by Frank's gentle visage. Laura came and went like a ghost drifting through Kate's nether world. Soft voices, whispers and the sound of machinery beeping confused her ears.

"Laura, I'm sorry for lying...well, especially to your father. I didn't think they would let me in, if I had said I was just a friend."

"It's okay, I understand. I asked Uncle Frank to call you. I knew Mom would want you here."

"Where did they find her? What happened?"

"She must have hit a patch of ice. The Beemer rolled over, maybe more than once. It's totaled. But the airbags...probably saved her. The EMTs didn't find any identification but the owner's manual was in the car and my dad's name and number were in it. So they called him. He came right away and called me from the E.R."

Kate heard the familiar "*O Dio*, my poor bambina."

Kate thought they might be talking about her, but she wasn't able to tell them they were mistaken. This was all just a bad dream. She would wake in her bed in Hackensack, Mamma would make espresso for Pappa and cocoa for Kate and the boys.

"Frank and I are going to go get some coffee. Nonna, come have a bite to eat with us. Sergio is waiting in the cafeteria. Brandon, can we get anything for you?"

"No, I'm fine. I'd like to stay...see if she wakes up."

Wake up. I'm supposed to wake up? They were talking to Brandon. Why is Brandon here?

She could feel his hand touching hers. Kate tried very hard to open her eyes. The lights were so bright. Tears overflowed her eyes and trickled into her ears. "Bran." Her voice cracked and it hurt to move her lips. "Bran?"

"Katie, I'm here. Don't talk if it hurts." He leaned over her and whispered.

"Thirsty...so thirsty." She felt his breath on her cheek, soft and calming. "I...need to go home." He momentarily slipped from her sight. "Bran?"

"Here, sip this. Take it slow. You must have bitten your lip, it's swollen. I don't want to hurt you." His hand supported her head while she tried to drink.

"You're not hurting me. Bran, what am I doing here?" None of this made any sense. She was on her way home...how did she get here...was this her bedroom? It was noisy and didn't smell like her bed.

"You were in an accident. But, other than being a little beat up, you're not injured badly. You hit your head pretty hard and you've been asleep for a while."

"A while?" Days, weeks, what?

"About eight hours. You've been coming and going, but don't worry, you haven't said anything I don't already know." He smiled, and she remembered how much she loved his smile.

"How long have you been here? Was Laura here? Frank? I thought I heard Mamma."

"I've been here a while. Laura, Frank and your mam are here. They just stepped out for coffee."

"I had this terrible dream. I was in hell. Jeffrey was there."

"Yes, well, don't worry about that now." He spread some soothing balm on her dry lips. "Here, this should feel better."

"So, I'm in a hospital?" It was beginning to make sense, the noises, the lights.

"Frederick Memorial, Intensive Care. You have a couple of intravenous lines, an oxygen cannula in your nose and...sorry to tell you...you've got a catheter in your bladder."

"Oh, that explains a lot." She felt an overpowering urge to pee. Oddly, she thought, it did not embarrass her that Brandon knew some rather private details of her situation. "Uh...when can I get rid of all this stuff?"

"Now that you're awake, probably soon. I would imagine it's not too comfortable."

"Ah, good to see you awake, Kate. I'm Cynthia, your nurse. Are you having any pain? Your doctor has medication ordered if you're uncomfortable."

"I'm sore. But I don't need anything, except maybe this damn tube out of my bladder."

"Sure, I can take that out. Dr. Cason wanted to be sure you had no blood in your urine. With this type of trauma, that's one of the things we need to watch carefully. Also, you will likely have some chest bruising, from the shoulder harness. That's one of the reasons you're being monitored...you can develop fluid around your heart. But so far everything looks very good."

"My face. I feel like I've gone a few rounds with Cassius Clay," Kate lisped.

She heard Brandon chuckle. "He's been Muhammad Ali for a while now, *Muirnín...* sweetheart."

"Oh." *I have lost my mind. What did he just call me?*

"Just bruises. The swelling and blotchiness will go away in a couple of days. I'll remove that cath now. Would you like your husband to leave or stay?"

"My what?" *What was she talking about...husband?* "What husband? I don't have a husband." She watched as the nurse looked at Brandon with an expression that Kate thought was sympathy.

"I'll just step out," he said.

"Just one minute. I've been hit on the head but not hard enough to forget my own wedding. What the hell is going on here?" Kate raised her voice. It hurt her throat and made her brain throb.

"Katie, darlin', I'll explain everything. Calm yourself now."

"Mr. Sullivan, maybe I should get her something to relax her," the nurse offered.

"Don't talk about me like I'm not here. I don't want anything to relax me. Just get this tube out of me." She reached for Brandon's hand. "Come back as soon as she's done. You have some explaining to do."

"I'll be right outside." He leaned down and kissed her above her ear and whispered, "I promise I'll tell you the whole story."

Brandon made a call to Annie letting her know that Kate was going to be fine. He talked to Kevin about which horses to ride, which to lunge and which ones got the day off. Everything seemed reasonably under control, so he grabbed a bite to eat and made his way back to check on Kate.

When Brandon approached the half-open door of her room he heard Laura talking and Kate laughing.

"Oh. Ow, it hurts to laugh this hard. I wish I could have seen his face," Kate was saying.

"Honestly, Mom, I thought Dad was going to faint. You know how his face gets so red when he's flustered? I about wet my pants trying not to laugh out loud."

"I can't believe Brandon would do that. He stood right there and introduced himself as my husband...to your father?" Kate laughed again and moaned.

Brandon knocked on the door jam. "May I join

you ladies?" He was relieved to see that Kate was sitting up in a chair; she had been bathed and was wearing running shorts and a T-shirt. Other than the bruises on her face and a few scrapes on her knees, she looked unscathed.

"I was just leaving. I need to let Daddy know that you're awake. Can I come back and bring you some supper tonight?" Laura offered Brandon her chair.

"I'm going home. I don't need to be here. I'm fine," Kate protested.

Brandon and Laura shared a concerned look. They both knew it was foolish for Kate to go home. She had suffered considerable head trauma and though she was now awake, she needed to be carefully watched for a couple of days at least.

"Mom, your doctor wants you to stay here tonight, and I'll come to stay at home with you for a few days. Nonna and Uncle Frank can stay a couple of days, too."

"No way. I'll stay one more night in this prison, but you are not going to miss the last weeks of the semester playing nursemaid to your mother." Kate was adamant.

"We'll talk about that. See you later." She left, closing the door behind her.

"She's right, you know?" Brandon reached for Kate's hand, examining it, admiring her long, graceful fingers. "You had quite the bonk on your head. You can't just go back home, alone."

"Brandon, there's something you need to understand about me. I'm the one who does the *taking care*. It has always been that way. It's what I do."

"I have noticed your tendency toward that particular approach." He couldn't help but smile. He loved that she was a nurturing woman who wanted those around her happy. But he wanted to help her

133

see that it needed to be a two-way street. "Think of this as a chance for those of us who care about you to give back a little."

"I'll try...It's going to be hard." She looked at him, silent for a moment. "So, why did you tell everyone, including my ex-husband, that you and I are married?"

"I wanted to see you and the watchdog at the front desk wouldn't tell me where they took you unless I was a relative. I saw Laura talking to this officious looking chap in the hall outside your room and assumed he was your doctor, so I fibbed again. By the time I told Dr. Cason who I was...it was starting to feel more like the truth than a falsehood."

"So...how does it feel to be a married man for a day?"

"Not bad, but I always was the marrying kind, you know. Your brothers would be thrilled to have me in the family...someone they can't drink under the table."

"They didn't see much of you sober. Maybe they'll find you boring."

"I am sorry, Katie, that I couldn't stay longer." He hadn't been allowed to explain his expeditious exit. "My daughter, Brighid, was terribly upset, about us...well...what she assumed about us. I needed to talk to her and I didn't feel comfortable—considering what I wanted her to understand—saying much over the phone."

"Brighid? Was that why Annie called? You needed to call your daughter?" Kate looked suddenly pale and sweaty. Her voice was thin as a thread. "You were talking to Brighid...on my phone...at Mark's house?"

"Katie, are you all right?" He thought he knew what was coming and grabbed a basin that sat by her bed, and at the same time hit the nurse call bell. "It's okay, take a deep breath." He put a cool cloth to her face and neck. "I've heard a concussion can make you queasy. Are you better, now?"

"Yes, well...I'm not sure. I think I need to lie down. Sorry for being such a wimp. Will you come back later?"

"Wild horses couldn't keep me away. Will you let me help you into bed?"

"No...Brandon, I'm...gonna puke and as much as it might not bother you, I don't think I can stand the humiliation right now."

He wanted to make her feel better, take away the fear of disgracing herself, if not the nausea that plagued her, but he just patted her trembling hand. "I'll be back tonight, but if you need me, I'll carry my mobile."

****

Kate's head felt like mush in a blender. The throbbing only got worse after everything she had put in her stomach made a return visit. She tried to sleep the rest of the day, thinking it would mend her body if not her mind. But sleep was elusive and her repeating thoughts, like seventies sitcom reruns, trampled any hope of peace.

Again she admitted to herself she had underestimated Brandon. She had jumped to a huge conclusion that he had been speaking to a lover that morning in Mark's house. The idea that it had been his daughter never crossed her mind.

Was it possible Brandon Sullivan was really just a very decent man? Was he as gallant and endearing as he seemed? Had she become so jaded that she suspected all men were clones of Jeffrey?

The fact that her two youngest brothers liked Brandon was not a vote of confidence. But the reality that Frank thought Bran was a standup guy Kate could not brush off so easily. Mamma would like almost any man who looked like he made Kate happy and Laura, well Laura thought Bran was hot.

135

Kate laughed out loud when she pictured Brandon introducing himself as Katie's husband, especially to Jeffrey. So let her philandering ex-husband think she had moved on and found someone to love, a man who would run to her bedside and worry over her. And if Jeffrey just happened to notice that Brandon was slim, handsome and obviously a few years younger than himself, all the better.

In the late afternoon Kate got up and showered. The water slaked her bruised body and bathed her tempestuous thoughts. She dressed in the pajamas that Laura had brought her, but she had to laugh at her daughter's taste in sleeping attire. The flannel bottoms were bright red and the white tank top had the image of Elmo begging to be tickled, but they were clean and soft on her tender skin, so Kate wore them with disregard for style.

She had just closed her eyes to block out the omnipresent light and sound when she heard a bustling presence enter the sphere of her quietude. "Catarina, Cara...You are awake. They let you out of bed? You should lie down."

"No, Mamma, I'm much better. It feels good to be sitting up." Kate made a quick decision to not let anything her mother had to say bother her tonight. "Thank you for coming all this way...you didn't need to you know. I'm not badly hurt."

"What kind of mother would I be if I did not come to the bedside of my child?" Silvana sat in the chair facing Kate. "Are they feeding you? I should go to your house and make you a *brodo di pollo.*"

"Maybe later Mamma...that would be good, thank you." *Chicken broth to heal every ill...that's my mamma.*

Nurse Cynthia stepped through the door and greeted the older woman. "You must be Kate's mother. I met your son earlier and your

136

granddaughter. It's nice to have family here." She checked Kate's blood pressure and pulse while she talked. "And, your son-in-law—Kate's a lucky woman to have such an attentive husband. Brandon...is that his name?"

Kate cringed as if struck by sudden, agonizing pain. "Oh...uh..."

"*O Dio*, husband? Catarina...husband?" Silvana's hand flew to her chest and she crossed herself. "*Ma...donna.*"

"Are you all right Mrs. Aiello?" Cynthia asked. "Are you having chest pain? Should I call someone?"

It took every resource Kate owned at the moment to remain calm. "No, Cynthia, she'll be fine. This has been a long day."

"I'll check on you later. If you begin to feel poorly, Mrs. Aiello, I can have one of the residents take a look at you." And she left.

"Mamma, I can explain."

"You would marry without your mamma present? Catarina, why would you do such a thing? *O Dio*, you did not have a civil marriage without a priest?"

"Mamma, stop, I didn't have a marriage at all."

"Oh no, Cara...you are living in sin...oh...I knew this man was trouble..."

"I'm not living in sin. Please just listen, for a change...Brandon and I are not married, we're not living together, we're not...anything."

It was after seven when Kate begged exhaustion and her mother let her be. Kate had dozed off in a recliner when she was awakened by a tapping on the door. It was Brandon, a bunch of multicolored flowers in his hand. He crossed the small room and gave Kate a light kiss on her forehead. "How's my wife?"

"Enough of that nonsense." Kate laughed. "Are those flowers for me?"

"Oh, when I saw your pretty face I forgot all about the posies. Are you good for a bit of company? Annie and Kevin are outside. They've been worried about you."

"My 'pretty face' as you so blithely call it, is a God awful mess, but you are kind not to point that out. I would love to see Annie and Kevin. Bring them in, please." She did not say it, but she was also eager to see his daughter and she wanted to know what he'd had to say to Brighid that he couldn't say over the phone.

It was good to be with people who cared. They talked, and Kate reassured them that she was on the mend and would be back to her usual self in a flash. Finally, it was Annie who asked the question Kate had not allowed into her consciousness since she awakened in utter confusion early this morning.

"Katie, did you think you might die...when you lost control of the car?"

Kate's first inclination was to brush off the question with a flippant answer, but she stopped herself, looked at Annie's concerned face and said, "Yes, I did. But I wasn't afraid exactly...it happened so fast and yet I had a moment to realize that I was in a very bad situation. Perhaps if I'd had time to reflect, I would have wanted to know that, in my life, I hadn't disappointed anyone."

"I doubt you've ever disappointed anyone, Katie. We're thankful you're alive. You should be, too." Annie touched Kate's hand and stood. "It's getting late. We need to let you get your rest. Brandon, see you at home, dear."

Brandon saw them out and closed the door. He returned to Kate's side and sat, silently looking at her.

"Don't you have to get home?" She finally had to ask. "Nurse Ratchet will be in here anytime to tell you visiting hours are over."

"No...I read the rules. Spouses are allowed to stay...all night if they wish."

"But does that apply to fake spouses?"

"Just don't tell anyone." He scooted his chair closer, lifted her feet into his lap and started to massage. "If you don't want me to do this, just say so."

"Huh, I'd have to be insane not to want a foot massage. Go for it." She thought she might melt to the chair from the heat trickling up her legs. "Brandon, tell me about Brighid. Why was she so upset?"

"Ah, my girl, what can a dad say? She's nineteen, overly sensitive, and has my penchant for exaggeration." He started on her other foot. "Kevin told her we were engaged. He thinks he's being funny, you know, and by the time he says it's just pretend, she's gone into a frenzy. Well, she called Annie, but wouldn't listen to any explanation her auntie had to offer, either."

"So, when you talked to her, did she understand that there's nothing between us?"

"That's not exactly what I told her, but I believe she has an insight into my feelings, now."

Kate wanted...needed to know what those feelings entailed and whether they included her. "I never told you how hard it was for Laura, when she thought I might want to be with someone other than her father. Even though Jeffrey betrayed me, I believe she thought that as long as I remained alone, there was some chance of our family being whole again. She's not a child. She had to understand."

"And do you think she does, now?"

"Yes, I believe she does."

He stopped rubbing her foot and closed his eyes. When he opened them he looked deep into hers. "Katie, do you understand? Do you know why I'm here? Why I was so terrified when I thought you were hurt? When I thought I might have lost you?"

Her heart stopped, and when it started it was thumping so loudly she was sure he could hear it too. "But I overheard you on the phone with Brighid...you said I was 'just a client'."

He stood and leaned over her, hands braced on the arms of her chair. "Katie, look at me." She did and his eyes were dark, passionate and riveting. "I can't say what will happen between us, but in the meantime I want to be very clear. You are not *just a client* to me."

"I understand...and it terrifies me."

He kissed her with such gentle care that it was a potion to sooth away the pain of her tender, bruised lips, a curative for the rift that had plagued her heart and a cipher to unlock the vault where she hid her deepest fears.

Chapter Fourteen

Brandon would have gladly stayed all night at the hospital; Kate made him leave, saying she did not think either would get any sleep if he stayed. He had to admit she was right.

Once home and in his bed though, he lay awake missing her, wondering what it would be like to have her warm and soft beside him and to awaken in the morning to the sound of her breathing, the fragrance of her skin. As slumber overcame him he questioned whether a relationship between them could last through the outbursts that would come of his quick temper and her volatile nature.

A mist so heavy it soaked through his coat and breeches rose like a grey sea around Carrick's legs. The turf muffled the sharpness of the hoof beats and accentuated the rhythmic breathing of horse and man. Without breaking stride, they vaulted over the rock wall, through the water and down the drop. Brandon glanced at his watch, his speed was good, his time perfect. He would have a clean ride. The brush fence skimmed under the belly of his horse and when they landed, he pressed his knuckles hard into the stallion's neck, leaned close and spoke words of praise and encouragement.

Through the haze, he could see the finish flags. Fiona would be there, waiting. His speed did not falter but the red and white banners failed to draw near. Carrick was tiring. Bran pressed his horse's heaving sides with his spurs and reached back with his crop to maintain their speed, but the more ground they covered the deeper into the fog the flags receded.

Brandon's eyes could not focus beyond the thickening atmosphere. He needed to get to the finish, to Fiona, to the comfort of her welcoming embrace.

Just as he felt his mount begin to stumble from exhaustion, the film that blinded his vision was swept away and he saw his objective. But Fiona was not there. He couldn't see the bright green slicker she always wore. Someone else was calling his name, waving her arms, chestnut hair whipping in the wind, red pajama bottoms and a white shirt with Elmo begging for a tickle. Brandon slid from the saddle and into her arms.

He awakened gripping his pillow like his life would skid into oblivion if he let it go. *Oh God, Katie, how I want you.*

The day dawned cold and urgent. There were horses to ride and people to coach. He swept away the cobwebs of fatigue and strolled out to face the day.

It had snowed and the sounds of Brandon's footfalls on the concrete of the barn aisle echoed loudly in the quiet of the morning. Murphy nickered to him as he walked past. "Are you lonely for your lady?" Bran reached in his pocket for a mint and gave it to the gelding. "I'm sure she won't be away for long."

He worked the young horses first, and at nine he taught Marsha Preston on Caddy. It was mid-morning when he heard Kevin mumbling to himself about the cold weather.

"I'm going to live in Florida for the winter, when I'm independently wealthy. I'm tired of freezing my butt off."

"Get busy, it'll warm you up," Brandon called from the arena.

"Hey, Dad, I didn't know you'd be here. I was going to go get Penny ready."

"I've been out here since before seven, so I don't

want to hear you bellyachin' about the cold weather. Yes, you can get Penny ready, thanks." Brandon thought it would be a good time to let Kevin get the feel of the mare's flat work.

It was almost noon when Brandon sat down in the corner of the arena to watch his son on the big grey. He made some suggestions, sat back and enjoyed the show. Kevin was a precise rider. The man and horse moved with fluidity together through the upper level dressage patterns that would be required at the competitions this spring. The sun had burned through the cloud layer, warming the walls of the indoor ring. The rhythmic beat of hooves lulled Brandon into a sense of wellbeing that tempted him to close his eyes, just for a moment.

A shriek that shook him so hard he nearly fell off his chair pierced the still air. "What the hell is that boy doing on my horse?"

Brandon stood, shaking the confusion out of his mind. *What was Felicia Dalwhinny screeching about?*

"This is my son, Kevin. He's here helping me with some of the horses."

"Brandon, I thought I made it perfectly clear that I hired you to ride my horse, not your underlings."

Her tone scratched a nerve in Brandon's head that threatened to burst into flames. "As I said, Felicia, this is my son. I asked him to run Penny through her work today because I have been at the hospital with an injured friend and I didn't get much sleep last night..."

"Well, I know all about your so-called friend. And, if you are too busy with your personal life to attend to your horse training business, I am not sympathetic."

Brandon clenched his teeth so hard he thought they might crumble. "You simply don't know how this works. I absolutely trust the skills of my son. I have a number of horses in training here and it is not humanly possible for me to ride every one, every day. Penny Lane is my responsibility. I supervise everything that happens to the mare."

"Regardless of that, Brandon, I don't know if I can continue with you. Don't think your private life has no impact on your reputation. I happen to know about you and Catherine Waldon and, frankly, I would have thought you had more sense than to get involved with someone like that."

"Just what do you mean? Like what?" Brandon was controlling his temper admirably, considering he wanted to strangle the arrogant bitch standing before him.

"My husband, Dr. Dalwhinny, is a colleague of Jeffrey Waldon. Dr. Waldon is an outstanding citizen and a gifted surgeon. I'm sure you're not aware that his former wife had quite the reputation. Well, I shouldn't say it, but since you are bound and determined to ruin your own name...she just never fit in...very working class, you know."

Her tone made Brandon want to retch. "Felicia, I think you've said enough." He turned to leave.

"You know she left her poor husband for another man? Well, I won't have my good name sullied by associating with people like that."

Brandon stopped, turned and faced Mrs. Dalwhinny. "Felicia, have your mare out of my barn by the end of the week. For the sake of the horse, I will recommend a suitable stable where she will get excellent care. I'm sure you will find a trainer with more respectable friends...elsewhere." He walked as calmly as was humanly possible out of the arena, across the paddocks and into the hay barn where he coolly extracted a baling hook from the tools that hung on the wall and pounded it repeatedly into the first available non-living thing...the side of the manure spreader.

When he had yelled every epithet he could come up with on short notice and his arms ached from wielding various farm implements into the walls, his anger was spent. He put his head in his hands and tried to come to grips with what he had just done. He had sealed the fate of Willow Creek.

****

Kate refused to go home without first stopping at the barn to see Murphy. And, if she just happened to run into Brandon, she wouldn't complain about that either. Laura agreed to stay one night and then go back to school, as long as Kate would keep her cell phone with her at all times and promise to call if she felt the slightest bit ill. The swelling of her face had gone but she had dark, raccoon-like circles around each eye that even the best makeup job couldn't cover. She wore sunglasses and skipped any other attempt at camouflage.

As they drove in to park, Kate waved at Felicia, who was just backing out. It did not completely surprise Kate that Felicia ignored the friendly gesture. Mrs. Dalwhinny had never been particularly cordial toward her. Today, nothing was going to make Kate sad, mad or disappointed. She was alive and considering the possibility that she might be in love. Even if it did not qualify as love, this pleasant tickle twittering around in her belly was worth taking the risk.

Kate and Laura walked around the main barn and toward the office just as Brandon rounded the corner from the hay barn. "Hey, stranger," she called. "Are you the boss?"

"Until the bank throws me out on my *arse*, I am." He slipped his arms around her. "What are you doin' here? I was going to come and take you home."

"They let me out early for good behavior. I made a deal with Laura that if I could come see my horse,

I'd behave for the rest of the day." Though Bran was smiling, she picked up a sense of unease from him.

"So, you came to see Murphy? When you're done kissin' on the old boy, I'll meet you up at the house. I suspect you should be taking it a bit easy. Annie can make you some tea."

"Brandon," Kate looked straight in his eyes, "what's going on? You look worried."

"Oh, nothing...nothing at all...I'm going to check on a situation over in the barn. Murphy is out in his paddock. See you in a few."

Murphy nickered to Kate when he saw her approach. She fussed over him, giving him mint candy and hugs. She told him all about her accident and that she was glad to be here.

"Mom, do you always talk to that horse like he understands you?" Laura laughed.

"He does understand me and I can tell him anything because he doesn't tattle." Right now she'd like to tell him that she was exhausted from just walking the distance to his paddock, but she wouldn't say it in Laura's hearing. Kate was hurting more today, now that sore muscles were added to the pain of the bruises on her chest and pelvis. "Okay, I've had my horse fix for the day. Let's go see Annie."

They stepped up on the covered porch of the house and Kate raised her hand to knock. She stopped when voices, projected in heated dispute, reached her ears.

"What do you mean, he sent her packing? He can't do that. We need that sponsorship or we lose the farm."

"Annie, you weren't there. She said horrible things...things about Kate. She...damn...the woman called her 'working class'...like that's some kind of sin or something. She more than implied that Kate was an adulteress."

"Kevin, this isn't going to work. He has to

146

apologize. He can't let her leave. Penny Lane is the best horse your da's had in years...she's his chance. Don't you see?"

"Then you are going to have to tell him. But you won't win this one."

Kate heard footsteps coming and stood back as Kevin flung the door open. He stopped and stared in horror at the two women on the veranda. "Kate, Laura...I didn't know you were here. Come in...please. Aunt Annie, Kate and Laura are here."

"Oh, my heavens. Come in, Katie. Why, I didn't expect that you'd be out and about."

Kate was confused, embarrassed and worried. *What did Annie mean, they'd lose the farm? Brandon's chance? What did this have to do with Penny Lane?*

Annie handed Kate a tea cup and set a plate of little sandwiches and cookies on the coffee table. Kate's hand was trembling so badly she thought she might drop the china cup. It clattered against the saucer. "I'm still a bit shaky, I guess." She tried to explain it away, but it was not from her trauma.

They visited about the mundane, Kate's stomach in a knot of confusion. Finally, the sound of Brandon pulling off his muddy boots at the back door broke the tension.

"The temperature is dropping out there. I think we're in for a cold night." He was blowing on his hands to warm them. "Umm...tea. May I join you?"

Kate scooted over on the sofa and made a place for him. "Please do." Annie went to the kitchen to get more sandwiches and an additional tea cup. "Brandon, we need to talk," Kate whispered. "Is there someplace?"

"Sure, excuse us." He stood and took her by the hand. They walked to the small office off the parlor. Brandon closed the door. "What's bothering you?"

"Me? I have the same question for you. You look

like you lost your favorite uncle." He started to turn away and Kate caught his hand in hers. "Brandon, what happened this morning?"

"I fired my most lucrative client. Felicia Dalwhinny got on my last nerve and I told her she had until the end of the week to move Penny Lane out of my stable."

"And, what does this mean...for Willow Creek?" She had heard what Kevin said. The disagreement was at least partly due to what Felicia had said about Kate, and Annie's words repeated in her head. *We'll lose the farm.*

"Katie, Willow Creek is a losing proposition. This ship's been sinking for a while now. The mess with Dalwhinny just finished it off, that's all."

Kate couldn't believe what she was hearing. It never occurred to her that Brandon was in a financial crisis. Knowing him, she shouldn't have been surprised that he would keep it to himself.

"Why didn't you tell me? What was she so upset about?" Kate started to waver on her feet. She felt slightly faint, but hoped he wouldn't notice.

"Come over here and sit down before you fall over." He led her to the window seat and sat down beside her. "She was upset because I had Kevin on her horse. The woman doesn't know a bloody thing about horses. I tried to explain that I was tired, that I felt Kevin would be more effective with the mare today." He reached up and touched her cheek. "I might lose Willow Creek...I'm not happy about that, but I won't let people tell me how to run my farm, or my life."

"I'm so sorry, Bran. Is there anything I can do?"

"Conjure up the winning lottery numbers for me." He smiled and shook his head. "I've been in worse trouble. I'll get through this." He brushed a lock of hair off her forehead. "You should be getting home to bed."

"I hate to admit it but I am sore and tired. I'm going to sit on my sofa and watch old movies until I fall asleep." She wished he would ask if he could come home with her, sit in front of the TV and snuggle, warding off the autumn chill.

He walked them to their car and helped Kate settle into the passenger seat. "Kate, call me when you get home, or I'll be worrying." He touched her hand. "Laura, let me know if your mom misbehaves."

"Good night Brandon." Kate looked in his concerned face, willing him to kiss her. Whether it was because he was shy in front of Laura or he simply was not in a kissing mood, he did not even give her a brotherly peck on the top of her head. Kate was uncommonly disappointed. She had, in a very short span of time, started to like his indiscriminate displays of affection.

****

She had no appetite, even for the *brodo di pollo* her mother had spent hours in the kitchen preparing. Kate did not know whether to laugh or cry. *Who spent all day making chicken broth, for God's sake?*

Though finally convinced that Kate and Brandon were not married, shacked up or otherwise headed for perdition, Silvana was very insistent that the wedding should be soon. Kate wished she had never proceeded with the crazy charade, but now she just wanted a couple of days of peace. She tried to humor Mamma with all the good reasons why spring would be a better time of year for a wedding.

They tried to watch a funny film, but it hurt to laugh and Kate finally gave in and admitted she just needed to go to bed and try to sleep. To her dismay, sleep would not come. She lay awake trying to think of ways she might help Brandon without pummeling his male ego into smithereens. Would he accept a loan? Not likely. Would he let her buy part of the farm, a joint venture? Kate had been thinking of selling her house; she could invest some of the money in Willow Creek. He would see right through that offer.

What was this *sponsorship deal* that he had with Felicia? The Dalwhinnys owned the horse. Brandon trained Penny and would ride her in competition. What did the owners get out of the deal? Was there prize money or just the glory of having a winning horse? What was a horse like Penny Lane worth? Surely it wouldn't be that hard to find Brandon another prospective winner. Kate had been thinking about a horse of her own for a while now. She loved Murphy, but there was something compelling about the idea of bonding with a horse who would be her very own. She would talk to Brandon about it first thing in the morning. He would love the idea, she was sure of it.

Chapter Fifteen

"Katie, that's a terrible idea." Brandon all but shouted into the phone. "I'm sorry, darlin', I didn't mean it like that. It's just that...well...first, one doesn't just go out to the horse boutique and pick up the perfect Eventing horse. Even if I knew of a good mount, this isn't a simple process. Secondly, we're talking about considerable expense, possibly six figures, to buy a horse who would be ready to go by spring."

"Brandon, money is not a problem for me. It's the one thing I will never need to worry about. I want to do this...for me." She didn't dare say she wanted to make him happy. That would stop the conversation in its tracks for sure.

"Do you realize that this horse would not be one that you could ride yourself? Is that what you want?"

Kate hadn't thought about that. She had ridden one horse, Murphy. "Well, I'll learn on Murphy and maybe someday I can be good enough to ride my own horse."

"Kate, listen to me. You could do this and gain nothing but a hay-burning hunk of horse flesh. There are no guarantees in this business. It only takes one injury for a horse to be knocked out of competition for life. I could make the best choices possible and we could still lose...badly."

"Okay, but what if I'm willing to take the chance because I want to, for once in my life, do something outrageously risky." She regretted trying to get her point across over the phone. "Brandon, hear me out. I could have died the other night, out there on that icy road. I've spent my life doing for other people and I don't regret that...well...other than I'd like to have the years I put into Jeffrey back to give to someone else who deserves it. But, now it's time for me to see if I can care for myself, give myself something I want. Not anything I need, not to impress anyone else, not to make someone else happy. Do you understand?"

He was silent. She was sure he was going to shoot her rationale down and she was not prepared to push much further. She heard him take a deep breath of resignation. "Katie, let me make some calls. I'll see what I can do."

****

Kate hadn't heard from Brandon by noon and she was getting worried. She wanted to call him, but knew he had horses to ride, lessons to give and barn chores to supervise. She tried to be patient.

Her mother was starting to drive her nuts with her overbearing concern, so Kate faked the need for a nap and actually did fall asleep for a couple of hours. She was annoyed at herself that this accident had taken more toll on her physical strength than she wanted to allow. When she had been a young woman, Kate could seemingly go for days without adequate sleep, bounce back from injury or illness quickly and look pretty good in the process. Now, her energy level had little room for discrepancies and it made her angry.

When she awakened, she heard talking and laughing from downstairs and, groggy though she was, she could pick out Brandon's voice among the rest. Kate splashed cool water in her face, rubbed vanilla scented lotion on her arms and legs and dressed in jeans and a sweater. She looked at herself in the mirror and tried to see what it was about her that Brandon thought was pretty, but she was unable to be objective.

Kate entered the downstairs sitting room and Brandon stood to greet her. "I hope we didn't wake you." He took her hand and led her to sit beside him on the sofa. "Your mam and Sergio have been telling me stories of Abruzzo. Sounds like a beautiful region."

"You didn't wake me, but I wish you had. How long have you been here?" She wished they were alone. She wished he would kiss her. It occurred to Kate that her mother thought they were engaged. If she wanted to give her *official* fiancé a kiss, who would object? She leaned into Brandon and whispered, "Aren't you going to kiss me? You're supposed to be glad I'm alive."

"Ah, that I am, *Muirnín*." He gave her lips a soft brush of a kiss.

"Why do you call me that? What does it mean?" He had used the word once before. She assumed it was Irish.

"Sweetheart. It simply means my sweetheart." His hand ran the length from her shoulder, down her spine and rested on her waist.

Kate shivered. "Mamma, what shall we make for supper?" She had to say something; food planning seemed like a good distraction. "Brandon, you will stay? I have a great recipe for white clam sauce linguini."

"Yes, but only if I can help you cook."

"Catarina, you shouldn't be standing in the kitchen. You will tire yourself. I will make the linguini."

Silvana knew her way around her daughter's kitchen and she wouldn't take no for an answer, so Kate didn't even try to dissuade her. "Sure, Mamma, but I really feel good. You're going to spoil me."

"No, no...you visit with your guests and rest. I am here to take care of my *bambina*." She got up and scurried into the kitchen. Soon they heard the clanking of pots and Silvana singing "*O Sole Mio.*"

Laura was busy practicing her Italian on Sergio when Kate took the opportunity to get Brandon away where they could talk privately. She took him to the solarium, a tranquil space and the only part of the house that Kate thought she would miss when she sold it. They sat on a bright blue fabric chaise.

"I never thought I'd get you alone." Brandon said and reached for her hand. "Please tell me how you're really feeling."

Kate's immediate response was to brush him off with her usual, "I'm just fine." But something compelling in his eyes, a depth of sincerity in the touch of his hand on hers, made her want to be completely honest with him. "I'm more exhausted than I thought I'd be. I've a bit of a headache and no appetite, but considering...well, I shouldn't complain."

"You never complain. That's one of your more endearing attributes."

"I learned early on that expressing any distress around my house meant the overbearing attention of my mother, and subsequent teasing from my brothers." It had been a good attribute to develop because Jeffrey was summarily unimpressed with Kate's need for comfort of any kind.

"You can always be honest with me. Do you believe that?"

She wanted to. "I'll try."

"Well, then, I have some of information for you. I called my old friend, Murt O'Brien. If there's anything goin' on in the world of horses that side of the pond, Murt'll know about it."

"That side of the 'pond'?"

"Ah, at home, *in Ireland*. Well now, my buddy Murt, we grew up together, you see, and he has a tack supply business near Ballyvaughan, County Clare." The man had a funny way of picking up more brogue than usual when he talked of his homeland.

"Ballyvaughan? Can't you find a horse here, in Maryland?" Kate thought Ireland sounded too far to shop for her horse.

Brandon laughed. "If I'm to ride the horse, he has to be able to understand a little Irish." Kate could see his point. She had heard Brandon mixing his languages, mostly when he was excited or angry. "Also, Irish horses have strong bones, we have high calcium in our soil, and they have heart. You need a horse who has all the bravery of a Celtic warrior."

And a man with the same characteristics, she thought. "So, does Murt have any specific horse in mind?"

"He does and he'd like to show him to me. He's emailing a video. He should have it ready tomorrow. Kevin will set it up for us to see." He paused. She could see the rising excitement in his azure gaze. He ran a fingertip over her bottom lip. "The swelling is gone."

Kate couldn't breathe. His touch was like a feather brushing its gentle kiss on her soul. "Yes, it is," she inanely stated the obvious.

"Will you come to Ireland with me? I would love to show you my homeland." His hand caressed her cheek, skimmed her ear and settled on the back of her neck. "We could be there for the solstice. It's magical, you know?"

"I don't believe in magic, Brandon."

"Maybe that's because you haven't had the opportunity...or a good reason."

She was almost convinced that Brandon could make her believe. She wanted to let his wizardry carry her off to mythical places. The few brain cells that still owned logic niggled at her and warned this could lead to disappointment or worse. "When would we leave?" Logic had just lost more ground and she surrendered to his persuasion.

"If we like what we see on Murt's video, by the end of the week, unless you don't feel ready to travel."

I can't believe I'm doing this. "I haven't had a real vacation in years. I think I'm due. Let me make the airline reservations. Do you know of a hotel in the area where we could get rooms at such short notice?" She was careful to say rooms, plural, no confusion as to her intention to sleep alone.

"I can do better that that. We can stay at my house."

"What do you mean your house? You have a house over there?"

"Yes, I do. Where I grew up, in North County Clare. I rent it to tourists during the summer months and Murt takes the folks out on horseback over the countryside. But it sits empty this time of year. I'll have Mrs. Connelly tidy it up for us. She's my neighbor lady."

"I can't believe I'm doing this."

"You'll love Ireland, but if you'd rather not go..."

"Oh no, you don't. I'm sold. It's time for me to get out of town anyway, before my mother locks me up in a home for wayward girls."

"Katie, I don't want to force you into anything. Not buying a horse, not going to Ireland with me...anything. Do you understand?"

His deep blue eyes captured and held her, invisible pinions arresting her thoughts. He was so close she could feel the warmth of his skin that accentuated his scent—clean, spicy and all male. Kate wanted to bury her face in his neck and breathe him into her. But, was he trying to tell her that whatever happened held no commitment for either of them?

"Brandon, I'm not as vulnerable as I might seem. You're not going to force me into anything that I don't absolutely want." Her heart was thumping

156

wildly from the closeness. She unconsciously licked her lips, not intending it to be an erotic gesture.

"Katie...when you do that, you make it terribly hard," he leaned to within an inch of her mouth, "to keep from kissing you." His right hand was on her back, gently pressing her closer.

"Uh...oh...excuse me...I...uh." It was Laura.

Kate pulled away, but a blush rose in her cheeks and she thought a hot flash was threatening. "Oh, Laura dear, come join us. We were just talking about...we were planning a little horse-buying trip."

"I'm sorry to interrupt. Sergio has a question he wants to ask Brandon and he needs you to translate. He wouldn't tell me what it was all about. I said I'd get you."

"Sure...just give me a minute. I'll be right there."

When Brandon and Kate joined the others in the living room, Sergio looked a trifle undone. Usually, he was the picture of the fashionable Italian, suave down to the trim of his fingernails and the shine on his shoes. Right now he was uncharacteristically rattled. Kate was alarmed when she noticed tiny droplets of perspiration on his forehead.

She spoke to him in Italian and listened intently to his request. When he had finished, she turned to Brandon and tried very hard to be serious. She could feel her face trying to twitch into a smile and knew she dared not start to laugh. Sergio was a kind and caring man and she wanted to do him this service.

"Brandon, my cousin is asking your permission, since you are Annie's brother..." She took a breath to stifle her impending giggles. "He would like your consent to court your sister."

Brandon raised an eyebrow and suppressed a smile. "Hmm, ask him...Oh God...ask him if Annie is aware of his interest."

Quick words passed between Kate and her cousin. She turned to Brandon again with a *don't make this harder for the poor guy* look in her eyes. "Sergio says he has expressed his interest to Annie and he hopes her feelings are mutual."

"Kate, does he know she's a nun? Was a nun, I mean. She's very inexperienced in these things." Kate just nodded and shrugged her shoulders. Brandon stood and offered Sergio his hand. "I would be pleased to have you court my sister, Sergio." And he whispered to Kate, "Lord help him if he causes her any hurt."

Kate asked Brandon to go and get his sister so that she could join the family for supper.

Annie was glowing and Sergio couldn't take his gaze off her. Kate was certain that the two were holding hands under the table between courses.

Mamma's clam sauce was perfect and the company lively, but by the time coffee was served Kate was starting to ache in her shoulders and her knees were stiff from sitting at the table.

"Annie, come upstairs and help me pick out some appropriate clothes for Ireland. I have no idea what the weather will be like." Kate wanted to have a chance to talk to Annie alone. Annie followed her upstairs.

"Oh dear, no one ever knows the weather, except it will rain, the wind will blow and the days, of course will be short this time of year. Let's see what you've got that might work."

They pulled out sweaters and wool trousers from Kate's closet, sensible walking shoes and a rain coat. Annie suggested a dressy outfit for dinner and Kate picked out a midnight blue wool dress that came to mid-calf and flattered her slim waistline. Finally, Kate had to ask the question that both women knew hung in the air between them. "Annie, if Sergio asked, would you consider marriage?"

"Well, I've been thinking about that since the night we were at Trapeze. Yes, I do think I would consider it. He's a lovely man...very kind and gentle."

"Yes, I know, but does he know that you..." Kate swallowed and cleared her throat. "That you were a nun?"

"Oh, of course. He asked why a 'bella signorina' had not married. I had to tell him. He's never married either...except, well Sergio is not a virgin. Not that I expected him to be...it's just that, well obviously, I am."

"Yes." Kate forged ahead. "Do you want to, well you know, ask me anything, Annie?" Kate wasn't an expert on the subject but certainly had more experience in bed than this fifty-two-year-old former nun.

Annie didn't look the slightest bit embarrassed by her innocence. "I know the basics." She laughed. "It's the fine points I might need some advice on. Kate, I never dreamed my life could take this turn. I was ecstatically happy in my life as a Sister of Clare. It never occurred to me to think I was missing anything. The students I taught were all the children I ever wanted. I had love every day of my life from my family and from the church. But, I look on this possible relationship as a new adventure. If Sergio and I could make one another happy, why shouldn't I allow it?"

"I can't think of any reason you shouldn't. If I had another chance, a 'do over' in my life, to be loved by a man who appreciated me for myself, I think I'd risk it."

"That's what I'm thinkin', too."

"Annie, I've gotta ask...where did you learn to speak such perfect Italian anyway?"

"Oh, well, I spent four years as a special envoy from the Sisters to the Vatican. I lived in Rome. I loved it there and if Sergio asked me to be his wife, I'd gladly go back to Italy."

"Annie, I guess that would make us cousins of a sort, wouldn't it?"

"Yes, but I like to think of you as a sister, Katie."

Kate was near tears at the idea. She had one sister-in-law, but Maria seemed to be of a younger generation. They were close in a different way, but not enough to be serious confidantes. She had her good friends, Ginny and Marietta, but they truly did not know her heart. Laura would always be supportive of her mother, yet there were some things Kate would never feel comfortable sharing with her daughter. Frankie would always listen to Kate's troubles and rarely, if ever, give unwanted advice, but he was a man and a priest. Yes, it would be nice to have Annie Sullivan for a sister.

Chapter Sixteen

As Kate often did when she was too wound up to rest, she filled her bathtub with lavender-scented warm water and immersed herself up to her shoulders. She turned on the jets and let the throbbing pulses massage her still-bruised muscles.

Her mind wanted to wander to Brandon and she had no good reason to halt its progress. What would it be like to let him make love to her? She instinctively knew he would be a combination of gentleness and fury. The mental image of him, the way he might look with the intensity of passion in his face, gave Kate an old familiar tickling in her low belly. There was a time, not all that long ago when Kate felt no shame in her secret fantasy world.

Jeffrey had left her wanting so many times that she had, rather early in their marriage, developed various scenarios that were guaranteed to bring about a mind-melting release. Her husband would never have suspected that it was not his prowess but the hot lovemaking of Antonio Banderas as Zorro fantasy that flung her over the edge of sanity. The thought of it now made Kate's hands flutter over her breasts and down her tummy, but it wasn't her fantasy man whose face she longed to see above her.

The pulsing of water against her back and legs were to Kate the embrace of a lover moving against her. She rolled on her side and shamelessly aimed one of the jet nozzles just below her pubic arch. The results were lovely—the pounding pressure and Brandon's searing touch imagined swiftly carried her on waves of pleasure until her mind and body

161

melded into a core of heat that burst like shards of the cosmos through every nerve ending. When the quivering stopped Kate was fully relaxed and more than a little satisfied. She was also vastly relieved that the connection between her imagination and her clitoris had not been severed along with her marriage.

****

The sun was shining through her bedroom window when Kate awakened. She lingered, enjoying the freedom of sleeping late. Already she could hear Mamma in the kitchen and smell the fragrance of espresso and pastries.

Showered and dressed, Kate made her way downstairs to face the day. Laura was sitting at the kitchen table with Sergio. Mamma was at the stove, doing God knows what, as she had done every morning as far back as Kate had memory.

"Mom, you're up. We thought you were going to stay in bed until noon," Laura teased.

"*Buon giorno*, Catarina." Sergio stood and pulled a chair out from the table for Kate.

As they had coffee with steamed milk, cornetti, jam and slices of fresh fruit, Kate tried to pay attention to the conversation going on around her, but her mind was caught in a web of feelings that pulled Brandon into her thoughts. Could she let herself float off on a magic carpet ride with a man who most likely wasn't ready for any level of commitment? Were her own wounds healed enough to allow rational decision making, or was she just so desperate for affirmation that any man could easily wheedle his way into her heart and her bed? Brandon had been sweet to her. He'd never given any indication that he would push her into anything. But he was a man without the available comfort of a wife, and Kate worried that she might look pitifully convenient.

Her rambling was interrupted by the ringing of the phone and before Kate could react, Laura was on her feet and answering the call.

"Oh...hi, I'm great...yes, she's right here...hold on a second." Laura covered the receiver with her hand and turned to her mom. "You'll never guess who just can't wait to talk to you. Damn, he has a sexy phone voice..."

"Laura!" Kate grabbed the phone and whispered to her daughter, "I had noticed that particular attribute, myself. Hello Brandon."

"Katie, do you really think I have a sexy phone voice?"

"You apparently have awfully good hearing, too. What are you up to this morning?" *Did you think of me last night like I thought about you?* "Have you already ridden five or six horses and cleaned twenty stalls?"

"Well, darlin' it's a nasty job, but someone's gotta do it. I have a couple of lessons yet before noon and I was hoping, if you feel up to it, that you'd come out and take a little walk with me. Murphy misses you."

"Hmm...well, if Murphy misses me how can I refuse?" *What will I do with Mamma?* "I think I'm up to a short ride. How about I come out about one? Sergio can drive me in the rental. I'm going to have to get a car of some kind here pretty soon. Would you like to help me shop?"

"I know nothing about fancy foreign sports cars."

"No more sports cars for this woman. I want something like a Sherman tank, indestructible and good on ice-covered roads."

"I'll warn my sister that her suitor is coming, so she can pretty herself up for him. See you at one?"

"Yes, you will. Bye for now." She almost automatically said *I love you.* It was the way she ended so many of her phone calls that it felt natural.

Kate virtually smacked herself on the side of her head and told herself to snap out of it. One slip of the tongue like that and she'd have the man running for cover before the flight to Shannon left the ground.

Laura agreed to take Nonna shopping in Baltimore so that her mother could be free to spend the afternoon at Willow Creek. Kate dressed in her breeches and took her boots. She preferred to drive, but Sergio insisted. Sergio drove like an Italian, or like a motorcycle racer, and she was just a little nervous with him behind the wheel, but nothing was going to spoil her mood today.

Brandon was just finishing with Marsha Preston and Caddy when Kate walked into the barn. She could hear him calling out instructions and he sounded on the verge of frustration with the woman. "Marsha, keep your legs close to his sides. You're confusing him with the way your legs bump him constantly. Be quiet with your hands...okay... okay...stop for a moment and reorganize. Don't be angry at him. He does not deserve that."

Kate never heard Marsha say anything and she worried that the woman might take her horse elsewhere and Brandon would be out yet another source of income. She walked to the gate and watched the rest of the lesson.

"Now there...that's a better trot...steady now...bend your elbows...good. Give us a nice square halt and you can be done." Kate couldn't help but wonder if he softened his words when he saw her at the rail. Or maybe he just knew it was time to call it a day with Marsha. Whatever his rationale, Kate was glad he was wrapping up his work and they could plan their trip.

Marsha dismounted and walked Caddy out of the arena, thanking Brandon for the lesson and giving Kate a little wave. It made Kate wonder what barn gossip was flying around about the *new student and the boss*. She was sure at least three other women who stabled their horses here would have liked to have caught Brandon's eye.

"Katie, I'm going to get Clancy. Murphy is in his stall. If you wait for me, I'll help you get him tacked up."

"Thanks, but I can manage." Kate walked the short distance to the tack room where Murphy's saddle, bridle and her helmet were kept, but as she approached she heard women talking. One voice was familiar. It was Marsha's. The other Kate wasn't sure of but thought it sounded like Brenda Weeks, a young, bitterly formal woman who liked to make it clear to everyone within earshot that she had more money than God and could buy her way into anything she wanted.

"What's the attraction, if I might be so bold? She must be well past forty and I heard she had a nasty but financially tidy divorce. Go figure. Maybe he needs the money...a sugar mamma," Brenda sneered.

"Oh Brenda, I don't know. Maybe she's just a nice person..."

"Nice? Oh please. She was on the make from the moment she stepped onto the property. From what I've heard it's not the first time he's screwed a client." Brenda laughed. "At least they've all been women...well, as far as I know."

"Who? Who was he boffing? Now you have to tell me," Marsha asked.

"Why do you think Lorelei left so quickly? She had to find a new place for her horse because Brandon wouldn't leave her be," Brenda scoffed.

Kate had heard enough to last a lifetime. She tied Murphy in the barn aisle and spoke loudly to him so she could be heard clear into the tack room. "Stay here big guy. I'm going to go get your saddle."

She tried to sound happy to see the other women, even though she wanted to set them both back on their heels. Kate had an almost overwhelming urge to strangle Brenda until she told the names of the supposed clients Brandon had been *boffing*, as Marsha had put it. Instead she smiled graciously at the snotty bitch and went about her own business. If Brandon had fucked every equestrienne in the state of Maryland, there was not a thing Catarina Aiello could do about it. And, in reality, she found it hard to blame scandalous behavior on the man who had sat by her hospital bed, claiming to be her husband so he could stay and comfort her; a man who liked her mother and laughed at being handcuffed and cop-napped by her brothers. No, if Brandon was a gigolo, he hid it well.

Kate had brushed Murphy's coat until even in its winter coarseness it gleamed. Brandon tied Clancy and reached for the hoof pick that Kate had just taken out of the grooming tray. "You are not cleaning this horse's feet. I'm not even sure you should be lifting a saddle."

"Bran...I'm fine...and I'm not just being self-effacing. I really do feel almost healed. You should see the bruises on my chest though, from the seat belt."

"Uh...I've got the time...but what are we gonna do with the horses?" he said in a poor imitation of Mae West. "I'm cleanin' the feet today, and don't argue with the boss."

It was a clear, briskly cold day and they rode the horses out and around the dormant hay field, circling around the practice jumps. "I can't believe you can jump a horse over some of these things. They look just huge to me." The rock wall seemed especially daunting, solid and as high as Murphy's shoulder.

"Oh, come next spring I'll have you hopping over

these like they're poles on the ground." Brandon stopped Clancy and turned toward Kate. "It's good to see you back on the horse, Katie."

"It's good to be back."

"Are you ready to see what Murt sent? Kevin is in the office doing his cyber magic on the computer."

"Sure, anytime." Kate tried to sound like she had her excitement under control, but the thought of seeing the video had her heart thumping.

Kevin was, like most young people, a whiz with anything digital and he had the video ready to view when Kate and Brandon joined him in the office. "Have you looked at it already?" Brandon sounded like he was asking if Kevin had peeked at a Christmas present.

"Yes, I have, but I'm keeping my opinions to myself until you take a look." Kevin clicked on the keyboard and the video started.

Kate saw a long-legged, rust-colored horse, running free in an arena. He looked pretty to her, but she had no clue what Brandon was seeing. Her eyes went from the computer screen to Brandon's face and back. He said nothing and his expression was unreadable.

There was a pause and when the action started again, the horse was being ridden by a man of such similar build to Bran that it could have been him, if not for the untrimmed red hair that stuck out from under his hard hat. He showed the horse at a trot and canter both ways of the ring. Still Kate saw no indication on Brandon's face that would tell her if this was good or bad. She was dying to ask him, but did not want to break his concentration. The rider circled the big horse and turned him to a fence that they jumped with ease, but two strides after the jump the horse gave a huge twisting buck like a rodeo bronc. Brandon's lips curved into a half smile as horse and rider headed toward another jump, a sizable triple bar. Like a blur of molten copper, front legs tucked tight to his chest, the equine's muscled body sprang over the barrier. Stretching elegantly through his back and landing, he galloped off to the next obstacle. One after another the fences were breached—walls, oxers, vertical spans so high they looked to Kate like the horse could have more easily gone under the barriers instead of over the top.

The video ended. Brandon kept staring at the screen, his jaw clenching and relaxing, his long fingers folded into soft fists. Finally he turned to Kate, locked his eyes on hers and a corner of his mouth twitched.

"Katie girl, pack your bags...we're goin' to Ireland." He drew her into his arms and kissed her mouth with complete disregard to her surprise and Kevin's laughter. When he pulled away from her lips he took her face in both hands and Kate saw such joy in him she nearly kissed him back.

Kevin smacked his dad on the back. "Damn, I thought ol' Murt was gonna get his arse bucked into the next county. Why does he do that?"

"Ha...because he always wanted to be a cowboy. It's how he gets a horse to buck like that I can't figure. So, what do you think?"

"Dad, if you don't want him, I'll take him. He's a son of his grand sire for sure. He might need some polishing in his flat work, he's a little strung out and I'd like to see how he handles the big solid fences, but from this...today...wow."

"Do you fellows want to give me a clue as to what you're talking about here? I thought he was pretty, but that's the limit of my understanding." Kate felt a little left out, but since she got a splendid kiss out of it, she wasn't really complaining.

"First, he's a grandson of my Carrick. His sire was a horse I'd sold as a weanling. I thought Clancy was a better prospect, so I kept him and sold

Clannad. Clann never did much more than pack his owner around in the amateur divisions and make a few nice babies. I had heard through the grapevine that Clann died last year, but I didn't know about Calypso." Brandon sounded like a kid telling about catching a home run ball at the World Series. "Second, I like the look of him."

"When do you want to leave? I'll have to see that my mother gets safely home...and what am I going to do with Sergio?" Kate didn't think she could just leave him on his own.

"Your mam can fly back to Hackensack in a couple of days. She won't mind your going off with your fiancé. Tell her we're checking out possible places to have the wedding...or honeymoon... whatever. I'm sure you can think of something. Sergio will be well entertained by my sister. I wouldn't worry about him."

"You've got it all figured out, don't you? I'll have to get flight reservations. Okay, I can do this." Kate was determined. She wanted to see this horse up close and personal *and* she needed to figure out where she was headed with Brandon Sullivan. "I absolutely have to be back by Christmas."

"I do as well. I'd like to spend my birthday here with my family."

"When's your birthday?" Kate asked.

"Christmas morning will be my forty-ninth."

Chapter Seventeen

Reservations in place two days later, Kate convinced her mother that a vacation with Brandon was just what the doctor ordered. She was fully ready to promise that they would set a date for the nuptials, if push came to shove with Silvana. Fortunately, for the sake of her conscience, Kate was not required to make any such vow.

Brandon had cajoled his son and daughter into helping around the farm in his absence. Annie was more than thrilled to make sure Sergio was not neglected while Kate was gone. The wheels were set in motion and any trepidation Kate might be feeling was outweighed by her enthusiasm.

Kate packed and repacked, trying to be sensible but wanting to take enough. She was as twitterpated as a new bride when it came to choosing underwear and sleep attire. If she should make the leap of intimacy she thought was a possibility, she did not want to do it in crummy old undies or a dumpy pair of flannel pajamas. She wondered if men thought about such details. Did Brandon care if his boxers had a rip in the seat? Kate doubted those indelicacies ever occurred to heterosexual males.

****

Kate's evaluation of Brandon's worries was close to correct—his underwear was low on his list of priorities. He tried to keep a positive outlook about his prospects for turning his luck around, and if ever there were a dark horse of a chance, Calypso was it.

If this gelding proved to be a brave and talented mount, if he was a good match for Brandon in temperament, they would still have to *click* and develop a partnership in very short order and that was a long shot.

And, to complicate matters, there was Katie—beautiful, tempting, vulnerable Katie. Could he manage to keep his hands off her? Perhaps the plan to stay at his childhood home was a risky one. Brandon was not a promiscuous man. He had been the faithful husband of one wife and, excluding a fling or two in his youth, he had not been intimate with another woman. His carnal need had all but vanished during Fiona's fight for her life and for months after she was gone he had not had so much as a morning erection to remind him that he was a man still. Now, Katie had awakened his need and he longed to bury himself in her warmth. But he would not allow himself to use her and throw her away. If she were not ready, if he couldn't give her what she needed, he would not cause her more pain than she had already endured at the hands of a callous man.

Kevin had asked his dad to look for one additional horse. It would be a gift for his bride, one that she would never suspect but that she would love. Barb had been riding and working for Brandon since she could saddle a horse on her own. As his working student she'd had the opportunity to handle some of the best horses on the east coast, and she had never complained that she hadn't one to call her own.

Barb had practically lived at Willow Creek for the past ten years, her family life being a nightmare for the young girl. Both parents were alcoholics and Barb took the brunt of their abuse. Fiona had seen the sadness in the girl and taken special care to include her in family activities. She became like a second daughter to Bran and Fi and a much-loved sister to Brighid.

Barb was never shy about making it clear what

she wanted in life: to be the best horsewoman she could be and the wife of Kevin Sullivan. Kevin's requirements for her gift horse were few—brave, bay and jumps the moon. He had no doubts his dad could find such an animal.

Brandon notified Murt of his intention to come to Ballyvaughan and see Calypso, as well as several other horses that his oldest friend was agenting. Along with the feed and tack store, Murt had made a respectable living as a sales agent and he was known throughout Ireland and Britain for being an honest and knowledgeable procurer of horseflesh.

"I'm bringin' a friend with me, Murt. Do you think you can find us a couple of quiet ponies for a day?" Brandon thought he'd show Kate County Clare by horseback. He wanted to do something romantic and if the weather wasn't too chilly, he knew the best locations for such an adventure.

"Oh, a friend have ye now? And, what kind of friend are we talkin' here?"

"A relatively new one, so watch what you tell the woman about our rowdy youth, if you don't mind." Brandon was half serious. He and Murt O'Brien had been babes in the cradle together and started causing trouble shortly after they learned to crawl. By the time they were teens, their parents were threatening to send the boys to a monastery, but knew no religious order brave enough to take them on.

They would sneak out of mass on Sundays and take off on the fastest horses in the stable. Jumping the rock walls and plunging down to the beach, they raced along the cliffs scattering the cows that grazed on the grass.

When they were in high school they started a rock n' roll band in a derelict cottage up the road from Murt's grandfather's farm, planning to be the new wave in Irish music. Bran played the drums,

Murt lead guitar and Fiona the fiddle, until the day what was left of the roof fell in on them and called an end to their careers.

Murt married his high school sweetheart, Nuala Ryan and they had three daughters in as many years. The girls were grown, but Murt and Nuala were still sweethearts and that would never change.

"Ah, it'll be good to catch up on old times. Will ya stay with us?"

"Thanks, mate, but I need to check on the old house anyway. I thought we'd stay there for a few days; maybe we'll travel about some." Nuala was a very religious Catholic. She would not consider allowing two unmarried people to sleep in the same room under her roof. If he and Kate ended up in the same bed, it wouldn't be at the O'Brien's.

"That serious is it?" Murt could read Bran's mind.

"Do you think a man could be blessed twice in his life? I guess we'll see how serious it gets. See you in a couple of days, mate."

Kevin drove his dad and Kate to the Baltimore airport late on Saturday afternoon. They would fly to Boston and take Aer Lingus from there to Shannon, Ireland. Kate had flown internationally and remembered it as boring and interminable, but the Boston-Shannon leg was relatively short and it was night.

Kate had wanted to be in first class, but when she saw the cost she just couldn't make herself spend it. She did confirm bulkhead seats, so that Brandon would have more room for his long legs. "Have you made this trip very often?" she asked him, partly to make conversation and quell her nervousness.

"I used to go home as much as possible, when my parents were living. But, I've not been back now for almost two years." He was solemn and Kate was sorry she'd asked. But he continued. "The last time was to bury my wife."

"Oh, I'm sorry...I didn't mean to bring up a bad memory." *Damn, why did I have to say that?*

"Katie, don't be worried about it. It's part of my life...granted a painful part, but it's in the past."

The flight was boarding and he helped her with her carry-on bags. "We're going to have a splendid time. There's so much I want to show you."

Whatever he wanted to show her, she hoped she was prepared.

Kate had tried to sleep on the plane but every time she drifted off, her head would fall onto Brandon's shoulder and she would lurch awake. He finally dozed off and she watched him as he slept, admiring the smooth contours of his face and the completely relaxed body posture. Brandon was not a man who sat immobile for long, so to see him at rest was a curiosity worth enjoying.

By the time the plane was on the ground, Kate was giddy with exhaustion and silly with excitement. They took separate lines at the immigration check point, Brandon to the queue marked "European Union," Kate the one marked "Others."

"How long do you plan to be in Ireland, Ms. Aiello?" the officer asked, looking from the passport photo to Kate's face.

"Just until the twenty-third."

"Business or pleasure?" he questioned.

"Oh, pleasure." *I hope.* "Yes, just a vacation, I'm with my friend." She looked over at Brandon who was through his line and waiting for her. He stood, smiling that half smile that made her pulse race, handsome in his grey trousers, jacket thrown over his shoulders and a shirt the color of his eyes.

The young man stamped her passport and wished her a lovely stay in his country.

"I thought he was going to take you into custody, or home to meet his mam. I guess I need to get used to other men noticing how exquisite you are." He took her shoulder bag.

"Bran, stop saying things like that. You're going to make me believe you, and I'll be hell to live with." In truth she wished he would never stop. He made her feel special and pretty, for the first time in her life. Right now, though, she was sure her face was a mask of tiredness and her hair was a mess. Her well-planned traveling outfit was wrinkled beyond hope and she was afraid she had morning breath.

With their luggage stuffed into the tiny rental car and Kate safely ensconced in the left-hand seat they made their way past long stretches of the most picturesque countryside in the world. Kate tried to rest but the uneasy feeling of traffic coming and going in what she determined was the wrong direction completely unhinged her and prevented her from keeping her eyes closed for more than one roundabout. The city thinned until they were surrounded by neat farm fields limited only by stone walls that skirted the horizon.

Brandon had told her of Black Bush Cottage. The home of the Sullivan family since 1892 sat on a knoll of brilliant green grass. The white-washed façade with red painted door and window frames was topped by a dark slate roof. Shafts of sunlight bounced off the glass of two dormer windows that looked out to the sea. Brandon searched in a terra cotta pot on the stoop and pulled out an ancient key.

The interior of the house was pristine and peaceful. White, plastered walls contrasted with a burnished, red brick expanse behind the fireplace. Tile floors gleamed and light shone from the large window that faced the north looking out toward the sea. Kate noticed a small boat aground in the low tide and wondered if Sullivan land extended down to the water.

A large trestle table with six chairs divided the kitchen area from the great room where a cozy mix of worn leather and gently used upholstered furniture called for weary family members to congregate at the end of a work or school day.

"Welcome to my home, Katie." Brandon said with a bit of a flourish.

"Brandon, this is so charming." She sat in an overstuffed chair and rested her feet on the matching hassock. "I'm so tired, I could just fall asleep right here."

"There are two bedrooms on this main level and two more upstairs. You can take your pick. The loft room was Annie's. It has a spectacular view."

"That sounds perfect. Honestly, anything will do as long as it has a bed."

"I'll take your things up. I need to get a fire going or we'll freeze tonight. There's a stove in the loft. I'll light that as well." He left her and set about the chores of getting everything in livable condition. By the time the peat fire was warming the great room and he had taken the chill off the loft, Kate was totally unconscious in her chair.

"Katie," he whispered. "Let me help you to bed."

"Umm, why am I completely trashed and you look unscathed?" He seemed energized by being in this place, like it was part of him, a puzzle piece set to complete him.

"Because I slept on the plane and you didn't." He pulled her up from the chair and took her by the hand. "Come now, fairy queen. Your bower awaits."

Annie's loft room was not a disappointment. The large window facing the south gave a panoramic view of a picturesque village and, out in the sea, a castle appeared to float in the tide. Kate had seen plenty of castles, Italy is dotted with them, but this grey stone edifice with its soaring watchtower pulled at her imagination with visions of fine-looking Celtic warriors on their brave steeds and the ghosts of star-crossed lovers waiting to reunite on mid-winter's eve.

The four poster bed was swathed in a quilt, a crocheted coverlet and delicately embroidered pillow slips on down pillows. A cobalt blue, enameled stove warmed the room with its fragrant turf fire.

"This stove can really put out the heat. If you get too warm, just close this little knob on the side, here." He showed her how to adjust the damper. "Brighid liked to stay in this room when we visited, but she was always too cold, so I added this little stove for her." He turned and faced Kate. "The toilet is at the end of the hall. If you need me...if you need anything, I'll be downstairs."

"Please wake me in a couple of hours. If I sleep all day, I won't sleep tonight and I'll be all screwed up for the rest of the trip."

"I will, and then we can talk about what you want to do for supper." He made no move to leave. "I'm happy that you're here with me, Katie."

Kate just stood there, looking at him, willing him to take the initiative and pull her into his arms. He did not, and she was not sure if she should be disappointed or relieved.

****

Looking out from the castle wall she could see the man riding toward her. His red cloak was blown back from his broad-shouldered body by the wind coming off the sea. He wore no head covering and his black hair had come loose of the lace that had tied the thick mane.

They called him Bran, the Raven.

Man and steed moved with the fluidity of one being, a centaur—the earth atremor from his power. Her heart pulsed with each stride of the beast, pulling the man in with invisible threads born of her desire for him. The memory of his hot touch, his warm moist kisses, the hardness of him pressing into her tender flesh formed a burning in her core that made her dizzy with anticipation.

From her high refuge she heard the chains that raised the gates, opening the fortress of her protection, the stronghold that guarded her heart. Spurs, scraping metal on stone as he took the stairs to reach her, rang out with his fierce intention. She knew he would not, could not, waste a minute more to hold her, bury his need in her until they both cried out in their joining. The scents of leather, sweat and musky male melted her bones and she leaned into him to keep from falling. Sapphire flames searched her face. Long fingers traced the line of her jaw and traveled to her neck, where her pulse beat in counterpoint to her panting breaths. "It has been too long, Muirnín." His whisper settled like a butterfly's wing on her ear. "I want you now, Katie..."

"Katie...Katie...wake up, sleepin' beauty. It's almost supper time."

Brandon sat on the side of the bed and brushed her hair out of her face. "I'm sorry. I meant to wake you sooner."

"Oh...oh, dear... I was having this dream." *My God, what a dream.* "I thought I was in that castle." She pointed out the window at the medieval fortress that was now a silhouette in the evening sky. "And you were there." *How much am I going to tell him?* "Well, it was...amazing."

"It's called Carraigdún." His fingers combed through her mass of curls. "Do you know you have such beautiful hair? It reminds me of a lioness—like you—wild and unruly."

Kate instinctively pulled the quilt up over her shoulders, a shield to protect her from his heat. "I've always thought it was a mess."

He ruffled her tresses. "I'll show you a mess."

She smacked his hand away, dropping the quilt and exposing the rise of her breasts. "Brandon, I'm not dressed." Kate tried to grab the quilt against her again.

"You might have forgotten, but I've seen you in less than this." He traced the line of her collarbone with one finger. "You still have a tiny stain of a bruise here." He touched the shadow where the shoulder harness had gripped her.

Kate's breath caught in her throat, and when she took her next gasp of air her chest rose against his hand. Molten waves of sensation rippled from breast to belly and settled in her cleft. "I need to get up," she barely whispered in a voice that sounded like it came from someone else's lips.

Brandon stood, walked to the door, and turned back to her. "We have a dinner invitation. Do you feel rested enough to meet my friends, Murt and Nuala?"

"Yes, that would be great. Do I have time for a shower?"

"I told them we'd be there in about an hour. Dress warm. It's chilly out tonight." He closed her door and she heard him humming an unfamiliar tune as he descended the stairs.

****

Kate slipped the midnight-blue dress of soft wool over her head and let it slide over her breasts and hips, enjoying the heaviness of the way it caressed her. She touched a minimum of lavender scent to her hairline behind her ears. It was a little odd, but she had always done it that way, stroked the cologne into her hair. She wore a plain strand of pearls and simple matching ear studs. Kate looked at her face and tried to decide if she needed make-up. She had naturally dark, rosy lips, so gloss was all she added, along with a bit of blush to mask the jet lag that made her feel otherworldly, rather than tired. *Okay, Catarina, time to face the music.*

Brandon stood when he heard her descend the stairs. He was a sight to behold. The crisp white shirt, red silk tie, dark trousers and his amazing smile caught her in mid-step and rendered her legs useless appendages that barely held her upright. He took three steps and held out his hand to her. "God, woman...," he breathed. "What are you trying to do to me?"

"Me?" She mocked innocence. "I don't know what you mean."

"I mean...I'm trying to be a gentleman and you're making it awfully hard." He started to pull her closer. "We had better get to where we have a proper chaperone."

"I think we'll be just fine. I'm a person of unmatched self-control, you know." But if he kept looking at her like this she would lose even that claim to fame. Bran was so close she was certain she could hear his heart beating against his chest. He smelled incredibly tasty. She had the irrational impulse to bite his neck, just below his left ear. "Your friends will wonder what happened to us."

"Oh...Murt knows me better than to expect me to be on time." His hand snaked around her back and nudged her toward him, closing the last of the distance between them. "Katie—"

Kate didn't let him finish. She tangled her fingers in the hair at the back of his head and pulled him to her lips, tasting, teasing, nibbling his warm mouth. The tip of her tongue trailed along his lower lip, savoring the contour and coaxing him to reciprocate. Give back he did, with interest, and Kate held onto him lest she crumple and melt to the floor in a pool of midnight blue wool.

He searched her mouth and trailed his lips to her ear and bit her softly. She let out a little squeak of pleasure and purred deep in her throat like a cat being stroked into submission. She knew she had to stop him or they would never get to dinner, but it was like separating two magnets, drawn to one another by mutual need and long-denied solace.

"Bran...," she finally said. "Let's go to dinner and later...we can...talk."

"Talk? Is that what you want, Katie?" His eyes would not let her go.

"I'm not completely sure what I want." Her body wanted to drown in his embrace, let him rekindle the fire that he had started when his lips branded hers with a burning touch. Only a faint remnant of her usual sensibility remained to tell her she was casting into dangerous waters.

****

They drove in silence the short distance to the O'Brien's. Brandon was not sure if he could continue to be alone with Kate without resorting to begging, which had never been his style. But, pride be damned, he wanted this woman and he had done everything but come right out and tell her. He momentarily considered giving her too much to drink so that his instinct to protect her from herself would kick in and he would just tuck her safely into her bed, alone.

"Here we are." He stopped the car in front of a stone house nestled in a grove of mature Dair ghaelach trees. Brandon was seized with a stinging memory of the last time he stepped foot in the O'Brien home, two years ago, in April. Now the winter chill had rendered the more tender plants to dormancy, but the garden was still as beautiful as it had been, though he had seen it last through tears of despair.

"Bran Sullivan, it's about time," Murt called from the wide front porch. "Man, it's good to see you." He and Brandon hugged, pounding on each other. Murt tried to punch Bran in his stomach and

Brandon caught the fist and twisted it behind Murt's back.

"Ah, Murt...when are you gonna learn that I'm quicker than you in a fight?" He turned to Kate. "Let me introduce you...Katie, this is my best mate, Murt O'Brien. Don't believe anything he tells you. Murt, this is Kate Aiello."

Kate offered her hand. "Murt, pleased to meet you."

"The pleasure is all mine. Come in..." He opened the door, sending Kate ahead, and turned to Brandon. "Jaysus, man, you've been holdin' out on me."

"Just a friend, Murt...don't go buyin' a suit for the weddin'...yet."

****

Nuala was a perfect foil for her husband—quiet, with a wit to match his boisterous one. She had a look about her that was all Irish. Red-gold hair with strands of silver, china blue eyes, fair freckled skin and a pleasantly rounded body made you want to cuddle up and tell her all your worries. She was also an excellent cook, which belied the myth that the Irish can't discern a gourmet meal from a pot of porridge.

Kate tried to concentrate on dinner and not on what she now thought might be dessert, Brandon Sullivan. He was not shy about watching her during the meal nor while they had coffee and whiskey after. His hot eyes perused her, taking in her every nuance, it seemed. In an attempt to escape his scrutiny, Kate offered to help Nuala clear the table while the men took their drinks in the front room by the fire.

"So, Kate, how long have you and Bran been together?"

Kate should have been ready for this by now: the Irish penchant for getting right at the truth of things. "We're not really together. I mean...it's not like we're dating...actually." She stammered, not knowing how to describe her relationship with Bran.

"Well, you might not be 'dating,' as you call it, but I've known Brandon Sullivan since we were both in nappies and I've seen that look in his eye before."

"Oh," was all Kate could come up with as an answer. "We haven't known one another very long. I've been taking riding lessons and I wanted to buy a horse...so that's why we're here."

Nuala smiled. "He's a good man, he is. It'd be hard for a woman to do better, but it's not a practical matter, now, is it? Loving a man, I mean."

"No...and...well, I'm just getting over..." *Dare she say it?* "A very painful divorce. I'm not at all sure I'm ready. And Brandon...well, he still loves his wife."

"Fiona was a wonderful woman, but she's with the angels now. Bran is here."

"Yes, he is." *And so am I.*

They joined the men and Murt offered Kate a brandy. She refused, worried that the jet lag and strong drink would render her a drooling idiot. It had happened before; she did not want to repeat that scenario tonight. "I'd take a cup of herbal tea if you have it."

Nuala went to put the kettle on and Brandon turned to Kate. "Are you getting tired? It's late and we have a big day tomorrow."

"I can have Calypso ready for you anytime. Don't get up early on my account. Just come by the shop and fetch me," Murt said.

Kate had her tea, sitting by the turf fire, listening to Murt and Bran reminisce, laughing about some stupid, and even dangerous, stunts they had pulled during their adolescent years. It was a wonder how they survived to be adults. Finally, Kate did start to nod off, but not from boredom. She could listen to Brandon talk and laugh all evening and be entertained.

Brandon stood, stretched and offered his hand to Kate. "I'd better get you to bed. Thanks, Nuala, for the lovely dinner. Murt, we'll ring you before we come by the shop."

Nuala handed Brandon a bag with brown bread, eggs, sausage, and a bottle of milk. "Breakfast," she said, and he thanked her and kissed her on the cheek.

"You're as beautiful as the day I stole your clothes when you were swimmin' in the pond behind your uncle's barn."

"And you haven't changed much in the last forty or so years yourself, Bran Sullivan."

****

The chill air stirred Kate fully awake by the time Bran pulled the car up to Black Bush Cottage. He got out, walked around to her door and opened it for her. Reaching for her hand he helped her to her feet. "I was beginning to wonder if I would ever get you alone again." His breath was hot against her cheek in contrast to the wintry atmosphere around them. They entered the cottage and stood facing each other, eyes locked in indecision as to the next move. "Let me take you upstairs, beautiful Kate."

She didn't say anything, but neither did she stop him from lifting her into his arms and carrying her to the loft room where she had dreamed of him earlier that day.

Kate was certain her heart was beating but apparently no blood was reaching her brain because she couldn't think and she felt faint. By the time he mounted the last step to the loft, his mouth was on hers, and his hands searched for the zipper of her dress.

His kiss tasted faintly of whiskey and she irrationally wondered if that could explain her intoxication. Her fingers twisted into his hair and traced the line of his neck and jaw, noting that he must have shaved just before they went out—his cheek was smooth.

"Bran, you're going to have to put me down," Kate gasped between kisses and his arms loosened and let her slide down the length of his lean body.

His voice was a rasping whisper against her lips when he spoke. "I want you so badly. I think I might die if I have to wait another minute." He grasped her hips and pulled her into him, pressing her belly against the evidence of his arousal.

She kicked off her shoes and ran her foot up his calf and thigh, wrapping her leg around him like a vine, trapping him even closer to her center. The hot hardness of him between them burned through layers of clothing, threatening to vaporize her from within.

Having succeeded in loosing the fastening of her dress, he slipped the gown off her shoulders one at a time, kissing and licking each inch of smooth flesh that he bared. "I've longed to kiss away that bruise since the day you woke in your hospital bed." His lips and tongue traced the mark and followed it to the top of her breast. "May I?" he asked, and when she gave a nod he freed her from her garment, letting the folds of indigo wool puddle at her feet. The peat fire in the corner stove had long since died to the merest embers, but his body was a blaze that nullified the chill of the room.

Her hand pulled his shirt free of his trousers and slowly trailed fingers from his belly to his nipples, feeling the ridges of rib and muscle, crinkly hair and hot skin. Inching the white cotton up, she bent and laid moist kisses on his torso. She felt him tighten and heard a soft growl from his throat.

His hands stroked her hair and he lifted her again to hold her against his body. "Katie, oh my

God, how you've bewitched me." His eyes were dark with need and he caressed her face, tipping her chin so that she had no choice but to meet his gaze. "Will you let me love you, like you deserve to be loved?"

No man had ever, in Kate's experience, cared one whit for her pleasure, until she met Brandon Sullivan. It was a completely new world that revolved beneath her feet; an orb where *she* mattered, where her desires counted for something. She was not sure how to respond. A simple "Yes," was her only answer; a word inadequate to a need that went so far beyond the carnal that it threatened to take her apart and reconstruct each molecule, building a woman who expected to be loved.

Brandon sat on the side of the bed, leading her to sit beside him as he pulled off his shoes, socks and trousers. He turned to Kate with such tenderness in his face, she thought she might faint from the sight of him. She unfastened his shirt, giving a kiss for each button, playing on his mouth with her lips and tongue as he chuckled under her ministrations. "You plan to take all night just with the buttons?"

"Never rush a woman at her work, Brandon." She opened the front of the shirt and started to pull it off his shoulders, but her next breath caught in her throat. Her hand went to her mouth and she stiffened. She wanted to continue, to ignore the obvious, and to allow him to convince her she was wrong.

"Sweetheart...what?" Brandon started to coax her into his embrace, but she stood, grabbed her dress from the floor and covered herself. Standing across the room with the bed between them, she trembled like a young foal on shaky legs.

"I...Oh, Brandon...I can't do this." She started to cry. "Please...you have to leave." Tears of shock and embarrassment at what she had nearly consented to burned down her cheeks.

"Katie...*muirnín*...it's all right. Please, talk to me." He stood and started to approach her, but she backed away and up against the window where the chill of night and remorse made her shiver uncontrollably.

She couldn't tell him, not without bursting into hysterical, convulsive sobs. How could she tell him that she couldn't make love to him when he did not, could not ever love her? He still loved Fiona. He wore her ring, on a chain around his neck, close to his heart.

He had not let her go.

What had made her think he would have left it behind since she saw it that morning in Mark's house? And why should he? She was his wife. Dead or not, she was his wife. He had vowed to love her forever, just as Jeffrey had vowed to love Kate. If Kate allowed Brandon into her heart, her bed, her body, she would be stealing him from Fiona, forcing him to break his vow to her. To be part of the destruction of a marriage promise, even if she and Bran both needed the solace, the comfort of joining their bodies, in Kate's thinking, rendered her no better than Jeffrey.

"I'll leave you, Katie, to sleep now, but I'm in the next room, if you want to talk. I didn't mean to rush you or frighten you. I hope you believe me when I say I'll never hurt you." He turned and left her.

****

Alone in his room on the other side of the thin wall that separated her from him, he could hear her weeping. He wanted desperately to go to her, comfort her, explain what he realized had upset her. Why hadn't he thought of it before? It had become such a part of him, the ring. He never imagined what it might represent to Kate. He had worn it around his neck from the day of Fiona's burial. After closing her casket the priest came to Brandon and handed him the ring saying, "I thought you might want to keep this." He started to protest, *No, it's her wedding ring, it should be with her...* but he was speechless, disoriented and incapable of decision-making. He went upstairs to the bedroom they had once shared, found a stout gold chain in her jewelry box and put the ring around his neck.

Some days it was a comfort—Fi close to his heart. Other times it was a reminder of his pain. After a time it became as familiar as his own skin, not thought about day and night, but an integral piece of him. Now he had to question what he might give up to have the happiness he so craved. Was this a simple piece of cold metal with meaning that only he could give it or a reminder of a love that was so giving and perfect that it deserved to be honored? Could he help Kate understand? Did *he* understand? Could he see the symbol of his love for his wife as Katie had seen it?

Brandon rolled to his back on the bed, his hand went to the place over his breast bone where the circlet lay. Tears stung his eyes and trickled past his ears. He could feel the beating, but his chest seemed hollow where his heart should have been, a black hole where love should reside. Was he wrong to want to fill himself with Kate? Did he love her enough to let go of the past? And, did letting go have to mean leaving Fi behind?

Chapter Eighteen

Dawn battled with the mist off the sea and won ground with tiny rivulets of light that crept through the window of Kate's loft room. She thought she might be dreaming when she heard the cottage door squeak on its hinges and close with a soft bump. The crunch of footsteps walking away from the house urged her to rise in the chill of the morning and peer into the haze to see Brandon's tall, lithe figure striding toward the road.

Where would he be going at this hour? It's barely light. Last night had been beautiful and terrible, comforting and despairing.

She threw a block of peat into the stove and tried to light it, but it took more skill than she anticipated. Her only salvation would be to get into some warm clothes and go down to the kitchen to make a pot of tea. As she descended the stairs the heat of the fireplace rose to meet her and she had to smile at how Brandon always thought to do the courteous thing. He had made sure she would have a warm welcome to her morning.

And, oh how she had left him frustrated last night. Kate, now you've gone and done it. Could you be dumber if your brain had been sucked out your ears? You've gone and fallen in love with the man. She wanted to run and hide, smack her ears like Mamma did to the boys when they were stupid, sit in the confessional and be ordered to say a million Hail Mary's and twice as many Our Fathers, possibly never to rise from her knees again in this lifetime.

Kate took her tea to the leather chair in front of the fire, pulled an afghan over her and watched the peat bricks glow. What would she say to Brandon when he returned? They needed to talk about what had happened, but she would not know where to start. Perhaps this trip had been a fool's journey, an attempt at happiness for which she was not ready—too soon for her, possibly never for Bran.

When she heard his footsteps returning, her heart leapt in her chest. Trying to remain calm, she did not get out of the chair, but watched the door open and was relieved to see his smile.

"I didn't mean to wake you." He shed his coat and hat, pulled off his wet boots and joined her to warm by the fire.

"You didn't. I was awake. Thanks for making the fire. There's tea. Can I get you a cup?" This was filler, meaningless chatter, words to ward off the fear of facing the reality of their need.

"No." He reached across the distance between them and took her hand in his. "I need to tell you where I went this morning and then I'll make a real breakfast for us."

****

Brandon had walked the half mile to the tiny, ancient churchyard where his family had been laid to rest since the early eighteenth century. Standing among the granite headstones, one of white Italian marble shone bright in the gray of the burgeoning day. The inscription was simple, "Fiona Flanagan Sullivan. Beloved wife and mother."

He knelt, removed his glove and ran warm fingertips along the grooves of the chiseled words, causing dew to drip like tears on the face of the marker. He spoke to her in the language he had always used in times of intimacy. He had made love to his wife in the Irish, soothed her childbirth pains with the soft tones, and whispered his love for her as she took her last breath. I'm here, *leannán*, my love. Oh, Fiona, what am I going to do?

Brandon's wife had been a good Catholic, but a devout Irishwoman. She believed in myth and magic, fairies and ghosts. He would tease her when she planted rosemary and thyme in their garden to attract good fairies. He laughed when she made him go to Home Depot and buy a pointed gate post for Willow Creek to keep bad spirits from sitting on the fence.

She had once told him the legend of a man who would not let go of his dead wife's spirit. He clung to her and became a ruinous drunkard out of his grief, neglecting their children as he mourned. "You must let me go or I'll wander aimlessly between the pull of your grieving and the glory of heaven," she had said.

"Is that what I've done, Fi? Held on too tightly? How do I give up the last remnant?" His fingers were cold with the dampness of the morning, or perhaps with trepidation as he found the clasp on the fetter that held the last bit of her captive to him. The band of precious metal nested, tiny and fragile, in the palm of his hand, the first glimmer of morning light dancing off the inner rim. *Gus an déan Dia*, it read, the words part of an old Irish wedding vow, *dhuitsa, gus an déan Dia leis a' bhás ar dealachadh*. "To you, until God shall separate us by death."

Brandon closed his fist, feeling the edges and smooth surfaces press an imprint into his flesh until the pain quelled. He slipped the ring and the gilded ligature that had bound it to him into the pocket of his coat.

The mist had cleared, the bright blue of the sky mimicked the hue of Fiona's eyes and he knew she was there and at peace.

****

"Brandon," Kate asked. "Do you still love your wife?"

191

"Yes, I do. I always will. But, know this, Katie, what happens between us is just that...between us...here and now. The past, both mine and yours, made us who we are. I would not change that. But I wish you hadn't been hurt so. The love I shared with my wife...can you see it as a gift, to me...to us?"

She wanted to. His experience of marriage had been so different from hers. "I'm sorry I never knew Fiona. Would we have been friends, do you think?"

He smiled and ran a finger along the palm of her hand. "You're very different in most ways...well except for your tempers, but, yes, I think you would have liked one another." He stood and walked to where he had hung his coat, reached in the pocket and pulled out the ring. When Brandon sat down his knees were touching hers. He opened his hand. "I'm going to give this to my daughter. I think she would like that."

Tears filled Kate's eyes. She reached for his hand and closed hers around it. His hands were brown, warm and slightly calloused between his ring and fifth fingers where he held the reins as he rode. Hers were cool, pale and still held the indentation of a wedding band on her left hand that had for twenty-five years identified her as Jeffrey's wife. Could she trust another man with her heart? One salty drop fell on the back of Brandon's hand, quickly followed by another, and then the deluge. Nothing short of the Great Barrier Reef was adequate to stem this flood. Nor did Kate want to try.

Brandon pulled her across the space between them, cradling her in his lap, stroking her hair and whispering as he might to an injured child or a frightened horse. "Katie, I know you're afraid, and I know why. Believe me when I tell you I won't measure you against Fiona. And, I'll ask you to try to never see Jeffrey in me."

Brandon held Kate until, exhausted from emotion, she fell asleep in his arms.

He awakened her with a kiss.

"Katie, let me go make you something to eat," he whispered in her ear. "And then I think we should go look at Calypso."

She unfolded herself from him. "Yes. We'd better get going or Murt will think we forgot about him."

While Brandon made his version of the traditional Irish breakfast—sausage links, eggs, grilled tomatoes, brown bread and tea, Kate took a shower and dressed for the day in her favorite jeans, a turtle neck shirt and a warm sweater. She hadn't known what Brandon was talking about when he asked her if she'd brought a *jumper*, which she finally figured out was what everyone in the British Isles as well as Ireland called a sweater. By the time she descended the stairs he had set their places at the end of the long trestle table. "Brandon, who's going to eat all this food?" Kate laughed. It looked like he planned on ten people, not two.

"I may have overdone it a little, but you should eat a good breakfast, you know." He sat and poured her tea.

"Try to remember, I'm Italian. Breakfast consists of biscotti and a cup of cappuccino." She took a bite of the eggs. "Interesting culture, the Irish. You do everything to the extreme."

"Hmm...that's an astute observation. We do have fun, though. I'd like to take you into the village tonight for an evening of pub crawlin'."

"What on earth is pub crawling? Sounds dangerous."

"Only for the fellas' who try to flirt with my Katie." He leaned back in his chair and watched her. Her face started to pinken and flush. She fanned herself with the cloth napkin. "Are you blushing...or flashing?" He grinned.

Kate dabbed the moisture from her face. "A little of both. So you'd best behave yourself. I can become quite irrational. I'm sure you remember that."

"I do, but I also think you look rather stunning with those little beads of sweat on your nose. So I don't mind," he teased.

"Enough of your nonsense. If you're done, let's go. I'm eager to meet my new horse."

Chapter Nineteen

They drove into Ballyvaughan and stopped in front of Murt's Tack and Feed. The store was cluttered from front door to back with every kind of horse paraphernalia one could possibly imagine.

"Ah, Bran, Katie, I thought you might have changed your mind and gone sightseein'. I'm ready. Let's go get a look at Calypso."

As they drove, Murt gave Brandon the details of what he liked about the horse and Brandon listened. Murt was an accomplished horseman, though he had often acknowledged that his skill was a poor second to Bran Sullivan's.

"I've taken him over a few solid fences, through water and down the big drop behind my paddocks. He's brave, quick and has a good sense for his own safety. I've not done much with his dressage...but you know me...not much of a one for the flat work."

Brandon did know and it had been, in his opinion, the one aspect of Murt's riding that limited his success on the circuit. But it was his choice and he didn't miss the competing. Brandon, on the other hand, was fiercely competitive and took it badly when he did not perform to his own intolerably high standard.

Murt had called ahead and Liam, the boy who worked for him as groom, had Calypso saddled and ready. Kate sat at the side of the ring, pulse racing like a trip hammer as she watched Brandon look at the gelding.

She was reminded of a friend of hers who was a pilot. Each time Max prepared to fly his little plane, he did what Kate called his *O.C.D. walk around*, checking every rivet, screw and surface for the slightest deviation from optimum. Now Bran was doing this to the equine that stood impatiently before him. Finally, Brandon adjusted the stirrups and swung up into the saddle. They fit each other, this horse and man, tall, long-legged and elegant.

Brandon worked the horse through basic dressage patterns, testing the way Calypso thought through the questions Bran asked with his hands, seat and legs. He answered calmly, and tried to please. Kate knew that was a good sign. The horse was smart and trainable, caught on quickly to new things and didn't freak out when he was confused.

Brandon did not punish for wrong answers, he simply asked again and rewarded when Calypso responded correctly. Kate wondered if Brandon had been this calm and encouraging with his children. Did his horse skills translate into people skills?

Stopping to shorten his stirrup leathers and don a hard hat, Brandon called Kate over to the horse's side. "He's a thinker. I like that. Did you notice how he tries, even when he isn't sure what I'm asking?"

"I'm impressed, but remember I only have the tiniest clue what you're doing up there." She was going to have to trust Brandon's skill and intuition.

"Okay, big guy, let's see what you can do over these rails." He turned the leggy chestnut and calmly trotted toward a moderately sized vertical. Calypso popped over it like it was a silly waste of time. "Not impressed unless it's a challenge," Bran commented.

Murt raised the top rail. Brandon circled and cantered the horse over the obstacle, muscles stretching and recoiling, arcing, giving and landing, both man and beast in fluid unison. They did the same with the combinations, testing the adjustability of the horse's strides, the sensitivity of his response to direction.

Kate watched in complete awe, happy that Murt and his groom could not read her mind. If they had, they would have found her wondering if Brandon could make her respond with such complete obedience and if he could perform his magic with hands, legs, hips and voice upon her body. She had almost found out last night and what she had experienced had been mind-melting.

Kate was so busy watching the man, she forgot about the horse, until Brandon pulled him up and vaulted off. He handed the reins to Liam and turned to Kate and Murt. "He's a trier, for sure. The bigger the fence the happier he is to jump it. Never even came close to touching anything out there. Tomorrow, I'd like to take him out on your cross country course...see if he has the guts for it, and the speed. What do you think, Katie?"

She was startled out of her reverie. She had only been thinking of how sexy Bran looked at the moment; blue eyes flashing, breathing a bit rapidly, hair sweaty on the back of his neck. He might look like this just after a lengthy tussle in bed. "Oh, I thought he was...you were both magnificent."

"Walk back to the stable with me," Murt said. "There's something else I want you to see."

The barn was dark with smells of hay, oats and horseflesh. Kate followed the men to a stall at the end of the aisle. "This is Beltaine." Murt smiled.

The men went into the stall so that Brandon could have a close look at this horse Kevin wanted for his bride. Kate walked down the row of stalls, peeking in to see what possible horsey treasures each might hold.

The box stalls were open to outside paddocks where the horses could sun themselves and visit over their fences. There was a small, dappled, grey mare with a black foal at her side, a bulky draft horse that Kate thought looked like the ones on the Budweiser commercial, and three almost identical bay thoroughbreds. She stood for a moment watching an overly fat and hairy pony munching his hay when she was bumped softly between her shoulder blades. Startled, she yelped and turned around to find herself caught in the gaze of dark brown eyes half covered by a fall of black forelock. The velvety nose nuzzled Kate's arm, begging for treats. "Who are you?" she asked, and searched in the pocket of her jacket for the ever present mints she had become accustomed to carrying.

The stall plaque said his name was *Samhain Eve*, his owner Emma O'Brien, his breed, Irish draft cross. *Emma? Could she be one of Murt's daughters?*

"You're a friendly one." Kate rubbed him behind his ears, noting the thickness of his mane. He had the look of a large pony, with a broad back and hooves that would cover a sizeable salad plate. He wore a tartan plaid rug with his name embroidered on the hip.

"Katie, who are ye chattin' up there?" Bran called as he strode toward her.

"Brandon, isn't he the dearest thing ever. He's been my best friend for the last thirty seconds. I gave him a mint."

"Ah, I see our boy has been begging again. He's a fine laddy, he is. It's a shame I have to sell him," Murt said as he pulled a halter off its hook and opened the stall. He slipped the restraint on the gelding's head and led him out into the aisle. "I bought the two of them together, *Samhain* and *Beltaine*. They grew up on the same farm, over in Wexford."

"I thought my Emma would love the pony so much that she would start ridin' again, but she's not interested." Murt shook his head as if in dismay. "A father's luck, here I have what most girls her age want, a barn full of horses, and my oldest comes to me and says, 'Da, I only ride to make you happy.' I hate to part with him."

Brandon ran a hand over each of the horse's legs. "Good bone. What's he used for?"

"Ah, he's been a Novice horse." He turned to Kate. "Done a bit of Pony Club, some hunting, dressage, hacking. He's ten years old and I had his legs x-rayed before I took him. He vetted perfect."

Kate was afraid to even ask what Murt might want for him. She had no business buying more than one horse and the trip had been to find one for Brandon to win with. No, she would not let another horse nibble his way from her hand to her heart, even though he had the softest nose in all the world and eyes that begged to be loved.

"Do ye like his name?" Bran asked. "You don't remember the first time you heard it, do you?" His mouth curled into the barest hint of a smile, he tilted his head and rubbed his chin with his knuckle. "*Samhain* is the Celtic New Year, pronounced *sawən*...so, *Samhain* Eve is...Hallowe'en."

Kate had never been a giggler, but she couldn't help it. "*I* think his name should be *Sam.*" The tickle of laughter rose in her like bubbles in a champagne glass, came to the surface and spilled over in joyous glee. "Murt, can I...oh my God, I can't believe I'm asking this...can I try him out?"

****

By the time they left Murt's farm it was well past lunchtime. They stopped at the Spar Mart and Bran bought brown bread, Irish cheddar, apples and bottled water. They parked the car at the cottage, Brandon grabbed a quilt from the back of the sofa and they hiked up the hill to the north of the house for a picnic. From the rocky outcrop they looked down on the beach where a fringe of silver sea foam caressed the pebbly strand and over to the

Carraigdún castle tower. It was idyllic. Kate could not imagine why anyone would live anywhere else.

Brandon rested his back against a granite erratic, stretching his long legs out onto the quilt. Kate lay with her head on his thighs and closed her eyes against the slanting rays of the setting sun.

"It gets late so early here," she mused. "Brandon, tell me the truth. How did I look on Sammy? I mean did we...match?"

"Sweetheart, you would look beautiful on a jackass and make the beast look bloody fine as well." He swept her hair off her forehead and looked down at her face.

"You know what I mean. Did he look like a horse I could ride...well?"

"Okay, purely as your riding instructor, you are a nice pair. He has a heart of gold; that you saw from the start. He looked easy to sit or I've just taught you so well that you made it look easy. I believe Murt if the man says the horse is sound and you probably won't ever need to put shoes on those fabulous hooves."

"He is smooth. I can sit his trot without bashing my...well, you know and his canter was like a rocking horse. Oh, Bran...I think I'm in love." She moaned and then laughed.

He bent over and kissed her laughing mouth, lifting her into his embrace and scooting her onto his lap. "I knew it from the first day I saw you on Murphy. You are a daughter of Epona, the horse goddess."

"Don't you think it's amazing that his name means Halloween, my birthday? I've always hated that I was born on Halloween. I got teased in school. My brothers called me *Witch Hazel*. You can't imagine how awful it was. But, do you trust in signs?"

"You said you didn't believe in magic. Are you

changing your mind on me?"

"It must be this place. I'm beginning to buy into your crazy old mystical world. Pretty soon I'll start seeing fairies at my garden gate." She twisted on his lap and straddled him, heart missing a beat when she felt how aroused he was, but leaning closer to his chest until her breasts brushed the wool of his coat. "It's getting late. Should we be getting back?" She brushed his lips with a feathery kiss.

An involuntary gasp escaped his throat. "Ahh, that would depend on how safe you feel being alone with me, Katie. I told you I want you." His lips were not tentative when he met hers, but urgent and demanding. "Every bit of you."

"There's not a human in sight. How safe am I right here?" she asked when he released her mouth.

He looked around, patted the ground as if testing it for comfort, and examined the sky with thoughtful pondering. "I would say you will have some bruises on your backside from the pebbles under this blanket and pneumonia from the damp. But you've nothing to fear from my touch."

As if he had read the clouds, one drop of rain splattered onto Kate's head. "Oh, how did you know?" She made no move to get off him as more big, wet dollops splashed off the rock and a rumble of thunder rolled off the sea.

He scooped her to her feet and started to gather their picnic together. "Forty-eight years of getting caught in the weather should teach a man something."

They scrambled down the path to the house as drops became slashing sheets of hard blowing rain. Kate had left her raincoat in the car and her sweater soaked through in seconds, the chill wet on her skin. Her shoes were nearly sucked from her feet as she jogged in the mud that settled in the low recesses of the trail.

They reached the house and Brandon searched in his pocket for the key, fumbled with wet hands shaking to get it in the lock. Finally, he pushed the door open and they burst inside, laughing, shivering, shedding wet clothing as they clambered up the stairs. Kate stood, wet tendrils of hair whipping about her face as she shook her head.

"I should get the stove going," Brandon offered breathlessly as he pulled Kate against his chest and kissed her.

She started to work on his shirt, yanking it up over his head, peeling the wet knitted garment off and flinging it across the room. She was stripped down to bra and panties and she was freezing, but the heat of his body was all she needed right now. "Forget it, we'll be plenty warm." Her arms snaked around his neck and she stood on tiptoe to reach his lips. His hand slid down her spine and between the wet silk of her panties and her smooth skin, cupping under her buttock and urging her to press into him.

Kate tugged at Brandon's breeches, forgetting he had a belt, struggling to free him. Finally, he helped her by unbuckling, unzipping and kicking the offending garment across the floor. She boldly inched his briefs down until they fell to his ankles. It was all a dream that was happening to someone else, as though the real Kate stood in the corner of the room watching this other Kate—Katie—undressing a man with a lack of restraint that was outside the authentic Kate's experience. She heard herself say, in a voice she barely recognized, "Bran, make love to me." And begging him, "Please, whatever you do...don't stop."

He lifted her in his arms and placed her on the bed, the naked length of him beside her. Reaching behind her back he unclasped her bra. In a flash of silliness, Kate was glad she had made the trip to Victoria's Secret for the bit of lace and silk that he now dropped on the floor beside the bed. Brandon's breath sucked in as he looked at her. "You are more beautiful than I remember."

"Oh, and what do you remember?"

"The morning sun shining in your bedroom window and you jumping out of bed, naked as a newborn babe. God, I knew you were a lovely creature then, but now..." He bent and laid moist kisses on one breast and then the other. "I can take my time and enjoy the view."

Hot trickles of sensation traveled from each inch of skin where his lips touched her, straight to that center low in her belly where a tension started to form, like the spring of a clock that would only wind tighter before it came undone. She wanted to look at him, explore his body, walk her fingers over the landscape of his chest, belly, and long lean legs. She wanted to touch everything, but held back from either shyness or fear.

As if he could read her thoughts he took her hand in his and led her to him. "Touch me," he whispered.

She wrapped her cool fingers around his phallus and felt the heat of him, hard and throbbing against her palm. His breathing quickened and her own body responded to the sounds with a rush of hot wetness. She lifted her leg and wrapped it around his backside, pressing her foot into him, urging him closer and positioning herself until his stiffness lay against her opening.

"Katie," he gasped, "tell me what you like. I want to please you." He slipped his hand between their bodies and cupped her mound, feeling her with his long fingers.

She wasn't sure at first what he was saying. *What I like? No one ever cared to ask before.* "What you're doing right now is...really...good."

Words were getting more difficult to articulate.

She buried her face in his shoulder, nipped him with her teeth, and kissed the spot. "I want you," she gasped, on the edge of incoherence. She rolled onto her back, urging him to cover her with his body. She kissed him on the mouth, searching, tasting, drinking in his breath, making it hers. She spread herself open to him, thrusting her hips up to meet him, taking him full into her, the length of him, until she was pinioned with his hardness.

He did not move. She could feel his heart pulsing where he was joined to her and when she looked into his face his eyes were like those of a feral beast captured—dark, pleading and slightly delirious. "*Muirnín*," he whispered, as if she would vanish if he spoke her given name.

By mutual need and consent he moved in her, hard steel sheathed in hot silk, each pass a word of love unspoken. She answered, enfolding him, letting him fill the void in her, the hollow left by years of emptiness. As they claimed one another there was no end to him or beginning to her. Their joined bodies moved hungrily, devouring any barriers that lay between, until the rhythm that matched their hearts burned a blazing mark into them that would never be erased.

Kate's rapid breathing became an unwilled panting. She gasped and tiny squeals of pleasure were replaced by unbidden wild creature sounds deep in her throat. All thinking ceased, the universe tilted and did not right itself before the planets exploded, shards of light and sound were sucked into a vortex that became a hard, hot ball of pleasure. She wrapped her legs around his hips, held him tight and deep, pulling him as pulsations shook her whole being, balancing the world and all its elements.

Before her own quaking settled she could feel Brandon's resolution building, pressing hard into her, only to withdraw to his length and plunge deep again, repeating the pounding, hard and furious. With a finality that buried him deeper than Kate thought she could accept, he groaned, his body shuddered and he gave himself up to let her own him.

The silence was broken only by the beating of the rain on the window, slowing and waning with the pulse of two hearts. Brandon thought he would be happy to never move from this position again. Slick and sticky with a mix of his fluids and hers, his flaccid member receding from her, he slowly rolled to her side, keeping her snuggled close. "Katie," he breathed, "I love you," and he knew he meant it.

"You don't have to say that." She buried her face in the damp skin over his breast bone.

"No, I don't." But he would continue to, until she believed him or sent him away. "Look at me, Katie." He needed to see her face, know she trusted him with her heart as she had with her body. "Have I ever lied to you?"

"Of course not."

"I never will. I'm as imperfect as a mortal can be. I have a penchant for putting my foot in my mouth. I'm a terrible money manager and I like to indulge myself in fine horses and expensive whiskey. I'm probably too old to change…but I do love you."

He couldn't stop looking at her. Her skin was wild honey and cream, smooth and luscious, her dark nipples a contrast that begged for his tender kisses. "Your skin is perfect. Why do you look so young?"

"Because you probably need bifocals."

"It's not just my eyes that helped me come to that conclusion." He ran a finger over her cheek and traced the line of her neck all the way to the tip of her left nipple. She smelled of meadow grass, rain and sex, an overpowering blend of olfactory stimulation that traveled from his brain straight to his cock.

She laughed when she felt him stiffen. "God, Brandon, you're not supposed to be able to do that so fast. We're not teenagers here."

"I can't help myself...the boy-o has a life all his own." He licked her neck and she shivered. "I know you don't want to, but, since we're here and it was...umm...very nice." He trailed a warm, moist line down the center of her ribs and circled her belly button with his tongue. He couldn't get the sounds of her out of his head, the little gasp and cry that came from her lips when he entered her and the deep, unearthly sigh when she climaxed and pulled him with her through time and space. "You never did get around to telling me what you like."

"I...well...no one's ever asked before." She blushed. Brandon was tempted to laugh at the contrast of her passion and her innocence. "And I can't imagine you'd want me a second time so quickly, or that you'd have the ability."

He kissed her, loving the feel of her lips on his. What kind of man had she spent half her life with anyway? One who hadn't asked her what she liked? Brandon could understand a man not being able to get it up a second time in quick succession. That particular problem had certainly happened to him more often than not. But not wanting her a second or a hundredth time was unthinkable.

"My ability, as you call it, might falter at times, but my desire for you will always be strong. Seeing as how I'm having an impressive moment here, you might like to take advantage of it." He had been holding her hand and led it to him in case she discounted his desire, or his capability.

Chapter Twenty

It was dark and though it was warm next to Brandon's naked body, Kate knew it would be terribly cold when she got out of the bed. "Brandon, I've got to get up."

"Why are you whispering? I'm not asleep and you aren't going to wake the children." He ruffled her hair.

"You're a real wise ass, you know. It just seemed like I needed to be quiet. Anyway, its freezing and I need to go wash up."

"Are you telling me to get my arse out of this nice warm bed and build us a fire?"

"Well, since you put it that way...yes."

"Stay here until I get the stove going and I'll go turn on the electric fire in the toilet for you."

She thought it was funny that what she called a space heater, he insisted was an electric fire. Basically she didn't care what he called it as long as the bath was warm and she could get up and pee without freezing her tush to the toilet seat.

It took no significant time at all to have the turf fires both upstairs and down blazing and the chill off the bathroom. Kate scooted down the hall and ran a bath while Brandon showered. He was dressed and waiting when she descended the stairs dressed in her warmest wool trousers and a sweater.

"Did you have any ideas for supper?" she asked, like this was just another normal day for her. Her insides knew differently. There was nothing normal or usual about this day. He loved her. The ache that he had left deep inside her and the rawness of her tender parts were a reminder of their joining, but his words rang and echoed in her consciousness, *Muirnín, I love you.*

Why had she not responded with the truth that she had been coveting since hearing his gentle voice calling her back to awareness in her hospital bed? Was it fear of losing herself to a man who might take her heart and use it as a trampoline to launch himself into another's arms? She had promised Brandon she would not compare him with Jeffrey; it was going to be a battle for her. Would Brandon be able to wait? Would he fight side by side with her or stand at the crossroads and watch her slay the dragons of her past by her own hand and heart?

"I thought we'd go into the village...unless you're too tired." His hand stroked her wet hair. "How long does this take to dry?"

"I forgot my hair dryer. But I can fluff it out by the fireplace...it'll be a horrible explosion of frizz, but it won't freeze to my head." Kate knew her hair would, if not tamed with diligence, take on a life of its own.

"We're not as primitive here in Éire as you might think. I've a hair dryer in my room. But, I've got to admit the visual of you, sitting by that fire, running your nimble fingers through that mane of yours...well..." He put her palm to his lips, "we might not get to dinner."

A tingle of electricity went straight from the skin of her palm to her tummy and threatened to travel further. "Brandon..." She looked from her hand to his face. He was barely breathing. "It's been a...well...long dry spell for me, until today, and I'm aching...in there."

"I'm sorry...if I hurt you. I could kiss it and make it better."

"I'm sure you could, but let's save that for later. Besides, come on Brandon, three times in as many hours?"

He hugged her to him and kissed the top of her wet head. "Talk about dry spells...I'm making up for years here."

"Not from what the gossips at Willow Creek say. I understand you've been 'boffing' everything with a pulse. Well, although they are pretty sure you don't do men."

"Oh, and do you believe these tales?"

"I might have a few months ago, but, no, I don't. In fact I've probably never known a more honorable man. After all, you did get me drunk, take me home to my bed, sleep beside me and, after this evening, I'm thoroughly convinced you did not have sex with me. I would definitely have remembered that, drunk or not."

"Ah, but do you know how hard it was to keep from touching you as you slept?" He chuckled and then became serious. "All I wanted to do, really, was stop your pain. If I could have done that by making love to you, I might have. It broke my heart to see you like that."

"I hope you've mended, because I'm healing nicely. Show me where you keep that hair dryer."

"Sure and it's a lovely night. We can walk the distance to Vaughan's Pub and have a meal."

The rain had stopped and the sky cleared. The blackness of the night was pierced by a trillion brilliant stars—light traveling out of time. Kate wanted to rewind those years and be with Brandon at the foundation of everything. Was it too late to begin again? She felt young tonight, like a girl who had just lost her virginity to this man who claimed to love her. It was a tempting and intoxicating thought, starting over.

"Katie," he said, "tell me what you did before you married. What were your goals, what did you want to do for your life?"

"I honestly haven't thought about that in years. Well, I wanted to be a ballerina, but that was when I was six." Her mother still kept a picture of Catarina, all pretty in a pink tutu and a toothy grin. "I was a boring, straight-A student. God, twelve years of Catholic school, no wonder I understand guilt so well. Anyway, I have a couple of college diplomas that say I know a lot about a little."

"What did you study?" He continued to encourage her.

"My undergraduate degree is in Italian language and I have a perfectly useless Master's Degree in Classics. It does qualify me to quote some obscure Latin poets, but that doesn't help much at hospital auxiliary dinners, neither does it come in handy at PTA meetings."

"I studied a bit of Latin myself. Although I seem to recall my mother threatening to nail my thumbs to the kitchen table if I didn't put more effort into it. I still don't recall much." He looked across at her. *"Omnia vincit amor et nos cedamus amori."*

"Virgil? 'Love conquers all; let us, too, yield to love.' If you're only going to remember one line of poetry, that's a good one." She wondered if Virgil had been right. She hoped so. "What else did your mother hammer into your head?"

"Oh, I'm one of those rare folk who can't claim family dysfunction for my malfeasance. Both my mam and da were loving and kind. I'm sure I stretched their patience. Annie was the perfect child...four years later they got *me*."

"Nothing you did in your childhood could surprise me. I have three brothers. Trust me, even Frankie was no saint." She laughed at remembering the trouble they found on a daily basis. "So, what about you? Did you ever want to do anything but ride horses?"

"Not since I have memory. My da was a trainer,

my mam rode jumpers. I guess you could say I learned to ride in the womb." He looked thoughtful. "I wasn't the best student, but I went to university because my folks expected it."

"What did you study?" Kate thought he seemed well educated, or at least well read.

"Oh...Irish history, culture, music. I suppose you could say I have a varied liberal arts education, but no paper to prove it. I never could sit still for long and I just wanted to ride and compete. My parents wouldn't have noticed at the time, but I watched and learned about life from their example. They kept their promise to never go to bed angry, at us or each other. I've a rotten hot temper, but they tried to teach me to balance that with respect and kindness."

Kate reached for his hand and wove her fingers between his. "I would have liked your parents. They did a good job on you."

****

It was well after midnight when Bran and Kate arrived back at the cottage. She was unsteady on her feet and he thought he might have to carry her the last few feet. One pint of Harp and pure exhaustion had rendered her senseless. "Can you make it the rest of the way?"

"Uhhh...yeah...sure...I'm good." She stumbled and would have done an inglorious face plant if he hadn't caught her.

"Has anyone ever suggested that you're a cheap date?" He lifted her and carried her the rest of the way inside, up the stairs to the loft. Her breath, laden with a hint of lager, was hot on his neck and her body, pressed against him sensuously close, sent familiar signals to his libido.

"Where are you taking me?"

"My room. It's got a nice electric fire and I won't have to start that turf stove." He laid her on his bed and started to remove her shoes. "Do you mind if I help you undress?"

She was suddenly more awake. "Oh. I can...in my suitcase I have my pj's." She started to get up.

"Stay here. I'll get what you need." He did not think she needed pajamas, but he aimed to please. He thought it might actually be romantic, although she wouldn't wear them for long.

"No, get in bed where you won't freeze. I'll be right back." She disappeared down the hall. He heard her talking to herself as she used the bathroom and undressed.

Brandon stripped and pulled the pile of quilts over him, hoping the bed warmed up fast. The sheets felt like slabs of ice. He had a brief fantasy of her standing in the doorway in some silky poor excuse for pajamas, but when she materialized she was wearing the red flannel things with Elmo on her chest. So much for that fantasy. *Is she trying to tell me something here?* "Sexy outfit," he teased.

"Nothing sexy about hypothermia." She snuggled in next to him. "Umm, you're nice and warm already." He ran his foot up her calf. "Yikes, except your feet!" She turned her back and they tucked up spoon fashion, his right hand resting between her breasts.

"Are you really worried about being cold or is this armor?" His hand strayed to her hip, slid inside her bottoms and settled on her belly.

"Brandon, I'm not one to make excuses. It's not going to be 'sorry, darling, I have a headache,' but I am tired and I think if your hand travels any further south, we're going to be awake for at least another hour."

"Okay, I know you're right. It's just going to be hard...to get any sleep." He had thought he was tired, too, but being this close to the prize stirred him despite his weariness. "Can you sleep if I hold you like this?"

"I'd like to find out."

"Promise me something, beautiful Katie. Wake me if you need me...for anything."

"You'll be the first person to know if I need anything." She placed his hand on her heart, covering it with both of hers.

Chapter Twenty-One

Like the silent paws of a gray cat, the mist of morning receded across the green slopes and settled into the crags that rimmed Galway Bay. In the quiet of the cottage loft the lovers lay, one asleep and dreaming, and the other awake in his own dream.

Dark chestnut locks twined about her delicate ears, long black lashes rimmed her closed eyes. Watching her sleep was a balm for his soul as surely as her laughter was a salve for his spirit.

Brandon was not a man who spent precious time wondering why fate had chosen him. It had never crossed his mind to ask *why me?* when he lost his first love and it wasn't his manner to question his blessing of a second chance at happiness. He simply wanted to savor the moment.

Her hand breached the few inches of distance between them and touched his face. "Brandon, are you awake?" she whispered.

"Yes, my love." The endearment came easily. "I've been awake for a while."

"Do you have any idea what time it is?" She moved closer, the curve of her body fitting into him.

"I'm guessing it's about eight. The sun is almost up. Did you sleep well?"

"Umm, better than I have in months. I guess it helps to have a man who can tire me out." She ran her tongue over her teeth. "Yuck. My mouth tastes like stale beer."

"Ah, the realities of true love...morning breath." His hand strayed to her thigh. "I'd like to pull those damn flannel knickers off you and give you a proper

214

good morning."

"I need to pee. God, I hate to get out of this warm bed." She flung the cover off, leapt up and sprinted down the hall. He heard her yelp, say something about the cold toilet seat, and then her bare feet padding back to the bedroom. To his surprise she had shed the pj bottoms and the dark triangle of hair at the apex of her long, shapely legs made him tremble inside.

The bed bounced as she jumped back in next to him. "I'm not getting up again until you build one of your toasty fires."

He traced the curve of her inner thigh with his fingers, while he pulled the offending pajama top off with his other hand. Brandon spread kisses on her breasts, watching one dark nipple contract before attending to the other. "I want you," he whispered against her ear, eliciting a shiver of response from her body and a quiet squeal of delight from her throat. Bending over her he ministered to her inner thigh with nips and kisses, making silvery snail tracks with his tongue to the center of her sex. He teased her with his lips, enjoying her gasp of realization when he found the little pearl of her pleasure hidden there.

Rising up on one elbow he looked at her—the long curving line of her hip, flat belly with just the hint of marking from bearing her child, her breasts gently rounded, each a perfect fit for his hands.

Kate became the aggressor. She rolled him onto his back and mounted him, easing her wet cleft onto him.

Brandon groaned with surprise and had to force himself to hold back his burgeoning culmination. "Have I been captured by an enchanted beastie, a forest muse to take me into her lair and use me so adeptly?"

As she moved against him he watched the

expression on her face change from captivating to startling. Her body appeared to transform from mere human to daughter of the Si, bewitching him into the sea of her imagination and drowning him. She rode him with untamed wantonness, her hair falling forward, masking the desire in her features until he felt her tighten deep inside and press hard against the root of him. She arched her back, hands on his chest, head flung back in a posture of triumph as waves of heat forced him to the unfathomable reaches of her core.

****

"Brandon, I just know I'm going to go straight to hell for having all this fun," Kate said rising from their bed. "I'm going to shower and get dressed and you are going to keep your hands off me for a while."

"Ah an' she's gettin' bossy already."

Kate really did have misgivings over being so happy. She simply wasn't used to feeling this content. Fear that it couldn't last wanted to creep up her spine and settle into her brain where it would worm around making her worry. She could wash the outward evidence of their joining down the shower drain, but they had forever branded one another with an iron forged by mutual need and longing.

If she were to look at this situation from a purely objective standpoint, Brandon was a fabulous find. Of course he was in virtual financial ruin, but she could deal with that. He was, by any woman's standards, a handsome man. He was kind and gallant when he wasn't having a fit of temper over something, and if he were using performance enhancing drugs in the bedroom she'd like to have the patent.

It was after noon when they finally got to the O'Brien Stables. Murt was waiting. "Is it jet lag or somethin' else keeping you up late these days?" He smacked Brandon on the back and gave him a knowing look.

"Just you mind your own business, mate," Brandon warned. "I'll ride Calypso first and Katie wants to have another go on Sam. Have your boy set up some small fences for her."

Kate overheard this direction and gave Brandon an 'are you insane' look. "Fences, for me?"

Bran just grinned as though he had a secret he refused to share until the time was perfect.

****

Brandon looked like he was dressed for battle when he came out of the barn office. Hard hat, flack vest, spurs, and a crop were his equivalent of armor, sword and dirk. When he mounted the copper gelding, all he needed was the blessing of a maiden to complete the fantasy.

He turned to Kate "Now you're going to see why I love this sport." He leaned down and kissed her lightly on the lips. "For luck."

Murt had built a number of nice obstacles of varying levels of challenge in the fields around his property. Brandon trotted and cantered his steed around and between the felled trees, rock walls and sod covered mounds. He looked relaxed, even lackadaisical.

Just as Kate thought this was going to be a rather boring little exercise, Brandon's posture changed slightly, and Calypso came alive. Speed increased, stride lengthened and they turned toward the rock wall. The half smile and look of determination on Brandon's face were mimicked in the body language of the horse as they flew over the barricade. When the horse had cleared the wall, Bran galloped on to a jump configured to look like a giant's bench. They cleared the red-painted monster furniture and Kate heard Brandon laughing as he reached forward and patted the horse on the neck. Without missing a beat they traversed the back of a sod-covered mound, leaping off into space on the other side, landing and taking two strides to a log suspended over a ditch that, to any horse, may as well have been bottomless. Calypso never faltered, questioned or misjudged a distance. Jump after jump—drops, water, walls and ditches, he flew as if he had the headless Dullahan at his heels.

Kate was astounded. She had seen Brandon jump horses over fences before, but this was thrilling and terrifying. This is what he did and it hadn't occurred to her to worry for his safety, until today. She tried not to think of the possibility of his being hurt, but now her life was complicated with the fact that this was the man she loved.

As though Murt had read her mind he put his hand softly on her shoulder. "He's good at what he does and he's as careful as he can be, but it is a risky business, Katie."

"I, uh...I know. Has he ever been hurt? I mean...has he ever fallen?"

"You ride, you fall. Sure an' he's been hurt, but not enough to stop him...not by a horse at any rate."

Brandon headed to the track that circumscribed the jump field. It was marked at intervals with metered distances. Kate saw him look at the big stop watch he wore on his wrist and nudge Calypso into a huge gallop. "What's he doing, now?" Kate questioned Murt.

"Wants to see if the horse has any speed. I told him Calypso was fast. He apparently didn't believe me. You'd better know Bran Sullivan is a damn perfectionist when it comes to horses. I'll go get Sam for you. When you're ready, meet me in the large arena."

When Brandon was done he vaulted off the horse, handing the reins to Liam, and strode over to Kate with a look she could only describe as satisfied. It was an expression that was alarmingly close to the one he'd had in bed that morning. "So, you like him, I take it?"

He closed his arms around her and lifted her off her feet. When he kissed her, his lips were warm and salty. "That...is only second to loving you."

Kate wasn't sure that, in reality, she came first, but for now she was willing to suspend her disbelief.

She changed into her breeches and boots, secured her helmet and met the men in the arena. Brandon held out his hand and pulled her close. "Hop up and I'll talk you through a warm up and then you're going to pop him over a few little X's."

"Brandon, are you crazy? Jumping? Me?" She would break her neck and never have another orgasm—it would be her punishment for indulging her fantasies.

"You've trotted Murphy over cavaletti. This is no different, but if you're really scared, I won't have you doing it."

"Well, I...if you think I can." She let him give her a leg up and adjusted her stirrups. Sammy stood solid as a granite boulder until she told him with a squeeze of her calves to walk on. They picked up a trot and then a slow rocking canter.

Brandon walked to the center of the ring next to a small barrier of crossed poles. "Now, Katie, just trot him over this. Nice and steady now. Grab some mane over the fence."

"Okay, big guy, do your best not to make me look incredibly stupid here." Kate said under her breath as they approached the poles. When Sam lifted his legs and jumped, Kate's hands had a white-knuckle grip in the thick black mane.

"Eyes up, looking straight ahead," he talked her through. "Perfect, now trot over the red and white."

After a few jumps, Kate's confidence soared as if she had sprouted wings. Brandon raised the fences to just over two feet and had the happy duo trotting them easily. "Pick up the canter and come around to this little oxer," Brandon said in a matter of fact way.

"Okay, but you'll have to explain it to my mother if I fall off and break anything."

"Sit up tall until he leaves the ground and just go with him. Grab a hank of mane if you want to. Keep your heels down...eyes up."

Sam took the fence in an arcing canter stride and landed them safely on the other side. Kate gave an involuntary squeal of joy. She couldn't say it with Murt within earshot, but this was almost as much fun as the ride Brandon had given her not so many hours ago.

"Sounds like you're enjoying yourself," Brandon called. "Have you had enough?"

Kate and Sam came to a stop in front of Bran. "Why didn't you tell me it was this much fun?"

"Maybe I was afraid I couldn't compete."

****

Kate was silent for a long time as they returned to Black Bush Cottage. It was late afternoon and the setting sun threw random rays of light across Brandon's face as he drove, emphasizing the line of his jaw. He did not have a face one would describe as rugged, but he was not soft either. Loving his smile was easy—he had straight white teeth and full lips that on a less defined face would have looked just a tad effeminate. They were nice lips to kiss and be kissed by.

"You're quiet this evening, Katie. What are you thinking about?"

"My horse," she lied. "And I think we need to call home and make sure all is well. I'd like to talk to Laura, see if she's heard anything from my realtor."

"Realtor?" He took his eyes off the road and nearly hit a sheep.

"Brandon! Please, let's not total another car.

Yes, realtor. My house is on the market and I have a nice offer. You didn't think I planned to live in that huge place all by myself, did you?"

As they sat sipping tea in the quiet of the evening, Kate knew she had to present her proposal to Brandon and she was sure he would fight her. Now, as they cuddled together on the sofa before the fireplace, she knew the time might not be right, but it wasn't getting any righter.

"Brandon, I have a business deal for you." She turned to face him. "I want to be a partner in Willow Creek."

"Okay, think of yourself as a partner." Bran kissed the end of her nose.

"No, you don't understand. I want to invest the money from the house into the farm." She knew she needed to talk fast. "I've told you I understood the risk and I want to do it."

Brandon looked at Kate and shook his head. "I understand that you want to invest in this horse, but the farm? Katie, we could still lose Willow Creek, and you'd lose everything you put into it."

"We won't. I know it. Calypso will be fabulous and the barn will soon be full of paying clients. Brandon, I believe we can do this...together."

Brandon had to think fast. His pride would not allow Kate to bankroll him. He would look to all the world like a gigolo. "Katie," he took a deep breath. "I would consider your offer, but I'd want to deed this house over to you as collateral."

"This house? I don't want this house. It belongs to your family. What about Annie?"

"It's just for security, until Willow Creek is in the black. This place is mine free and clear, to do with what I wish."

"Do you make these kinds of offers to all your investors? Did you tell Felicia Dalwhinny you would guarantee her investment or she could have your home?" Her voice had an edge of danger he had heard in her before.

"No, of course not. Katie, this is completely different."

"Why, because you didn't sleep with her? Look, Brandon, I have the money, I want to invest it." She pulled away from his arms and looked straight into his face.

Her comment hit a nerve and it stung, flying away with a piece of his restraint. "All right, if you really want to know...I won't be taking Jeffrey's money." He knew the moment the words left his lips it was an incredibly stupid thing to say, but his pride and temperament were in a clashing battle with his sensibility.

"Jeffrey's money? Jeffrey's money! Well, Mr. Sullivan, let me just clarify something for you. I earned every nickel. Just what price would you put on twenty-five years?" Kate's voice was rising and her hands emphasized every word. "That's half my life, mind you, the half that should have been filled with the best of everything love and marriage had to offer." She rose to her feet.

"Katie, you're taking this all wrong." He tried to backpedal, but wasn't fast enough.

"I am, am I? And what do you know about it? I tried, every day, to make him love me, to be exactly what he wanted me to be. What is that worth...in dollars?"

Brandon saw a hot flash stirring and it was not hormonal. Kate was furious. "Now, Katie."

"Don't 'now Katie' me. I've spent all my life kowtowing to that. 'Now Catarina, watch your temper, *basta cosi.* Now, Mom, you're overreacting, it's just a little tattoo. Now, Catherine, I'm in love with another woman and you're going to sit there and take it like the nice, sweet fool you've always been.' *Jesus Christ,* can I just be let alone to throw a fit now and then?"

Brandon saw her hand reach for his Waterford crystal sculpture on the table and thought she was going to throw it at him. She must have seen the look of terror in his eyes because she retracted her hand, turned on her heel and stalked out of the house, slamming the door behind her.

The night was cold and it didn't take long for Kate to regret rushing out without her coat. Anger kept her warm until she reached the skiff that was tied up below the cottage. It did not look at all seaworthy and there were no oars or Kate would have tried to row the disreputable craft all the way back to Baltimore. As it was, all she could do was sit in the empty hull and sulk.

Sulking, a state for which she would have been solidly berated by her mother, was a hard-won luxury and one she thought she deserved right now, but physical discomfort has a way of redirecting wanton anger. Kate soon enough found herself wishing Brandon would come and beg her forgiveness so she could get back in where it was warm without destroying what was left of her ephemeral shield of pride.

Just about the time she thought she'd start to walk back, before she was too far gone with cold to move her legs, she spied Brandon's shadowy form striding toward her.

"Here's your coat." It was clear by the illumination of the full moon, he was not smiling. His jaw was set in a mask of determination that she had seen before.

"Thank you." Kate answered softly, not wanting to ignite an explosion by shooting flaming arrows of verbiage.

He sat in the boat, facing her, putting his hands in his coat pockets. "Katie, I think we need to come to a compromise here."

It did not sound like the voice of a man who was going to back down easily. Kate knew he was proud. She loved that part of him, when it was not a barrier to common sense. There was a fine line for Kate, the difference between doing the right thing and being a doormat. She was done letting everyone dictate her next action, even Brandon Sullivan. "What kind of compromise do you propose?"

Bran took her nearly frozen hand in his, lifting it to his lips and blowing warm breath on it. He kissed her knuckles lightly and looked into her eyes.

"Marry me."

"Marry you? Are you insane?" Kate was shivering from the cold and now shaking from surprise.

"I love you."

"We barely know one another."

"Marry me and I'll put your name on the deed to Willow Creek. Have your attorney draw up an ironclad pre-nup that protects every cent you invest in our farm." He moved to sit next to her. "Call it a marriage of convenience." He opened his coat and snuggled her next to his chest. "May I?"

"You're trying to distract me, confuse me so I agree to your preposterous proposal."

"It's more sensible than you think. But, take your time, think about it. I'm going to be here. I'm not going away, unless you send me packing."

Yes, she could. She could take her time. She *should* take her time. She tried to remind herself that this was an experiment, an adventure to regain her independence. It was her search for Kate, a Kate who had been pulled apart and pieces scattered to the four winds. *Marry him? Ridiculous!*

"Are ye goin' to answer me?"

"No. No, Brandon, not tonight." Kate leaned into his warmth and let the moonlight bathe her face. "Is the moon always this big, or are we closer to it here, in Ireland?"

"Hmm...same moon, I believe. The full moon of December is called the Wolf Moon, but I'm not sure why."

Brandon's arm snaked around Kate's hip and nudged her into him. The boat rocked and canted with the shift of weight. "If you succeed in tipping this boat over, we'll both freeze to death before we can drag ourselves out of the water."

"Not necessarily. Here, put your hand in."

Kate reached over the side and dipped her fingers in the blackness, rippling the reflection of the moon. "It's warm. How?"

"Ha, another bit of Irish magic. This time thanks to topography. I've stood on the Giant's Causeway, up north, and you can see the line where the North Channel meets the Gulf Stream. The waters are of different colors. The Atlantic side is warmer and it moderates the climate."

Kate wondered if the tides that moved in her could mellow her own temperature changes—cool her anger but not her ardor, warm the chill that had been left by years of disappointment, allow the heat of a man's love to melt her without taking her identity and rendering it to ashes.

****

Kate had smiled so much during dinner her face hurt by the time they arrived back at the cottage. "Brandon, I haven't laughed this much in years, maybe in my whole life," she said to him as they walked up the stairs to the loft.

He stopped at the top and turned to her, looking very serious. "Katie, I'd like you to sleep with me tonight."

At first she thought this was an odd thing for him to say, but Kate realized he meant it. He was not just going to assume that they would share a bed and he was willing to give her the choice. "Yes, I'd like that, too." She took his hand and led him to her room.

Touching him, being touched by him, was a feast for a starving heart. They were far from home and the worries of everyday life and she chose not to be denied.

They lay nested, a tangle of limbs, tired from their mutual delight in one another and not wanting to break the spell by moving or talking. Finally, Kate whispered, "Bran, I don't want this to end. I know it must, but I can't think about going back to my real life."

"It's not going to end, Katie. I'm in this deal forever. I'm trying to understand your fear of a relationship. I have ghosts, too. But you're not alone now."

"It may be too soon, for me. I don't know. I'm still trying to figure out how I went so wrong. You know, in the beginning, I think Jeffrey must have loved me. I can't get over the feeling that I did something to destroy that."

"Were you much different when you married him than you are now?

"I suppose so. I was naïve, idealistic. My family was always warm and loving. I thought my marriage couldn't be any less. Jeffrey was charming. He's from old money, he was well traveled and I was...well, impressionable. I never thought of marrying as giving up anything. I'm a capable woman. I could have had a career, but I primarily wanted to be a wife and mother. If I had given a moment's thought to my needs, maybe he would have had more respect for me."

Brandon moved so that he could see her face clearly. "I'm sure we were both different people twenty-five years ago, but we walked the paths that we chose at that time and somehow we ended up here. When I lost my wife, I thought my life was over, but I couldn't lie down and quit, I had my children to consider. How was I to know you would come along?"

"Yeah, you ran right into me. Maybe I should thank that squirrel, he did sacrifice his life for us," Kate mused. "Brandon, will you be able to be patient with me?"

"I'm going to try." He kissed her and let his hand rest possessively on her hip. "Sleep now. I have a beautiful day planned for tomorrow. There's so much I want to show you."

"Good night, Bran."

"Wake me if you need anything."

Kate thought about that simple statement. *Wake me if you need anything.* She believed he meant it and it was the kindest offer anyone had ever made her.

Chapter Twenty-Two

Kate was terrified and thrilled. She had an irrational feeling that if she stepped an inch closer to the edge she would jump off the precipice and fly out over the Atlantic Ocean. The Cliffs of Moher, rising seven hundred feet from the sea, pulled at her in a way Kate had rarely known. Brandon had brought a picnic supper, spread a quilt on the meadow grass and held her in his arms as they watched the mid-winter sun extinguish in the swells that met the western sky.

It had been a day of magical places. They had risen early, driven to Poulnabrone and held one another as the winter solstice sunrise set the Burren afire with an aureate glow. They walked the limestone slabs and explored the megalithic stone circles and ring forts, some older than the pyramids in Egypt. Bran explained that the area was known for its unique flora and concentration of Fairy Folk who, he claimed with feigned seriousness, take offense at being disturbed. Kate stepped lightly with that in mind.

Now, she sat leaning back into his embrace, dreaming of the night to come and conflicted about returning home.

Kate had given Murt a certified check for an amount that, though enormous, turned out to be less than Brandon had first estimated. The three horses would be flown to the U.S. as soon as possible. To Kate it was all a technical nightmare of paperwork, licenses and veterinary clearances, but Brandon had done this dozens of times and assured her it was routine.

There was nothing routine about the decision for Kate. Never had she done anything so selfish, and let it feel right. Not that she had ever wanted for much in the way of material things, especially when she was married. She had a closet full of expensive clothes, a house worth a clean million dollars and she could replace her automobile without much of a dent in her bank account when the time came. No, it was the act of making a decision that even months before would have been deemed frivolous, and allowing it to make her deliriously happy.

"I'm going to worry about Sam until I see his smiling face in a stall at Willow Creek," she said like a true horse mother.

"He's a good sturdy lad. He'll be fine." Bran tucked her closer to him to ward off the chill of the night air. The moon had risen, waning but still huge, in the eastern sky. "It's getting colder. We should get back."

****

He loved her gently and slowly, savoring her every nuance, each breath that caught, the sounds he elicited from her throat. He took her to the verge of a precipice and held her as she fell, balanced and was lifted again. And when she had tumbled through space in his arms, their bodies locked in a timeless battle to possess and be possessed, she cried out to him, in a wordless plea that dwelt so deep in her only he could call it forth.

She was golden, a gilded scabbard, slick and hot to sheath his hardness in one smooth stroke. Together they ascended, bound flesh to flesh, a burning singularity pulsing between them until they burst into a million stars and floated back to earth, embers on the wind.

Kate lay very still and listened to him breathe; the slick, warm testament of their joining was fresh on her thighs and her lips still tingling from his last kiss. He had her tucked into him; his hand, even in sleep, caressed her breast and one long leg was wrapped around her hip. She tried to banish the question that popped into her head, *had he held Fiona like this?* More than likely he had. It was just the way he was—openly affectionate, giving and not afraid to throw himself on the altar of chance for what he wanted in life.

They had talked about how to handle their situation once they were back home. Brandon wanted Kate to move in with him at Willow Creek right away. She told him in no uncertain terms that was not going to happen. She was concerned about the reaction of his sister and his children.

"And do you think they don't already know? One look at us and I would think it's going to be awfully obvious what we've been up to these last days."

"Well, I guess I hoped they would think this was...platonic. Oh God...you mean...Kevin and Brighid know we're...intimate?" She suddenly thought she would not be able to face them.

"Katie, this isn't something I do with clients, take them to Ireland to stay in my home, my bed. My children are adults, and they both know how I feel about you."

"You told them? Before you even told me?"

"Not exactly like that, but, Katie, I'm not going to sneak around in order to be with you." He touched her cheek with his knuckles. "I'm not going to be able to keep my hands to myself."

They agreed to disagree for the present. They would get home and see what happened next. But this night was theirs and Kate wouldn't spoil it by worrying about the reactions from family, friends or Brandon's other clients when it became the hot topic of gossip at Willow Creek.

He awakened her long before the sun chased the

blackness of night out to sea. They showered and dressed, trying not to look at one another for fear of the distraction. Finally, he took her into his arms. "Katie, this is only the beginning for us. You'll see. We're going to make everything work. Calypso is a great horse, you're going to have fun on Samhain and I'm not going to let you down."

Brandon had a renewed conviction to keep Willow Creek. This time not only for himself or for his children and the memory of Fiona, but for Kate. It could be a future for them, together. He simply had to make it profitable, somehow.

Chapter Twenty-Three

"Kevin, shut your bossy mouth. I'm not your slave, dammit," Brighid yelled across the barn. "I'm going to get Da at the airport and I'm not going smelling like horse shit." She stomped off toward the house.

"Okay, smart ass. And how are you going to get them and their luggage in your car?" Kevin snapped back at his little sister. "Damn, she's a single-minded brat." He followed her back to the house.

They had been cleaning stalls since six o'clock this morning, getting everything in perfect shape, worried should their father find even one item not up to snuff in his barn. Kevin and Brighid had an ongoing feud with their dad about the need for a barn to be immaculately clean, but they knew their opinions were a waste of time. Now they were at each other's throats from frustration and glad their dad would be back today to run the place himself.

"Brighid, could you be reasonable for about thirty seconds, please. If you want to pick them up, you can take my 4-Runner." He knew he would get nowhere if he did not compromise. It was good practice for marriage, he figured. "Barb is coming over in about an hour. I should be here anyway."

"Oh, yeah, everybody's out of the house. You two can fool around. Just remember, our Aunt the nun will be back from shopping anytime, and she probably thinks you're a virgin."

"Maybe I am." He laughed.

"Sorry, Kev, your girlfriend tells me everything. Wow, the things she tells me. I'm shocked."

"Well then, don't be too shocked when Dad comes home with a real satisfied look on his mug, because I am more than sure he's—Ouch! Don't do that." He grabbed his shin where she had kicked him.

"You don't know anything, you dumb ass."

"Their flight is in at one. They're gonna be tired, so don't be late. Annie's making dinner and Mr. Italy will be here, too."

"God, Kevin, any other orders? I'm not a child, you know."

He hoped not. Kevin knew his sister would fight the idea of their dad being with Kate. He had seen them together, his father and Katie Aiello, and Kevin was certain they couldn't keep their hands off each other. Whether or not this was going to be any kind of a permanent arrangement, who knew? He liked Kate. He just hoped she wouldn't distract his dad from his goals.

Brighid hadn't wanted to say it to her brother, but the reason she wanted to go to the airport was not only because she missed her father, but she needed to get a look at this Kate. It had been going on for some time now and the lady wasn't going away. If she was a typical *barn bunny* looking for a quickie from the boss, Brighid would know immediately. She had grown up around women who made no effort to hide their flirting with her father. He was a good-looking man and even when her mom was around women came on to him. Brighid had asked her mother once if it bothered her. Fiona's response surprised her daughter, "Not at all. Your father is devoted to me and he has never given me any reason to doubt him." It was pure and simple, never any question.

When she drove up to the loading zone, she instantly saw her father. He was standing hand in hand with a slender woman with dark, curly hair.

This must be the *famous* Kate Aiello. Brighid noticed immediately that the woman was pretty; with an oval face, straight nose and very dark eyes. She reminded the girl of the Da Vinci sketch *La Scapigliata*. Her father would be glad to know that her study of Renaissance Art was worth what he was paying.

"Daddy!" she called, parking the SUV and hopping out.

"Hey, baby, I didn't expect *you*." He hugged her and turned to Kate.

"Katie, this is my daughter, Brighid. Brighid...Kate Aiello."

Kate took the girl's hand in both of hers. "I'm so happy to finally meet you. Your father has been bragging about you since I met him."

"Thanks Da, now I have to live up to your propaganda. Glad to meet you, too. May I call you Kate?" *So far, not bad, seems nice enough.* "I have strict orders from my obnoxious brother to get you two home as soon as possible. Annie is cooking. Sergio and Barb are coming. We want to hear all about the trip."

****

"Kevin, you're an animal," Barb giggled and shoved him off the bed. "This is gonna look sweet when your Aunt walks in on us."

"You're virtually my wife and she's busy ogling her Marcello Mastroianni." He lay back down beside her and ran his hand up her spine. "Love is definitely in the air this winter."

"I think the thing with your dad and Kate is just too cute. Do you think they had fun in Ireland?" She kissed him.

"Not as much fun as we had right here." He breathed the scent of her hair. "If you're the one who wants to look respectable when my aunt shows up, why are you kissing me and not getting up and putting your clothes on?" His knee slid between her thighs, ready to pleasure her again.

"Because you are tempting me beyond my ability to resist...because I love you...because you have the best lips for kissing...and...umm, let's see...a few other body parts a woman finds attractive."

"Kevin, Barbara...are you here?" It was Annie.

"My family has the worst timing," Kevin groaned. "We're here, Auntie, just going over some wedding plans."

"Liar." Barb grabbed her clothes and jogged into the bathroom.

"I'm not lying. We're planning the sex part," he said while he zipped his jeans.

****

Kate's fears about returning home, facing family, were unfounded. They ate, laughed and listened as Brandon and Kate told about their trip. After dinner, Brandon stood and raised a glass in salute.

"Listen up all of you. I have an announcement to make." Kate had a moment of fear wondering what he would say. He was tired and a little relaxed from the wine. She was not ready for him to announce their wedding plans.

"This is a truly momentous occasion for my Katie...our Katie. She has acquired her first horse. To Katie and Samhain...*Sláinte*." They drank to the occasion and Brandon bent down and kissed her full on the mouth. Everyone cheered, with the exception of Brighid, who smiled politely.

Brighid's coolness did not go unnoticed by Kate. When she thought about it, she wasn't surprised. Counting back, Kate realized Brandon's daughter must have been only sixteen or so when her mother became critically ill, a devastating time for a girl to lose a parent. Kate knew she would have to be tactful, and if not win Brighid's trust, at least try to

235

not offend the young woman.

Annie stood and started to clear the table and Kate was surprised when Sergio immediately pitched in to help. It was completely out of character for an Italian man of his generation, raised the way he was, to help with domestic tasks. They disappeared into the kitchen and Kate looked over at Brandon who had a wry smile on his lips. "Should I go make sure they behave?" Kate suggested.

"I'm not sure either of us qualify as chaperones, after this last week," he whispered. "Do you want to get home to bed?"

"Soon, but what about Sergio? He's staying at my house. He should take me home. You need to sleep." She knew if Brandon took her home, he would want to stay.

"Do I have to admit that you're right? Okay, you go with Laura and Sergio. I'll see you tomorrow."

They got ready to leave. Everyone said good night...glad you're back...congratulations on the new horse...get some rest. Brandon walked Kate to Laura's car and tucked her into the back seat. He surreptitiously ran his hand over her hip and down her thigh in the dark of the car's interior and kissed her behind her ear as he whispered, "I love you."

The words both thrilled and terrified Kate. It hadn't seemed so daunting in the unreality of the loft in Ireland, snuggled into his hard body, the idea that they could make a life together. Now, the choking sensation of doubt, the cold fingers of fear...the fear that she would disappoint him and he would find his needs fulfilled elsewhere, crept over her heart.

She looked over to Annie and Sergio standing in the shadow of the porch, his arm encircling her, a hand stroking her cheek. Did they have any reservations? Was there any doubt in them? They seemed to Kate as innocents, never having been betrayed. They simply allowed the tide of their mutual yearning to carry them along. She prayed to recapture that lack of guile in herself, to let go of the constraining noose of distrust.

****

Her house was quiet as a tomb and twice as cold. To Kate it accentuated the reality of being alone. Her bed seemed huge and empty without Brandon's arms around her. She wondered if he was thinking of her—if his bed felt just as vacant.

To keep her thoughts off the craving in her body, Kate tried to mentally organize her Christmas celebration. Every Yuletide for the duration of her marriage had been Kate's sole responsibility. Since her husband would not spend the holiday in Hackensack, and his parents always used the time to travel abroad, that left the Aiello brothers, and they all came to Kate and Jeffrey's.

This year things would be different. Kate had been in the hospital and then away in Ireland. Not only did she not have the time to fuss about the plans, she hadn't been in the country. Each year Kate purchased plane tickets for her family. It had become part of her gift to them. They would all descend on her home Christmas morning come hell, high water or lack of planning on Kate's part.

The cooking usually began two weeks before the big day and Kate left the kitchen only to shop or go to one of the many parties associated with Jeffrey's work at the hospital. This year the food would be delivered to her door by a catering service and the only event that she planned to attend was Brandon's birthday celebration on Christmas Eve.

Since she had precious little time and absolutely no desire to shop, Kate had sat at her computer in the days following her hospital stay and shopped online for everyone. Yes, it was impersonal by her usual criteria, but it was done and she had not had to fight for a parking spot at the mall. The one exception was browsing the shops in Ballyvaughan for just the right gifts for Brandon and Laura.

Did Kate feel guilty about dropping the ball like this? Terribly, but it was a change that had to happen and there was no better opportunity than this year. Next year, the whole *fam damily* would celebrate elsewhere.

****

Bran sat stunned for several minutes before opening his phone and hitting the speed dial for O'Brien's.

Murt answered. "What are you up to this fine evening?"

"I need some advice. Are ya up to it?"

"If it's concerning horses, I'm yer man. If it's on the subject of that lovely woman you're courtin', well...good luck is all I can offer."

"I want her in my life...not just in my bed."

"Ah, and I'm seein' the truth of it now...got yerself a taste of heaven, have ya? Let me think on this a moment."

Brandon was ripped back to a time when he and Murt were young and infinitely more stupid. Murt had come whining to Bran that he was hopelessly in love with Nuala Ryan. Of course, O'Brien had known the Ryan girl since infancy. They fought like siblings, loved like sister and brother, but she had gone off to school in Dublin for a summer and come back a woman. Murt, overcome with her loveliness and a Guinness or two, caught her off guard in the doorway of the Pub and kissed her, in a very unbrotherly manner. Nuala, being a girl known for her virginity as well as her strong arm, knocked him flat.

They were married the next summer, after a courtship that had poor Murt fevered with need. She, of course, made him wait until their wedding night, but it had been well worth the wait and he never forgot she could still bash the stilts from under him, if he'd had a bit to drink.

"Here's my thought on the subject, Bran. The filly's been spooked. That I can see in her eyes, genuine fear she has. If you force her into a corner, she might bolt and run you down." He paused. "On the other side of it, some need to be coaxed more strongly than others. You are going to have to decide if you have the patience, the agility, and the love to ride out her startles."

"A wise man you are, Murt. You know, I've learned over the years, I can ride as fast as a horse can run away with me; but I've never met a challenge quite like this one. Say a prayer to St. Brigid for me, my friend."

Brandon sat in his favorite chair, feet propped up on the fireplace hearth, glass of Midleton warming in his hand. He still had his farm, he had a new and impressive horse to start the year, Kevin was in love with a woman who could kick the boy's ass and Annie was smitten with her Italian gentleman. Even Brighid seemed at ease.

Bran Sullivan should have been deliriously content. He was not. He wanted Katie, wanted her here, now and forever. Instinctively, he knew he should not push her, but the thought of sleeping alone, especially now, remembering the way she fit to him so perfectly, caused him a palpable ache in his gut.

The marriage proposal had been a shock to her, he had no doubt of that. He saw no point in putting off the sacrament and making it official. Kate, he was almost certain, would not want to be rushed.

Annie came and sat beside him, cup of tea balanced on her lap. "You have a troubled look to you, Bran."

She could always read his face. He never could

get anything past his big sister. "Annie, what if I told you I'm in love? What would you think of that?"

"I'd say if it's with our Katie, it's about time you admitted it to yourself."

"Damn, has it been that obvious?" He gave her a sideways grin and rolled his eyes.

"Only since the day I found you two screamin' at each other in the office over the car insurance. So, brother, what do you plan to do about it?"

"You know, thirty years ago, I'd know just what that answer should be. Now, I'm not so young and smart. I don't want to scare her away."

"I may not be very experienced in the ways of romance, but I've learned a few things over the last weeks. I'm pretty sure I know what love looks like in a man's face, in his voice, his touch. And, I see the way you are with Kate. She sees it, too. Kate's no fool and she loves you."

"She hasn't told me that." Brandon had not wanted to admit to himself that she might not ever be able to. "I miss her tonight. Annie, I loved Fiona, I still do, but I also loved being a married man. I don't like sleeping alone and I've had too much of it. I want Katie as my wife. Until that time, I asked her if she'd come stay with me here. She refused, of course. She thinks it's improper."

"Well, it is. But if the two of you feel strongly that you want to be together, I'll look the other way. This is your house, Brandon, and you are a grown man."

"You know for an old nun, you're not too bad." He leaned over and kissed her on the cheek. "I love you, Annie."

She pinched his nose. "Don't call me old and I'm no longer a nun. I'm a woman with a handsome Italian boyfriend. You're not the only one lookin' at a weddin' in the near future."

Brandon pulled her into his arms and hugged

her so hard she squeaked. "And just when is he going to ask my permission to marry my only sister?"

"Hold on to your hat. He is planning to do that tomorrow night." Her face was pink and glowing. Brandon had not seen his sister this happy since the day she took her vows for the Church, more than thirty-five years ago.

****

Kate flung her arm out across the void that was her bed. All she encountered was the cold side of the sheets. *How could I get used to waking with arms around me so quickly? Had it all been a wonderful dream: Ireland, the loft with its fragrant peat fire, the musky scent of a man, his body hot against hers?* Maybe, if she just rolled over and went back to sleep, she would wake to find that this lonely room was the dream and Brandon beside her the reality.

As if she bid him come to her, the phone jingled. "Good morning," she said with a sleepy whisper.

"Umm, you sound like you're right beside me. Did I wake you?"

"No, I was awake. I was thinking about our trip." *I was craving your touch.* "What are you doing awake so early?" *Any chance you were dreaming of me?*

"Missing the enchanted forest nymph who stole my heart and used my body with such care," he confessed.

"Go on, keep that up, we'll never get through the day ahead. Can I come help you this morning? Now that I'm an investor, I think it's time to learn to clean stalls."

"I'm getting started in a few minutes here. Barb, Kevin and Brighid are already feeding and cleaning. I'm not riding any horses today. The stable is closed to clients at six tonight."

"And then?"

241

"I'll come get you. Annie's cooking, the rest of us are riding. That's the tradition."

It sounded simple and fun to Kate who had always been in such a dither over party plans that by the time the guests arrived all she wanted was an antacid and a nap. "I'll be waiting for you. It's going to be a long day."

"Yes it is, but tonight will be worth the wait."

Chapter Twenty-Four

He was right. They took the trail that wound through the woods near the farm. The silence was broken only by the crunch of crusted snow beneath hooves. It was a cold, clear night. Black silk spread above their heads. The Milky Way, a bottle of silver glitter, spilled across the expanse.

They rode for an hour and then put the horses away and joined Annie and Sergio in the house. Brandon poured himself a whiskey and, for Kate, a cup of hot tea.

"So, what do you think of the Sullivan traditional Christmas Eve ride?" He handed the cup to Kate.

"Aside from the fear that I'll never get warm again, it was beautiful. Thank you. Next year I'll be riding my very own horse." Assuming, of course, that there was still a Willow Creek, and that she and Brandon did follow through with their marriage plan.

The meal that Annie had prepared was perfect down to the last crumbs of Brandon's birthday cake. They were enjoying coffee in the living room when Laura came to her mother with a request from Sergio. "Mom, Cousin Sergio wants you to interpret for him. I guess he doesn't quite trust my Italian with the big question."

"What big question?" Good God, if he's going to propose to Annie, he can do it himself.

"You'll see. Get Brandon and bring him to the library. Sergio is waiting." Laura had a silly grin on her pretty face and it had Kate just a bit worried.

When Kate and Brandon entered the library, Sergio was standing at the window looking out at the night. Turning to face Bran, he had an expression Kate could only describe as a blend of trepidation and contentment. "Sergio, Laura said you wanted to say something to Brandon."

"*Yessa*, Anna is a helping me with a my *Inglese,* but I *ama* not so sure *yeta*." He struggled with the words.

Kate went ahead and spoke in the man's native tongue before he completely embarrassed himself trying to get it right in English. "That's all right, Sergio. Just tell me what you want to say to Brandon, and I'll put it in the right words."

When he explained his request, Kate thought it was so sweet she almost couldn't say the words to Brandon without starting to cry. "Sergio says he is happier than he has been in his entire life since meeting Annie. He is asking your permission to propose marriage to your sister."

Brandon was silent for what seemed like an eternity. Then he spoke, "Sergio, my sister has always given herself for others, first for the Church and then for me and my family. I would like nothing more than to see her happy. If you can give her the love she deserves, I will be pleased to call you brother." He offered his hand, but Sergio grabbed him by the shoulders and hugged him, kissing him on each side of Brandon's surprised face.

Kate had tears dribbling down her cheeks and her nose was running when they joined the others. Brandon turned to her and wiped a drip off her upper lip with his thumb. "This means we'll be related by marriage. I hope these are tears of joy."

"I...uh...just think...it's so sweet." She was smiling and choking back a sob. "What will you do when she moves to Italy?"

"I'm going to have to find a new accountant," he

half joked. "Who will keep me in line without my big sister to nag me day and night?" He turned again to the guests and raised his glass. "Sláinte."

Kate locked her eyes on his and spoke softly. "If you want your birthday present now, you have to take me back to my house."

"Oh, not a gift I can open in front of our family?" He raised one brow in query.

"You could, I suppose, but I left it in my bedroom."

"I'll get your coat."

Kate said goodnight after inviting everyone to the Aiello home for Christmas dinner. "You can meet my family. Bring ear protection and a big appetite."

Sergio was going home with Laura for a few days, to make room for the Aiello bunch at Kate's. Tonight was a rare chance to have the house all to herself and she wasn't going to waste the opportunity.

They were both shaking with anticipation when they parked the pickup in Kate's driveway. Brandon tapped the numbers out on the keyless lock with trembling fingers.

Kate's pulse was racing and she was slightly out of breath when they finally got up the stairs to her room. "Sit down and I'll get your present."

He grabbed her hand. "Where are you going?" He kissed her on the mouth and his hand slipped under her sweater. "This is the only gift I want from you."

"Well, too bad, because it's not what you're getting...yet." She handed him a flat box, gaily wrapped in birthday paper. "Go ahead and open it. We don't have all night."

"Okay, let's see what you got me." He removed the wrapping and tissue paper to reveal an original watercolor. It was one he had admired in an art store in Ballyvaughan. "Katie, this is perfect. I didn't know you even saw me looking at it." It was a simple scene, green hills, stone walls leading down to the sea, a flock of sheep on the road. "It reminded me of the picnic we had on the hill behind my house...the day you let me love you the first time."

"Me too. That's why I wanted you to have it." She took the painting from his hand and set it aside. Kate sat across his knees and put her arms around his neck. "Happy birthday, Brandon."

An hour later, Kate lay naked and warm, her cheek against his chest. "You need to go home," she murmured.

"I can't move...I've lost all willpower where you are concerned." Brandon combed his fingers through her curls. "Katie, marry me."

He was wearing her down. "I need more time."

"I want you in my bed...every night...not just when we can steal a moment here and there. And I love you. I want to be part of your life, not just looking in on it from the outside."

"Brandon..."

"Marry me New Year's Eve."

Kate raised up on her elbows and looked in Brandon's face. "I knew you were insane the day I met you. I should have run the other direction while I still had the chance." She hoped she wasn't making her decision based on her past mistakes, on loneliness or because her brain was shriveling from age. "Will you let me invest in Willow Creek?"

"Within certain limits...if I must."

"I don't know, Bran. What about the kids? Brighid seems suspicious of me. How do you think she'll handle it?"

"Leave Brighid and Kevin to me. You have Laura to explain to and maybe Frank. Your mother will be thrilled to know you're not headed for damnation and your other brothers...they just want you happy." He reached out and cupped her chin with his hand. "Kate, we don't have to please our children. They have their lives...we have ours."

How did this happen? All she wanted was riding lessons. The whole thing felt out of control, wild and crazy. Could she take this chance, this leap of faith?

"Yes. I'll marry you. On New Year's Eve."

****

It was past one A.M. when Brandon drove in to Willow Creek. The light was on in Brighid's room. Brandon tapped on the door. "Baby, are you still awake?"

"Yes, Da, come on in."

She was in bed, reading. She looked like he remembered her at about twelve years old, before she knew about grief and loss. Brandon sat on the edge of her bed. "It's nice to have you home. I miss you when you're away at school you know."

"It's good to be home. I had fun tonight. I've been thinking about it. That's why I can't sleep." She set her book aside. "Daddy, I like Kate. I'm sorry if I was skeptical at first."

"It's okay. I know you're looking out for your old da." He looked at her and saw Fiona. "Sweetheart, when your mam passed, I thought I could never be happy again. If I hadn't had you and Kevin to keep me grounded, my life would have spun off into oblivion."

"I know, Daddy. Sometimes I forget how hard it was, it still must be, for you."

"The kind of love I have for your mam, it's special and only she holds that place in my heart...forever. But, Brighid, I love Katie, too. She makes me laugh, gives me hope, let's me believe in my dreams."

"You mean you're in love with her? Like...for real?"

"Yeah, baby...like for real." Brandon brushed Brighid's hair back away from her eyes. "I have asked Katie to be my wife and she has said 'yes'. I hope you can, over time, come to love her, too."

"Wow, Da...if she really does make you happy...I'll do my best."

"I went to mam's grave and I talked to her." Brandon reached in his coat pocket. "I have something for you." He took her hand and put the ring in the palm, closing her fingers over it. "I believe she wants you to have this."

"Oh, Daddy...her wedding ring?" She put her hand to her chest. "Are you sure?"

"Yes, with all my heart."

"Da, I'd like to wear it." She held it up to the light and looked at it in wonder. "On my right hand. Is that okay?"

He took the ring from her and slipped it on her right ring finger.

"It's more than 'okay'. It's the right thing to do."

Chapter Twenty-Five

"*Buon Natale*, Catarina." Mamma squeezed Kate's cheeks between her hands and laid big smacking kisses on her face. "You look fabulous, Cara. You are in love. I can see it in you."

"*Buon Natale a te*, Mamma." She wasn't willing to confirm or deny her mother's speculation about the state of her heart, but it was a tickle to think someone noticed a difference in her.

Everyone else crowded around Kate, kissing, hugging, thanking her for hosting the party another year. Joey immediately asked where Brandon was. "Hey, you haven't broken up with him have you? I liked the guy." And the twins were eager to show Laura their new outfits and iPod accessories. The unremitting talk, laughter and noise had begun. There would be no respite until every Aiello was sated with holiday feasting and their jaws ached from speaking their mixture of *Abruzzese* and Hackensack dialect.

While everyone was distracted, Kate pulled Laura aside. "Come to the solarium for a few minutes. I want to talk to you about something."

"Sure, Mom, what's up?"

Kate had poured herself a glass of wine for courage. They sat. Kate sipped from her glass, took a deep breath and spoke as calmly as possible. "I...have decided to marry Brandon. New Year's Eve." She waved her hand in dismissal of the comments she was sure would come. "Don't bother to tell me I'm crazy. I already know that."

"Jesus...Momma! What are you thinking?"

"Now, Laura...hear me out. He makes me happy. He loves me...and...Oh, my God, I can't believe I'm telling you this. The sex is great."

"Mother! How much wine have you *had*?"

"It's not the wine."

"Okay, be reasonable. If you like his company...and all that...why not just live together? You don't have to *marry* him. This is the twenty-first century. People can have sex and not be married."

"Well, I know that. But, I can't. I can't sneak around and I can't lie to your Nonna. She'd drop stone cold dead if she thought I was living with a man outside of marriage. And what kind of example would we be to you and to Brandon's children."

"Mother, I'm not a virgin, you know."

"No! I didn't know, but..." Kate felt faint at the thought. How could she have been so naïve?

"And Brandon's kids, they're adults, too. You shouldn't commit yourself to something on the basis of being a good example to any of us."

"Laura, I'm going to do this. I want you to know that Brandon has insisted that I have a pre-nup that protects all my assets. If something happens to me, everything that I brought to the marriage goes directly to you. And..." It was hard to say the next words, but Kate had to be sensible. "If he should leave me, if we...divorce, I lose nothing... financially."

Laura shook her head. "I don't understand the whole thing."

Kate waited.

"Okay, Momma." Laura sighed in resignation. "But only if he makes you happy."

"He makes me feel alive. More alive than I have in years."

****

By the time Brandon and his family arrived everyone was in full party mode. Mark's girls were pounding out Christmas carols on the piano. Mamma Aiello was fussing about the food. Sergio looked uncommonly nervous, wouldn't remove his jacket and kept checking his inside pocket for the engagement ring he had there.

Maria had already collapsed on the sofa, looking unusually wan, worried and listless. Kate noticed that her sister-in-law hadn't eaten but a few crackers from the buffet table. Sitting down beside her, she asked, "Maria, can I get you a drink, some tea or a soda?" "Catarina, can we go somewhere quiet. If I don't talk to someone, I'm going to have a meltdown and it's not going to be pretty."

"Sure, come upstairs. No one will miss us for a few minutes."

By the time they got to Kate's room and shut the door, Maria was shaking with uncontrollable sobs. "Oh Kate, you won't believe what's happened. Oh, my God..."

"Hey, slow down, what's going on? Is it you and Mark? If my stupid ape of a brother hurt you, I'll kill him." Kate's first thought was divorce, but it would be so much out of Mark's character to do that to his family.

"No...oh...no, it's not Mark. He's a wonderful husband. Maybe too wonderful. Kate, I didn't think it could happen...I'm forty years old, for God's sake, my girls are practically grown..."

Even though Maria was making little sense, Kate feared she was getting the picture. She took a good look at the woman she had loved as a sister since Mark first brought her home to meet the family. Maria was a perfect counterpart for Mark's boisterous humor and he had loved her instantly and passionately. Apparently that had not changed over their twenty year marriage. "Maria, are you pregnant?"

The younger woman flopped face first onto

Kate's bed. "How could I have been so dumb?"

Kate didn't know whether to laugh or cry along with Maria. "Does Mark know?" She doubted it. Mark would be announcing it to anyone who was willing to listen and he would be overly solicitous toward his wife. "You haven't told him?"

"I just found out. Get this...I actually thought I was having menopausal symptoms. I missed a couple of periods before I started to feel a little nausea and my boobs started to tingle. Here I am almost three months along and I just figured it out. Damn, I feel so stupid. I got one of those home tests, it lit up brighter than my Christmas tree!" She was starting to get control of her hysterics. Kate handed her a box of tissues.

"Listen, Mark's going to be thrilled. You need to tell him."

"What about the twins? They're going to be completely shocked."

"Well, I guess when you're sixteen the last thing you want to know is that your parents still do 'it', but they'll adjust. Look at it this way; in two years they'll be off to college, you won't have an empty nest."

"No, I'll have a toddler. *Jesus Christ*, a toddler."

"If I go downstairs right now and send Mark up here, will you tell him?"

"Oh...okay, but I need to wash my face, and Kate can I borrow some blush and lip gloss. I don't want to look like a schlumph."

"Yes, of course, but obviously my brother still finds you attractive or you wouldn't be in your current state." She hugged Maria and showed her where the makeup was. "I'll send him up in ten. Don't worry, everything is going to be better than you think."

Brandon was looking for Kate when she descended the stairs. "I've been searching for you."

"Have you now? I've been consoling my sister-in-law." Kate slipped her hand into his.

"Consoling? Is something wrong?"

"No, just surprising. Come with me." They walked into the kitchen where Mark was entertaining Kevin with tales of cops and robbers—Hackensack style. "Hey, sorry to interrupt your crime education, but Mark, Maria needs you for a minute. She's upstairs in my room."

"Oh, sure sis. Is she okay?" A look of loving concern crossed his face.

"She's fine. Just has a little Christmas gift for you. It's personal."

His expression changed from concern to delight and it occurred to Kate that he probably thought he was getting a pre-gift exchange quickie. She momentarily thought of offering him a shot of *grappa* before he joined his wife, but reconsidered. He should be sober for this news.

Mark strode off toward the stairs and Brandon turned to Kate. "A little present, huh. And am I getting one, too?"

"Brandon, believe me when I tell you that under no uncertain terms are you getting anything like what my brother is about to get."

"Now I'm curious. Would you like to find a nice quiet place and tell me all about it?" His hand surreptitiously slid down her back to the place just below her waistline that he knew was especially sensitive to his touch.

"Maybe, when the rest of the family has slipped off into a well-fed coma. Right now, we need to gather everyone together and do the traditional toasts, and then we'll have presents."

"You sound like you have this all well-orchestrated. I have an announcement and toast of my own, and I'm ready." He grinned that killer grin of his and Kate felt her pulse quicken. *Damn, it's hard to keep my hands off him.*

They gathered near the Christmas tree. Kate made sure everyone had champagne or sparkling grape juice. It was a remarkable sight, the Aiellos and the Sullivans. Mark stood with his arm around Maria, a ridiculous smile of manly pride on his handsome face. Maria looked vastly relieved and, if not happy, at least content for the moment. Sergio, his hand resting lightly on Annie's shoulder, looked down at her upturned face with blatant adoration.

Brighid had taken a liking to Silvana and the two stood together, Silvana leaning possessively on the young girl's arm. The twins thought Kevin was just too 'hot' and wouldn't leave him alone. They had him surrounded, giggling, nearly spilling their grape juice. Barb came and stood next to Kate. "I think I've lost my fiancé to a couple of sixteen-year-olds," she whispered.

Joey raised his glass to Kate from his place across the room. "To my big sister, thank you for having us all, *Buon Natale. Cin cin.*"

They all drank and Kate felt Brandon squeeze her hand. "I'm gonna do this now before I lose my nerve." He lifted his champagne glass and turned to Sergio and Annie. "I have the honor of making an announcement. Sergio Di Benedetto has asked for my sister's hand in marriage and Ann Caitilín Bhriain Sullivan has accepted.

Sergio...*Sláinte fo saol agat, bean ar do mhian agat, is solas na bhflaitheas tareis antsail seo agat.* Health for life to you, a wife of your choice to you, land without rent to you and the light of heaven after this world for you. *Sláinte.*"

There were hoots and calls of *sláinte, cin cin, salute*! Every one rushed over and hugged and kissed the couple saying, "Congratulations," "what a surprise," "*auguri*," "*O Dio*," and "good luck."

Kevin shouted above the din, "*Nollaig shona*

duit, Happy Christmas." The twins giggled and begged him to teach them the Irish words.

Brandon turned to Kate, "*Tá mo chroí istigh ionat.*"

"Would you mind translating?" It was such a strange language, lyrical and ancient sounding.

"My heart is within you."

He kissed her lightly and waved Kevin over. "Fill everyone's glasses again, I have another announcement."

Kate sipped her champagne and leaned into his warmth. *This is it,* she thought. *Too late to change my mind, even if I wanted to.*

He raised his glass, looked down at Kate, tightening his grip on her hand and spoke. "Now that I have everyone's attention." He took a deep breath that seemed more like a silent prayer. "Katie and I have set a date for our marriage. We will be wed on New Year's Eve." And, then, Brandon Sullivan embraced Kate Aiello and kissed her, bearing witness to the fact that he meant to make her his.

When he released her mouth she was wobbling so badly he had to hold her to keep her from falling. The room receded, and voices were muted into background noise. All Kate could see were dark blue eyes, all she could hear was a heart beating. Was it hers? She wasn't sure. His hand burned into her back between her shoulder blades. The heat of it passed through her chest and melted her fears, denials, reservations and doubts into a mist. For that one moment in time she felt a rush of love so all-consuming it would be despoiled by nothing in this realm.

Mamma was overcome with joy at the thought that her Catarina would wed the Irlandese. Kevin and Barb shared knowing glances over the announcement. Brighid was quiet and serious, but hugged her father and Kate, wishing them well. Kate's brothers were typically slap happy and shared a round or two of Jameson with their new *cognato*.

All said and done, it was beyond any doubt the best Christmas of Kate's lifetime. And to add to the glory of it was the fact that Kate had not lost weeks of her life preparing for it. She actually enjoyed her own party. Everyone offered to help clean up and she just sat back and let them do it. If the china didn't end up in the right cupboards, if the glassware was spotted, and the silver upside down in the dishwasher, so what? She hadn't suffered one holiday blowup or even a minor meltdown.

Chapter Twenty-Six

The last week of the year brought a new level of work. It was physical and relentless for Brandon. He never complained, but Kate often saw the exhaustion in his face at the end of a long day. He trained horses and riders from dawn to late in the evening, and though Kate was at Willow Creek every day, she felt like they spent precious little time together.

This was his real life, not a vacation or a holiday, and she was beginning to gain an appreciation for just how much effort it would take to make Willow Creek profitable.

She had just finished riding Murphy and putting him in his stall when Kate heard Brandon's unmistakable footsteps on the pavement of the barn aisle. "I'm looking for a woman I used to know. Her name is Katie." He opened the stall door and shut it behind him. "There she is. Come here, I have something for you." He pulled her toward him and kissed her. "Damn, I've been missing you. Let's leave this place to the kids and go back to Ireland where I can cuddle with you all day without interruption."

"Are you almost done for the day?"

"Yes, that's why I came lookin' for you. I have a proposition. Let me take you out to dinner and we can hide out at your house tonight."

"That sounds nice, but Sergio is back from Hackensack, so we won't be alone. I'm sorry."

"The pain of being responsible working adults," Bran moaned melodramatically. "Then it's dinner and you can stay at my house tonight. Kevin and

Brighid are back in school and my sister's not known to be a light sleeper."

"You're tempting me beyond my ability to resist. I've got to admit, I had no idea how hard you work." Kate removed her gloves and slipped her hands under his jacket and sweater. He was warm and it made her tingle clear to her toes to touch his skin.

He shivered and groaned, taking her mouth gently with his lips and plying her with feathery kisses. "I've wanted you so, but I've been too tired by the end of the day to even get off with a fantasy. How's that for pitiful?" His hand caressed her backside. "I want to be with you, see if I can still get the old boy-o to perform." He pressed her close.

"I would venture to guess that 'the old boy-o', as you like to call that part of your anatomy, will perform with perfection if we just give it a chance." Her fingers slid over the front of his breeches, just to be sure she was having the desired effect. "Apparently, you're not all that tired right now." She turned and gave Murphy a pat on the neck. "See you later, handsome."

"Do you have a change of clothes with you? Not that I mind going out with you in your britches, but I might not like the way the other men ogle you."

"I have jeans and a sweater, but I didn't plan on a sleepover...no flannel pj's."

"There is a God." They walked, hand in hand out of the barn. "What do you want for supper?"

****

In the stall adjacent to Murphy's, Brenda Weeks stood silently eavesdropping on the conversation between Bran and Kate. Anger and jealousy welled up in her like nausea, burning in her throat. Brenda did not understand what the attraction was, why Brandon Sullivan would shackle himself to this Aiello woman. It was probably just one of the many flings he had indulged in. The man was shameless.

Even before his poor wife was in her grave, Sullivan had been flirting with the barn help.

And Kate, she had no idea of what she was getting herself into. Brenda's first marriage had been to a professional rider on the hunter circuit. He was arrogant and single-minded, but not as focused on fame as Brandon. Kate would have one big rude awakening when she discovered she couldn't compete with the thrill of winning. Kate Aiello would always be a poor second place. This Brenda had learned the hard way.

****

Brandon had no appetite for anything but being with Kate. Food, at this point, was simply sustenance to satisfy his body until he could fill himself with this woman. He watched her as she ate and talked about Sam. She was a constant joy of animation, her face and hands a symphony of expression.

"Brandon, I just love him. Waiting for him to arrive here and knowing he's safe is just killing me. I want to continue learning to jump. I feel safe with Sam, like he wouldn't let me get hurt. That's probably foolish, I know, but that's how it feels." She stopped and looked at him, just now noticing how he was watching her. "What? You think I'm crazy, don't you?"

"I think you're perfect, and, yes, a little crazy. Other women would be planning the wedding. Are you done?"

"Done? Talking about my horse?" She looked a bit piqued at the inference.

"No. Done with your salmon?" he said with a slow smile. "You can talk about that horse of yours as much as you like. You deserve to be excited about him."

"Oh, yes...do you want to go?"

"It's been a long day. A very long and rather

259

lonely day. I don't know if I have the self- control to keep my hands to myself much longer and what I want to do with them might be quite inappropriate in a public place." He reached across the table and played his fingers over her outstretched palm.

"Well, when you put it that way...by all means, let's get out of here." She stood and he helped her with her coat. "When we get back to the house I need to make a call to Laura, just to check in. She's making the plans for New Year's Eve."

They drove the short distance to Willow Creek, chatting, catching up on the family news that they had not had time to share, Brandon hoping Annie had retired to her room for the evening. With relief, he noticed that her bedroom, which was downstairs adjacent to his office, was illuminated by lamplight, a sure sign that his sister was awake reading, prior to going to sleep for the night.

Brandon slept in the largest of the three bedrooms on the upper level of the old farmhouse. The floorboards creaked and the walls were paper thin, the bath was shared by all, but tonight he and Kate would be blissfully alone. "Do you want anything from the kitchen before we go upstairs?" he asked her.

"No, go ahead and get comfortable, I'll be right up after I talk to Laura." Kate ran her hand along Brandon's cheek. "You might want to shave. I intend to do some serious kissing on that face of yours."

"Your wish is my command." His lips brushed hers. "Don't be long." He left her to her phone call.

Kate called Laura's apartment, but the message machine came on. Deciding not to leave a voice message she went ahead and called her cell.

"This is Laura." The voice of her daughter brightened the other end of the line.

"Hi, sweety, this is your mom."

"Oh, Mom. Gosh...I didn't expect you to call.

Wow...what are you up to?"

Kate thought Laura sounded odd. Something about the tone of her voice set Kate to worrying. "Brandon and I just got back from dinner. How are the plans coming? Have you talked to Frank?"

"Sure, uh...everything is perfect...look, Mom, I can't really talk right now. Can I call you back?

Why was she being evasive? Kate's motherly instinct kicked in and she was not letting this call end until she was satisfied that all was well. "What's going on, Laura? You sound like something is wrong."

"I'm at the hospital...but..."

"You're where? Laura, for God's sake, are you sick, hurt, what?" Kate's heart rate accelerated.

"No...Mom...it's not me. I, well, I didn't want to say anything. Daddy's wife just gave birth to a baby boy."

A bolt of pain pierced Kate's head. She thought she had been struck by ball lightning. When she spoke, it took great restraint to keep from screaming. "Oh, okay, give them my regards, will you? I should go...we...I was just headed to bed...it's late." Kate couldn't think of her next words, language was failing her, she was forgetting how to breathe and felt she was about to vomit.

"I know this is hard for you, Mom, but please understand. I'm excited. I have a brother."

Kate could barely hear for the tinnitus that had started in her head; blackness was stealing her peripheral vision. Laura sounded happy and Kate wanted to be joyous for her daughter, but the pain in Kate's gut was trying to destroy her. "Good night, sweetheart. I'll talk to you again soon." She did not wait for her Laura's reply. She closed the phone and silently, as if swept into a trance, treaded the stairs.

"Katie, what's happened?" Brandon reached for her, but she shrank from him. "Sweetheart, please, tell me what's wrong."

Kate wanted to be alone, she wanted to go home, to her room, close the door and scream until the demons scattered from dread. She did not want to have to explain herself to anyone, even Brandon. "I need to be alone." Not wanting to alarm him, she added "No one's sick or hurt, nothing is...wrong, really."

She simply could not move. *Get a grip, this is not unexpected...you knew it was happening.* Was it Laura's reaction that hurt so? Or the last moment of closure, the fruition of Jeffrey's betrayal.

"Please, Katie, try not to shut me out." His arm encircled her. "Let me hold you."

Her shoulders started to shake with uncontrollable sobs. "I can't...right now." Kate wanted to trust Brandon to make the throbbing ache go away, to let him possess her flesh and blot out the last ten minutes. But the romance of the moment had been crushed. She had been ripped through a wormhole back to bleak reality.

"I am not leaving you to cry alone. Tell me what's happened." He pushed her hair off her face and studied her eyes.

The embarrassment was excruciating. Kate felt selfish, mean, and bitter. "Jeffrey's new wife just succeeded in giving my daughter something he would not allow me to give her...a baby brother." It was irrational, but Kate started to laugh. Hysteria was so close to the surface it threatened to well up and snatch her soul, tearing it to pieces and feeding it to the monsters in her nightmare.

He held her, let her sob, scream, beat on his chest and claw at him in desperation, a substitute for the bastard who had used her so cruelly and thrown her away.

When she ran out of tears, when her throat was raw and her voice a whisper, he continued to hold her, stroking her hair. They lay down on the bed and he held her close, speaking to her in Irish. He could have been telling her of an ancient legend, the lyrics of a bawdy song or simply babbling nonsense, she did not care; his voice was soothing as a lullaby.

"I don't want to be hateful. I'm not like that." Kate spoke so quietly it was like hearing only her thoughts. "It's just that...I wanted another child. For years I would cry myself to sleep. He either never noticed or simply did not care." Dry, wracking sobs shook her again. "I had my tubes tied. I didn't want to. I did it to make Jeffrey happy."

Brandon kissed the top of her head. "I'm sorry, so terribly sorry."

"I hated myself for it. Now, I just want to hate him, but I can't even make myself do that."

Brandon held her until she calmed. He stood to remove his clothes and she stirred. He lay back down beside her. "Katie, let me make love to you," he whispered against her soft curls.

Kate knew he could make her forget the pain. She wanted him to erase every smudge of anger and resentment that had ever marked her. But she did not want to give herself to him, not tonight, not with Jeffrey so close to the surface of her being. "I...I don't know. I'm not sure I can be completely in the moment." God, she hated to disappoint him. He had waited, been patient, kind and loving. She knew he would not force her. "Uh...well...okay." Rolling toward him she pulled him to her.

He propped himself up on one elbow. "Okay?" he said in disbelief. "Okay?" He sat up on the side of the bed. "Kate, 'okay' isn't enough for me. What do you mean? You'll consent to have sex with me, but don't expect that you'll actually be 'in the moment'? Whatever the hell that means."

"That's not what I meant. I just...well...don't exactly feel in the mood, but I don't want to disappoint you." *And make you mad and have you go looking elsewhere for comfort.* "I'm sorry. Of course, I want to be with you. Come back to bed."

"Katie, that's not good enough for me. Don't you see? You'd have me, because you don't want to disappoint me, not because you love me, not because you need me to be part of you. I want more than your body, I want *you*." He ran his hand through his hair in a gesture of frustration. Bran started to reach for her, but snapping his hand away, grabbed his clothes and headed for the door.

"Brandon, can't we just talk about it?" Kate begged.

"No. I know you've been through a lot. I'm trying to understand. I just need to be able to think and I can't while I'm in the same bed with you. I'll be downstairs." He closed the door and she heard the footfalls of his stocking feet until the sound vanished, to be replaced by silence and the sting of her tears staining the pillow of Brandon's bed.

The darkness closed in on Kate like a shroud of blackest wool, a cover so thick she could not find her way through it, even to tarry into oblivious sleep. Hurting Brandon was unthinkable. Now she had done it. She had tried to promise him that she would not let Jeffrey divide them, but there the scoundrel was. She had invited him in and he was settled into the bed between Kate and Brandon, like a houseguest who wouldn't take a hint and vacate the premises.

Kate sat on the side of the bed willing her legs to support her and carry her to Brandon to give him the one part of her she had denied him. Giving him her body had been easy, a mutual gift they had shared with abandon. Vowing her love for him—lowering that last bastion of her defenses and letting him in to rend her in two if he chose, leaving herself open to complete destruction with no paths left for escape—for this she had not been brave enough.

The office door was ajar. One light on the desk illuminated the recumbent form, slumped onto the sofa with legs dangling off onto the floor. Kate stepped softly toward him, her vulnerability bared. She knelt and put her hand on his arm. "Bran, I need to tell you something." She wasn't sure if she said this out loud or imagined it.

He opened his eyes and reached his hand to touch her face. "You don't need to, *muirnín.*"

She wasn't sure he was fully awake. "No, I want to. But, I'm so afraid."

Brandon lifted her into his arms as he sat up on the sofa. "You don't have to be afraid of me." He stroked her hair. "What do you want to tell me?"

"I, oh Bran, I...I love you so much." She pressed her face into his warm chest for a moment, letting the feeling of the words she had uttered penetrate every cell of her body and mind.

He lifted her face by one gentle finger under her quivering chin. "Look at me." The love in his face was beyond any words he could speak.

"I love you, Bran Sullivan. God help me, I love you," she repeated, her dark eyes locked on his. She held onto him as though he were a life ring tossed into the current that threatened to suck her under its murky waves. She drank in his warmth like a potion to bring magic into her life.

He kissed her lips, her ears, eyes and neck and when she reciprocated, his face was streaked with salty moisture. Whether the tears were his or hers made little difference. The silky wetness was a shared testimony, a silent prayer of thanks.

****

The morning light wove ribbons of gold across the floor of the room where Brandon and Kate lay tangled together on the sofa. An observer might have had trouble discerning which appendages belonged to which lover and where he ended and she began. Her tousled chestnut locks splayed over his cheek and her face was nuzzled securely under his chin. Brandon had a long leg tucked around her hip, preventing her from tumbling from their precarious nest and his right hand was cupped over her left breast.

They had talked and kissed, touched and explored, but had not breached their clothing. There would be plenty of times for hot, naked sex; this had not been one of them.

"Bran, I need to get up, but if I move we'll both fall off the sofa," she said, whispering into his neck and kissing him there, just for good measure.

He managed to sit up, holding her and not spilling them both onto the floor. There was a tap on the door a second before Annie walked in.

"Brandon, what are you doin' sleepin' on the...Oh, Katie, you're here early." As if a light bulb popped on in her head, she smiled. "My dears, come have some tea. You both look like you need it." She retreated and left them to sort themselves out.

"I'm gonna go pee, and I'll meet you in the kitchen. Do you have a spare toothbrush?" Kate stood and stretched to work out the muscle stiffness that came of sleeping wrapped up in a man.

"Not a spare, but you're welcome to use mine." Bran ran his hand over his chin. "I've no horses to ride today, other than my own. Do you want to have a lesson? A very private lesson?"

"You mean on a horse? Because I'm sure there are a couple of other things you could teach me...and we wouldn't have to leave the house."

"I meant on the horse, but I have all day." He rumpled her already disheveled mass of curls and patted her on the bum. "Go freshen up. I'll see you in the kitchen."

Chapter Twenty-Seven

Kate had demanded a quiet, simple saying of vows at Brandon's house, in the front parlor, with Frank to officiate. That is not exactly what she got. If anything could ever be said of the Aiellos and the Sullivans it was that they knew how to throw a party. The result of Laura's planning was an Italian *Festa*, Irish *Ceilidh* and New Year's Eve bash to be remembered. Kate taught Brandon to dance the *Tarantella*, a tradition at Italian weddings, and he tried to teach her enough words to give a toast in Irish. They all ate, drank, sang songs both romantic and bawdy in Italian and Irish and danced until the light of dawn turned the old year into a new day.

The newlyweds dragged themselves up the stairs to the bedroom they would share, flopped onto the bed and fell asleep fully clothed. When Kate awoke, Brandon was sprawled on his back, arms outstretched and snoring like a chain saw. "Wake up, Sullivan. If I'd known you were a snorer, I might not have married you." She rolled onto his chest and gave him a kiss.

"I don't snore. You must have been dreaming." His arms closed around her. "I think we should consummate this marriage as soon as possible, so you can't back out." He started to unzip her dress.

"And you think we're in any condition to do that just now? I'd like a cappuccino and, no offense, but you need a shower."

"Saints preserve us. You try to make a woman happy and all she does is complain." Brandon reached for her, tracing the line of her cheek with

267

his fingers. "I've married the most beautiful woman on the planet. Did you really promise to love me forever, or was I dreaming?"

"You weren't dreaming. *Ti adoro, mio marito.*" I love you, my husband.

****

The horses arrived just after the first of the year. For Kate, it was nothing short of heaven. Sam was fat and healthy, none the worse for the long flight or the quarantine. When the van arrived at Willow Creek, she was there to meet it.

Kevin had not told Barb about Beltaine, so he took her away for the day, but there was no keeping a secret like the big bay for long. Kev put a fancy white lace ribbon fit for a bride on the stall, made his lady close her eyes and walked her down the stable aisle. She opened her eyes and screamed, then cried, kissing the man, the horse and anyone else within reach.

Calypso had lost some weight during the trip. It was not unusual, Brandon explained to Kate. Thoroughbreds were often hard keepers, meaning they didn't keep their weight on easily.

"Your boy Sam, on the other hand, will outlive any horse in a hay shortage."

"Sorry to muddle up your day, Bran, but Brenda Weeks called and she wants to do a pick up lesson for the one she missed over Christmas," Annie said as she joined the couple in the kitchen for breakfast.

"When?" He wasn't particularly fond of Brenda, but he had told her he would let her make up the lesson, so he was going to try to be pleasant about it.

"She wants to do it today, at eleven. If you can't, you can call and tell her." Annie didn't like getting between Brandon and his students.

"Damn, I was looking forward to a day with my new wife. Katie, do you mind sharing a jump lesson with Brenda? I'll keep the fences small; we can run through some gymnastics." He was sorely tempted to lick the smidgen of jam off her bottom lip.

"Sure, that'll be fine with me, but will Brenda mind? I don't think she particularly likes to share you."

"Well, today she isn't getting a choice." He had always felt somewhat uncomfortable around Brenda. She was an average rider and had a good horse who would jump just about anything, but Brenda was openly seductive toward Bran. She tended to get into his personal space, touch him on the arm or brush past him so that her body glanced off his. It only made him avoid her. "I'll help you get Sam ready. It'll be fun."

"I'm ready for anything you have to throw at me, Mr. Sullivan," she replied with a smile that made him want to rip her clothes off and have her right there in the kitchen.

****

He wouldn't throw anything at her that he wasn't completely confident Kate and Samhain could handle. Brandon set the cross rails low to start and had them trotting over them easily before he raised them to just above two feet. Brenda and her horse, Bear, had competed at novice level. She was openly annoyed at having to jump lower than she thought she should because Kate was such a beginner. She didn't say anything because she knew Brandon would simply tell her to use the opportunity to improve her technique.

"Katie, that last one was grand. Come on through again." He raised the back rail of the oxer she was about to approach. "Nice steady trot now, heels down; grab some mane over the fence." He watched the pair as they arched over the barrier. "He can take a break now. Brenda, canter Bear to the red and white, circle and come to this oxer. Watch his pace now, you need a steady canter. Don't worry about where he takes off, let him make his choice, and you just go with him."

She took the first fence beautifully, but then pulled on the reins to slow her horse before the next. He put in an extra stride and jumped too close to the base of the oxer. It was as ungraceful as it was dangerous.

Bran grimaced. "I said, leave him be. You're gettin' in his way. He has a good sense of findin' a spot if you let him."

"He was going too fast," Brenda whined. "He'll take a huge spot and leave me behind."

"If you know better than I what to do, what are ya payin' me for, Brenda?" He raised the oxer one more hole on the jump standard. "Now, come around again. Stay out of his way. Let him take the big spot if he needs to." She did as she was told, but did not look pleased. "Now, was that better?"

"Yes, but it isn't like that every time."

"Not every fence needs to be pretty, but remember the pretty ones are also the safe ones, for you and your horse." He turned to Kate. "You two come and canter the oxer. Same as before. Just go with him, grab a hunk of mane."

They continued like this for nearly an hour. Kate was having a blast and Sam would have had a silly grin on his face had it been possible. Brenda stopped whining, but her face was grim. Brandon didn't care. The woman paid for his help and expertise, not his praise. "Great job, all of you. Brenda, are you going to the horse trials at Southern Pines?"

"I'm planning on it. I want to ride Novice. Are you coming to coach me?" She gave him one of her most seductive smiles and Brandon cringed.

"I'll be there. Get your entry in on the opening date or you'll never get in," he warned.

"Of course," she said as she headed back to the

barn.

Bran turned to Kate and put his hand on her thigh. "You looked fabulous. I was afraid to say much with Brenda around, she's the jealous type, but you and Sam are quite the perfect pair. I think you could do a Beginner Novice course with no problem."

"Oh, Brandon, do you think so? I just can't imagine...competing."

"It's not a requirement, but you might find it fun and, don't quote me, but I understand a good cross-country run can be near orgasmic." His hand slid from her thigh to her hip.

"Oh, and who told you that, if you don't mind my asking?"

"Ah...yes...well, common knowledge, you might say. If I were a man of less self-confidence I might be quite emasculated by the idea that a woman could be so moved by a good ride...on a horse."

"And what will you do if I find the sport all that stimulating? I mean, look at this big, hot beast between my thighs? Can your male ego stand up to this?"

"Katie, let's go put your horse away." He encircled her waist and lifted her off Sam's back. "We have the rest of the day to ourselves and I happen to know that my sister and your cousin are going to the museum this afternoon. They plan to be gone several hours. You can make all the noise you want."

"Are you saying I'm noisy?" Kate's gloved hand reached under his sweater.

"Only enough to wake the ghosts in that old farmhouse and make them moan with jealousy." He was aroused at the thought of how she cried out when he was inside her, taking her to the height of ecstasy and falling together in a dance older than humankind.

Chapter Twenty-Eight

Kate and Brandon tried to be tactful around the stable, lest they offend their clients. They stole moments like two young lovers forbidden to touch. His hand would slide past her hip in the barn aisle. Her breath would tickle his neck as he sat in the office perusing the day's schedule. He'd try to concentrate on a lesson he was giving and then would hear her little squeal of joy when she landed her horse after a fence—the same sound she also made when Bran's body entered hers—and all his focus would be blinded.

Each secret tryst, every clandestine meeting, all the furtive touches would be consummated in the nights when they could finally be alone. He would kiss every inch of her flesh that he bared as he stripped her riding breeches, shirt, and socks from her.

Kate trembled as he licked her ankles and his tongue traced a path up her calf to her inner thigh. He nibbled his way across her pelvis, tasted the piquant flesh that stretched over her belly and pressed his lips to her mouth to drink in the salty sweetness of her. He would let her slip off the edge of oblivion, settle for a moment and raise her again to her peak until she was soft and pliable, her barriers melted by his touch. He would bury himself in her silky center and they would come together, crying out in words translated by their joined hearts.

It took trust, but she did finally start to tell him what she liked. Little hints at first—'touch me here, kiss me there,'—and then boldly, 'let me come with your fingers in me first, then I want you deep and hard.' No matter what she said, he was never shocked, embarrassed or hesitant. This was between them; her secrets were safe. She even told him about Antonio Banderas, the rubber ducky and why she missed the jetted tub in the bathroom of her house.

"You know, Brandon, when I was a little girl and I first learned what men and women do, I was horrified. I thought I would never be able to let a boy, a man, even *see* my naked body, let alone enter it with such intimacy. I don't know if young women think that way now, but for me, for my generation, that was a *huge* step. Now lying here in your arms feels so natural, so right."

Sometimes all they did was lie in bed and talk, sharing their day, before falling into exhausted rest. A few times Brandon was so knackered from long hours of teaching and riding, he was interested in sex but admitted the boy-o had a mind to take a hike and come back stronger another day. Kate laughed inside, but tried to look sympathetic. But, after holding him naked in her arms, she would notice his wayward member would gradually come to life. "Hmm, another world heard from. So much for a night of just cuddling." And he would pierce her to the hilt of him until she cried out for his release into her depth.

****

"So, Brenda, are you going to Southern Pines?" Marsha's voice could be heard over the sound of water running in the wash stall where Brenda Weeks was hosing Bear's legs.

"You bet I am. I actually have a chance of winning if I can keep Brandon focused on helping me."

"What are you talking about? He's not riding."

"Oh my God, get a clue, Marsha. The man is trying so hard to impress Mrs. Moneybags, he hasn't given any other students their fair share since November."

"You mean Kate? You think he only married her for her money?" Marsha said. "No way...you can't...possibly think...oh, Brenda. He wouldn't do that...would he?"

"Look, it's obvious. He meets her right after her divorce. She's vulnerable. Everyone knows she has big bucks from her ex. I heard she sold her house for over a million."

Kate had been trying not to listen to what she thought of as the rantings of the jealously insane, but what Brenda was concluding cut into Kate's gut. She stood in Sammy's stall and leaned her cheek into his warm shoulder, letting a wave of nausea wash over her. Brandon wasn't that kind of man. He had not wanted any of her money. She had practically pushed it on him. *Ridiculous*, she told herself, and she would not insult the man she loved by bringing it up. She was so deep in this uncomfortable thinking she did not hear Brandon until he spoke.

"At least I always know where to find you." He leaned over the stall door.

Kate turned around but did not meet his gaze. "I was just putting him away and I was going to go up to the house and...uh...I'll start some water for pasta." The sting of burgeoning tears threatened to undo her.

Brandon stepped into the stall. "Are those tears I see, Katie? What's troubling you?" He brushed her hair away from her face and held her chin in his hand. "Talk to me," he whispered.

Kate brushed his hand away. "It's nothing. Just a hot flash. Please, I'm fine."

"If you say so, but I've not known the flashes to cause you tears."

"Well, get used to it." She turned back to run a

brush over Sam's coat. "I'm sorry, Brandon, it's just making me emotional and grumpy. It'll pass...in a few years," she groaned in resignation. Turning back to him, she reached for his hand. "I'll go make you a nice lunch."

Walking toward the house, Kate wanted to smack her own ears. *Don't let those stupid gossiping bitches ruin your day.* She fought the urge to confront Brandon with Brenda's cruel words, but it was the eight hundred pound gorilla in the room—hard to ignore.

As she bent to the task of boiling a pot of water, choosing pasta and preparing a *soffritto*, she tried to focus on the domestic venture, mentally thanking her mother for teaching her to cook. Her pulse sped up and she knew she was sweating. The now-familiar prickling sensation in her face forced her to steady herself against the kitchen counter. The buzzing in her ears blotted out the creaking of the door and Brandon's footsteps.

"Oh my God, Katie, what's happened?" His arms encircled her and eased her into a chair. "You're pale as a ghost." He filled a glass with water and knelt beside her. "You're scaring me. I want you to see your doctor."

Kate waved him off with a flick of her hand. "Please don't be worried. This isn't anything unexpected." Tears threatened and she choked them back.

"Here, I want you to just sit here and let me take care of you." He returned to the sink and dampened a tea towel. "Let me see you." He mopped her face and cooled the back of her neck.

"Bran, I'm all right, I was just making pasta. The *soffritto* will scorch." She tried to get up, but he put his hand on her shoulder.

"I am perfectly capable of stirring your sauce. Just stay put...for me."

Kate was nearly paralyzed, not only with her temperature change but with self-hatred. She had allowed herself to doubt the man she loved, the man she wanted most in the world to trust. Bran loved her.

He served the pasta and made a small salad for them. Kate picked at her food, watching him, trying to ferret out any reason to question his sincerity. She found none. "Kate, are you not well enough to eat? Let me get you something else. How about a glass of juice?"

"Brandon, stop being so nice to me. You're making me feel guilty as hell."

"I can't stop. I like being nice to you. Would you prefer I knock you around a bit?" He tilted his head to catch her eye. "Besides, you deserve to be treated well. You've spent your life making others happy. If you're a little grumpy, I can take it...as long as you love me."

"You know I love you. Maybe too much." She finally couldn't stop herself from smiling back at him. He was irresistible.

Chapter Twenty-Nine

Red and white flags waved gaily from the jump standards and the parking lot was full of horse trailers of every description. Brandon had barely stepped out of the truck before being assailed by persons of every size, age, shape and gender. The characteristics they all had in common were the breeches, boots and baseball caps they wore and the smell of horseflesh on each one's person.

"Hey, Sullivan, good to see ya...are you riding or just coaching...how many students did you bring? Who's the babe with the cute draft horse? Rumor is you got married." The men smacked him on the back and the women hugged him shamelessly, some not stopping until they got a kiss on the cheek.

Kate led Samhain to his stall and spread fresh shavings for him. She filled his water bucket and threw him some of the hay they had brought from home. He was his usual overly-calm self, munching away at his horsey lunch and completely oblivious to the fact that he would soon be the center of attention.

Kate was not so calm. She had ridden her dressage test over in her head until it was branded onto her memory forever—twenty meter circles rolling around in her brain at the walk, trot and canter. She memorized the section of the rule book pertaining to her division, not wanting to flub up and be disqualified for some dumb infraction.

She had glanced at the cross-country course on the drive in and Brandon had said he would walk it with her this evening. He would point out the approach to each fence and the best way to jump every barrier. "Don't worry over it much," he had told her. "Just keep a steady pace and Sam will do the rest. This is nothing new for him. You tell him which way to go, he'll take care of you." Kate believed this to be true, but she still had whirligigs in her gut at the thought of being in the start box for the first time.

She was sitting on a bale of hay outside Sammy's stall, browsing through the prize list and pondering her fate, when Brenda Weeks strolled by and pulled up a lawn chair. "Oh, Brenda, I was daydreaming. I didn't even hear you," Kate lied. She had seen and heard Brenda, but wished her away. It didn't work...the wishing.

"So what do you think so far? Brandon is certainly the popular guy at these things."

"I guess so. He seems to know everyone, anyway. Are you going to walk the course later?" Kate didn't really give a rat's ass, but was trying to be polite. She didn't trust Brenda or like her much.

"Brandon will walk it with all of us. That's what we pay him for...those of us who still have to pay."

That stung and Kate wanted to sting back, but did not think getting into a cat fight with Ms. Weeks would help Brandon or herself. "I'm excited. Sammy competed in Ireland, but I've never even dreamed of this myself."

"Sam's a packer. That's what we call a horse like him. He'll pack his rider around the course and make you look like you know what you're doing."

Another barb from Brenda's quiver. *Does the woman even know how insulting that sounded?*

"I may be out of line here, Kate, but, woman to woman, I've just got to say it." She spoke in a conspiratorial manner, like she was only here to help the poor, easily deceived Kate out of certain heartache. "Brandon...gets around. I mean, he has an eye for good horseflesh and pretty women. He has been known to...well...use women who seem needy."

"What exactly are you saying, Brenda? You think he's taking advantage of my 'neediness'? He's my husband. We take care of each other." Kate tried to keep her tone even, but her blood was beginning to boil.

"Look, it's none of my business, but it's no secret that you had an ugly divorce and that you have plenty of cash to spend. I'm just saying he might take advantage of those facts."

Kate wasn't worried about her blood scalding because it had already boiled over. She had never been skilled at the instant and biting comeback, she left that to women who needed it, but she did have a hair trigger when it came to defending those she loved.

"You'd best be careful, Brenda, someone might just think you're jealous of what I have...be it horse or man. I won't be discussing your comments with Brandon. He has enough to think about this weekend and I am pretty sure you'd like his help to prepare yourself for this competition. But, if you have a mind to set me straight again concerning my personal life, you might want to reconsider, because I'm absolutely confident that if Brandon has a choice between you and me, you will no longer be welcome at Willow Creek."

Kate leaned back, picked up her competitor's packet and started to leaf through the contents. There was no way she was going to get off her hay bale, in front of her horse's stall, or budge one inch out of her way to dismiss the likes of Brenda Weeks.

"There's the woman who owns my heart. Take a walk with me, *muirnín*." Brandon's blue eyes sparked and he reached for her hand. "I want to walk the course with you now. Just the two of us."

"Am I the teacher's pet then? Won't your other

clients be put out?"

"Sure and I don't care. If they don't like the way I do things, they can all go hire someone else." He slipped a possessive arm around her shoulder.

They started at the beginning, the start box. "Just like we practiced at home. The starter will count down, he'll say 'have a good ride' and off you go. Come straight out of the box at a trot. The pace is two hundred fifty meters per minute. Your horse has a nice big trot. So for him, that's an easy pace."

"What if I want to canter between some of the fences?"

"Sure, but you will be penalized for too much speed, so use your watch and don't get ahead of the time." He walked briskly to the first fence, a small log on the ground. "This is no bigger than a *cavaletti*. You just point Sam past it and keep your eyes up. Look at the coop, that's where you're headed next."

They walked the whole course this way: "ride this drop by slipping your reins...remember you lose momentum in the water...don't let him get flat over this long open stretch...remember to half halt, set him up just a bit, but don't get in his face."

"Bran, there's so much to remember. How am I ever going to keep it all straight?"

"Just have fun. Walk this course a couple more times by yourself. Memorize it, so you can come out here and not have to think about more than one jump at a time."

"Am I allowed to kiss my riding instructor?" Kate put her arms around his neck and gave him a big, sloppy kiss.

He walked courses with his other students that evening after everyone practiced through their dressage tests one last time. They fed Sam and Beltaine, tucked them in for the night and headed to their motel.

"I'm excited...and wiped out," Kate confessed.

"Here's what I recommend." He flopped back on the bed. "A good supper and an early night."

Kate kicked off her shoes and joined him. "Don't feel rejected, but I think I need to sleep tonight, not tumble or be tumbled by my husband."

"I will try to behave myself. Do you know your dressage test and your ride times?"

"I do." She turned over and looked in his eyes. "Brandon, thank you, for all the things you've taught me and for being so patient...with the horse things and everything else."

He removed the cap from her head, loosed her hair from its ponytail, tangled his fingers in the soft curls and urged her to his lips. "You taste like you've been into the horses' mints. We had better go get some supper."

****

The mist lay like a foot-deep blanket on the earth, muffling the hoof beats as Kate groomed Sam for their dressage test. It was eerily quiet, the day just waking with sounds of soft rumbles and excited whinnies from the barns where competitors' horses were readied for the day.

Kate and Sam were Brandon's only Beginner Novice pair for this event, and the last of his students to ride this morning's dressage. Traditionally, the higher levels rode earliest. Barb and Beltaine had gone first, then Brenda, Suzanne and Carla, who rode a level up from Kate. Brandon had also agreed to help a former student who had been away at college and was without a trainer. Karen was a fine rider and a fun girl to visit with around the barns. Her horse, Scimitar, was what Brandon called a 'fairy horse,' an Arabian who had the ability to disappear out from under his rider without prior warning. Karen handled the grey gelding well, and was proud of the fact that, though he was smaller than the thoroughbreds, he could jump anything and make the time and distance without breaking a sweat. Her boyfriend, Tom, was not a rider, but Kate thought it was incredibly sweet the way he catered to Karen's every need from polishing her boots to wiping the green slime from Scimitar's mouth before he was trotted into the ring.

Barb had shown Kate how to plait Sam's thick mane into a kind of French braid that complemented his neck. He was all spit and polish and so was his rider. In her white breeches, black coat, and black velvet helmet, Brandon thought she looked about fourteen years old and twice as beautiful. "People are going to think I've seduced a teenager, or that you're my daughter."

"Maybe you should start telling all those Brandon Groupies that you're a married man now. Not that it will make them keep their hands off you, but they might feel a *little* guilty," Kate teased. In truth, she felt proud that this man who attracted females of all ages belonged to her... and she had the paper to prove it.

Kevin, Barb and Brandon watched as Kate trotted down the center line, halted and saluted the judge. "Nice halt," Bran said under his breath.

"You sound more nervous than when I was seventeen and going Advanced," Kevin commented.

"I had been teaching you to ride for fifteen years by that time. And, you wouldn't have dared screw up or your mother would have strangled you with her bare hands." Bran didn't take his eyes off Kate while he spoke softly. "That was a perfect circle, now sit and canter...yes...yes...grand...lovely...this is nice."

Kevin turned to Barb: "Does he always talk through the test like this?"

"Shut yerself up, Kevin...I'm concentratin' here," Bran snapped.

"Well, you sound like a fuckin' horseshow mother," he chuckled.

Barb gave Kev an elbow in the ribs. "I hope you worry a little bit about me when I'm out on the course," she glanced at her watch, "in about one hour and thirty-two minutes."

"Ah, sure an' I'll worry if ya want me to, darlin'," he said, imitating his dad's brogue because he knew it would make Barb laugh.

Brandon was oblivious to everything but the woman and horse in the ring. "Grand, now, sweetheart, straight down that center line...and... halt...salute...yes! Nailed it." He walked to the out gate, and took hold of Sam's reins while Kate leaned down and kissed him, knocking his hat off his head.

"You did a lovely job, Katie," he said, pulled her out of the saddle, embraced her and kissed her sweaty neck. "I'll take Sam and brush him down for you. You get yourself a fresh bottle of water out of the cooler and meet me back at his stall. I have a few minutes before I have to start out to the cross-country for coaching the other riders."

When it was Kate's turn to ride the course, she was jittery but confident, thinking perhaps it was beginner naiveté that allowed her to believe she would survive this adventure. She wore her flack vest with a bib tied over it sporting her number on her back and chest. Forty-two. She laughed in her head at that. Forty-two, the answer to life, the universe, and everything.

Brandon helped her with her warm up, watching and coaching as she trotted and cantered Sam over the cross rails, a vertical and an oxer before helping her check her girth and walking with her to the start box. "Heels down, head up, not too fast," he warned. "Do you need a sip of water?"

"No, I'm fine." But she didn't look at him as she patted Sam on the neck, more to calm herself than her horse.

"Thirty seconds, number forty-two," the starter

called.

"Go on into the box now and when he says 'have a good ride' you just take a nice big breath and go have some fun." Bran patted her leg and sent her to her fate.

Kate did exactly as she was told; she went out and had herself some fun. Sam obediently trotted over the fences, down the embankments and through the water. They picked up a canter over a long rolling stretch of grass and she slowed him again before a little hop over a log and then continued on.

Her heart was pounding out a rhythm that matched Sam's strides and she imagined he was having as much of a blast as she. Kate glanced at the big stopwatch on her wrist only once and noted that their pace was adequate, not fast, but at her level fast was not always a good thing. At each fence, a judge in a lawn chair watched as the pair, steady as a grandfather clock and just as solid, breached the obstacle. Kate's only regret as she saw the last jump, a red painted bench, was that it was the last and her ride was over. Crossing the finish line, eyes focused on Brandon, his smile a reflection of her triumph. She pumped her fist in the air in a victory salute.

"I want to do that again. Right now," she said breathlessly. "Oh, my God, Bran, you were right. It's orgasmic," she said louder than she meant and then flopped herself onto Sam's neck and wept with glee. "Oh, Sammy, how I love you. What a good boy you are. You get a million mints for this."

"I don't recall you ever offering me a million mints for a good ride," Bran commented with a sly grin, reaching for her.

Kate leaned over to kiss him and he grabbed her out of the saddle and into his arms. Her legs wrapped around his hips and nearly knocked him to the ground. "You...hmm...I'll have to give that some serious thought."

"Let's go put your pony away. He needs a hosing and you can relax until stadium, which is in three hours." Bran would have to keep his hands to himself until after the competition, but afterward he'd be giving her a celebration that he alone could provide.

"Yes, sir!" She gave him a mock salute. "You're the boss. I feel like the queen of everything right now. Nothing can spoil this day for me."

****

Whether it was beginner's luck, the right trainer, the best horse or a combination of all those, Kate ended her day in third place over all the many adult amateur riders in her division. She won a bright blue halter and rope for Sam and the good-natured envy of the other riders.

Brandon knew Kate did not represent much of a competitive threat at the higher levels, Sam had no speed for that, but at Beginner or Novice they had potential to shine. He had no need to push Kate beyond her desire or ability and in that way this experience was worlds different from the kind of relationship he'd had with Fiona. She had been a fierce competitor and had literally grown up on the back of a horse. Fi could outride even her husband and she never showed a hint of fear or hesitation. Kate was brave but he had to be cautious to not over fence her and scare the fun right out of the sport.

They celebrated with dinner at a steak house where groups of riders took up nearly every table. Barb had finished in the top ten with Beltaine and was thrilled with the potential he showed. Karen had a clean ride on cross-country but a spook and a rail down in stadium put her out of contention. Bran talked to her about ways to prevent future mishaps and she was ready to go home and work on the fine details. The only completely disgruntled participant from Willow Creek was Brenda Weeks. She had gotten around the cross-country, barely, and then Bear had three refusals in stadium. She was eliminated, and livid. Brandon knew that the horse was sick of Brenda yanking on the bit in his mouth, but decided to avoid the subject until her next lesson.

Finally, when Kate looked as though she was about to fall asleep in her dessert, Brandon reached for her hand under the table. "I think I'd better get you back to the motel before you're too far gone for our private celebration."

"I think I'm brain dead, but maybe you can revive me."

He turned to Kevin. "We're off. See you bright and early. We need to get the horses loaded by seven."

"He's a slave driver, my da," he said to Barb. "We're doing late feeding, so the old folks can go get some sleep." He and his fiancée would be cuddling up in the goose neck of the horse trailer tonight.

"Ah, youth is so wasted on the young," Bran shot back. "Get some rest yourself." He doubted they would.

All attempts at sexual merriment aside, Kate was truly exhausted. Brandon was going to have to be content with snuggling her body into his while she dreamed. "Wake me if you need me," he said as she slipped into sleep.

Chapter Thirty

Spring was both an exciting time at Willow Creek and a season of increased work and additional stress for everyone. Kevin had a few weeks before graduation from Georgetown and Barb was starting to get flustered over the wedding plans. Whenever Kate tried to calm her down, the girl would swallow back her tears and rush off to groom the next horse for Brandon.

Annie had gone to Italy to meet Sergio's mother. Upon her return, having left Sergio behind, she stumbled dreamily through her accounting tasks, her heart lost at sea until she could go back to him after her nephew's nuptials. Brighid kept her distance and Kate hoped it was simply that the youngest Sullivan was busy with her studies. Bran had said not to worry; his daughter would soften to Kate as soon as they had a chance to spend more time together. Kate hoped he was right.

But, beyond any doubt at all, the next most exciting event would be the Rolex Kentucky Three Day Event. It was coming up in April. Brandon and Calypso were on the competitors' list. It was a ballsy move on Bran's part, taking a horse he had spent barely three months with to the only four-star event in the United States. But they had qualified and he had high hopes for a decent placing. Even more important than winning would be the fact that the world would know that Bran Sullivan was back in the saddle and that he had a horse who could take him to the top rankings. To ride at a prestigious international venue like Rolex put you in circles where connections were made, names were spoken and business deals were struck. Sipping Bourbon under the same tent with Buck Davidson or Olympic Gold Medalist David O'Connor was where Brandon wanted to be. Having Kate by his side made it all the sweeter.

"Are you excited?" she asked him the night before they left for Kentucky.

"Yes," he said as he stepped out of the shower, towel around his hips, hair wet, his skin flushed and warm. "Come, sit next to me. I want to tell you about it."

Kate sat on the edge of the bed next to Bran. "Go ahead. Impress me with your 'adventures in the big time'."

"I hope I can explain to you why this is such a big deal for me. On the surface, it's obvious. I like winning and my business depends on having my name out there. But there's more to it than that.

"The last time I was at Rolex, Fiona was the one riding. I hadn't qualified with Clancy, he just had no speed. We kept falling behind in the endurance phases and I was in the process of looking for client horses to ride. Fi qualified with Murphy and they finished in the top fifteen. That probably doesn't sound very impressive, but trust me, it's very good."

"Hey, I'm impressed. I've seen some of those fences...they're daunting."

"Other than when our children were born, Fiona was the happiest I'd ever seen her." He smiled at the remembering and then his expression turned wistful. "She was diagnosed two weeks later."

"Bran, you don't have to talk about this if it's painful."

"No...no, I do. This is part of me you need to understand. By the next time Rolex came around, Fi was barely holding on to life. I didn't compete that year and the next season I couldn't make myself even show my face at the big events. I was afraid that the people who knew us would either avoid me, because they wouldn't know what to say, or they would ask about her and it would cause me fresh grief. Anyway, I simply couldn't face them."

"But, at Tamarack, everyone was perfectly comfortable, kidding with you, friendly...what's different now?"

"Time, I guess, or enough of them know I've moved on with my life. Everyone loves you. The people who care know you're good for me." His arm slipped around her and drew her near. "Now I feel like I can be back in it and I need to...want to do it for us, for our future and for Fiona's memory. I need one or two advanced horses, with owners who want to win enough to invest in me. If Calypso and I can even be in the top twenty, it could turn things around for me financially. I don't have to win, but I do have to finish. It's absolutely vital."

"Do you have any doubts that Calypso can finish? I thought he was doing well. All your qualifying rides were great." She was just learning how the whole sport worked. It was sometimes as simple as not being eliminated, or having a horse who wouldn't pass the inspection the morning of the third day.

"He's strong and so am I. Barring the unexpected, we have as good a chance as I've had since Carrick. I can thank you for that." He kissed the palm of her hand.

"Maybe you'd like to show me just how appreciative you are, right now...while you're all clean and fresh from your shower." She untucked his towel and slid her hand over him, eliciting a shiver as he responded to her touch.

"I believe in always showing my appreciation," he said as his fingers found their way to the buttons of her blouse.

****

It was a carnival atmosphere at the Kentucky Horse Park in Lexington. Booths, concessions and tents set up with food and drink hosted thousands of Eventing fans, horse lovers and competitors. In contrast, the barns were quiet except for the sounds of horses munching hay, snorting, pawing, and the constant clip-clop of hooves on the walkway to the arenas. People spoke in more hushed tones here behind the scenes, where riders, owners and grooms moved in their own private world.

Kevin was in charge of technical details, using his laptop to coordinate the activities of the next three days. Barbara would, as usual, be head groom, having responsibility for Calypso's care and preparing him for each phase of competition. She would braid him for dressage, making certain his coat shone like a new penny, adding the shamrock quarter mark that was the Willow Creek trademark to his rump. Knowing she could not possibly handle all the work herself, she had asked for Brighid's help.

Brighid would be in charge of tack: three different saddles, two bridles, pads, girths, galloping boots, all the paraphernalia essential for each day's riding. Kevin claimed Kate had the hardest job of all. She was in charge of Brandon. Making sure he ate, stayed hydrated, wasn't distracted by inconsequentials and that he was rested; these were her bailiwick.

Kate couldn't decide who was more handsome, Calypso or Brandon. The horse was blindingly clean and polished from his braided mane to his gleaming hooves. Brandon, in his Shadbelly coat with the long tails, white breeches, black silk top hat, looked to Kate out of another time and place. And she thought he was drop dead gorgeous. Brighid had rubbed his tall dress boots until they squeaked and reflected her smile back at her. His hands were gloved in white kid leather. He carried no whip and wore no spurs.

When the pair entered the ring, Kate saw a side of her husband she knew was there, but it never ceased to intrigue her: the consummate professional, the unyielding perfectionist. She had seen him schooling Calypso and had been at all the qualifying events, but something about the ambiance of Rolex brought everything into sharper focus, even to eyes blurred with tears.

The test was beautiful in its precision and when they cantered down the center line, halted and Bran saluted the judge, the applause from the grandstands was affirming. He presented a good, solid start to the three days of trials. This phase set his score. Any penalties over the next two days would be added and like golf, Bran had explained, the lowest score wins.

At each qualifying competition Kate had walked the course once with Bran and then he would walk it alone. So as not to break tradition, they did the same this time. But this time Kate had to work much harder at hiding her anxiety at the size and scope of the obstacles. She tried to keep the fear out of her voice when she asked him, "Do these fences seem any bigger than...oh, Fairhill or Radnor?"

Putting his hand on the grass topping a massive bank, he turned and looked at her. "If you're asking if I'm intimidated or scared the answer is 'no', I'm not particularly concerned. Yes, this is more technically challenging than some." Bran took her chin in his hand and tipped her face to meet his eyes. "Worry for me if you must, this is a risky sport, but you'd best accept that this is what I do. It's bred into me as much as it is into Calypso."

Kate closed her eyes and swallowed hard. "It feels like I'm sending my man out, sword in hand, to war. Is this some substitute for that, a need to put yourself in danger, fighting an unseen enemy?"

"Ah, and maybe that's it. Would you rather have me sitting behind a desk?" He raised one brow and smiled. "Here's my advice for you. Have one of those mint juleps, sit at the finish line and picture me flying over the course. I'll look for you beyond the last flags." He took her hand and started to walk. "Let's get done here and get some supper. I'm hungry."

How he managed to be so relaxed she had no idea. Her stomach was in such knots she could only pick at the meal they had that evening. Brandon ate like a starving wolf. Likewise, Kate's libido had been kidnapped by her anxiety and she'd thought Bran felt the same until he awakened in the night and took her powerfully and with such force that it thrilled and left her aching.

He slept soundly the rest of the night. Kate was certain of his somnolent state because she had lain awake listening to him breathe. Her philosophy had always been that if others were too oblivious to worry properly, it was her job to fret for them. She knew it didn't help, but it was how Kate was hardwired and she wasn't about to change now.

When Bran virtually bounced out of bed at five o'clock in the morning, Kate was smoosh-faced into her pillow and drooling with exhaustion.

"Katie, wake up, you're droolin'." He gave her a kiss on the back of her neck.

"I don't drool," she mumbled.

"Sorry, darlin', you do, but only when you lie awake all night and fall asleep ten minutes before you have to get up."

Forcing herself to sit on the side of the bed, she watched his naked backside as he walked toward the shower. Damn, no man should get to look that good at this time in the morning.

The second day at Rolex would separate, cull and carve the field down to the toughest horse-rider teams the world had ever seen. It was truly a test of teamwork, stamina, skill and bravery. When Brandon mounted Calypso to walk to the first venue of the day, they both looked almost too blasé.

Finally Kate turned to Kevin and asked the obvious. "Okay, so is he really as unconcerned as he looks, because I'm about to have a nervous breakdown?"

Kevin just laughed. "This is how my dad deals with his anxiety. It's a waste of energy to get worked up and today he'll need every ounce of strength he has. I learned early to stay out of his way. I leave it to Barb to read his mind if he or his horse needs anything. She's good at that."

"Da, you're on deck for Roads and Tracks," Brighid called to Bran.

"Thanks. Katie, come here a minute," he said as he adjusted the chin cup on his helmet. Bran leaned down and took her hand. "Go now and get that mint julep. Be here when I finish Steeplechase. I'm off to work now. Give me a kiss for luck."

She reached up on tiptoe as he leaned down. "Have fun out there. Show them the Sullivans are back." Kate kissed him and watched as he trotted to the start area.

"Brighid, would you walk over to the tents with me?" Kate asked. "Your dad thinks I need a drink."

"Sure, Roads and Tracks is pretty boring and you can't see much. Let's go."

They walked in silence until Brighid spoke. "Are you worried about Da?" When Kate nodded, Brighid shook her head in agreement. "You're not alone. Before my mam died, I wasn't ever scared. Now I know how fragile life is. If anything ever happened to my da..."

Kate stopped walking and looked at the young

woman. "Brighid, I know you miss your mom. Please don't ever think I'm trying to replace her, but I would like to be your friend."

"I've gotta be honest. I really freaked when my father told me about you. He's always been my hero. I compare every man I come in contact with to him. Makes it hard for me to date anyone more than once." She laughed. "I hope you will always appreciate what a great guy he is, that's all." Her expressive blue eyes, not the dark azure of her father's but light with an underlying tendency to turn stormy grey, riveted Kate's gaze. "I would consider it an honor to call you my friend, Kate."

Mint julep in hand, Kate watched as Bran and Calypso appeared to melt into a copper streak as they galloped past, skimming the brush fences of the Steeplechase field without breaking stride. Then they traveled back out to the roads for approximately seven miles of slow trotting while horse and rider relaxed in anticipation of the extreme efforts of the cross-country phase.

Brandon had a ten-minute break while a veterinarian examined Calypso for any problems before they set out for the most grueling part of the day. As much as Kate wanted to talk to Bran or simply touch him to assure herself he was managing, she kept her distance, watching as Barb offered him water and adjusted Calypso's tack.

To Kate, he looked like a warrior fresh from a fight, unscathed and ready for more. His focus on the task at hand was extreme and she thought he was avoiding looking her way until he turned and waved her over.

"He feels fantastic, Katie, strong and so willing." Bran grabbed her and gave her a quick kiss. "Gotta go. See you in a little while. I love you."

Barb held Calypso's reins as Bran mounted and settled himself in the saddle. The horse started to fidget and prance, feeling the energy of the moment as they made their way to the start box.

When Calypso leapt from the box and the timer started there was nothing for Kate to do but watch, her heart thumping with fear for the man who owned it. Her only reassurance came from the speakers that broadcast the announcer's voice as he told the tale of Brandon's ride.

"Number ninety-three, Bran Sullivan on Calypso...out of the start box now...safely through the Rolex Arch and headed into the trees." And moments later..."at the head of the lake...now looks like Sullivan is taking the shorter, more difficult route through the water...he'll save time there...two grand efforts at the big combination...Sullivan is back at Rolex after a long hiatus from the sport and making a nice comeback today with this Irish Thoroughbred...we understand the horse is owned by Sullivan's wife...that's keeping it in the family...and there they go over the covered bridge...oh, a slight bobble at the drop...but... recovered...might have lost a little time with that stumble...mighty effort at the sunken road..."

Yes, he was back, Kate thought with pride as she listened to the disembodied voice following the progress of her very own Celtic knight in shining armor as he slayed the dragons of the day.

"Here he comes," Kevin shouted. "Damn, they're blazing. Barb, what's his time?"

"He's gonna be a little over optimum...but...he's good. I can't believe it. That horse is *fast.*" Barb jumped onto Kevin's back, laced her legs around him and threw her arms in the air in triumph.

As Bran crossed the finish line, Kate saw him glance at his watch and push the stop button to freeze his time. She hoped he was pleased. They had finished the day with few, if any, penalty points. To Kate, it was magic.

When Brandon dismounted it wasn't his usual graceful vault from Calypso's back. He slid down the horse's sweat-soaked side and staggered before handing the reins to Barb, who would cool the horse out and hose him off. He removed his helmet and wiped his dripping brow with a gloved hand. Kate handed him a towel and a water bottle. She wrapped her arms around him and held him to her. "You are amazing," she said, and helped him to the shade where he sat to catch his breath.

"Okay, now I can admit it to you. I was a smidge nervous. Now, God...I can't believe what a horse he is, Katie...he did it!"

"You both did."

Chapter Thirty-One

They hadn't been back at the hotel for more than the few minutes it took for Bran and Kate to strip out of their clothes when his cell phone rang. Looking at the caller ID, he hesitated a moment before he answered. "Kevin, what's up?" he asked, at the same time reaching and pulling Kate onto his lap.

"Sorry to bother you, but I wanted to warn you that I gave your number to a guy who came by the barns looking for you. The name is Wendell Brownstone. He seemed to think you knew him."

"*Christ*...yes, I know him." Brandon had not thought he would ever hear from Brownstone again, not in this lifetime anyway. The man had once solicited Brandon as a trainer for two horses he had purchased. Rumor had it that money was no barrier to what the man wanted, and he wanted winners. The last time they had talked was at Rolex the year Fiona had been the Sullivan in the limelight. "Did he say what he wanted?"

"Nope...just that he'd like to talk business. Well, I gotta go or my lovely fiancée will kick my ass for not helping her clean your horse's stall. *Ciao*."

"Yeah, sure and I'll see you at the inspection tomorrow. Bright and early." He closed his phone and snuggled Kate closer to him.

"So, are you going to tell me what that was all about?" Kate queried.

"Not sure really. This bloke had wanted me to train a couple of horses for him. One I would ride and the other for his daughter. I was planning to do

297

it and then...you know, everything got put on hold when Fi was ill. He called a few times, but there was surgery, chemo...all that. I never returned his calls."

Kate pushed him back on the bed. "Roll over and let me rub your back." He did. "Are you tired?"

"If you're asking if I'm too tired to have sex with my wife...no, I'm not that tired."

"Well, that wasn't exactly what I was asking, but it's nice to know that's an option." She straddled his legs and was working her thumbs into the muscles along his spine when his phone jingled again.

"If that's Kevin, the boy is not having enough fun."

"I don't recognize the number," Kate said as she opened the phone. "This is Mrs. Sullivan."

"Oh, Mrs. Sullivan? I was trying to reach Mr. Sullivan." The words were spoken with a quiet and formal Georgia drawl.

"Sure, he's right here." She covered the phone with her hand. "This must be your Mr. Brownstone." Kate removed herself from Bran's naked body and handed him his phone.

"This is Brandon. Oh, well, good to hear from you, Wendell. Uh, sure...no, no problem. We're at the Sheraton Four Points...we could do that. Yes...see you then." He closed the phone and put his arms around Kate. "He wants to talk business. Pretty yourself up, my darlin'. This is what we've been waiting for."

****

Wendell Brownstone was a short, stout man, balding and bespectacled. He introduced the young woman at his side as his daughter, Rebecca. "My daughter has been riding Preliminary. She wants to move up, but she needs the guidance of a man of your caliber, Mr. Sullivan."

"Please, it's Brandon. Well, Rebecca, I'd like to

298

talk to you about your plans." He tried to engage the young woman, but her father interrupted.

"Yes, you'll have plenty of time to do that. I want to commend you, Brandon, on your ride today. That's a fine mount, Calypso. I understand he belongs to you, Mrs. Sullivan."

"Yes, we purchased him in Ireland this winter. He's lovely, isn't he?"

Ordinarily, Brandon would not have been pleased at all with the way Wendell Brownstone was eying Kate, but in this case he was glad to have his pretty wife to keep the man a bit off balance.

Brownstone explained his proposition. He would like Bran to train his daughter and her thoroughbred to the next level of competition and he would sponsor Brandon to take his other horse Advanced next season. Bran knew the horse; Lions Gate was a stallion who had done well at Intermediate and then faded from the radar. Now he was back, just like Sullivan. Maybe they were fated to be a team.

While Kate and Rebecca sat talking over their iced teas, the men went into the bar for drinks.

"Sullivan, let me be blunt here." Wendell looked at Brandon over his whiskey glass. "You've the reputation for being a fine rider and trainer. You are also rather well known for being a...well...a hot head."

Bran gave him a sardonic grin. "I don't pale for lack of enthusiasm, Wendell."

"I need to be assured that you are a man who will follow through, that I can depend on you." He paused to sip his drink. "Your wife...I seem to remember she's quite a fine rider."

"Kate is a beginner. You might be remembering Fiona. She passed a couple of years ago." He sipped his Glenlivet, wondering where this was going.

"Sorry, I hadn't heard about that. Well, I'd like

to see how your horse does tomorrow and I will decide if you can help us with our endeavor."

So, that's it. He wants to see what I have in me. Fine, that I can show him. "I have grand expectations for Calypso. This is our first season and he's not let me down. But, as you know, we are all subject to the unexpected in the Eventing world."

"Yes, that is the only thing we can be sure of, isn't it? Good luck." He shook Brandon's hand. "Tomorrow...I'll be looking for you."

****

They rolled around on the bed like teenagers—laughing, kissing and undressing one another with spectacular abandon. "I knew you could do it, Bran. I knew someone would see how incredible you are. This is just the beginning."

"I'll have to ride with care tomorrow. We're not all that far down in the standings. He'll trot out sound. Of that I'm almost certain." He held her close. "I'm wearing my lucky hat in the mornin'. With that and my beautiful wife at my side, I can't lose."

"Do you think we should get some sleep?"

"I'm a superstitious man, Katie. The night before Show Jumping at Radnor, when I qualified for this event, you made love with me. I don't think we should change anything and possibly jinx the day tomorrow." He kissed her neck.

"I must be hanging around with too many Irish folk. I'm getting rather superstitious myself and I don't want to be responsible if you knock down a rail." Her legs opened to him.

"You're a wise woman, Mrs. Sullivan."

****

Calypso did trot out sound the next morning and passed the inspection without a question. Brandon was in tenth place overall and the rides were in reverse order of placing. It was going to be a long day.

Kate was wandering around, shopping and browsing at the many vendors that had set up their tents, just enjoying the friendly ambiance, when her cell phone rang. She considered not answering it, but glancing at the caller ID, she recognized Frank's cell. It was not unusual for him to call on a weekend just to chat or give an update on the family.

"Hello, favorite brother, how's it going?" She couldn't help but smile into the phone.

"Kate, where are you? Is Brandon with you?"

Frank sounded strange, worried. "I'm at a horse show. Brandon is back at the barns. Do you need to talk to him? Frankie, what's going on? You sound funny."

"No...I just...I have something to tell you. I didn't want you to be alone. Kate, it's Mark."

"What? What's the matter? Frank, you're scaring me. What's happened to Mark?" A hot knife of fear cut into Kate's chest making her shiver.

"Kate, Mark's been shot. He's in surgery right now. Kate, oh God," Frank's voice shook. "It looks pretty bad."

Kate's legs gave way. She leaned unsteadily against a folding table full of souvenir shirts and hats. With two brothers in law enforcement, it was a nightmare Kate had pushed deep into the back of her mind for years. Now, it was reality. "Frank, I'll leave right now. I'll get the first flight to Newark. I need to go find Brandon."

"Call me from the airport and let me know when you're coming in. Kate, I talked to Mark before they took him to the operating room," his voice broke. "I told him we...we all love him."

Kate's legs were shaking so badly she barely made it to the barns. Brandon was not there. She looked in their tack stall for Brighid, who had been there earlier cleaning her father's saddle. "Oh...you *are* here! Sweety, I need to find your dad. Do you know where he is?"

"God, Kate, what happened?"

"It's my brother. I need to go...right away. But I can't find Bran."

"He said he was going to take a walk, just chill out. Last I saw he was headed toward the Man o' War statue." She reached for Kate's arm. "Wait here, I'll go find him."

"No, I'll go." She had to find him, let him know she needed to leave, hold him close and let him give her strength. "If you see him, tell him to ring my phone and I'll come back."

"Hey, Kate, where ya headed?" It was Kevin.

"I need to find Brandon. Do you know where he is?"

"He went for a walk, said he needed some solitude. I think that's a good idea. He needs to concentrate."

Kate tried to collect herself. She wanted to be sensitive to Brandon's needs, but she *needed him*...now. "Kevin, my brother Mark is in surgery. I've got to find Brandon. I have to leave. Bran should know."

Kevin looked at Kate and then at his feet, thinking, struggling with the words. "Kate, you gotta understand this. Dad can't be distracted right now. I know this sounds cold, and I'm sorry. This competition is everything he's worked for. Please, if you've gotta leave, I'll talk to him...right after he rides."

Kate felt the wind knocked out of her. How could she leave without letting Bran know what was going on? Wouldn't he ask where she was when he was ready to ride? Maybe not. What Kevin was saying was true. This was Brandon's world. Kate would always come second. She tried not to let the thought that dwelt in the back of her mind intrude. But it did. *She was second, just like she had been with*

Jeffrey.

"Okay, Kevin, whatever you think is best." She gave him a brief hug. "Tell Bran to have a great ride. I'll call him later."

Blinded by a kaleidoscope of emotions that she did not want to name, Kate ducked into the women's restroom, splashed water in her face and tried to gain a modicum of control. *Brandon be damned*, right now she needed to get to the airport and find a flight to Newark. "Focus," she told herself; she needed to focus on Mark, on her family, on the people who would always be there for her. She had the keys to their rental car in her pocket and she decided to just get down the road and figure out what to do next while she drove.

****

"Da, Kate was looking for you. She said she's on her way to catch a flight to Newark. What's going on? Didn't she find you?"

"No. What are you talking about? She *left?*"

"Yeah, Kevin talked to her. She said she had to go to New Jersey. Her brother was hurt or something. I thought she would find you."

Bran wasn't able to make any sense of this. Kate wouldn't leave, not without telling him. Why didn't someone let him know what was going on? "You say Kevin talked to her? Why didn't he come and get me?"

Brandon flipped open his phone. He tried Kate first. No answer. Was she out of range or just not answering? *Katie, answer your phone. I need to talk to you.*

He hit the numbers for Frank Aiello.

"Father Aiello is unable to answer your call at this time. Please leave your name and number and he will return your call as soon as possible. If this is an emergency, please call Father O'Keefe at—"

Brandon snapped the phone closed. *I don't want*

to talk to the damn O'Keefe. He tried Kate's phone again, but there was still no answer.

He called Laura. "Hello," the familiar voice picked up.

"Laura, this is Brandon."

"Are you with Mom? Where is she? Is she coming?" She sounded like she'd been crying.

"Whoa, slow down. I called you because I don't know what's going on."

"Oh, Brandon. Mark was shot. He's critical...in surgery right now. I guess they don't expect...oh God. Uncle Frankie said he talked to mom. Where are you? Why aren't you with her?"

"I'm calling from the Horse Park. Your mom is on her way. I'll be there as soon as I can get away. Kate's got her phone...but I haven't been able to reach her. I should go now. I'll see you soon, Laura." He closed the phone. Anger welled up inside him. *Why didn't someone find me before Kate took off?* He considered putting his fist through the barn wall. Instead he went to find Kevin.

"Dad," Kevin called. "Where the hell have you been? Barb is getting Calypso ready. You've only got about an hour." Kevin had been following the progress of the show jumping on his laptop and had calculated exactly when his dad should get to the warm up ring,

Bran looked at his son and hoped he wasn't about to make the biggest mistake of his life. "Kev, I've gotta leave. Go to the Technical Delegate and tell him I've scratched from the competition."

"You what? Have you lost your fuckin' mind?"

Usually Brandon wouldn't tolerate his son's lack of respect. Right now Kevin had a right to be confused and infuriated. "Kate's brother, Mark, has been shot. He's critically injured."

"I know, I talked to Kate. She can handle this. She has her whole family to support her. I told her

304

not to bother you."

Brandon grabbed Kevin by the collar. "You *talked* to her! You told *my wife* not to bother me? Kevin..." Bran tried to breathe, get control of his anger, fear and disappointment at his son's callousness. "I need to be with my wife. That's the way it's going to be." He turned to leave.

Kevin grabbed his father by the arm, swinging him around roughly. "Dad, you can't do this. You can't walk away from this. Two or three hours isn't going to make a difference. This is everything you've worked for, everything Mom wanted. If you walk away now...you'll look like a quitter."

Bran shook free of Kevin's grip. He knew Kevin was right on several levels. If he pulled from Rolex, he would risk losing everything—his place in the sport he loved, his reputation, his life's dream...Fiona's dream.

Kevin had his fists balled at his sides and he was shaking with fury. "Well?"

It wasn't an easy choice he was making here. It was a decision that would seal his fate in more ways than one. "Kevin, I don't have much time." Brandon was sure his son would someday understand. "If Kate has to face her brother dying, she's not going to do that without me by her side. I need to leave right away. I've got to get to the airport and try to get a flight now, not two or three hours from now."

"But, Dad, this is *Rolex* and you're in the top ten. Dammit, this has to come first!"

Putting both hands on Kevin's shoulders, Bran closed his eyes and tried to organize his thinking. "Listen to me, son. Katie needs me now. You are about to commit your life to a woman you claim to love. Before you do that, read over those marriage vows and think about what you would be willing to give up to keep them...to keep her. I'm willing to give up everything...the least of which is this chance at recognition."

"I'm not sure I could do it. What kind of man am I that I'm not sure?"

"Ah, Kev...just a young one. Sooner or later you will be asked to make these kinds of choices and you'll choose wisely. You'll be a fine husband." He hugged his son, this young man so much like himself. "I'll call you. Take care of Brighid for me now. *Slán abhaile*...safe home."

****

Kate was able to get the last seat on a Delta flight to Newark at two P.M. She had an hour before she needed to check in at the gate so she stopped at a kiosk, purchased a bottle of water, and some wet wipes. There was not much hope of washing away the evidence of her tears, but she needed to freshen up as best she could. The line at security looked like the most popular ride at Disney World, so she went ahead and joined the crowd.

The adrenalin surge had left her drained. The echoes of Frank's news bounced from one side of her consciousness like a cannon shot to be volleyed back by the unreality of Kevin's utterance. *Mark's been shot*, broadsided her. *This competition is everything,* split her asunder.

"I need to see identification and your boarding pass, Miss."

"Oh...yes...sorry, I have them right here." Kate handed the young man her passport and her paperwork from the airline.

"You're Kate Aiello Sullivan?"

"Yes, I am."

"You'll need to remove your shoes and put your purse through the scanner."

She did as she was told, feeling like an automaton. On the other side of the scanner she sat to put her shoes back on and headed for the concourse.

She did not hear him call her name.

"Katie!"

Bran was running, full bore, through the line, tripping over baby strollers and rolling luggage, moving people out of his way as politely as possible but offending everyone who had waited for close to an hour to get to the front of the queue. "Katie, wait!"

"That's as far as you go. I'll see your boarding pass and I.D."

"I don't have a ticket. That's my wife...Katie!" She didn't hear him or turn when he called, but kept walking toward the stairs that led to the gates. "I've got to get through here. I need to talk to my wife. You don't understand."

"Buddy, this is as far as you go."

Brandon hadn't meant to shove the young security guard, he had just wanted to get by, but push him he did and the fellow went sprawling to the tile floor. Bran rushed to the metal scanner, but got no further. Two burley guards assailed him from behind, throwing him face first against the conveyer belt of the x-ray machine. One shoved a knee into Bran's back and twisted his arms behind him. The other was on a walkie-talkie calling for backup.

Chapter Thirty-Two

The elevator doors opened onto an unreal scene that screamed at Kate to run, but her legs wouldn't carry her anywhere but where she was needed most. Mark's daughters sat, arms twined about each other, looking for all the world like conjoined twins who were permanently fused at the heart.

"*Zia*, oh, *Zia* Kate," Julie cried.

"You're here!" Cathy croaked, her voice gone from weeping.

"Oh, babies...I'm here." She held them, these children who had yesterday been young ladies, who were her godchildren as well as her nieces, who had been named for her—Catarina and Giullietta.

"Mamma's in with Daddy. He's out of surgery, but he won't wake up. It's horrible, *Zia*." Julie, the more vocal of the two, told the story. "It was a robbery. But, Daddy...he was just off duty...and...and he left his Kevlar vest at the station."

"Where's Nonna, sweethearts?"

"She went with *Zio* Frankie to the chapel. We wanted to stay here and say a rosary. We didn't want to leave."

"Will you be all right if I go in to see your dad now? I won't leave you if you want me to wait." Kate brushed the dark curls out of twin faces and looked at the sad golden eyes that belonged to her brother.

"It's okay. Mamma wanted to see you as soon as you got here. She's real worried," Cathy finally spoke.

"Okay, I love you two. Wait here. I'll be back in a

bit."

The room was dimly lit, a monitor beeped out a steady pulse, a ventilator pushed air into the chest that rose and fell beneath the clasped hands of Maria Aiello. Her head rested against him, waiting.

"Maria?" Kate was afraid to even whisper for fear that she wake her sister-in-law from a much needed rest. Maria looked up with eyes swollen with tears, but not with sleep. Kate sat in the empty chair beside her brother's wife and laid a comforting hand on her arm. Neither spoke for several minutes. They watched as the machine breathed for the big, boisterous, loving man they both adored.

Finally, she spoke in a voice that came from another place and time, a poorly forged replica of the girl with the easy laugh and cutting wit that had been Maria Aiello. "Mark doesn't usually work the night shift, but Rusty Puglisi needed the time off...his wife's been ill." She shuddered, composed herself and continued. "I had an ultrasound yesterday. I hadn't had time to tell Mark. It was routine because of the trouble I had carrying the twins to term. I expected him home at eight in the morning and I made a *timbale*, set the table with candles, a little wine for him. It was going to be a surprise...because, I found out...it's...it's a boy. We're going to have a son." She reached for her husband's hand. "I didn't have the chance to tell him. Kate, what if he...never knows?"

"He'll know. We have to believe he'll know, Maria."

****

When Brandon finally convinced airport security he wasn't a terrorist, they allowed him to purchase a ticket to Newark. It was well past four. He had called Kevin and given him the latest on his flight and where he would be when he got to Hackensack. "You can reach me on my phone. I'm not sure where

I'll be staying."

Brighid wanted to talk to her dad and Kevin put her on the phone. Bran could hear the sorrow in her voice. "Da, I can't believe what you did. I'm so sorry. Please call us right away and let us know if Mr. Aiello is going to be okay. Tell Kate I'm praying for him and Da…give her my love."

"I will, baby. Everything's going to be okay. Brighid…Rolex will be there next year as well. I love you."

"Daddy, what are your plans? Where will you be?"

Brandon had no plan of action to tell Brighid at this point. He would get to Hackensack and figure it all out from there. He had finally reached Frank, who explained the circumstances. It was a sorrowful event in the lives of this loving and close knit family. Mark had been shot at close range, in the chest, during a convenience store robbery. He had been off duty, but still in uniform and carrying his service revolver. He never got a chance to use it. The punk who shot him got away with thirty-five bucks. The entire Aiello family was holding vigil at Hackensack Memorial Medical Center. That would be Brandon's destination.

****

"*O Dio*, Cara. *Mio figlio*, my Marco. What will I do without him?"

"Mamma, he's going to be okay. He has to be. Where's Joey?" Kate hadn't seen her youngest brother yet. She worried that he was out searching for the monster who shot Mark.

"*O* Giuseppe, he will be back soon. He went to make some calls. Cara, where is your husband? It is not like our Brandon to leave you in your sorrow."

"He's coming later, Mamma. He couldn't get away." She swallowed back the tears that gagged her. "I need to talk to Frank. Will you wait here for me?"

"*Si*, Cara, you go talk to Frankie. He is in the chapel. I asked him to say Padre Pio's Novena to the Sacred Heart of Jesus. You should go to him."

"Yes, Mamma, I should." Frank would know what she should do. He understood where she hurt, where her scars were hidden.

"Frank," she whispered, sitting next to her brother as he knelt in prayer. He crossed himself and gathered her up into his arms. "Frank, help me understand."

"I'm not sure I can, *mia sorella*. It is the nature of the world." His elegant fingers stroked her cheek. "I have no greater knowledge than the poorest of God's servants, when it comes to this."

"Frankie, I think I've made a terrible mistake. I wanted to be happy. I tried to put myself first, but it wasn't enough. I want to be first to someone other than myself. Is that wrong?"

"Kate, why isn't your husband here with you?"

"That is my worst mistake. I acted so quickly. I thought he loved me. I know he loves me, but he has other commitments that I can't compete with. I'm always going to be a cheap second place. I'm not sure I can live with the knowledge of it. It makes me feel like my insides are shards of broken glass, cutting me to pieces every time I move." Her tears spilled onto his prayer stole making dark ovals on the ivory silk.

"Do you want to tell me what he did? It will be between us, alone."

"He didn't do anything, really. I just don't feel like I matter. Kevin made it clear that Brandon's career would always take precedence. I'm not Fiona. I can't ride like her. I worry about him when he's out there risking his neck. I'm afraid I'll make him hate me.

"Now, I want to be here for my family, for Maria

and the twins, for Marco. I don't want to be grieving over my mistakes, my rushing into something because I was so terribly lonely, because I needed a man to love me, to tell me I was beautiful and desirable. I was determined to find myself after Jeffrey. Now I've misplaced Kate, again."

Frank held her as she wept.

Neither Kate nor Frank heard Joey slip into the back pew to pray. They did not hear him leave. They had no knowledge of what Joey had heard, but the youngest of the Aiello brothers had heard enough. Another bastard had hurt his sister, his beautiful Catarina. This was Kate who had helped him with his math homework and told him how to behave on his first date. Fifteen years his senior, she had taken the role as *little mother* to him, and he loved her more than his two languages had words to describe.

Joey had been tempted to beat the shit out of Jeffrey Waldon when he'd found Kate in tears after the jackass humiliated her at some stupid hospital social function. Joey should have held a gun to the coward's head or threatened to shoot one of his balls off before Waldon had a chance to divorce Kate and break her heart.

Now, another bastard had made Catarina cry, one too many if Joey had a say in it. The Irishman had better not show his face in Hackensack, or Joey would rearrange it for him.

****

The picture that met Brandon when he stepped into the intensive care waiting room was as beautiful as it was pathetic. Kate sat, her head nodding in exhaustion, her arms cradling twin angels with curly dark hair, asleep across her lap. Raphael could not have painted a more poignant portrayal of devotion.

He stepped to the sofa where she rested and started to reach for her.

"Brandon," she whispered. "I don't want to wake the girls."

"We need to talk." He touched her. She stiffened.

"Just give me a moment." She ran her hand through the ebony ringlets of one of her identical nieces. "Julie, I have to get up for a minute. Here sweetie just lay your head down." Kate slipped out from under the girl and tucked her close to her sleeping sibling.

They walked silently out into the hallway. "Is there somewhere we can go, where we have a bit of privacy?" he asked.

"There's a conference room. My family has been using it...to discuss things." She led the way to a small room off the hall, shutting the door behind them.

"Brandon, it's three in the morning, my brother is struggling for his life, my family is terrified. Thank you for coming. You didn't need to."

"Of course I needed to. I want to make this easier for you. That's why we have each other. It's what family is, Katie."

"Yes, I know that. That's why I came looking for you. But then Kevin said..."

Maybe it was fatigue, getting knocked around at the airport, the look of hurt in her eyes or just plain Sullivan pride, but he could feel his temples begin to throb and his blood pulsing anger to the surface. His hands reached for her and bit into her shoulders, forcing her to look at him, not allowing her to ignore his presence or deny his power. "Look at me. You shouldn't have listened to Kevin. He's young and he was stupid to tell you to leave without me. I'm the man you claim to love, the person to whom you pledged your life not three months back. Katie, I am a patient man when it comes to those I love. Why can't you learn to trust me?"

"I don't know what you mean." She tried to back

313

away. "I was just trying to...well...do what Fiona would have done."

"You're not Fiona!" Rage rose in his throat along with the fury that ignited in his heart. "You don't *know* what she would have done." He held her at arm's length and tried to calm the demon that made him want to shake her until her teeth rattled. "I promised I would never compare you to her. I've kept that promise. Why can't you believe me?"

"Brandon, I..." Her lips quivered and tears made silvery tracks down her pale cheeks. "I don't know what to believe. The doubts I have..." The harder she attempted to back away the stronger his grasp became. "Let me go," she begged.

Just as Brandon started to loosen the grip he knew was far too strong, a whip of a hand snapped him off his feet.

"Get your fuckin' hands off my sister."

Before he could gather his balance or defend himself, Brandon saw a fist coming at his face. The impact snapped his head back and he hit the wall with a sickening crack. Stunned, he tried to shake off the blackness that threatened to consume consciousness. Somewhere, it seemed, he heard Kate scream.

"Stand up and take this like the man you think you are, asshole!" Joey grabbed the front of Brandon's shirt and dragged him to his feet. "You are the last person who is ever going to hurt my sister." A meaty fist was rammed into Brandon's ribs. He heard a sound like dry branches snapping, and did not have the awareness to connect the sound with the pain in his chest. "Never...," another blow hit, bouncing its recipient against the wall. "Never...will you lay a hand on my Catarina, again. Not while this brother is alive."

Brandon had a history of being a brawler and a quick hand in a fight, but against the anger of Kate's brother he was powerless. "Look, man, I..." Bees began to buzz, darkness started to close in from the periphery of his view, sounds receded to a distant space and he thought he heard Kate crying, but it could have been the disjuncture of synapses in his head deceiving his ears.

"Joey, stop, you're hurting him...stop...you don't understand." The sound of her weeping was a knife in Brandon's side, stabbing him with each breath he took. "Please, Joey...leave him...leave us...you can't do this."

Moments before oblivion yanked the last shred of sentience from his grasp, Brandon thought he saw Joey pick Kate up in his arms and carry her out, flailing, pounding, begging him to release her. The door slammed shut behind them as the portal to Brandon's awareness closed with his own final slide into insensibility.

****

"Kate...Joey...where have you been?" It was Frank, he was smiling. "Mark's awake." Then he took a good look at his sister. "Kate?"

She choked out a response that was hindered by confusion, overwhelming joy and sadness. Her voice was next to useless. "I...need to...see him..." *I need to go back to Brandon.* "Frankie, Brandon...he's in the conference room. He's hurt. I need to make sure he's okay."

"What's the matter with Brandon? I didn't even know he was here." He reached in his pocket for a packet of tissues and handed it to her. "Here, I'll go see to your husband. You go say good morning to Mark. He's asking for you."

Mark was awake, but the only evidence of it was his half-open eyes and the relieved look on Maria's face. He was still intubated and that in itself gave a grim picture of his tenuous hold on life. When Kate sat down and took his hand he gave hers a squeeze

315

that threatened to crush her fingers together. "So, this is a hell of a way for a middle child to get attention," Kate teased through her tears. "You scared all of us to death."

His hand lifted and pointed in Maria's direction. Kate thought she saw a smile in Mark's eyes. "Maria, did you tell him the news?"

"Yes, it was the first thing I told him." She stepped close to the bed so her husband could lay his hand on her abdomen. "And I told him if he died on me, I'd kill him."

"Your girls want to come see you. They're with Mamma and Joey. I'll go now and send them in." Kate stood and leaned over her brother. "I love you, Marco. Glad you're back with us." She kissed his forehead.

Walking out into the hallway, the floor seemed insubstantial and shifted beneath Kate's feet. The walls closed in, tilted and the last thing she heard was the sound of her own body slumping onto cold linoleum.

****

When Frank opened the door of the conference room and switched on the light he did not, at first, see Brandon. He heard him. Sprawled in the corner like a broken Ken doll, mumbling in Irish, left eye swollen shut, blood dripping crimson rivulets from his nose onto his white shirt. He was a sorry sight.

"*Madre di Dio*," Frank exhaled. "My sister did this to you?"

Speech was painful, laughing was unbearable. "She might have...but Joey beat her to it."

"Dear Lord...the only Aiello with a temper hotter than Kate's is my youngest brother. So, do I dare try to move you? Can you stand?"

"I'm damn sure I've a busted rib or two. The rest of it is just the humiliation of losing a fight. He's fast. I never even got in a lick." Brandon let the priest help him stand on legs that felt like overcooked spaghetti.

"He's a cop, a big ape, and he loves his sister. I'd like to say I can't believe he would do such a thing, but yeah...he would. I don't know whether to be a brother here, or a priest. Would you like to talk about it or would you rather keep it for the anonymity of the confessional?" He deposited Brandon in a chair and went to the small sink to get damp paper towels and a cup of water.

"Father...Frank, I haven't been to confession in years. I may be guilty of a multitude of sins, but I love your sister more than life." He took the water, tried to drink and dribbled it out of the side of his swollen mouth. "Thanks. Look, I know Kate's been hurt. I knew that going into this relationship and I knew I'd have to win her trust above anything else. I thought I'd done that." Brandon looked at Frank out of his one good eye, the other completely useless. "Is it too much to ask for her to simply decide to trust me? I believe she should know me well enough by now."

"Brandon, my sister loves you. I've no doubt about that. I believe she wants to put her faith in you, because she needs the healing that comes of learning to trust again. That journey for her is going to be taken in little steps. You may have to do more than meet her half way. Pride has no place in this, only love."

Tears stung Brandon's good eye and burned behind his traumatized one. "I'd like to clean up before I go to her." He started to stand and groaned in pain. "I haven't been in a brawl for a good long while. I'm getting too old for this kind of abuse."

"Let me take you and get those ribs x-rayed, and you should have some ice on your face. You do look like you ran into the mean end of a rhino."

Chapter Thirty-Three

"Mrs. Sullivan?" The young emergency doctor pulled the curtain open and offered his hand. "Are you feeling better?"

"Yes, thank you. Please call me Kate."

"Certainly, Kate," he looked at her chart, not at her. "Your lab reports tell me you are dehydrated and your blood sugar is low. Looking at you tells me you're exhausted and emotionally drained."

"My brother is in the intensive care unit. I haven't had much time or inclination to eat, drink or sleep. I'm better now. I need to get back upstairs and find my husband." She swung her legs over the side of the gurney, sat up and immediately a wave of dizzy nausea swept over her.

"I'm not comfortable letting you go quite yet. You need some fluids in you and you need to get home and to bed. Is there anyone who can drive you?"

"My whole family is here. I'm expecting my daughter. I'll be fine."

A nurse pushed the curtain aside and poked her head in. "Doctor, there's a guy who just came in with facial trauma and what looks like rib fractures. Do you want me to get x-rays before you see him?"

"Sure, I'll be right there." He turned back to Kate. "Someone will be right in to get an IV started. You may as well take a nap. It's going to be an hour or so here before I can let you leave."

Kate did not want to give in to the wisdom of medical advice or the calling of her body for respite. Sitting up again and dangling her feet over the side of the cart, she tried to fight the weakness that called her to lie down and submit. The nurse came in, stuck Kate's arm for the intravenous fluids she needed, and left her to rest; rest and ponder the injuries recently inflicted on her husband and the trauma dealt to her own heart.

"Kate, Mamma said you were here." It was Frank. "This is like musical hospital beds. I just left Brandon at radiology."

"You what? Radiology? Oh God, something's broken?" The panic rose in her chest and pounded like rubber mallets in her brain. Once again she started to hop off the gurney, but Frank stopped her.

"Lie back down before you fall on your pretty face. We don't need both of you with an eye swollen shut. Brandon has probably got a couple of fractured ribs, his face looks like...well, I've seen him looking better. He'll recover from the physical beating. He won't recover if you break his heart."

"Frank, I was trying to do the right thing."

"Yes. There's no right and wrong here. What would it take for you to simply trust him?" Frank pulled up a rolling stool and sat, taking Kate's hands in his.

"I...I don't know."

"He wants you to respect the kind of man he is. And, Kate, he *is not* Jeffrey. Rest now. It's almost daylight. I'm going to check on Mark. When you feel up to it, come back to the I.C.U." He kissed her on her head and patted her hand. "You'll make the right decision. I've never known your heart to be wrong. Listen to it."

****

Brandon sat holding an ice pack to his face, the entire troupe of River Dance tapping a jig on his head. He was trying to pay attention to the physician who had just come in and tossed an x-ray up on the viewer.

319

Pointing and squinting as if the damage were not clearly visible he finally spoke. "Mr. Sullivan, you can see here...a fracture of the fourth rib. I'll have to send this to a radiologist, but I think I see a hairline crack in the fifth." He snatched the picture off the lighted screen. "Hmm...Sullivan? Odd, I just admitted another Sullivan. Well, common name, I suppose."

"Whatta ya mean?" Brandon's attention was caught. He stood. "What Sullivan?"

"I shouldn't have even mentioned it... confidentiality, you know." He backed away, appearing like he wanted to flee. "A...Kate Sullivan...do you know her?"

"That's my wife." Personal space be damned, Brandon was right in the man's face. "What's happened to her? Where is she now?"

"Calm down, Mr. Sullivan. She's fine... dehydrated, exhausted, needs a good meal and some rest."

Brandon pitched the ice pack in the waste basket, snatched his coat off the chair and left the doctor, bewildered and mumbling to himself, "Who are these people?"

Kate's eyes were closed but she was awake. She heard the curtain sliding on its metal track and, assuming it was the nurse come to check on her, she feigned sleep. She may have felt him, or more accurately perceived his presence, just before his hand whispered over hers. His touch was an infusion of strength that, even in her current state of confusion as to their status, made her want to drink him in, an elixir for her wounds.

"Sweetheart?" His lips skimmed her cheek.

"I'm so sorry he hurt you." Her voice wanted to break like carnival glass in an earthquake of emotion. "Are your ribs broken?"

"One or two. Don't be afraid when you open your

eyes. My ugly kisser is a bloody disaster."

When she did look at him, she tried not to gasp. "Oh, Brandon, I married you for your pretty face. Now look at you." She was afraid to touch him for fear that she might hurt him.

"Oh, did you now. And here I was thinkin' you only wanted me for my money. Or was it the boy-o?"

"At least you haven't had your sense of humor beat out of you." Joey was going to pay for this, she decided. "You should have stayed in Kentucky. How was your show jumping?" There was no energy left for anger, just an emptiness inside. Kate wasn't ready to address the possibility that filling the hole would take more effort than she had strength to commit.

"We can talk about that later. We're a fine pair, Katie, beauty and the beast." He sat next to the bed. "We need to make peace between us. I need you. You look like you could use a bit of comfort yourself. Why are we making this more difficult than it deserves?"

Laura burst into the cubicle. "Mamma...oh, Brandon...what the hell happened to *you*? Look at the two of you. Damn. You're both a mess."

"It's been a long night. When did you get here?" Kate sat up on the side of the bed, forgot her IV line, tugged it loose and flinched in pain. "Brandon, get someone in here to let me off this leash."

He gave Kate a quick kiss on the top of her head and went to find help.

"Momma, I went straight to ICU. Uncle Mark is awake. I was looking for you and Nonna says you're in the ER, that you fainted. Brandon looks like he was hit by a Mack truck. Will someone let me in on all the craziness?" She gesticulated with her hands in a way that reminded Kate of Mamma.

"Just as soon as we figure it all out," Kate told her daughter.

The nurse removed Kate's IV and discharged

her with instructions to keep up on her fluids and get something to eat. Kate was considerably perkier and starting to catch a second wind, but she wanted to get back to Mamma's house, give Brandon one of the pain pills the doctor had ordered for him and put him to bed. There would be time to sort themselves out when they'd had a meal and a good sleep.

Replacing her distrust for nurturing had been a resource Kate had used in the past to get through relationship problems. It might work this time, but it would be temporary. Eventually, the bond between them would have to be chiseled down, sanded clean and rebuilt without guile or reserve, or it would crumble for lack of foundation.

The family was gathered in the hallway outside Mark's room. Laura was still fresh and would stay with her uncle Mark while everyone else got some much needed sleep. Maria finally agreed to go home for a few hours and rest. Kate and Brandon would stay at Mamma's. Kate was so angry at her youngest brother, she wasn't at all sure she could be in the same house with him without causing him bodily injury, so Joey was relegated to the rectory to hang out with Frankie for the duration.

Chapter Thirty-Four

Brandon looked at Kate's childhood bed and then at her. "This is going to be cozy." He sat down, tried not to wince in pain, and pulled her down beside him. He watched her hands as she unbuttoned his shirt, remembering the first time she ever attended to him so. "Brighid asked me to give you her love. After you've rested, maybe you can call her."

"I will. Your daughter is a lovely woman. Oh God, look at you." Kate gasped when she saw the purple flesh stretched over the left side of his chest. She worked his shirt off his arms, trying not to jostle him, and then she started on his trousers. "Lay back, I'll help you out of these."

"I certainly can't argue with that." Lowering himself gingerly, he leaned into the bed pillows as she pulled his pants off one leg and then the other.

"Now, stay put. I'm going to get you a pain pill and an ice pack for your face." She stopped at the doorway and turned to him. "Bran, my days of taking responsibility for everyone are over. I made that mistake with my first marriage and I won't do it again."

"Wait, Katie. I don't need anything for pain. It's not that bad. I just want you to lie down with me and give me a chance to explain."

Kate gave him a look somewhere between annoyance and amusement and started to peel off her jeans, sweater and socks. She had to lie on her side on the narrow bed to make them fit as she pulled a quilt over the two of them.

"Katie, I have to tell you something. If I have to swallow my pride to comfort you, I'll do it." Frank's words hummed in Brandon's brain, meet her more than half way.

Her leg slid against his and twined around his calf, pinning him softly to her. She lifted on one elbow and looked at him. "I'm not sure I want to hear any explanations."

"I won't have a wedge between us, especially if it's a spurious one. Listen to me. When I was in such pain, after losing Fiona, I tried to date. I took one woman out to dinner. She was young, pretty, she liked me. Men need affirmation, too." He was unable to roll to his side to see her face so he nudged her closer. "I don't know if I can communicate to you how lonely I was. In a moment of weakness and too much whiskey, I kissed her...rather thoroughly as I recall."

"Brandon, why are you telling me this?" She wanted to pull away, cover her ears and sing loudly.

"Because you need to know. It left me more bereft than ever. I realized she was only a substitute for Fiona, a warm body. I was embarrassed that I let it get as far as it did. I sent her away and I swore it would not happen again."

"But then I came along and it did happen again."

"No, it did not. You are no substitute. You are my fate. We have belonged together, from the beginning of time. You are the magic in my life." His fingers tangled in her hair, reveling in the silky feel of it.

"I told you once I didn't believe in magic."

"Yes, but you're married to an Irishman now." He tried to kiss her with his bruised lips. "Ow...I never thought kissing you would be painful."

"You can't imagine how furious I am at Joey." Kate lifted up on an elbow and looked at the face of this man she knew she would always love. "Are you ever going to tell me how Rolex turned out?"

"I didn't stick around to find out." He was intentionally evasive, not sure how she was going to react.

"Cut it out, Brandon, tell me now. What happened?"

"Nothing, I didn't ride." He watched her face change from amused to confused.

"You *what*? What do you mean 'didn't ride'?"

"I withdrew. I needed to find you, be with you. Kate, I was afraid that Mark wouldn't make it. I couldn't let you be alone."

Tears filled her eyes and spilled over to drop onto his chest. "You missed your ride...for me? Bran, what about winning, making a name for yourself, for Willow Creek? What about the offer from Brownstone?"

"Brownstone will make his own decisions. I can't change him or the world. God willing, I'll be back next year. You will never come second to anything, for me." He brushed her hair off her face so he could see her eyes. "Do you believe me, Katie?"

"This has been a horrible twelve hours or so. It's like the bumper sticker that says, 'Oh my God, not another learning experience.' I have been living that very sentiment for so long now, I should have it tattooed on my ass."

"That would be spoiling a fine ass." He patted her tush.

"Thank you. Bran...I set out on a journey last October. It was not one I started willingly. I was pushed out in the middle of a road I would not have taken on my own. And, before I could get very far, I swerved to miss a damned squirrel and there you were."

"Ah, so you finally admit it wasn't my fault," he chuckled.

"Don't push your luck here. I'm not sure if I should be mad at you. I had no hopes, dreams or designs on falling in love. The riding lessons were a way to say to everyone, including myself, 'I have power over my life. I can do this one little thing without a note from home.' Going to Ireland, buying not one but two horses, having sex with you...those were all decisions I made for myself."

Brandon reached for her and drew his finger across her cheek. "People do those things everyday without giving much thought to it."

"Not me. I tried to tell myself that the time in Ireland was just a fling, but in truth, I knew I loved you and it scared me...because I didn't think I could stand to be hurt again." She shivered as his hand slid from her cheek to her neck and down her collarbone to her breast.

"The challenge for me, Brandon, is standing on my own. You would gladly prop me up and keep me from falling on my face, but what I need from you is that attitude you have when I take a tumble from a horse. Check to make sure I'm not dead or horribly maimed and tell me to get back in the saddle. Life is not a sport for wimps."

"I can do that if you can remember that life is also a team event. You're not in this alone."

"No one has ever wanted me on his team before. I was always the last kid picked. They'd whine, 'ah come on, do we have to take Aiello?' Maybe that's why, when Jeffrey chose me, I went so blindly and worked so hard to win his love and respect. You were so different. You simply loved me. I didn't even have to promise you breakfast. It seemed unnatural."

"Katie, it's the most natural thing in the world, loving you. The first time I saw you, I knew you'd haunt my dreams. When you showed up at my barn, I nearly fell off the horse. I told myself it was anger that unsettled me, but it was the thrill of seeing you again that sent me flying over a triple bar like a flaming beginner, letting the mare pull a rail.

"The night I saw you at the Greek restaurant, your cheeks flushed with wine, lips sweet with honey from the baklava, if we'd been alone, neither of us would have been safe. You had a temper to best me, a vulnerability to let me know I was still a man and a love vast enough to encompass two big, crazy families. How could a man not treasure you? I was hopelessly at sea in you. I still am."

Kate looked at this man to whom she had lost her heart, found it again and now willed it into his safekeeping. "Tell me again, the words you said in Irish, on Christmas, when you announced our wedding date."

"*Tá mo chroí istigh ionat*," he whispered.

Catarina Giullietta Aiello Sullivan lay gently against her husband's chest and listened.

"My heart is within you."

Epilogue

Santo Stefano di Sessanio, L'Aquila, Abruzzo, Italy

The Church of Santo Stefano sat atop a rocky outcrop, standing sentinel over the verdant valley where the Di Benedetto family had prospered for over seven hundred years. Tracing their history back to the third century BCE, when the Vestini occupied the region, they were a people of tradition and pride.

And...they did know how to throw a party!

When Brandon arrived at the house he found his sister, stunning in her bridal finery. With her red-gold hair topped by a ring of white roses woven with pearls and her gown of gossamer ivory silk, she looked the part of a fairy queen from Irish myth. He escorted her down the street of the hill town, musicians playing, children skipping along and the entire family parading to the ancient church together.

Kevin and Barb had spent their honeymoon in Sorrento on the Bay of Naples and then traveled to Abruzzo to attend this celebration. They were as fresh and new as young lovers could be, unable to stop catching glimpses and smiling that secret smile that couples in love wear like neon signs across their faces.

Brighid, flaxen hair shimmering in the morning light, was attendant to her aunt. Brandon saw a look of appreciation on Joey Aiello's face when Brighid walked past and, not wanting to start a family brawl in the middle of Annie's wedding, made a mental note to have a little talk with his brother-in-law right after the ceremony.

The church was cool and fragrant with flowers and candle wax as Brandon's eyes adjusted to the dimness of the light that was filtered through ancient stained glass. Kate stood on the aisle in a gown of turquoise gauze, her hair wild and free about her classic face. The Triskele, nestled in the hollow of her throat, and her wedding band of Celtic knots were her only adornments. Laura stood with her mother, a reflection but for the fairer hue of skin and hair.

The Aiellos, Sullivans and Di Benedettos filled the space, but when Ann Caitilín Bhriain Sullivan's bright green eyes caught and held the golden ones of Sergio Massimiliano Di Benedetto, other beings ceased to matter. Today they would be one flesh, she and her handsome Italian gentleman.

Brandon kissed Annie's sweet face and placed her cool, delicate hand in Sergio's warm and waiting one. If a picture had been ordered to be painted epitomizing the faces of love, the honored pair would have been the models. Any doubts that Brandon might have had for the happiness of his beloved only sibling were laid at the altar when he turned away to stand with his own wife.

Immediately after the sacrament was sealed, the party began. Wine started to flow, toasts and pronouncements were articulated, food was served. Music played, dancing commenced, and celebration rang out over the valley with the peals of church bells from the medieval campanile.

"Come with me. I want to show you something." Kate took Brandon by the hand and led him up the brick-paved streets, past stone domiciles that had sheltered families for centuries in this enchanting place. Baskets of geraniums and lobelia hung from balconies along with the ubiquitous laundry on lines above their heads.

"I was here once when I was young," she said, as she ascended a narrow stone stairway that snaked steeply at the end of the street. They came out at the top of a *torre*. The tower commanded a view of the red tiled roofs of the village and guarded the valley to the peaks of the Gran Sasso.

"Bran, what were you talking to Joey about right after the ceremony? He looked worried."

"I strongly suggested that if he wanted to keep his cullions connected to his cock, he'd keep his hands off my daughter."

"Bran, Joey wouldn't...he's fifteen years older than Brighid. He's got more sense than that. You're imagining things," she hoped.

"Brighid is a woman, a beautiful woman, and your brother is a man. If you were twenty and I was older, I still would have been tempted." His finger drew a line along her jaw. "Even if your father had threatened to castrate me," Brandon whispered.

"Do you want me to have a talk with Brighid? I could try to tell her what a rotten guy Joey is. Although it would be a terrible lie."

"I'll leave the fibbing up to you." He turned her so that her back was against his chest. "It's going to be hard to go back to reality after being here with you."

"Yes, but when you get back you'll have two new horses to train."

When Brownstone, being a family man himself, found out why Bran had withdrawn from Rolex, the man was uncommonly impressed and his decision to have the Sullivans train his horses was sealed. Brandon would ride Lions Gate and coach Rebecca for a lucrative sum, assuring the financial security of Willow Creek, at least for the near future.

Kate shivered from the chill and Brandon enfolded her closer in his arms, silently watching the evening stars beginning to burst through the black of the night. "You look stunning tonight, my love," he whispered against her hair.

"And I think I'll insist you wear an Armani suit at least once a week, so I can admire my ability to choose a man and dress him well."

"Should I worry about Annie tonight?" The idea of the wedding night of his sister still made his stomach churn.

Kate chuckled at his protective instinct. "We talked, Annie and me. You've nothing to be concerned about. I wouldn't tell you before, but they've been sleeping together for some time now. She said she'd waited long enough and, well, she didn't go into any detail, but I'm certain she's…shall I say, satisfied."

"Okay, I don't want to hear anymore, thank you."

"My, you're prudish for a man who was not at all shy about taking me to Ireland and seducing me."

"I thought you seduced me. I was helpless to resist you. I'm rather helpless right now." He nuzzled her neck where she was especially sensitive.

They could hear the sounds of the festa. It would continue late into the night. "Do you think anyone will notice that we've gone?" she wondered.

"The very old will have fallen asleep, the very young will think *we've* fallen asleep, those who are in love won't be wondering about us at all. That leaves the few who will be so lost in drink they won't be noticing anything." His lips teased across her cheek, breathing a path down her jaw and nibbling the tender flesh of her throat. Like a thief waiting for the opportune moment to take her treasure, he waited, lingered, before his mouth covered hers, warm and sweet with wine and wedding cake.

The air was cool, but a heat in the core of her traveled cell by cell to the surface of Kate's skin.

This fire did not come like a rampant beast from the depths of despair or the sickening waves of a life gone awry. Instead it was a mantle of molten silk, wrapping her in its cocoon while she imagined herself a butterfly, her wings still wet with the newness of loving.

A word about the author...

Clare Austin has been courting a love of literature since reading *The 500 Hats of Bartholomew Cubbins* in primary school. Now, inspired by a belief in a happy ending and a passion for lyrical prose, Clare spins her own tales of romance with a touch of humor and pathos.

Clare makes her home at the foot of the Colorado Rocky Mountains with her husband, their three horses and Maggie the Cairn terrier.

Visit Clare at www.ClareAustin.com.

Thank you for purchasing
this Wild Rose Press publication.
For other wonderful stories of romance,
please visit our on-line bookstore at
www.thewildrosepress.com

For questions or more information,
contact us at
info@thewildrosepress.com

The Wild Rose Press
www.TheWildRosePress.com

LaVergne, TN USA
07 April 2011
223312LV00001B/6/P